THE LOST LEGION: AN ARCHAEOLOGICAL THRILLER
THE JACK REILLY ADVENTURES - BOOK 6
BY MATT JAMES

SEVEREDPRESS

THE LOST LEGION

Copyright © 2024 Matt James
Copyright © 2024 by Severed Press

WWW.SEVEREDPRESS.COM

All rights reserved. No part of this book may be reproduced or transmitted in any form or by any electronic or mechanical means, including photocopying, recording or by any information and retrieval system, without the written permission of the publisher and author, except where permitted by law. This novel is a work of fiction. Names, characters, places and incidents are the product of the author's imagination, or are used fictitiously. Any resemblance to actual events, locales or persons, living or dead, is purely coincidental.

ISBN: 978-1-923165-09-0

ALSO BY MATT JAMES

THE JACK REILLY ADVENTURES
The Forgotten Fortune
The Roosevelt Conspiracy
The Dorado Deception
The Undying Kingdom
The Venetian Pursuit
The Lost Legion

THE CHARLEE FLYNN ADVENTURES
The Cursed Thief
The Golden Tiger (2024)

RELICS OF GOD
The Blood King
The False Prophet (2024)

THE UNSEEN
Origin
Desolation
Perseverance
Inferno
Nightmare: A Short Story
Petrified: A Short Story

THE ZAHRA KANE ARCHAEOLOGICAL THRILLERS with Nick Thacker
Empire Lost: A Prequel
The Anubis Plague
The Sixth Seal

THE ALEX WAKE THRILLERS with Richard F. Paddon
Midnight Mass

THE DANE MADDOCK ADVENTURES with David Wood
Berserk
Skin and Bones
Venom
Lost City

STAND-ALONE TITLES
Dark Island

Cradle of Death
Sub-Zero
The Dragon

THE HANK BOYD ADVENTURES
Blood and Sand
Mayan Darkness
Babel Found
Elixir of Life

OTHER STORIES
The Cursed Pharaoh
Broken Glass
Plague
Evolve

PRAISE FOR MATT JAMES

"The words of a Matt James story flow like the best rivers. Smooth and subtle at times, interrupted by danger and thrills at every churn of whitewater. This guy is the real deal!"
—Ernest Dempsey, *USA Today* bestselling author of POSEIDON'S FURY

"Matt James is my go-to guy for heart-stopping adventure and bone-chilling suspense!"
—Greig Beck, international bestselling author of TO THE CENTER OF THE EARTH

"If you enjoy globetrotting adventures jampacked with over-the-top action, then you'll love Matt James' work!"
—Nick Thacker, *USA Today* bestselling author of THE ENIGMA STRAIN

"If you're looking for a fast-moving tale with action to spare, give Matt James a try!"
—David Wood, *USA Today* bestselling author of SERPENT

"Searching for relentless action and harrowing adventure in dangerous locales? Look no further than Matt James!"
—Michael McBride, international bestselling author of CHIMERA

"Matt James is a must-read! The thrilling action, unexpected turns, and rip-roaring chases across the globe are fantastic adventures every time! You won't be disappointed."
—Andrew Clawson, bestselling author of THE ARTHURIAN RELIC

"Matt James is the gold standard for archaeological thrillers!"
—Luke Richardson, international bestselling author of THE TITANIC DECEPTION

"Matt James writes thrillers that define the genre! Neck-breaking speed and hairpin plot twists. Top notch!"
—Craig A. Hart, bestselling author of SERENITY

"Matt James is the Michael Bay of action-adventure authors!"
—Richard F. Paddon, author of *Cash is King*

"Matt James reminds devotees of Indiana Jones and Nathan Drake why their love for rock-solid action-adventure springs eternal!"
—Rick Chesler, international bestselling author of ATLANTIS GOLD

"Matt's novels need a pause button. They do not stop!"
—Lee Murray, *Bram Stoker Award* winning author of INTO THE MIST

"A talent voice in the action-thriller genre!"
—Richard Bard, *Wall Street Journal* bestselling author of BRAINRUSH

"If you like thrills, chills, and nonstop action, then Matt James may just be your next favorite author!"
—John Sneeden, bestselling author of THE SIGNAL

"Matt James has proven that true adventure is found in the fine line between myth and reality. James walks that tightrope with a master's touch."
—J.M. LeDuc, bestselling author of SIN

For Riley, Daisy, and Wyatt.

THE LOST LEGION
THE JACK REILLY ADVENTURES - BOOK 6

BY MATT JAMES

PROLOGUE

Rome, Italy
67 AD

Quintus Petillius Cerialis looked out over Rome from its imperator's balcony. Even though he faithfully served Nero, Quintus despised the man. Very few men had ever rubbed him the wrong way and none as much as the tyrant king himself. He was selfish and someone who gladly stood atop other people's accomplishments.

But, as General of the Ninth Legion, Quintus was forced to bite his tongue. Unlike Nero, Quintus didn't act out of self-centeredness. He served Rome as a whole, not just his imperator. His loyalties were typically unshakeable.

But not Nero.

The doors to Nero's room opened and in walked the man himself. Quintus had been sent for and, as usual, Nero wasn't even there. Quintus knew the man well. Nero loved to make an entrance. He also saw this type of treatment as a power move.

But Quintus wasn't some rookie. In his career, he had served Rome in both the role of military commander and politician. He was very familiar with the game.

Like now.

"General," Nero said, "I thank you for meeting with me."

Quintus turned, his regal robes billowing as he did. "It is my pleasure, Imperator. What is it I can do for you?"

It pained him to be so formal with the man.

"My scholars have unearthed some interesting information."

Quintus was actually intrigued. "Oh?"

"Yes." Nero's face darkened. "It seems that you have not been entirely forthcoming with the empire about your…background."

Quintus hid his surprise. Had Nero found out about Quintus' other life?

He relaxed. "I'm not sure what you mean."

"Oh, I think you do." Nero produced a scroll from inside his robes. "This is a signed confessional. The man who these words belonged to has named you as his commander."

Quintus deflected the accusation. "I command many, Imperator. What did this man do?"

Nero eyed Quintus again, no doubt studying him for faults.

You won't find any. This isn't my first interrogation.

"Before his life expired, he said that you also command a secret detachment of men within the Ninth."

Quintus couldn't hide his shock. Nero had, indeed, discovered his deepest secret, something he and countless others had kept in the dark for centuries.

"Private treasure hunters, hmmm?"

The general looked out over Rome, picturing his men now—his other men. They did not *hunt* treasure. They did something infinitely more important.

Fine, I'll play your game.

"And not just any treasure," Nero continued. "Your little band of treacherous legionnaires have their sights on one treasure in particular."

"Which do you speak of?" Quintus asked, refusing to meet Nero's manic gaze.

Nero pounded the top of the marble banister. "Do not play dumb with me, General! You know of what I speak." Quintus could see the man seething with rage in his periphery. "Not only do I have evidence of these secret tasks, but I also know, without doubt, that you yourself have taken part in them." Quintus turned to face Nero. "In the years I have been imperator, you have not once offered me this information. Why?"

Quintus sighed. He had no reason to lie to the man any longer. As imperator, Nero could just as swiftly order Quintus' execution for no other reason than it being his will. Nero had ultimate power.

The general's defenses broke. He would tell Nero what he wanted to know, but he wouldn't tell him everything. If he thought that Quintus' men were fortune seekers, then that's what he'd tell the man.

"And what would you do with the Macedonian's treasure?"

Nero smiled smugly, perceiving victory over Quintus. "Add it to my own, of course. As imperator, is that not my right?" Quintus didn't reply right away. "General? Is that my right?"

Quintus gave him a small bow, all while gritting his teeth. "Your will is the will of Rome."

He was stuck in a bad place. If Quintus openly defied Nero, he'd be executed, much like the man who had signed the confession. Unfortunately, now, Nero owned Quintus' life until either Quintus died—

Or he dies.

"Would you not share it with Rome, as your predecessors would've done? You would not use it to enrich your empire?"

Nero grinned. "*I* am not my predecessors, General."

Clearly.

Quintus took in a deep breath. The next question would alter the course of his life, and the lives of many others. "What would you like me to do?"

1

Rome, Italy
Present Day

Home to a myriad of architectural wonders, near-unmatchable cuisine, and the perfect Mediterranean climate, Rome, Italy, was still missing something vital: the blues. And Jack Reilly was the answer.

He'd like to think so, anyway.

Jack sat outside, on the balcony of his third-floor suite, blowing into his brand-new harmonica, relentlessly attempting to play a tune from *The Blues Brothers*. Mimicking Elwood wasn't easy, especially for someone who'd only been playing for a couple of weeks.

"Why don't you pick something easier to play, like *Mary Had a Little Lamb*?" May had asked.

Jack shook his head. "Only the classics for me." He shrugged. "Sue me for being ambitious."

"Our neighbors might just do that."

He hit an off-note with a shriek, driving May back inside their room. Now, the only living beings that could interrupt him were the soaring birds...and anyone within earshot of his *novice* playing.

Like the elder statesman in the room above us.

The past three weeks had been the happiest Jack had felt in a very long time. He loved his job, and the friends he'd made along the way. And, of course, there was May... She'd given him something he'd desperately been missing.

She'd given him intimacy.

Jack had always scoffed at the idea of ever needing it. His mentor-mentored bond with Bull, back home in Wyoming, was all Jack had needed at first, but even it had its limitations. That friendship was built on trust and admiration, not emotion. Jack and Bull respected one another for who they were as men. Even now, blowing into his *harp*, Jack felt a rising anxiousness even thinking about his recently uncaged feelings.

But that's where May came into play.

The former Chinese intelligence officer needed Jack in the same way that he needed her. They were, honestly, perfect for one another. They each had skeletons in their closets, and they each still suffered from varying cases of post-traumatic stress disorder, though Jack's had lessened since joining up with TAC. His PTSD had been caused by his years of service with Delta. The things he'd done. The things he'd seen. Then again, May had done even more and seen even worse.

Jack was happy to pay it forward too. He was May's Bull in a way. He was also her...boyfriend.

Weird, he thought, hitting another off-note. He winced, feeling a pinch deep in his eardrums.

An annoyed mumbling picked up above him. Jack sighed and pulled the harmonica away from his lips. He'd give his neighbor a break. Plus, he and May needed to get ready for tonight's festivities. He checked his watch, eyes opening wide.

Right now!

He stood, yanked open the sliding door, and dashed inside, tripping and falling when a mostly nude Mayleen Wu turned to greet him. Jack went down on his hands and knees, dropping his harmonica. It skittered across the laminate wood floor, stopping directly between May's bare feet. Jack crawled to them, but didn't reach for the instrument. Instead, he stroked May's freshly shaven right leg, continuing up it until he got to her inner thigh.

May giggled, then squirmed back a step.

Jack looked up, thanking whatever god it was that allowed him to be in this woman's presence.

"See something you like, Agent Reilly?" she asked.

Jack grinned and blindly picked up his harmonica. "Yeah." He held it up. "This."

May rolled her eyes and turned but didn't get far. Jack scrambled to his feet and playfully hugged her from behind. May immediately shrugged out of his embrace...and hip tossed him onto the bed.

Jack let out an "Oof!" when he landed. He blinked, staring straight up at the ceiling. A now upside-down May leaned into view above him. "Well, that's one way to get me into bed."

She leaned in and gave him an inverted, *Spider-Man*-esque kiss. It was awkward, but Jack didn't mind.

May released her lips and stared deep into his eyes. "There will be time for this later." She stood tall. "We need to get ready."

With that, Jack's dreams were crushed. But May was also right. Back at home, Eddy had worked her ass off to get Jack and May's aliases on the guest list for tonight's soiree. The black-tie affair was scheduled to begin at eight o'clock, but the invitation had stated that guests needed to arrive two hours early for dinner and time to mingle. Security was going to be tight too, and, from what Eddy had found out, the team in charge were thorough.

It also meant that Jack and May would be going unarmed.

Still on his back, Jack lifted his hands and inspected his scarred knuckles. He and May didn't need weapons to win a fight.

Well, a brawl.

Jack reluctantly rolled off the king-sized bed. He stood with a slight groan. His back was pretty balky from his and Raegor's escapades a couple weeks back. Luckily, Jack was a quick healer, even with him approaching forty years of age. He attributed it to his can-do attitude, including a wicked, albeit juvenile sense of humor. He was also an expert at backseating pain. Besides the childlike comicalness, May was exactly the same. She complemented Jack in that regard, keeping herself on task, at all times.

Jack was closer to a dog seeing a squirrel.

This evening's event was being hosted inside the Roman Colosseum, of all places. Jack had been to Rome twice before, but never the Colosseum. He was beyond pumped. A few days after arriving, Jack had seen an advertisement announcing the already sold out, archaeological showcase. The subject had piqued his interest so much that he had called in a favor to Eddy who was at TAC HQ in Colorado.

"*Alright, Jack,*" Eddy had said, her southern accent bouncing along with her words, "*because you asked nicely, I'll see what I can do about getting you two on the guest list.*"

"Thanks, Ed. By the way, where the hell did they find an *aquila* headpiece?"

The *aquila* was the royal eagle standard of an Imperial Roman Army legion. And not just any legion, in this case. Once Jack found out which legion this particular headpiece, the eagle, belonged to, he understood why security was going to be so tight. Not only was this legion's eagle found, something that had never been recovered until now, but it belonged to another of Jack's favorite missing persons.

The Ninth Legion, he thought, smiling.

It was said that, sometime in the second century, the entire legion had just up and vanished from record. Jack could understand the lack of proper record keeping back then, if this had been some hole-in-the-wall, war-torn, Medieval village community, but this was Rome. How could thousands of the empire's men disappear?

"*Outside Rome somewhere, beneath a factory that was being demolished. The find was a complete fluke. Diggers hit stone, thinking it was bedrock. Except it wasn't! Only once they dug around it a little did they discover that it was a large stone container, not unlike a coffin.*"

"Funny how that happens sometimes," Jack said.

"*I know, right? The lead archaeologist said that the site reminded him of a secret storehouse. Picture a smuggler's hold on a ship.*"

"Really?"

"*Yep. Whoever built the storehouse, obviously didn't want what was inside to be found. Maybe ever!*"

Jack squinted, staring out his hotel room window. "I think you and I can understand why…"

"*Yes, we can. Usually, when someone goes to this much work to hide something, it's for a very particular reason.*"

Jack chuckled softly. "And rarely a good one at that."

"*More often than not.*"

Jack looked over his shoulder at May. She'd been listening in on the speaker phone conversation. She was now an agent of the Tactical Archaeological Command, after all, same as Jack. There was nothing Eddy could say that she didn't deserve to hear.

"So," Jack continued, eyeing May as he spoke, "looks like we're back on the clock, huh?"

May lightheartedly pouted her lips.

"*Not necessarily. We could also just be overthinking this.*"

Jack turned and faced May. "Or…it's exactly what we suspect."

"Yeah, Jack. That too." Eddy sighed. "*As always, stay on your toes. Unfortunately, there's nothing I can do about security, so you'll have to go in with nothing but your fists and wits.*"

"No problem, Ed. I'm sure this is all nothing."

"*Let's hope. And Jack?*"

"Yeah, Ed?"

"*Try and enjoy yourself. As of right now, you're still on vacation.*"

Jack laughed. "Are we ever really not working?"

Eddy sighed again. "*No, I suppose not. Still, be safe and have fun. That's an order. And, May?*"

"Yes, Eddy?" May asked, stepping closer to the phone.

"*Take care of our boy. Eddy out.*"

A creek in the floorboards pulled Jack out of the memory. May had left him and entered the bathroom. Jack hurried around their bed, sliding to a stop inside the doorway. May had yet to put anything else on, standing with her back to him in only her lace underwear. She gazed over her shoulder.

"Uh, um," Jack stuttered, "what are you wearing tonight?"

She gave him a mischievous smile. "You'll see…" May turned, grabbed the doorknob, and slowly shut it.

Jack's body broke out into goosebumps. He shook them away and stepped over to the wardrobe. Opening it, he spied its contents. It had been quite a while since he'd worn a tux.

"My name is Reilly, Jack Reilly."

2

They waited at the edge of the grand capital; a sprawling metropolis that had been known as Rome for over 2,500 years. And since its founding, Rome had been at the center of human advancement. But it had also been at the center of many battles, namely the Macedonian Wars (212-168 BC) and the sacking of Corinth in 146 BC.

From that point forward, Rome ruled Greece, the once formidable kingdom led by some of the most influential and powerful people in mankind's history, including a great military strategist, Alexander III of Macedon.

Alexander the Great, he thought, loading another cartridge into his rifle's magazine.

In fact, the clicking noise of round after round being loaded was the only noise emanating from within the warehouse. Seven other men were doing as he did, preparing for their group's triumphant catapulting out of the shadows and into the light. He and the others had been waiting for this day all their lives.

Their families had been waiting for this day for almost 2,000 years.

He checked his watch. They still had four hours before it was time to move. The men, as well as their support transportation, were ready and waiting for his signal.

He took a deep breath, lifted his hand to his neck, and checked his pulse. He grinned when he found it to be slow and steady. Nowadays, it took a lot to get his blood pumping harder than it would during a brisk walk.

One of his men stepped up next to him. "Sir?"

He paused what he was doing and set down the half-filled magazine. "Report," he ordered, gazing up at the soldier.

No, not soldier. We are legionnaires.

"Helo is fueled, ready, and awaiting your command to move in."

"Very good. Tell Zayn to keep waiting. We will not rush this operation."

The other man stood at attention. "Yes, sir. *Gaudere Legio Nona!*"

The team's commander gave his subordinate a simple nod, though to them he was more than just their stoic leader. They saw him as more of a godlike figure, someone ordained by destiny to be in his station. His blood, and it alone, had led this detachment since its inception two millennia ago.

And I will be the last.

If everything went as it should, this would be the Legion's last operation in their current state. They would then be large enough, and powerful enough, to expand into something closer to an army.

He glanced over at the legionnaire who had reported to him. Theo was his second in command. Like him, Theo was of Italian birth, as were his parents and grandparents before him. The other members were of multinational origin, which meant nothing in the grand scheme of things. It had been centuries since most of the other men's ancestors had immigrated to other countries. In doing so, they had blended their bloodline with that of other nations.

But their connection to the old ways, to the teachings of their ancestors, were as rock-solid as his were. As was their unwavering loyalty to him.

He thought back to the words Theo had recited before returning to his duties. Their team spoke Latin fluently, as did their ancestors before them.

He smiled wide. *Yes, Theo. Gaudere Legio Nona.* The Legion's commander—their general—picked up his magazine and continue to load it. *To rejoice the Ninth Legion.*

3

Their taxi pulled up to the Colosseum with plenty of time to spare. Not only were they early, but they were twenty minutes earlier than the invitation had instructed. Luckily, it was clear to see that there were already dozens of people here. Jack had dreaded showing up and being the first to arrive. After all, he and May weren't supposed to be here, and if everything went as planned, then their only enemy here would be *questions*.

As soon as Jack climbed out of the taxi, he gave May his hand and helped her out, doing his best not to ogle her.

First came her high-heeled foot. Then, her perfect leg. Her dress sported a slit that continued all the way up to her hip, showing off everything the toned appendage had to offer. Her dress also matched Jack's black tuxedo. He had no idea who had made it or what it had cost. All he cared about was how amazing the woman on his arm looked in it.

The pair stepped up onto the curb.

"You gotta admit," Jack said, looking around. His eyes ended on May. "We look good."

She grinned. "Damn good."

May's backless, one shoulder number caught the attention of several attendees as Jack led her down the first of two flights of stairs.

"You okay?" he asked.

She nodded. "It's just... It's been a long time since I've worn anything like this."

"Same, but I was mostly asking about the stairs. Those are some *high* heels."

She glanced down. "You don't like them?"

Jack snickered. "You couldn't pay me enough to say that—about anything you're wearing."

She blushed and looked away.

"What's wrong?" he asked, unsure about her reaction.

"Nothing's wrong, Jack." They made it to a landing and followed the flow of foot traffic down another set of stairs and to the left. May looked around. "It's this place. This life. I never thought I'd ever have," her eyes met Jack's, "this."

Jack smiled. "Ditto."

Men and women alike eyed May as she passed. Most of the women glared at May with disdain. Jack found it humorous that he could clearly spot which guy was with his wife. The ones who were single couldn't pull their eyes off May. The married ones only gave her short, secretive glances.

Even from outside the tall, stone walls of the Colosseum, Jack could hear the music. It originated from a string ensemble, though Jack had no idea what song they were currently playing. Unless it was a badass movie score, he didn't pay attention to orchestral music. That didn't mean he didn't like it. He just didn't appreciate it to the same level as someone else.

The cobblestone road between the bottom of the staircase and the entrance into the Colosseum was closed off on either side, and teeming with security. There was also a heavy-duty red carpet rolled out. It was smart on the host's part. The carpet would make it easier on someone in heels, like May.

Not that balance is an issue for her.

May was an expert in the Korean martial art of Taekwondo. It was a fighting discipline that relied heavily on powerful kicks, while also maintaining perfect balance. She'd been taught by her late mother who had been a champion, as well as a renowned instructor.

Before her asshat father brainwashed her into becoming an operative for the MSS.

The Ministry of State Security was China's version of the United States' CIA, and it had been run by Jin Zhao, May's father, until recently. Minister Zhao had been murdered by someone on the inside, someone loyal to May.

"It had to be done," May had argued. "My father would've never rested until he discovered what we found."

Jack nodded in agreement. "And until you were dead."

"Yes, that too."

While Jack had once fought the war on terror in the Middle East, May had been used as Zhao's personal James Bond, including a license to kill, since she had been a teenager. Jack refrained from asking her about the missions she'd been tasked with. The only time she and Jack talked about it was when it came up organically. Just like her, Jack did not enjoy reliving a lot of his past.

He looked at her. *The present is so much sweeter.*

May passed through security quickly, having nothing on her except her dress and heels. Jack carried her fake passport. It took him a moment to clear, but he inevitably did.

"Enjoy your evening, Mr. Jones," the guard said in heavily accented English.

Jack gave him a wink, then tipped his chin toward May. "How can I not?"

The security guard grinned, giving Jack a nod goodbye. Once more, May took Jack's arm, and they began their entrance into one of the most magnificent structures in the entire world. The sheer size of the Colosseum was what struck Jack the most. He tried to picture what the place looked like back in 80 AD, when it had been completed, before earthquakes eventually shook much of it to pieces.

"It's a shame," May said as they crossed the entrance platform. "Why are the pretty things always the most damaged?"

"Says the pretty, damaged thing."

May elbowed Jack in the side. Jack moaned, playing it up a little too. "Security!" he playfully called out, being sure to keep his voice down. "I've been assaulted!"

"Keep it up, and I'll be forced to turn it up a notch."

Jack smiled. "Promise?"

May rolled her eyes. "Boys…"

Jack took his eyes off May long enough to absorb his surroundings. The tall, arched entry made Jack feel downright miniscule. As they continued forward, the music grew louder as it was funneled through by a soft breeze. Jack felt May's skin react to the coolness.

"You okay?" he asked.

"Fine."

"You sure?"

She looked up at him. "A little chill doesn't bother me. It's very refreshing, actually. Keeps me focused."

Jack knew what she was getting at. "We're fine. Nothing is going to happen."

"How do you know?"

"Because of this." Jack placed a finger on his temple and closed his eyes. A second later he opened them, pulling his finger away. "Done."

"And that was?"

Jack motioned to the other attendees. "I just sent out a telepathic message to everyone here and told them to keep things civil."

May shook her head and looked away. "Why do I like you so much?"

Jack patted her hand. "Best not to think about it."

"Agreed."

They exited onto the partially restored arena floor. This was where the showcase was being held. In its current state, only one quarter of the floor existed. Partially hidden beneath it was the *hypogeum*—a two-level subterranean network of cages and tunnels that had been primarily used during gladiator matches.

The front half of the floor was empty and currently contained a few couples dancing with one another, while quietly conversing. The back half of the arena floor was where the historic presentation would take place. Rows of seats had been set up for the guests, complete with a central aisle to make things easier on everyone.

Up against the railing at the edge of the arena floor was the reason everyone was here. Displayed atop a low stage were beautifully preserved scrolls. The scrolls, as well as a handful of random trinkets, bordered this evening's main attraction. At the center of it all was a stout display case holding the all-important, golden eagle. And even from across the arena floor, Jack could see that it was, indeed, incomplete.

Damn, Jack thought, hoping Eddy's information had been wrong.

The eagle was missing its base and pole. Jack had read up on exactly what an Imperial Roman *aquila* looked like so he could fully appreciate the sight.

May had not.

"That's it?" she asked, obviously unimpressed.

"Yep. The only eagle ever recovered."

She looked away from the display. "Neat."

Now it was Jack's turn to roll his eyes. Since the presentation wasn't scheduled to start for another two hours, Jack and May had some time to kill. A seven-piece string group sat off to the left. Jack also spotted a bar off to their right.

"Drink?" he asked.

May nodded. "Please."

The pair headed that way, lit in shades of purples and blues. The lighting being used made the arena floor feel more like a nightclub than a protected UNESCO historical site. It's not that Jack didn't like it, either. He just hadn't expected it.

"Welcome," the bartender said. His eyes flicked off Jack and onto May. "What can I get you two?"

Usually, Jack would've just ordered a beer, but since he was inside the Colosseum and dressed in a tuxedo, he decided to step up his drink game.

"Gimme the best Old Fashioned you can muster."

The Italian nodded. "And for the *signora*?"

May glanced at Jack. "The same." She winked. "But make mine a double."

The bartender's eyes flashed over to Jack. He didn't say a word. He was just giving him an *attaboy*, congratulating him on having a woman like May.

"Shall I make yours a double too?"

Jack shrugged. "Eh, why not. When in Rome, right?"

The bartender smiled wide and got to work.

4

Jack and May did their best to avoid conversation with anyone else, but as the last stragglers entered, there were just too many people to ignore. Jack's cover was that he was here on behalf of the Smithsonian, and, of course, he was a historian.

"Jack Jones, I specialize in World War II history, though who doesn't love Ancient Rome too?"

"And your friend?" the older, Italian gentleman, whose name Jack had already forgotten, asked. All Jack could remember was that the guy was a researcher who focused on the early years of the Roman Empire.

May held up her hand as Jack introduced her. "This is May Zetian, she represents the Ministry of Culture and Tourism."

"Quite an interesting pair you two make. An American historian and a Chinese cultural expert."

May smiled. "We have a mutual friend who was gracious enough to help us out."

"Oh, you don't have to explain things to me. It was just an observation." May gave the Italian a small bow. He held up his wineglass. "Yes, well, I believe I am in need of a refill. Enjoy yourselves."

"Same to you," Jack said, quickly turning away, along with May. He sighed. "That was excruciating."

"I agree. My cheeks are killing me from smiling so much."

The corner of Jack's mouth lifted. "Yes, God forbid you smile." May swatted at him, but Jack caught her hand. "Dance?"

"You dance?" she asked.

"Nope, but the bourbon in me wants me to give it a shot."

May didn't look as confident. "Jack, I—"

"Need to relax."

Jack turned when they got to the center of the dancefloor. He clutched May's right hand in his left hand. She stepped in close, allowing Jack to wrap his right hand around her lower back. They pressed into one another, but didn't meet eyes.

Jack tried, but May didn't.

"Why does this feel like middle school all over again?" May still didn't meet his gaze. "Hey." May reluctantly looked up at him. "See, was that so hard?"

"It's not you." Her eyes darted around. "It's them."

"Them?" Jack asked, looking around.

"All of them. It's this dress. It's this place."

Jack was confused, but he could tell that May was uncomfortable being here.

"Why'd you wear it if you don't like it?" May glanced at him, then looked away. "Oh, I see. You wore it for me."

"Yes," she replied, still not looking at him.

Jack released her back and took the tip of her chin in between his forefinger and thumb. He forcibly made her look into his eyes.

"You're beautiful, May."

The ice-cold killer blushed again. "You're not too bad on the eyes, either."

Jack tilted his chin toward the encased eagle. "See that thing?"

May looked at it as they continued to dance. "Yeah?"

"I think it's safe to say that it's stuck playing second fiddle to something else tonight." May didn't immediately get what Jack was implying, not until his eyes darted down to her dress.

May instantly looked nervous. Then again, Jack couldn't exactly blame her. She'd spent a lifetime purposely working from the shadows. Being out in the open, exposed, not to mention unarmed, must've been hard for her. It made Jack understand, even more, how much she had sacrificed to be here with him, and wear what she was wearing.

It goes against everything she knows.

"Excuse me, Dr. Jones?" Jack blinked, then brought his eyes back to May.

"Yeah?"

"Where were you just then?"

He re-wrapped his hand around her lower back and pulled her in tight. "Right here. That reminds me. May Zetian, who's that?"

"It's a nod to the only female emperor in Chinese history, Wu Zetian."

"Her first name was Wu?" he asked.

"It was. You want to know something even spookier?"

Jack snorted. "*Pff.* Of course, duh."

"Before she was crowned, her given name was Wu Zhao."

"Your father's surname?"

She nodded. "Mmhmm."

Jack felt his skin tingle. "Whoa, that *is* spooky." His eyes opened wide. "So, does that mean I'm dating royalty?"

May's laugh was cut short by a PA system squealing.

"*Apologies,*" a local woman announced. Jack looked around and saw that the speaker was over near the stringed septet. "*Would you please take your seats. This evening's presentation of 'Relics of the Lost Legion' is about to begin.*"

The female, spectacle-wearing Italian was short, lean, and possessed curly, shoulder-length, dark hair. Like everyone else here, she was dressed to impress. And like May, she looked incredibly uncomfortable in her own skin. As Jack and May *broke formation*, he watched a portly fellow march over to the woman and berate her over something.

Jack didn't like that.

Jack got the attention of a waiter as he passed by. "I'm guessing that's our cultural expert?"

"*Sì.* Alberto Lombardi is not only an expert in Ancient Rome, but he's also the Director of the National Museum of Rome."

"Oh, a bigshot, huh?"

"No one knows more about Ancient Rome than him."

Jack nodded. "Gotcha. Thanks. What about the girl?"

The waiter turned and squinted. "I'm sorry, but I don't know her."

"No worries. Thanks."

Before the waiter walked away, Jack caught him checking out May. It shouldn't have bothered him as much as it did. If he was going to drool for May, he could've at least waited until Jack turned around.

"Hey, *Georgio*, eyes off my prize."

The waiter became flustered. "No, I wasn't—"

"Do it again, and I'll have her kick the shit out of you." Jack jabbed a finger in the man's face. "And not in a *Fifty Shades of Gray* kind of way, you filthy kink."

The beet red waiter huffed and stormed away.

"Was that necessary?" May asked.

Jack shrugged. "What? I can get very possessive over things I love." His eyes opened wide and he looked down at May. She was staring up at him. He'd just used the all-powerful L word. "Let's, uh, find our seats."

"I don't think they are assigned."

Jack pulled her to the central aisle and into the third row. "This'll do!"

He fell into the aisle seat, face flushed, heart beating a million miles a minute. His right leg shook and his palms were drenched in sweat. Jack had no idea what to do or say next. So, he just sat, spine rigid, and waited for the Ninth Legion showcase to start.

May leaned in close, gently squeezed his left thigh, and whispered something that rocked Jack's world.

"You know, I get very possessive over the things I love too."

Jack snapped his attention over to her and met her striking eyes and warm smile.

"*Good evening, and welcome to a most grand occasion.*"

Jack's shoulder fell. The rotund museum director had moved over to the stage. He had also just ruined an absolutely perfect moment.

May slid her hand into Jack's as Lombardi continued to speak. She leaned in close again. "Let's just enjoy the rest of the night here. We'll have plenty of time to talk about it later." She squeezed his hand hard. "I plan on staying up very late."

Jack's eyebrows lifted high and he smiled like a child on Christmas morning.

To Jack, Paris had just lost its title as the City of Love.

To him, it was Rome.

5

The first thirty minutes of Lombardi's presentation was unbelievably long-winded and self-indulgent. He went on to say that without his museum's aid, the excavation team would've never found the eagle. That, of course, was ludicrous since the stone container housing the artifact had been found by construction workers while doing routine demolition work.

Jack whispered his thoughts to May. "I think someone is a little butthurt that he wasn't included in the find."

"Just a little?" May mockingly asked.

Jack laughed a little too loud. Lombardi tripped over his next words. He gave Jack a death stare before moving onto the first of six scrolls.

At this rate, we'll be here all night, Jack thought.

If Lombardi had been on Jack's immediate shitlist, he would've heckled the man into moving the showcase along, and getting straight to the eagle. It made sense why he didn't, though. The *aquila* headpiece was the real reason everyone was here. It would've been unwise for Lombardi to lead off with his best hitter. So, Jack patiently sat through the first three scrolls.

He did have to admit, they were also pretty impressive. Each one contained information relating to the Ninth Legion's roster construction, ranks, and time served.

"I personally find it very interesting that the eagle was found outside of Rome, considering history tells us that the Ninth Legion was stationed hundreds of miles away at the time of their demise."

Huh. That is pretty interesting, Jack thought. *Why bring it back here if you were trying to hide it?*

Maybe his and Eddy's hypothesis was wrong. It would make more sense to bury it farther away from the Roman capital, instead of in its backyard. But then there was the idea of hiding it where someone would never think to look. Jack wasn't exactly sure where the Ninth's last assignment had been, but if it had been hundreds of miles away, as Lombardi had said, then hiding it on the borders of Rome might have been the smarter move.

Happily, the next couple of scrolls went by fast. Lombardi then strode up to the encased eagle, standing beside it with pride.

For no reason other than it being an important piece of Italian history. Jack squinted. *But that's not why you care. You just want the credit.*

"To understand why this seemingly inconsequential emblem is so important, one must understand a Roman legion, specifically the Ninth Legion."

Here we go. Jack sat up straighter now.

"Finally," May mumbled, rubbing her lower back. "The man has talked in circles all night."

Jack grinned, but kept his eyes on Lombardi.

Lombardi began to pace as he spoke. "There are many outlandish stories swirling around about the Ninth Legion and their eagle. My personal favorite, and the most fanciful, is that once it is reconnected with its base, and the pole of an *aquilifer*, an eagle-bearer, it is supposed to lead to a vast wealth—a treasure of some kind."

The museum director scoffed, laughing so hard that his belly bounced.

"Yes, well, let me tell you, that it's nothing more than a child's fairytale, despite what a few of my colleagues may think..."

Lombardi glanced to his right, to the same woman from before. She was currently standing offstage, looking very nervous. Everyone in attendance was now staring at her.

So, she's an expert on the subject too? Jack thought. *Hmmm. Good to know.*

"Though, interestingly, *aquilas* of the era were typically made of bronze or silver, but as you can clearly see, this particular one is made of solid gold. Beautifully preserved, I might add. If you look closely, you can see evidence that the eagle and its base were separated with great care. There was little force behind the action."

Lombardi produced a handkerchief and blotted his forehead before continuing.

"Some say that gold was used because of the Ninth's over-the-top beliefs. There is evidence—murky as it may be—of zealous behavior deep within their ranks, borderline spiritual extremism, not unlike a cult full of madmen."

Lombardi stepped up to the front edge of the stage, holding his hands behind his back.

"Nevertheless, the eagle standard was considered to be the legion's most important possession. It was sacred to them. And if a legion should misplace theirs or lose it in battle, they would be disgraced...forever."

The most bizarre thing happened next. Jack thought he heard someone cough behind him. By the time his brain registered the noise, Lombardi was struck in the forehead by something fast-moving and unseen. The back of his head exploded in a gore of blood, coating the eagle's casing. The museum director flopped backward.

Jack and May jumped to their feet. Someone had just shot and killed Alberto Lombardi. Before Jack could rush to the stage to check on him, however dead he was, a voice boomed through the archaeological showcase.

"Do not move!"

Everyone in attendance screamed in response to the abhorrent act. Everyone except Jack and May. They spun to look for the shooter, but instead found a single man standing just inside the gloom of the shadowy entrance tunnel. Despite the poor lighting, Jack could see members of the security staff lying on the floor. He couldn't tell if any of them were just knocked unconscious or worse.

The newcomer stepped into the light, showcasing his own marvel of Ancient Rome. He wore a beautifully polished, golden gladiator helmet. To Jack, it reminded him of the one Russell Crowe wore in *Gladiator*, when he was known as the Spaniard. However, this one covered the man's entire face, whereas Russell's mouth and chin had been exposed. Also, the Ninth Legion was technically called *Legio IX Hispana*, the Ninth Spanish Legion.

Is that why they call Maximus the 'Spaniard?' Jack asked himself.

"Please, sit," the newcomer said.

No one argued. Everyone sat.

The man's clothes were that of an armored tactical unit, and were well-worn. It meant he wore them often and had for some time. His all-black BDUs screamed former military, and in this case, *current* mercenary, more than likely.

He did not hold a weapon. However, Jack did spot a rifle tightly slung on his back and a sidearm holster on his right hip.

"He's not the shooter," Jack whispered.

"I know. He's too close."

Jack glanced at May and continued his assessment of the situation. "Definitely suppressed, and from far away." His eyes darted into the stands above the entry point. The Colosseum had several levels to choose from. "Up there somewhere."

Despite what Hollywood poured down people's throats, *silenced* weapons were not silent. Even the most advanced suppressors could only do just that, *suppress* the deafening report of a firearm. Typically, when a suppressor weapon went off, it would sound like two pieces of wood slapping together. Another reason to use them was to hide the explosive muzzle flash caused by the projectile violently leaving the barrel. It was a very handy accessory to have in covert situations.

Or when taking hostages.

This was eerily similar to what had happened to Jack back in Poland. There, an armed band of Neo-Nazis had taken over Auschwitz. Jack doubted that was the case here—the Neo-Nazi part.

"I'm guessing he's their leader," May whispered.

"Thank you, Captain Obvious."

"Jack, look." A red dot winked to life forty feet up in the stands. A second one ignited off to their left. "And another."

Jack looked up and to his right. "Over there too."

Each one of the lasers had landed on a random member of the audience.

"I'd like you to meet a few of my friends," the masked man said. "If you cooperate, they will not shoot. If anyone attempts to contact the authorities, not only will you die, but so will the people on your left and right."

Jack looked around, happy to see that no one was going for their phones.

Jack refocused his attention on the man himself. Even though his face was hidden, he was still giving away plenty about himself that Jack could use later.

First off, he spoke English, which was great, and it was accented in Italian, same as the staff. The biggest difference with this guy was that his accent wasn't as heavily accented. That meant he used the English language often.

Okay, so he's a local that travels, Jack thought.

Jack had taken into account that English was the common language of the world when making this assumption. Not everyone spoke Italian, but a lot of people, especially in other countries, spoke English.

Second, his gait was identical to his words, calm and stiff. None of this affected him emotionally. As Jack had suspected earlier, this was old hat for him.

Definitely ex-military.

The way he commanded the *room* was telling too. This guy was also used to being in charge. If Jack had to guess, he'd say this one had been a team leader in the Italian Special Forces, perhaps the 9th Paratroopers. They were a Tier 1 assault team.

"Awfully dramatic," May quietly added.

Then there was that…

Jack had no idea why this guy was wearing a golden gladiator mask, and as he neared the central aisle, Jack saw he was wearing eye black too.

"Was he a theater major?" Jack asked.

May could only shrug.

The skin around his exposed eyes was jet-black, painted with a substance that was more commonly used in sports. Traditionally, eye black was painted on beneath the person's eyes. It was used to absorb the intrusive light as it struck your eyes. In doing so, it reduced the glare bouncing off the wearer's skin, chiefly an athlete's sweaty skin.

But that wasn't this guy. This was all for show.

Jack had no idea what to make of him. He could've just as well been a whack job, modern-day, legionnaire cult leader.

Jack closed his eyes and sighed. "Why do I always get the crazies?"

"What?" May asked.

He shook his head, staying quiet as the "whack job" neared them. Jack noticed something else about him. He was staring at the eagle up on stage. He hadn't once looked at anyone since appearing from out of the shadows.

Jack looked back and forth between the gladiator and the eagle.

Oh, crap. I'm right, aren't I?

6

So far, the event's captor had not made any kind of demands from anyone except the part about not contacting the police. Jack watched him mount the steps up to the low, hip-high stage, passing by Lombardi's petrified colleague. The only move she had made was to get out of the murderer's way. Jack was stunned to watch him nod his thanks to her.

Oh, so he's a gentleman now?

The lone sound in the entire Colosseum was this man's footsteps. His combat boots clunked across the hollow stage until he approached Lombardi's body. The helmeted man stopped, bent over at the waist, and put his hands on his knees. He quietly examined the corpse for a moment. When he next spoke, he did so while still staring at the body.

"A disgrace, huh?" he asked Lombardi. Jack's eyes were glued to the scene. "Does anyone else share his sentiment?" He stood erect and faced the crowd. As he did, four more men entered the arena, appearing as if from nowhere. They held beefy assault rifles at the low ready and wore similar gladiator masks, though these were matte black, not gold. "Does anyone else believe that our ancestors are disgraces?"

May leaned in closer. "Ancestors?"

Jack didn't respond. His mind was now picking through its deepest recesses. In all his years of serving in the military, he had never heard of an outfit quite like this.

Jack squinted hard. *Who are you?*

"We need to do something," May whispered.

"Like what? There's two of us and five, six, seven—Goldie makes eight—of them. Oh, and we're unarmed, remember?"

May's fire dimmed. "What can we do then?"

"Survive," Jack replied, not liking his own words. "Then we can call the cops."

May looked at Jack, then back over to their abductor. "I have a better idea." She stood.

"May, no," Jack hissed, pulling on her wrist.

She ripped out of his grip. "You aren't going to get far without our help."

Jack watched in horror as the three red dots left their initial targets and centered on May. With nothing else to do, Jack raised his hands and slowly stood.

"And why's that?" the enigmatic man asked.

"Because we have the means to get you what you want."

The helmeted leader stepped closer to the edge of the stage. "Do you now?" He turned his hard gaze on Jack. "Do you?"

Jack gritted his teeth and quietly asked, "What the hell are you doing?"

"Doing what I do best," May replied. "I'm improvising."

"Do you?" he asked again.

Well, I guess we can at least delay these guys a little and give the police more time, Jack thought, relenting.

"Yes, we do," Jack replied, putting it together in his head. "We can help you find the other pieces of the *aquila*."

"And what makes you think we are pursuing them?"

Jack grinned. "The way you've been looking at it. It's the same way one might stare at a beautiful woman. And like the late Dr. Lombardi said, the royal standard was expertly divided. It would only make sense that you guys are trying to put it back together."

The other man tilted his head to the side a little, then stood tall. "Very impressive, Mister…"

"Jones—Dr. Jack Jones."

"And what exactly are you a doctor of?"

Jack looked around. "My education is in United States military history."

"Which means you probably served at some point."

Jack waggled his hand. "A little."

The other man stepped even closer to the edge of the stage. "Oh, I think it was more than just a little. A man of your stature and education…and fortitude…was most likely Special Forces of some kind. Am I right?"

Jack couldn't help but smile. "Not bad." He glanced left and spotted the waiter from earlier. He was now staring at Jack with a frightened look on his face. Before returning his attention to the helmeted man, Jack gave the waiter a quick wink.

"Now, who's your friend, and why does she say you can help us?"

May stuck her chest out, throwing her shoulders back at the same time. "I am May Zetian, formerly of the Ministry of State Security."

Their abductor looked back and forth between them. "Interesting… Tell me, what are a Chinese spy and an American soldier doing in Rome—in the Colosseum—tonight?"

"Former spy and soldier," May corrected. "We don't do that stuff anymore."

"Apologies, excuse me, though the question still stands."

May glanced at Jack for help.

Here we go, Jack thought. *Time to really sling some bull.*

"We're here for those," Jack said, pointing not at the eagle, but the scrolls.

"The scrolls?" he asked.

Jack shrugged. "Why not?"

"Because," he replied, turning and stepping over to the eagle, "this is infinitely more valuable than any one scroll."

He shouted something in what Jack recognized as Latin. Two of the four arena gunmen jogged forward, joining their boss onstage. Then, just as quickly as they had made it onstage, they gripped the edges of the protective casing and pushed it over. It fell backward with a crash, falling into the dark recesses of the *hypogeum* below.

The eagle was now exposed.

The leader carefully picked up the priceless artifact, turned to face the crowd, and hefted it high over his head.

Eyes glued on *his* prize, he shouted, "*Gaudere Legio Nona!*"

The four nearby gunmen repeated his words, standing at attention as they said them.

More Latin. But unfortunately, Jack didn't understand a lick of it.

When they quieted, Jack looked around. "So, the scrolls?"

"I'm curious. Why the scrolls?"

"Our buyer is very particular," May replied. "If he wants the scrolls, then he wants the scrolls."

"Yeah," Jack added, "we don't argue the *whys* and *whats*. We just do our jobs."

Another of the men rushed down the center aisle, carrying with him a large, square case. To Jack, it looked like one of the foam-lined weapon cases he had back home, a Pelican case.

"Very admirable…for a couple of thieves."

For some reason, Jack went on the defensive. "Takes one to know one, pal."

"I am *not* some simple thief." The other man's eyes grew more intense.

Jack held up his hands in mock-surrender. "Oh, I never said you were *simple*, but yeah, by definition, you *are* a thief."

The man in charge shouted another order in Latin. The lasers shifted off May and onto Jack.

Jack held out a pleading hand. "Whoa, buddy. I never said you were a bad thief." He motioned to the other helmeted men on the stage. "You seem like you have all your ducks in a row."

The leader huffed a heavy breath, then set the eagle down into the now open case. The soldier who had brought the case forward, shut its lid, then whispered something to his commander. Jack could've sworn he heard the other man call the big shot "*Legatus.*"

What the hell does that mean? Jack thought.

He didn't get the opportunity to think it over any further. The telltale *whup* of an incoming helicopter drowned out his thoughts. The black wraith slid into position directly above the arena floor, hovering fifty feet off of it. The rotor wash caused everyone in attendance to duck down and cover their heads.

But not Jack and May.

They stood and watched through squinted eyes. Both were visibly angry that there was nothing else that they could do.

Come on, Jack mentally pleaded. *Someone on the outside must've noticed all this going down, right?*

As if answering his prayers, a line of armor-wearing policemen, the equivalent of a United States SWAT team, came barreling into the not-so-private event. Several of them held riot shields. All of them were armed with a variety of rifles, shotgun, and pistols.

Now, not only was everyone ducked down, most of the hostages dove to the ground and curled in on themselves—Jack and May included. However, the duo kept their eyes up and on the mysterious armed unit.

The man with the case ran back toward the middle of the central aisle just as a line was dropped from the aircraft. It also just so happened to be right next to Jack and May.

The gladiators opened fire on Italian police, keeping them from advancing any further into the Colosseum. As of now, the incoming force was taking cover behind their shields within the entry tunnel.

Ah, to hell with this, Jack thought, deciding on a course of action.

He climbed to his feet and tackled the man holding the case.

7

Jack landed atop the bigger legionnaire and instantly went for the man's jugular and eyes. Punches to the face and ears would only injure Jack's hands, so would body blows, for that matter, unless he slipped in a shot between the bottom of his plate carrier and his belt. Last Jack recalled, body armor was still fist-proof.

But his armpits aren't!

The gladiator swiped at Jack's neck with a knife. Jack blocked it, giving the guy's wrist a stiff palm strike. Then Jack balled his fist and drove it into the other man's left armpit. Jack personally knew just how painful of an area that was to get hit. The energy transferred caused by the force of the impact went straight into your lungs, not to mention the plentiful number of nerves, as well as the lymph glands, located there.

The punch landed solidly, but so did his foe's rising knee strike. The *cup check* crushed Jack's privates. He also took the hard, plastic case across the temple, dazing him good. The results were almost painful enough to make Jack vomit, mostly from the shot to his groin. He lost his breath and rolled off his opponent. His head swam, and he lost all ability to do anything expect breathe.

The thickly built gladiator stood, drew his sidearm, and aimed it at Jack. "*Gaudere Legio Nona,*" he repeated. His eyes were filled with mania.

But then something struck him in the chin with the force of a mule kick, causing the soldier to drop his pistol. Jack snapped his attention over to his savior in time to see May retract her bare foot, instantly returning herself to a perfectly balanced fighting stance.

The kick not only saved Jack's life, but it also jettisoned the matte-black helmet from the other man's head. It went sailing into the seating behind him, revealing one of the hostage takers for the first time.

Huh.

Besides the eye black and manic expression on his face, the guy looked downright normal. Then again, what else was Jack really expecting?

"Theo!" The de-helmeted gunman glanced over to his boss. The gilded man's next words were back in Latin, but he was pointing down at the case.

With both Jack and May still unarmed, the unmasked man snagged the fallen case and bolted back toward the stage. While he, Jack, and May had been busy beating on one another, additional rappelling lines had been dropped. More and more armored policemen funneled in through the entrance. Soon, the criminal force would be overrun.

But not soon enough, Jack thought as the guy with the case skidded to a stop. Then he heaved the load up to his commander.

Jack struggled to his feet. "We gotta stop 'em." He was still trying to catch his wind.

May looked down at Jack, then took off barefoot after the case.

"May, no!" Jack shouted, stumbling after her.

The unveiled man clipped onto one of the available lines, then accepted the case back from the group's leader. He was quickly whisked away into the night sky a second later, prize in hand. The leader was still present, laying down cover fire for the other men present. One after the other, the ground force was yanked skyward. The only men Jack had yet to see were the snipers.

They must be getting out another way, he thought.

The stage lights must've concealed May's advance, because she arrived unharmed, diving headlong into the much bigger man's knees. She took him down, causing him to drop his *Heckler & Koch* rifle. Jack limped forward, quickly watching the other man overpower the slighter Mayleen Wu. The commander simply absorbed May's quick strikes before reaching out and grabbing a handful of her hair. Then he pulled her in and drove his elbow into her face.

"May!" Jack shouted, hurrying forward.

But it was too late.

The leader stood with his elbow hooked around May's neck. He secured a line to his belt and gave May a massive bearhug. Then, *both* of them were reeled in.

"May!" Jack shouted, sprinting forward, hand reaching to the heavens. "May!"

"Jaaack!" May replied, disappearing into the inky blackness hanging over the Colosseum.

With the gunmen gone, the shooting subsided. From what Jack could see, none of the legionnaires had died. He looked around and spotted several policemen on the ground, as well as a handful of innocent bystanders. This wasn't what Jack had expected at all.

He removed his phone from his pocket and called the only person he could think of. Even though it was just after four in the morning back at the office, he knew his boss, Solomon Raegor, would pick up. Eddy too. Their jobs forced them to be on call twenty-four-seven most days. While he waited for the international call to connect, he spotted a lump in the floor, back where he and the gladiator, Theo, had fought. Jack headed for it, hearing a familiar voice on the other end of his call pick up.

"*Jack?*" Raegor asked. "*Aren't you supposed to still be at the Colosseum?*"

"I am, sir," Jack replied. "But there's a problem with that…"

He knelt and picked up the matte-black helmet. He was surprised with how light it was. Whoever designed it had clearly spared no expense. Jack flipped it over and inspected the inside. There was a high-tech comms system and ergonomic padding.

"*What problem?*"

"A group of modern-day gladiators took over the event at gunpoint, stole the eagle, injured—possibly killed—several cops and attendees, oh, and they kidnapped May."

Raegor groaned. "*Uh… Give me a moment.*" Jack could hear him doing something on the other end. A few seconds later, he could hear Raegor speaking to someone else on another phone.

"*Hey, Jack*," Eddy said. "*Are you okay?*"

"Yeah, besides getting a sledgehammer to the junk, I'm fine."

"*Good to hear*," Raegor said flatly. "*Eddy's already on the horn with Italian intelligence. We'll find May.*"

Jack took a deep breath, waving away an incoming medic. Jack was sore, but otherwise, fine. "What in the actual hell, sir?"

"*Yes, 'what' indeed.*"

"*Jack?*" Eddy asked.

"Yeah, Ed?"

"*Tell me everything, and I'll get it to the Roman authorities, ASAP.*"

Jack chuckled. "Right. Well, this is what happened—"

"*Hang on,*" Raegor interrupted. "*Get moving first, Jack. We don't need anyone overhearing us and asking questions. For now, this is just a local issue. Having two U.S. operatives involved would be a bad look.*"

Jack knew the game, and he knew Raegor was right. He was dancing the optics dance. And honestly, like he had said before, were people like him ever truly off the clock? Jack also knew that, if he got detained, it would take *that much* longer to figure out what was going on.

And to find May, he thought, trying to relax.

"Okay. Let me get out of here and I'll call you back."

"*Copy that,*" Raegor said. "*And Jack?*"

"Yeah?"

"*We'll get her back. I promise.*"

Jack sighed and joined a crowd of panicked attendees heading for the main exit. "Yeah, sir, I know. Okay, gotta run."

There wasn't a real reason to hang up except for the possibility of there being curious ears in the arena. Jack just needed to get his thoughts straight. Right now, they were squarely on May. While good and all, he also needed to focus on the men who had abducted her. If he could find them, he'd find her.

Hotel first. Then something heavily caffeinated. Jack wouldn't be going to bed anytime soon. He felt the left side of his face swelling a bit from the hit he had taken. *And maybe a couple of ibuprofen too.*

He begrudgingly dropped the helmet. Getting caught with crime scene evidence would also be a bad look. Jack retraced his steps back up to street level and declined to hail a taxi back to his hotel. He needed the walk. Plus, it would give him time to talk it out with Raegor and Eddy.

Speaking of which...

Jack checked his immediate surroundings. When he confirmed he was clear, he redialed the home office.

"Okay, Jack," Raegor said upon answering, "*start from the top.*"

"*Don't skip a single detail, either,*" Eddy added.

"Oh, that won't be a problem. There are a *lot* of details."

8

Jack slapped his keycard onto his hotel room door's magnetic key reader, deactivating the deadbolt. He turned the handle and pushed it open. He continued inside, allowing the overhead, hydraulic door closer to do its job and shut it without a bang.

Jack tossed his ruined jacket on the bed and quickly went about changing his clothes. Raegor and Eddy were due to call him back at any moment, and he needed to be ready to leave at the drop of a hat. Jack went to the closet safe and retrieved his gun as his first order of business. There was no telling who was looking for him at this point. If the gladiators could take over an event at the Colosseum so easily, then they could've also had people on the streets searching for him. The helmets made even more sense now. Not only were they a homage to who these guys believed they were descended from, but the helmets also hid their identities.

"I dare you to come," Jack muttered to himself, glancing at the door. "I'm begging you."

He hadn't felt this level of a call to violence in years. Jack prayed someone was stupid enough to come up to his room, looking for a fight.

"Relax, dude. They aren't coming."

Jack had a feeling that whoever those people were, they didn't operate like intelligence officers. They were more military than anything else. They weren't plainclothes spies.

Then again, Jack could also be entirely wrong.

He double checked the weapon, making sure there was a round in the chamber. Glocks had no manual thumb safety, so he didn't have to worry about disengaging it to pull the trigger. Satisfied, he tossed the pistol onto the bed next to his jacket. Next was the rest of his clothes. Jack swiftly threw on his regular attire: t-shirt, jeans, sneakers, shoulder holster, and leather jacket. The gun went into its place beneath his left armpit just as his phone vibrated in his pocket.

"This is Jack," he answered, sitting on the edge of the bed.

"*Hey, Jack,*" Eddy said. "*You haven't by chance heard from May, have you?*"

"I wish."

"*Thought so.*" She sighed. "*Figured I'd ask, just in case.*"

Eddy went silent.

"Something on your mind, Ed?"

"*You mean besides all this?*"

Jack grinned. "Yeah, besides all this."

"*Actually, there is. Look, Jack, despite what I might think of May's past, I really do hope she's okay.*"

"I know, Ed. And thanks. So, how exactly are we going to find her? Don't suppose you implanted tracking beacons in our dental work, or something?"

"Um, what?"

Jack rubbed his face. "Nothing. It's a *Spy Kids* thing."

"*Spy Kids? The children's movie?*"

"Yeah," Jack replied quickly, feeling a little ashamed. "It was written and directed by Robert Rodriguez, ya know?"

"*But for kids.*"

"Yeah, Ed, for kids…"

Another line picked up. "*Raegor here.*" Jack sat up straighter. He bet Eddy did too, even though their boss couldn't see them. "*Based on your debrief, Jack, it looks like the only real way you're going to find May, is to figure out where this fabled treasure is.*"

Jack flopped back on his bed and closed his eyes. "I was afraid you'd say that."

"*Oh, come on, Jack,*" Eddy teased. "*Are you telling me you aren't up for another treasure hunt?*"

"That's *exactly* what I'm saying." Jack opened his eyes but didn't sit up. "I'm also hoping May will keep us in the loop. Remember her background…"

"*How can I forget?*" Eddy said. "*Recently retired Chinese agent.*"

"*Put away the claws, Eddy,*" Raegor warned. "*Jack's right. If there's anyone who can keep us in the loop despite their circumstances, it's May.*"

"Yeah," Jack said, chuckling, "I'm actually starting to feel sorry for those guys. Sir, are we really going with this whole 'secret fortune' thing?"

"*We are. I don't believe for a second that these guys would go to all this trouble, and dress as you say they did, for a quick in-and-out artifact heist.*"

"*I agree,*" Eddy said. "*Makes no sense if they aren't pursuing something else. Like you said during your debrief, these guys are, more than likely, looking for the other pieces to their eagle thingy.*"

"That was all bullshit, Ed. But I don't necessarily disagree."

"*Oh, I know it was bullshit. But I'm starting to trust your bullshit more and more as time goes by.*"

"Uh, thanks, I guess?"

"*The biggest issue I have with it,*" Raegor said, "*is that the only information we have to go on is a couple of far out theories about these modern-day legionnaires and their ancestors.*"

Jack snorted. "Yeah, and good luck finding anything useful about the Ninth Legion on the net. It's nothing but hearsay and useless factoids."

"*And they killed our best chance at getting help,*" Eddy added. "*A Dr. Alberto Lombardi, Director of the National Museum of Rome.*"

Jack sat bolt upright. "That's not entirely accurate."

"*It's not?*" Raegor and Eddy asked together.

"No," Jack replied. "I, uh, may have left out a small detail."

"*Why don't I believe you?*" Eddy asked. "*It's never just a small detail with you.*"

"*Enough, you two,*" Raegor snapped. "*It's still very early in the morning here. I'm not in the mood, okay?*"

"*Yes, sir,*" Eddy replied.

Jack stood. "Yeah. Sorry, sir."

"*Go ahead, Jack,*" Raegor said, moving them along.

Jack began to pace the room, focusing on the detail—the person. "During the presentation, when Lombardi mentioned the theory about the treasure, he said it came from his colleagues."

"*You already mentioned that,*" Eddy said.

"I know, but the small detail I forgot to mention earlier was that he looked offstage at a woman."

"*Who?*" Raegor asked.

"No idea," Jack replied. "Never got a name. Lombardi was a little too high on himself to introduce her."

"*Okay, Jack,*" Reagor said, "*your top priority is to find this colleague. Once you do, we can go over the next move.*"

"Copy that. I guess I'm staying put, huh? At least, until you dig up something juicy."

"*Correct,*" Raegor replied. "*We'll look into who was scheduled to work the event.*"

"*Already on it,*" Eddy said. "*Shouldn't be too long before we have something for you, Jack.*"

Jack stopped and looked out his window. He could just see the top of the Colosseum from here. It was now completely lit up, no doubt crawling with police. Jack had slid out before anyone could pull him aside for questioning.

"Alright, guys. Let me know. I'll be here...waiting."

"*We'll find her, Jack,*" Raegor restated. "*We're prepared to call in everyone we have in the area for this.*"

Jack's reaction to that statement should've filled him with joy. But it didn't.

"Hold off on that, sir. These guys are major players, and based on their firepower, and their willingness to use it, I don't want to do anything to alert them."

"*Hmmm...*" Raegor grumbled.

"Please, sir. Only my boots on the ground for now. Just get me a name and an address, and I'll handle the rest."

"*Fine. For now.*"

Jack took a deep breath. "Thanks, guys. Talk soon."

He hung up and pocketed the device. Jack stepped over to the slider and stared out over Rome. The feelings he had for this city had changed drastically in the last couple of hours. He was also distracted, thinking mostly about what he and May were supposed to talk about tonight. Jack had incidentally revealed his true feelings for her. *But* she had also revealed hers. They felt the same way about one another.

Thank God, Jack thought. He couldn't imagine how he'd feel if she didn't feel the same way.

"It doesn't matter," he told his reflection. "She's a part of the mission too."

But unlike other missions, if someone were to die, in this case May, it would ruin Jack. He pictured himself slipping back into his former depressive

state, waking up in cold sweats as a result of the night terrors.
Every. Single. Night.

Jack turned away from the slider. "No. That's not happening."

Jack drew his pistol, removed the magazine, as well as the chambered round. Until Raegor and Eddy called him back, he'd dry fire and attempt to keep his mind off the worst-case scenario.

He looked down at his clothes. Since he wasn't going anywhere right away, he'd get cleaned up too.

I'm coming, May. But first, a shower. He glanced down at the room's mini fridge, opened the door, quickly snagging a beer. *And you're coming with me.*

9

It had been just over an hour since May had been abducted by the ancestors of the Ninth Legion. At least, that's who the leader had said they were. May had no reason to believe him one way or the other, and frankly, it didn't matter. These guys were high-end antiquities thieves, and what had stolen was something May, and her new employer, had sworn to protect.

History.

It was weird being on this side of the coin. For all of May's adult life, and parts of her teen years, she had been on the reverse end. She had been the thief, the spy, even the assassin, though not as often. The MSS had specific people involved in that field. May had always had a knack for recon operations—intel gathering—using her quick thinking and laundry list of aliases to good use.

Since being yanked skyward, tossed into the cargo hold of a blacked-out helicopter, then having her head covered, May had kept track of the time by simply counting up from *one*. It wasn't a perfect method, but it worked well enough.

3,759... 3,760... 3,761...

It also helped that these guys weren't big talkers, so interruptions were few and far between. Even when she had been manhandled out of the aircraft and back onto solid ground, May had only lost a couple seconds of counting. Keeping track of the time in this manner also kept May focused. It kept her thoughts on the situation and off of things like—

Jack, she thought, picturing his face.

She replayed the scene with the waiter in her head. He had been ogling her from behind, and had been caught by Jack. She had known from the get-go that people would be looking at her. A dress like that would naturally draw the attention of everyone. May's confidence while wearing such a thing would also draw people's attention. It had all been done to tease Jack too. She adored his boyish charm and enjoyed making him squirm.

Well, it was mostly to tease him.

May had also wanted to give him a show in a way. She wanted *him* to ogle her, which he did, of course. But ever the gentleman at heart, Jack had frequently complimented her too, telling her that she was beautiful. Lots of men had told May that over the years, but she knew that Jack actually meant it. It had been from the heart, not the pants.

3,777... 3,778... 3,779...

Currently, May sat in a chair with her wrists zip-tied behind her back. She wasn't lashed to the chair in any way, and her legs were free. She was still in her destroyed dress too. A novice would've thought that these guys were being lazy, or had very little experience when it came to detaining captives. But May wasn't a novice. She knew someone was in the room with her.

And where are my heels?

Most likely armed too, she thought, trying to pick out his location.

So, she just kept counting, staying silent. She would force them to make the first move.

3,784... 3,785... 3,786...

A door squeaked open behind her. The noise had honestly startled her, but she kept calm and didn't show it. Heavy boots entered the room. The door stayed open too. This lot was confident. May assumed they were trying to bait her into moving for the door.

She wouldn't.

Sorry, boys.

The owner of the heavy boots strode past her, slowing as he neared. She figured it was a man since all the gunmen she had seen at the Colosseum had been big, burly males. He kept moving, stopping once he was directly in front of May. Then he spoke, but not to her. His voice was low, and once again, he spoke Latin, not English or Italian.

Romans spoke Latin. Who are these guys?

The question was rhetorical, of course. She already knew who they were— who they believed they were. These guys were 21st-century Roman legionnaires. They were heavily armed, well-trained, well-funded, and obviously well-connected. In all the years May had spent deep inside the world's intelligence community, she had never heard of a group like this. To her, it meant they weren't newbies. They had learned, long ago, to expertly cover their tracks. They probably didn't show themselves often, either. Sure, in some local circles, there were undoubtedly myths about these guys that popped up from time to time, but nothing that had made its way around the globe.

She sighed. *I need to call Li.*

Li Huang was one of a handful of people May could still trust inside the MSS, and someone that could get her answers.

The last time May had spoken with Li, she had ordered the assassination of her father, Jin Zhao, head of the Ministry of State Security, as well as the owner of BIOfintiy Genetics, David Cho. Though, as it turned out, Zhao had already killed Cho by the time Li had entered the picture. Regardless, with them out of the way for good, May could safely disappear.

3,798... 3,799...

"Gemma Conti."

May stopped counting upon hearing the two words. The way the speaker had said them made her believe they were a name, not just additional jumbled Latin. It was the same way she would say a name if she were speaking Mandarin to someone, having to break stride and pronounce a name in another language.

So, who is Gemma Conti? she pondered.

Big Boots turned, while another set quickly circled around her. Then the door shut.

"Time to start talking."

May's hood was ripped away from her head, but she still couldn't see much of anything. There were no windows in the ten-by-ten room, and the only light source was coming from directly above her in the way of a dim lightbulb.

"Classic interrogation setting," May said, blinking hard. "Goes along with your performance back at the Colosseum. Very dramatic."

A single man stepped into the low light. Gone was his helmet. His expression was deadpan, unamused by her verbal jabs. The man's eyes were still outlined with eye black. Oddly, May was pretty sure she recognized him.

"You," she said, thinking back to her and Jack's fight with him. The leader named him. May looked away as she thought, but quickly recalled it. Her eyes darted back to him. "Theo, right? The guy with the case." She grinned. "The guy I kicked in the face." She mocked him by looking around. "Where's your hat?"

Theo moved like lightning, and he backhanded May across the face. The impact stung like hell, but it wasn't anything she couldn't handle.

She opened and closed her mouth, feeling a slight discomfort in her right cheek. "Not bad."

"Start talking," he said, showing off Italian-accented English. "Convince me why I should keep you alive."

This was where May shined. No one could out-intense her. "My global connections are second-to-none."

"So are ours."

May studied him, replaying everything she knew about them so far. Their group was dramatic, yes, but they wholeheartedly believed in what they did. They were extreme, zealots even. Insulting them any further would be the wrong move. It would only enrage them more. That would be bad since May needed more information.

"Mostly confined to Europe, I bet," she said, keeping her voice calm. She didn't know a lot about Ancient Rome, but she did know that they ruled everything surrounding the Mediterranean Sea, as well as up into the United Kingdom and over into the Middle East. "Perhaps you have some decent contacts in the Arab world too, but who wants to go there nowadays?"

Theo gave her a small smirk. "Impressive. Yes, wherever Rome once ruled, so do we have a foothold there."

May listened to the sounds in the environment as they conversed. She needed to figure out where she was. Sometimes, all you needed was a specific sound to give away your location, like the deep bellow of a ship's horn, or the rumble of a train passing closely by.

"And let me guess, this treasure you're looking for—the one Dr. Lombardi was talking about before you killed him for no reason—it'll help finance some massive operation you have planned."

Bright lights burst to life, blinding May. It also nearly concussed her. The sudden switch in brightness had been like a sucker punch to the temples. She quickly shut her eyes and gritted her teeth as another set of heavy footfalls entered the room.

May looked at the floor, opening her eyes just enough to see the newcomer's legs continue around her. He stopped next to his friend. May's head still hurt, but she needed to push it aside.

She looked up. The newest arrival was wearing a gold helmet.

May grinned. "I was wondering if I'd see you again."

He knelt in front of her, staying out of kicking range. "Who are you really?"

May sat back and relaxed. "You first."

The team leader reached up and slowly removed his helmet. Like his buddy, this one also possessed an unwavering stare. The similarities were uncanny, almost as if they were related.

No, May thought. *That's not it. These two are just guzzling down the crazy Cool-Aid.*

The thought made May mentally roll her eyes. Jack's personality was definitely rubbing off on her.

This one's jawline was squarer, and his nose was slightly longer. His, otherwise, chiseled good looks were marred by a deep scar running from his left cheek down to his neck. May guessed that he'd seen battle.

Military?

He stood tall. "I am Marcus Cerialis, descendent of the great Quintus Petillius Cerialis, General of the Ninth Legion."

"The Ninth Legion?" May asked, remembering tidbits of Dr. Lombardi's presentation. "Correct me if I'm wrong, but didn't they go missing two-thousand years ago?"

Marcus smiled. "Not all of them. Some have always been here, waiting for this precise moment, doing as our ancestors did."

"This moment?" May asked. "Which one are we talking about?"

Marcus' eyes narrowed. "This one." He and Theo stepped aside to reveal the stolen eagle. It sat on a thin stone pedestal carved into the shape of an ancient column. "We have been waiting for *this* exact moment ever since our standard was stolen from us."

What have I gotten myself into?

"What are you talking about?" May asked, voicing her confusion. "You've been waiting two millennia for a broken eagle statue?"

Marcus' eyes lit with fire. "This is not merely a logo or family crest!" He slammed his fist into his broad chest. "This is our identity! We are what's left of the Ninth Legion. Without this standard, we have been lost—nothing!" He turned to face it, giving May some relief from his frenzied glare. Marcus held out his hands as if basking in the eagle's glory. "But now, with it finally in our possession…"

May's right eyebrow crawled up her forehead. "The treasure, right?"

"And with it, our return to glory. With it, we will take back what is rightfully ours."

May looked back and forth between the two fanatics. "And that is?"

"The world, May Zetian, starting with the Mediterranean nations. We want what Rome, and the Macedonian before, failed to accomplish all those years ago."

"Global domination?" Both men stared at her, nonverbally confirming the answer to her question. Something else he just said stuck out. "The Macedonian? Are you talking about—"

"Yes, I am," Marcus interrupted.

May couldn't believe it. She didn't need to be a Greek or Roman scholar to put two and two together.

Instead of continuing along this crazy topic, May decided to veer down another one.

"Not to sound ungrateful, but why am I still alive? I'm not exactly an expert on Ancient Mediterranean civilizations. Now, transport us to China—that would be different."

"You are still alive because I am not a fool. Whoever it is you work for will surely come calling, eventually. You are our shield against them…for now."

"They won't come," May lied. She knew, for a fact, that Jack would come for her.

The thought made her smile. Unfortunately, Marcus and Theo both noticed.

"Your expression says otherwise. And based on the way your Jack looked at you, I have a feeling he will try to come in guns blazing."

Damn, May thought, once again cursing herself for having feelings.

"He's smarter than that. If he does come, you won't see it coming."

Marcus squatted in front of her. "Perhaps. America owns some of the best soldiers on the planet. I respect that. But, let me ask you, is it commonplace for one of those men to have skin in the game? Soldiers are trained to never make it personal. In this, he has failed."

"Tell us more about him?" Theo asked, speaking for the first time since Marcus entered.

"I told you, he's nobody. Former Special Forces. I'm not even sure which one; SEALs, Delta, Army Rangers? He also knows some interesting characters in the Italian underworld." That was a lie. "It's how we found out about the scrolls. Other than that, he's nothing to me."

"Is he now?" Marcus asked, not believing her. "What about your public display of affection? That looked pretty convincing."

They were watching us before the presentation even started! May realized.

May didn't respond. She was speechless. She didn't know what else she could say to sway the guy's opinion of her and Jack.

Marcus shrugged. "Fine, if he really is nothing to you…" He removed his phone from his pocket, dialed, and lifted it to his ear. He smiled wide. "Kill him."

May leapt out of her seat. "No!" Before she could get to him, Theo shoved her back into it and drew his sidearm.

The Legion's leader held his smile as he showed May his phone's screen. It was black. He had faked making the call to kill Jack.

May shut her eyes and dipped her chin. "Bastard." Her heart was hammering on the inside of her chest. "Played me like a fiddle."

Marcus stepped up close to her, then leaned in until they were eye to eye. "Tell me who you really work for."

May sighed. "You might want to get a chair."

Marcus stood tall, towering over her. "And why's that?"

She looked up at him, getting ready for what was about to come. "Because I don't typically talk this early in an interrogation." She leaned back, relaxing some. "You boys have no idea who you are talking to." She let out a fake yawn. "We might be here a while."

Marcus stepped away.

Theo came in with a hard right to her face. The impact sent her careening out of her chair. She hit the floor hard, unable to break her fall since her wrists were bound.

Damn. This guy doesn't hold back.

But she wouldn't give Theo, or Marcus, the satisfaction.

"Correction," May said, spitting a dollop of blood on the floor. "We *are* going to be here a while, especially if you hit like that." She lifted her head and gazed at Marcus. "If you guys use callsigns, I'd change his to 'Grandmother.'"

Theo growled, balled his right hand, and continued his *interrogation* of Mayleen Wu.

After two more strikes, Marcus shouted, "Enough!". Theo looked up at him, fist cranked back. "We need her alive still…for now."

Interesting… May thought, licking her bloodied lips.

Marcus did not partake in the violence against her, nor did he seem to appreciate what Theo was doing to her. May needed to remember that…if she could stay alive long enough for it to matter.

10

Eddy had called back with the ID of Lombardi's female colleague. She also had the woman's address handy.

Jack stood outside Dr. Gemma Conti's three-story apartment building. He double checked the street and building number.

"12 Via Giovanni Faber," he said to himself. He looked up into the night sky. "Thank God for Google Earth."

Jack had used the overhead satellite mapping system to scout ahead a little from afar. This neighborhood was made up of cookie-cut, salmon-colored buildings. The area was quiet, which was a nice touch after everything that had happened three hours ago.

And still no word from May, he thought.

As much as it pained him, Jack pushed aside his worry surrounding May. He studied the front entrance to Conti's building. All that stood in his way was a six-foot-tall, worn gate and a call box. Navigating them both would be easy. The fence to either side was the same height.

Jack scaled the right-hand barrier in seconds.

He dropped to the other side, landing in a squat. He stayed put, making sure he hadn't been seen by anyone. Not only was this breaking-and-entering, but Jack had no way of knowing whether any of the legionnaire thugs had beat him here.

Jack thought back to the way the leader had eyed Conti as he had made his way onstage. Jack's gut was telling him to be extra cautious. If they could identify her, then they could see her as both a liability and an asset. The latter was what Jack, Raegor, and Eddy were hoping. Either way, Jack needed to contact her before the legionnaires did.

He stood. *And, unlike me, they don't mind kidnapping people, obviously.*

On the other side of the gate, was a communal area. The manicured grounds acted as a natural separation between Conti's building, the one on Jack's left, with the back of the neighboring building to his right.

He kept to the outer edge of the ground's single light source, a faux antique lamp. Jack dashed across the central, brick walkway, diving to the lawn as a figure stepped out of the lit, doorless entryway. Then he heard something he dreaded.

A dog.

Its owner spoke in Italian, quietly shushing it. The animal obeyed and calmed. Jack currently hid out in the open, over near the front fence. He needed to find somewhere proper to hide fast, just in case they came this way. Luckily, it didn't look like the dog's owner had brought a flashlight. He'd have to rely on the short range of the lamp positioned at the center of the communal area.

Using his environment, Jack army crawled further to his left, toward the front façade of Conti's apartment building. The grass beneath him was short and made very little sound while he moved. Jack silently thanked the lawn maintenance team for doing their jobs well.

But then the dog had to go and look Jack's way. It sniffed, then whined. Its owner asked it something, not that Jack spoke the language. The tone of the man's voice was enough, though.

The dog whined again. Now the man turned and looked Jack's way.

He froze, still out in the open but covered in darkness. His clothes were dark blue and black, adding to his camouflage.

The dog whimpered loudly, pulling its owner forward, deeper into the shadows. Jack moved as quickly as he could, while also staying quiet. A row of hedges grew along the front of the building. He headed for the back of them and immediately entered the tight space. He was forced to roll onto his left side, making his movements more chaotic and, unfortunately, louder.

The dog's owner asked a question, causing Jack to freeze in place. Even though he was speaking Italian to his pet, Jack still had an idea of what was being said.

Someone there, Rigatoni? Jack asked internally. He closed his eyes and sighed. *Rigatoni. Really, Jack? Out of all the names for a dog you could come up with, you named this guy's dog after pasta?*

The man repeated the same incoherent-to-Jack question. The dog whined again.

"Go away," Jack silently mouthed.

After a few excruciating seconds, the local pulled his dog back toward the lamp, despite the animal's insistent whining. Jack clunked his head back against the concrete wall. Then, he waited for the dog to do its business.

Once he was done, both man and beast retreated indoors, leaving Jack alone in a bush.

"Right," he said, climbing to his feet. A pair of voices picked up just outside the gate. "Oh, come on…" Jack returned to cover, kneeling and ducking his head this time.

Two men monkeyed over the fence line, just as Jack had. Whoever they were, they didn't belong here, either.

Has to be the legionnaires, he thought.

Jack mentally cursed the dog. The delay it had caused might've now cost Gemma Conti her life.

Once the duo was on this side of the fence, they quietly conversed with one another. Jack tried to listen in, but couldn't hear them. Plus, he doubted they were speaking English. Jack guessed it was Italian or Latin. Those languages seemed to be the running theme. It made sense too. But that didn't mean it wasn't annoying.

Jack felt his Glock holstered beneath his left armpit. If these guys were legionnaires, he could easily shoot them both from his hiding spot. But he couldn't risk it. The report of the shots would bounce around the communal grounds like crazy. Police would then be called.

Gonna have to do this quietly, he thought, scanning the pair, *which means one at a time.*

They stopped between the lamp and the building's front entrance. Jack heard them whispering to one another. Then one of the men headed inside.

Huh. That'll do.

Jack needed to make this quick. The legionnaires now had a head start on him.

"Stupid dog," Jack muttered, standing, and edging out of the shrubs.

He quietly looped back around to the gate, bypassed it, and continued over to the rear of the neighboring building. He stayed low and kept to the darkness. So far, everything was going smoothly. His foe had yet to notice him. Jack's biggest obstacle was going to be getting in close. The second legionnaire stood just inside the aura of the lamp. Sneaking up behind him was going to be a challenge since Jack would have to enter the light to do so.

The inside of the building's entrance came into view for the first time too. Jack spotted four doors, two to either side of a central staircase. If there was an elevator, Jack didn't see one.

He scanned the area directly around the lamp first. There were four benches situated around the base of its post. Each one faced away from it, pointing to the north, south, east, and west. Right now, Jack faced the eastern bench, kneeling some fifty feet away from it. His target stood twenty feet in front of the western bench.

Okay, let's call it seventy-five feet... he decided, *across open grounds with no cover.* Jack started to hate this more and more. His eyes fell to the benches. *Hmmm, there's an idea!*

Jack used his keen night sight and scanned the earth around him. To his right was a small garden filled with potted plants and white pebbles. Jack tiptoed over to it and grabbed three, quarter-sized stones.

"Time to go fishing," he whispered.

Jack tossed one of the pebbles at the lamp. He didn't need to hit it. He just needed to get close. The stone vanished into the night sky. Jack didn't see it land, but he heard it hit near the southern bench.

So did the legionnaire.

Jack grinned when the other guy turned, asking a question in Italian. After a couple of seconds of silence, he repeated the question.

"Is someone there?"

Jack was stunned. The legionnaire spoke English. His words carried a Spanish inflection, to boot. He thought back to what the leader had said, that they were descendants of the Ninth Legion.

Roman legions had marched all over Europe, settling wherever they conquered too. It would actually make sense if these modern-day legionnaires weren't all Italian. Even Jack's grandfather and grandmother on his dad's side weren't American by birth. They had been British and Polish. Then add in 2,000 years, and the Ninth Legion's descendants could've now hailed from anywhere in the world.

Like Spain, Jack thought, also appreciating that English was the most widely used language in the world. It was one of a handful of things that made his job a little bit easier.

The legionnaire gave up and turned back toward Conti's building. Jack growled, then lobbed another pebble at the lamp. It clunked off the backrest of the western bench. His foe spun, quickly drawing a pistol as he did. Jack was thankful that this guy didn't own an itchy trigger finger.

Easy, buddy. Next, he willed the gunman to move. *Come, step into the light.*

He did. The legionnaire moved toward the origin of the sound, keeping his aim low. His actions were slow, showing off his training. He listened for movement in between his footfalls. Whatever Jack decided to do, he'd need to be precise.

The legionnaire stopped directly beneath the lamp. He was dressed as an ordinary citizen. He wore no tactical gear, no eye black, and no helmet. Jack assumed the *uniform* was for public appearances only, not undercover operations like this.

The other guy waited for something to jump out at him. When it didn't come, he holstered his gun back beneath his coat, huffed out a breath, and turned.

That's when Jack made his move. He threw his third and final stone, flinging it over the legionnaire's head. It clattered over near Conti's building somewhere. Jack launched out of his kneeling posture, and into a dead sprint. He wouldn't have time to skirt around the lamp and benches. Jack needed to continue in a straight trajectory, which meant he was going over them.

His steps grew noisy, but the legionnaire's attention had been on the third stone, not what was behind him. As he turned, Jack's left foot found the eastern bench. He carried his forward momentum into his leap, diving headfirst past the lamppost, over the western bench, and into the unaware man. Jack struck his inert foe in the chest, driving all of his weight into him and the brick pathway beneath them.

They landed awkwardly, Jack's right shoulder took a beating, but so did the back of his target's head. The single attack put the legionnaire down for the count. Jack quickly checked his vitals, finding a pulse.

"Have a nice nap," Jack said, searching his body.

The only thing he found, other than a gun, was a keycard of some kind. The lone markings it possessed was that of VIIII, the *original* Roman numeral for 9. Jack couldn't remember when it had been changed to IX, and it didn't really matter. He pocketed the keycard, relieved the legionnaire of his weapon, and rushed through the doorless entrance to Conti's building.

11

He made it through the arched entryway and looked up, seeing the bottom of another flight of stairs. The first-floor stairs dead-ended up at the western wall of the second story. Then two paths broke off from there, one heading around to the right, and another going left.

Jack's intel said Gemma Conti lived on the top floor, and he got moving. He took the first flight two at a time, breathing hard already. He and May had admittedly kept very inactive since arriving in Rome. They were on vacation, after all. Jack's cardio was always the first thing to go, and it was the case now.

He didn't stop, though. He headed left and around to the beginning of the next flight of stairs. The second floor was set up exactly as the first floor was, two doors on the left and two doors on the right. And no, there was no elevator.

Bringing up groceries must be a pain in the ass, Jack thought as he began his climb. *And I'd hate to be a delivery driver.*

When his foot struck the second stair, he heard a female voice cry out. Jack bolted up the rest of the stairs in record time. When he made it to the top, Jack stopped and spun so he could see all four doors.

Two on the left. Two on the right.

"Marco…" he quietly said, grinning to himself. *What a couple of days that was.*

Jack spotted Conti's apartment number. "3A. Gotcha!"

He drew his gun and ran to the left, around to the northeastern corner of the building. When he got there, he stopped, pivoted, and drove his foot into the door, aiming two inches to the right of the deadbolt. It cracked open with ease. The lock hadn't been reengaged.

Lucky me, he thought, entering, gun up, index finger flat against the side of his Glock. Laying your finger on top of the trigger as you moved was a stupid, and dangerous, way to work. He entered a minimalistic living room. Jack immediately got the sense that Conti didn't spend a lot of time at home.

"Sounds familiar," Jack mumbled. She reminded him of himself nowadays.

There was a hallway straight ahead and a small kitchen to his right. Since there was no one in the living room or kitchen, he headed for the hallway. Jack would need to be very careful now. The tight confines would make things more difficult, as would the potential of an errant bullet passing through drywall and into a neighbor's home.

Jack bit his bottom lip with his top incisors and pressed on.

All was silent, and it bugged the crap out of Jack. The hallways contained three shut doors. There was one off either side, and one at the end. He guessed the door on the end belonged to Conti's bedroom. But Jack still had to check the others too.

He slinked up to the right-hand door and tried the knob. It opened quietly, swinging in with ease. Jack turned and backed away from the opening, keeping his gun leveled at it as he sidestepped around in a halfmoon arc. This method kept a wall between him and whoever else could be in the room. When he cleared the center of the room, he edged forward, then darted inside.

Nothing.

Damn.

He turned and faced the door across the hall. This time, Jack didn't proceed with caution. He went about it the same way he had at the front door and kicked it in. The room was Conti's home office, and it was empty, save for some very impressive artifacts. If Jack ever had a home office, this was what he'd want it to look like. Gorgeous photos of exotic places dotted the walls. Jack had a sneaking suspicion that it was Conti who had taken them.

The bedroom, Jack decided.

He wheeled around and slowly stuck his head and gun outside the doorway. He also checked the front door again too, just in case the other legionnaire had recovered sooner than expected. The front door was still wide open and empty, though. He also needed to speed things up a bit. Between the unconscious legionnaire, the scream, and Jack kicking in not one, but two, doors, the police were no doubt on their way, or would be soon.

He walked heel-to-toe, stalking forward at a nauseatingly slow pace. Once he was just outside the door, he leaned in close to it and listened, just as a body came crashing through. Jack's gun was knocked out of his hands, flipping end over end back toward the living room.

Both humans went to the ground in a flurry of motion. Jack caught a forearm across the jaw, but he also got an elbow up into the other man's face, particularly the bone just beneath his left eye. Jack rolled left, through the strike, squirming his way on top of his opponent. The legionnaire went for the gun holstered beneath his left armpit. Jack met his gun hand, pinning it against the pistol's handgrip.

The other man's free hand went for Jack's throat, and he squeezed. Luckily, Jack was prepared, and he didn't panic. Jack brought up his left hand and grabbed his opponent's wrist, gripping it hard. Then he dug the tips of his fingers into the bundle of tendons positioned there.

For good measure, Jack snaked his right hand around the legionnaire's gun hand, found the weapon's magazine release with his thumb, and pressed it. The magazine slipped free and fell as both men still fought for possession of it. When it did, Jack purposely wrapped his finger around the trigger and pulled, harmlessly expelling the chambered round. Jack prayed there was concrete present beneath the floor, to absorb the fast-moving round.

The close-quarters report hammered both men's ears. They each flinched, relaxing their grips for a moment.

Jack shifted his attention to the gunman's wrist, wiggling his fingertips around and driving them in deeper into the tendons, waiting for the guy's chokehold to weaken. When it did, Jack tore the legionnaire's outstretched hand away from his neck and quickly popped him in the nose with a jab.

The guy responded by grabbing Jack's jacket and rolling backward. He tossed Jack ass-over-tea-kettle, back toward the front of the hallway. He quickly rolled over and climbed to his feet, staring into the muzzle of the legionnaire's pistol.

The other man didn't waste any time. He pulled the trigger.

But nothing happened.

He glanced down at the weapon, which was currently in slide-lock and empty.

"You're missing something," Jack said, breathing hard. Jack held up his hands. "Here, I have something for you. Got it off your buddy downstairs."

At the mention of the other legionnaire, this allowed Jack to do whatever it was he was about to do. Jack reached into his inside jacket pocket, removing his harmonica. He cleared his throat and put the instrument to his lips, then immediately hurled it at the other man's face. It struck him square in the forehead. Jack rushed his opponent, bulling into his chest with his shoulder.

Jack gripped the sides of the legionnaire's belt, lifted him off the ground, and smashed him back first into the doorframe of the bedroom. Both men entered, spilling to the floor from the abrupt, awkward-as-hell impact. Jack spun and bonked the back of his head on the left-hand bedpost. The legionnaire landed flat on his back, wheezing heavily.

Jack blinked away the birds circling his head. "Coulda done without that."

He moaned as he got back to his feet.

So did his assailant.

"C'mon, man. Do us both a favor and stay down."

The legionnaire cringed when he tried to stand upright. "Never. You will not stand in our way."

The man's accent confused Jack. "You're French?"

"We are everywhere."

"Yeah, I kinda figured that out." Jack raised his fists. "So, are you going to do what the French always do when they see conflict?" The legionnaire squinted at Jack. "You know, surrender?"

That got the reaction Jack was hoping for. The other guy rushed Jack, similar to how Jack had rushed him. He ducked his head and shoulder into him, only, this time, Jack wrapped his forearm around the legionnaire's windpipe, rocked back, and fell to the floor. Then he wrapped his legs around his back and locked his ankles, executing a near-flawless, guillotine chokehold.

The legionnaire thrashed, but couldn't break Jack's grip. And all Jack had to do was wait and allow his opponent to expel the rest of his air himself.

"Before you go night-night, I have a message for your boss." He squeezed harder as the legionnaire fought to free himself. "I wasn't finished! Tell him that if anything happens to May, he'll have to answer to me."

It only took a few more seconds for the other man's movements to slow. Then his growls and snarls vanished and his arms flopped down to the floor. Jack gave him another couple of seconds before releasing him and rolling him off. Jack took a moment to catch his breath. When he did, he realized something. There was someone else in the room with him—besides the unconscious, possibly dead, legionnaire.

Laying on his back, he rolled his head to the left, finding the apartment's owner cowering in the corner of the room.

Jack gave her an exhausted wave. "Hi." She didn't reply. "You Conti?"

She nodded, showing off a welt on her left cheek. She'd been hit.

Bastard, Jack thought, picturing the legionnaire striking her.

Jack tapped his own chest. "I'm Jack," he explained between breaths. "I'm…the good guys." He sat up, taking a mental inventory of his injuries. Besides the graze across his jaw and the knock to the back of his head, he was fine. "Get some things together. We need to leave."

She didn't respond again.

"Dr. Conti?"

"Gemma," she replied, finally speaking. "Where are you taking me?"

Jack got to his feet and held out his hand. She cautiously took it. "I'm not going to hurt you, Gemma. I'm not like these asshats."

Gemma gave him a small smile and took Jack's hand. He pulled her to her feet. "Oh, and I'm not *taking* you anywhere. You don't have to come if you don't want. But—"

"But what?" the Italian asked.

"But I suggest that you do. More will come."

Her eyes darted down to the man that had attacked her. "Is he dead?"

Jack shrugged. "Could be. I did hold on for two extra Mississippis." Jack turned and headed for the door. "If you are coming, I suggest we get moving."

Jack reentered the hallway, searching for his new favorite toy.

"I recognize you," Gemma said, following him out of her bedroom. "From the Colosseum."

"Yeah, I was there." Jack bent over and retrieved his harmonica. "Aw, man."

Gemma leaned around him. "What's wrong?"

Jack held up the instrument. "Dinged my harp."

She gave Jack a questioning look, then gazed past him. "Where's your lady friend, the one you were dancing with?"

"May," Jack replied. "Her name's May." Jack tipped his chin back toward her bedroom. "These guys took her."

Gemma was honestly saddened. "I'm sorry to hear that."

"Yeah," Jack turned away, "so am I."

He continued into the living room, finding his Glock in the middle of the floor. He retrieved it, checking over the weapon closely. Luckily, the Austrian-made firearm was stout and could take a beating. He slid it back into his holster and found Gemma staring at him.

No, not him. His gun.

"Are you sure you're with the good guys?"

Jack shrugged. "There isn't anything I can say to convince you other than simply asking you to trust me."

Feet came pounding up behind Jack. He spun drew his pistol and gunned down the second legionnaire with two rounds to the chest as soon as he entered Gemma's home.

Gemma jumped back, crashing into the wall outside the hallway. Jack

holstered his gun again and faced her, waiting for her to speak.
 Jack folded his arms across his chest and waited.
 She swallowed. "Give me two minutes."
 "You have one."

12

Jack and Gemma exited her apartment fifty-seven seconds later. Jack decided to do something a little atypical and give the Spaniard back the gun he'd taken. The police would undoubtedly treat this situation differently if the body lying inside the open doorway was armed versus not. For good measure, Jack placed the weapon in the man's limp hand, closing the legionnaire's lifeless fingers around it the best he could.

Gemma gave him a questioning look. "What? It was his to begin with."

"But you just sullied a crime scene!" Jack looked up at her. "You planted evidence."

Did I? He stood. *Yes. Yes, I did.*

"Eh," Jack said stepping over the corpse. He motioned to the body. "It's not like he cares." He stared at Gemma. "He was here to hurt you, remember?"

She gently touched her cheek. "How could I forget?"

Jack placed a reassuring hand on her shoulder. "Come on. We gotta go."

They hauled ass down the stairs in full view of her neighbors. Unfortunately, there was nothing Jack could do about it. They would both be ID'd by witnesses. Jack wasn't really worried about it, when it came to himself. Jack's real identity had been a closely guarded secret of the U.S. government since he had joined TAC. But for Gemma, this was very bad.

Can't worry about it now, he thought.

They rushed for the gate and threw it open. Gemma pulled out her keys.

"No," Jack said. "We'll take mine." She eyed him. "Can't be traced back to me."

She nodded and dropped her keys back into her small shoulder bag. The pair took off at a steady jog. They turned right, heading south down the main road in the area, Viale Alessandrino. Sirens blared somewhere behind them and Jack made the decision to slow up a bit. They were out in the open and lit by streetlights.

"Take my arm," he said. Gemma didn't look so sure, but she did. "We need to look like we're just out for a late-night stroll."

"Hiding in plain sight, is it?"

Jack patted her hand. "It is."

He dug into his pocket and held up the keycard he had pilfered off the Spaniard. "Any idea where this goes?"

Gemma took it and looked it over. "No. The only thing I recognize is the early form of the number nine, VIIII. It didn't change to IX until long after the Roman Empire fell."

Jack glanced down at the much shorter woman. "Right... Expert in Ancient Rome."

"Greece too."

"Really?"

She nodded. "I believe that in order to properly understand Rome, you also need to understand Greece. The two cultures are heavily intertwined with one another."

"Fair enough."

"So, what about you, *Jack*? Where does your expertise lie?"

Jack glanced behind them. The police sirens were getting closer. Still, they didn't speed up.

"Counterterrorism and search and rescue. Oh," he gave her a wink, "and you can't forget about rock 'n' roll." Gemma opened her mouth to ask a question. He stopped her. "Look, all you need to know is that I was Special Forces, and that I love history, and that my current job is to protect it, without remorse if it comes to it."

"Like what you did to the men in my apartment?"

Jack looked away from her. "Worse, if needed."

Gemma bit her lip, deep in thought. "And the attractive woman you were with? May, right?" Jack was taken off guard by the question. Gemma laughed softly. "Don't pretend she wasn't noticed by everyone in attendance. She could not *not* be noticed. Like a sunflower in a field of ash."

"She's my, uh…"

"Wife?"

Jack's eyes darted down to Gemma. "No!" His blurted reply embarrassed him and he looked away from Gemma.

Thankfully, Gemma didn't push the topic. "So, which one is it? Do you need my help to get your lady friend back, or to find wherever the keycard goes?"

"Both?" Jack replied.

Gemma nodded. "I suppose that's fair. You did just save my life. The least I could do is help you find your…May."

"This is going to be incredibly dangerous. You know that, right?"

She shrugged. "And where would you like me to go? Who can I trust? Tell me." Jack had no idea. "Exactly. Those men obviously wanted something from me."

"Information, most likely," Jack said. "They must've done their homework and discovered that you are an expert on all of this too."

Fifty feet in front of them was Jack's rental, a newish, gray Fiat Panda. He fished his keys out of his pocket and hovered his thumb over the key fob's unlock button. But before Jack unlocked his rental, he did one last looksee to make sure they hadn't been spotted or followed.

Sirens blared off in the distance. Jack could see them further to the north and coming in hot.

Gotta go.

He unlocked the car, and they climbed in. Jack quickly started it, giving the economy puddle jumper a little gas when he did.

"Where are we going?" Gemma asked, tying her shoulder-length hair up into a messy bun.

"Right now, anywhere but here."

Jack got them moving, heading further south. He obeyed the speed limit, keeping their escape as leisurely as possible. He took the first turn he could, then snaked his way right and left until he put a decent enough amount of distance between them and the scene of the crime.

"Okay," he said, pulling them off the road again. In front of them was a sign that read, *Parco Bonafede*. Jack didn't need to be able to read Italian to see they were outside of a park.

"Okay, what now?"

Jack turned and faced her. "In a few minutes, I'm going to have to contact my bosses back home."

"Where's home?"

"Not important right now. What is important is that I have as much intel as I can before I make that call."

Gemma nodded. "Right. Yes, of course. What is it that you need to know?"

Jack started at the private event. "Back at the Colosseum, the leader shouted something that got quite the reaction out of his troops."

"*Gaudere Legio Nona*. It's Latin for '*To rejoice the Ninth Legion.*'"

"You speak Latin too?"

Gemma shrugged. "I mean, I read it fluently, so I guess I could speak it if I needed to. But it's a dead language!"

Jack snorted. "Tell that to the guys back at your place." Jack gazed into the darkness of the park. "There's something else…" He looked at Gemma again. "Back at the Colosseum, the guy with the case called his boss *Legatus*. What does it mean?"

"*Legatus*, really?" she replied. Jack nodded. "Well, that's what the commander of a Roman legion was called. He'd be the equivalent of a modern-day general."

"A general?" Now it was Gemma's turn to nod. "Oookay."

They sat in silence for a few minutes, contemplating what to do next. Honestly, Jack had no clue, and he didn't have enough information to warrant calling Raegor and Eddy, not even after his scuffle with the legionnaire pair.

"So," Gemma said, breaking the silence, "where to from here?"

Jack shrugged. "No idea. I was hoping you could tell me."

Gemma retied her hair. "Sure, of course. But where do I begin? There are so many prevailing theories when it comes to the Ninth Legion."

Jack pictured Lombardi chuckling when he had been onstage. "How 'bout we start with the one Dr. Lombardi openly ridiculed? The leader, the *Legatus*, didn't take too kindly to the insult."

Gemma puffed her cheeks and blew out her breath. "*That* particular theory is the most outlandish of them all. But I don't disagree with you. That man's reaction to what Alberto said was rather interesting."

"Why do you say that?"

"He took it personally. He really thinks he's the descendent of one of the Ninth's legionnaires." She readjusted her posture and continued. "Do you recall Alberto mentioning the radical nature of the Ninth?"

"How could I not? He called them a zealous cult, right?"

"More or less, yes. Well, my research has led me to believe that there were such goings-on deep within Rome's legions, but even more so in the Ninth, especially their hierarchy." She heaved a sigh. "Most of my colleagues would disagree, mind you."

"Thankfully, I'm not one of them."

"No, you are not. Thank you for that." She sat straighter and faced Jack. "I've seen bits and pieces of scrolls and engravings depicting the Ninth's mysterious behavior. One scroll even talks about them being blessed by Nero and given amnesty, regardless of their misconducts."

Jack's right eyebrow raised high. "They were given a license to kill?"

Gemma scratched the back of her head. "In a way, yes. What I personally believe, after careful consideration, is that the Ninth Legion, or perhaps a detachment within it, at the very least, was used as a private army of sorts."

"Nero?" Jack asked. "That was around 70 AD, right? There's nothing earlier?"

Gemma smiled. "Smart man."

"Eh," Jack said. "I know a little about a lot, but not a lot about one thing."

"Even so, still, you are a very impressive individual."

Jack gave her a curt nod of thanks. "Tell me, what changed during Nero's reign? Why did all this start then and not sooner?"

Gemma nearly deflated. "I don't know."

Jack gripped the steering wheel. "Okay, so what you're saying is that there may have been a black-ops team within the Ninth Legion of the Imperial Roman Army, and none of the emperors up until Nero knew about it?"

Gemma grimaced. Even she knew this was way out there. "Yes?"

Jack stroked his chin. "Sure, I can believe that."

"You can? Just like that?"

Jack glanced at her. "I've seen some pretty crazy things."

"Care to share?"

Jack glared at her. Gemma looked away, dropping the line of questioning.

"Back to the theory Lombardi scoffed at. He said that when the eagle standard was fully reassembled that it would lead to treasure. Which one exactly?"

"Technically, the word treasure is never used in the original translation. In ancient times, words had various definitions depending on context. And just as Alberto had said during his presentation, before he was…" Gemma took a deep breath. "He said it was a *vast wealth*. Regardless of what word is used, what I can tell you is that it is the single greatest *wealth* of the time." Gemma faced Jack again. "The lost tomb of Alexander the Great, King of Macedon."

13

All was quiet. It had been for some time now. May still sat in her chair, wrists bound behind her back. The heavy sack was back on her head too. Her eyes were closed and all she thought about was her breathing. Her meditative state kept her calm. Like counting the seconds, it kept her focused.

In all, May's interrogation had only lasted seconds. Marcus had oddly pulled the plug on it as soon as it had started. That was good news to May. It meant that they still needed her alive. Marcus had said as much. It also meant that Jack was still out there.

May allowed herself to smile. Her split lip stung with the movement. If their roles had been reversed, she would've been doing everything she could to find Jack. She knew he was doing the same thing, right now. She just hoped that he was doing so in an intelligent, systematic way.

But she also recognized that Jack was a bit of a cowboy at heart. He listened to his gut and heart more than he did his brain. May enjoyed that about him. It was refreshing. She'd spent so much time with straightforward thinkers with no concept of "adjusting on the fly" as they went.

That was Jack's specialty.

It was one of the many things May had grown to love about him.

14

With nothing else to go on for the time being, Jack made the decision to head back to his hotel room. Gemma was an emotional wreck, and both she and Jack were exhausted. Until now, the Italian historian had kept it together, but Jack had known that it was only a matter of time before the ramifications of everything that had happened came crashing down on top of her.

"Alberto's dead," she said. "He's dead."

Jack glanced over to her while making a right turn. "Yeah, and?"

Gemma looked at him. "He's dead!"

"I'm sorry for your loss?" Jack asked, confused by the sudden timing of her statement. "Are you okay?"

Gemma was wide-eyed and staring straight through him. He was about to pull off so he could give her his undivided attention, but she snapped out of it. She blinked and took a deep breath as twin streams of tears rolled down her eyes.

"Gemma?" he asked, applying the brakes.

"I'm…okay," she said quietly. "I…" she looked down at her trembling hands. "I have to be."

Jack sped back up and got them to his hotel as quickly as he could. Jack didn't need for Gemma to have a full-blown meltdown inside his rental. Jack did have to give her some credit. Even though she had finally come to grips with what had happened, she was keeping it together better than most would. It was an admirable quality.

He pulled into the parking lot, found the first spot he could, and stopped the car.

Jack threw the Fiat into park and looked at Gemma. "Were you two close?"

Gemma snorted. "As close as a king could be with his royal jester."

"That bad, huh?"

"Yes." Gemma nodded, but then changed her tune. "No, well, sometimes. I swear, that man must've had an undiagnosed mental condition. It was infuriating! One moment, he was encouraging. Another, he was ruthless. Have you ever met someone that could turn it on and off so easily?"

"I have. I was in the military, remember?"

She gave Jack a small smile. "I learned a lot from him over the years, and liked my job too much to quit."

"So, you just dealt with it," Jack said.

"Yeah, you could say that. He was still a few years off from retiring and I thought that if I gutted it out long enough that I would be named as his replacement." She sighed and opened her door. "Now I see that all of this could've been avoided if I had quit. I wouldn't have been there to watch him die."

"Yeah," Jack said, opening his door and climbing out, "sorry, but life doesn't work like that. You *are* here and thinking otherwise isn't going to help anyone."

As they entered the lavish lobby, the hotel staff that was present at this hour gave Jack a bevy of sideways glances. The only woman he'd been seen with until now had been May. The only thing Jack could do was focus on the floor in front of his feet and head for the elevator.

But Gemma didn't. She shrank beneath their gazes. "This is…uncomfortable."

"For you and me both." Jack pressed the up arrow and the doors behind them immediately dinged open. "Come on."

He half-dragged Gemma into the lift and repeatedly hit the door close button until, finally, they shut. When they did, Jack leaned against the rear mirrored wall, clunking the back of his head against it as well. He took a deep breath and closed his eyes.

"I'm sorry for that," he said, not looking at Gemma.

"Do they know you well?"

Jack shrugged. "We've been staying here for a couple of weeks. May… Well, you get it."

"Why do you care what they think?" she asked. Jack opened his eyes and lowered them, finding the much shorter Gemma staring up at him. "When this is all over, you'll more than likely never see them again."

She was right, of course. Jack shouldn't have cared about the looks he had received.

"My dad and grandpa were honorable men. They each loved one woman their entire lives." He had no idea why he was telling Gemma this, but he was. "May is the first woman that I ever really—"

"Loved?" Jack looked away. "Ah, and you feel like you're betraying her by taking me up to your plush, ritzy Roman hotel room. Is that it?"

Jack nodded.

"Well, Jack, I'll have you know that I don't find you attractive in the least." He snapped his attention down to her. She was miserably failing at hiding her smile. "I think you are a horrid creature to look at. Absolutely repugnant." She backed up and hovered her finger over the door open button. "So much so that I'm going to march right down there and tell them that." Now, she had a full-fledged smile on her face.

He rolled his eyes and pushed himself away from the mirrored wall. "Here, let me help you with the button." But just then, the elevator dinged, and the doors slid open. "Oh, would you look at that, too late." He tipped his head to the side. "Let's go. We could both use a beer."

Her shoulders sagged as if the stress had just lifted away from them. "Thank God for you, Jack." She stepped out, then allowed him to lead the way. When he did, she sniffed. "Another thing…"

"Yeah?"

"You need a shower in the worst way."

Jack looked over his shoulder. "Thanks, *Mom*."

Eight doors later, Jack produced his room key, a keycard similar to the one he had confiscated off the legionnaire back at Gemma's place. The hotel card displayed the company's logo rather than a mysterious Roman numeral nine. The room key was plastic too, and white. Jack removed the legion's black, metal keycard and re-examined it as he shoved open his door.

In hindsight, he probably should've been more cautious, but he was too engrossed in the possibilities of where the keycard would lead.

In the morning, he thought. He checked his watch and groaned. *In a few hours...*

It had been a long, *long* night.

"Take the bed," Jack said, as he rifled through his bag. He grabbed some clean clothes and headed straight for the bathroom. "I'm gonna get cleaned up."

"You sure? About the bed, I mean."

Jack waved her question off. "Yeah, I'll take the floor. I've slept on a lot worse. Just toss a pillow on the floor before you settle in, okay?"

"What about your friends back home?"

Jack poked his head back out of the bathroom. "What about them?"

Gemma sat on the bed. "Can't they help?"

"Believe me, they are. We have people all around the globe. I'm sure they're casting whatever nets they can." Jack re-entered the room. "Until they come up with something, or exhaust their resources and find out nothing, there really isn't anything they can help us with. We can't let these legion cultists know what we're doing by making a show of it."

"So, we're on our own?" Gemma curled her knees into her chest. "What about May?"

"Yes, we are, for now. And she'll be fine." Jack gave Gemma a wink. "Now, get some sleep, we may need to get moving early."

Jack left Gemma alone just as she turned and crawled up to the top of the bed. He knew she'd be out in seconds. Jack, on the other hand, doubted he'd get much sleep at all, not with May's life still in the balance, and her whereabouts unknown.

For all Jack knew, she was already dead.

The thought of May being dead gave Jack the willies. He reversed course again, opened the door, and found Gemma kneeling in front of the open mini fridge. She looked up at him and smiled sheepishly.

"Beer?" she asked, holding an open one out.

Jack forgot that he had mentioned having one with her. Apparently, she didn't. He grinned and took the offered bottle. Gemma plucked a second one out of the fridge and opened it with a keyring bottle opener. Jack had one on his keys too.

"Cheers," Jack said, holding out his bottle.

Gemma clinked the top of his with her own. "*Salute.*"

Jack tipped his beer back and took a long pull from it as he turned and re-entered the bathroom.

15

As Jack expected, he didn't sleep much. After only a few minutes of lying on the floor, he got up and headed outside. He sat alone with his thoughts and the Roman skyline. The night was cool and quiet, two things Jack could appreciate even more than usual right now. When he did finally doze off, it had been right where he sat.

Something grabbed Jack's shoulder, spooking him. He snatched it, eyes wide. In the millisecond it took him to react, he quickly deduced that he wasn't in any danger, and the thing that had attacked him, was just Gemma's hand touching his shoulder.

Jack released her hand. "Sorry."

"Good morning to you too," she said, stepping up beside him. She lowered a steaming mug of coffee in front of his face. "Here."

Jack audibly moaned. "Bless you, my child."

"Yes, well, you look like you need it." She sat across the small patio table and took a sip from her own mug of hotel room coffee.

Jack snorted and motioned to his sleep deprived eyes. "This is how I always look."

Gemma didn't argue it. "Can I ask you something?" She took another small sip.

Jack shrugged and took a sip of his own. "Shoot."

"How long have you and May been an item?"

Jack choked on his coffee. He spit it back into his mug and coughed hard before getting his breathing under control. When he did, he stared down into his mug with a lot of disappointment.

Eh, what the hell? he thought, drinking it. *What's a little backwash, right?*

"I'm sorry, I didn't mean to pry."

Jack held up his hand, then swallowed. "No, it's fine. I just didn't expect *that* to be the question." He set down his mug. "We've only been together for a couple months. Less, actually."

"Really? I would've pegged you guys as a more seasoned couple with how you talk about her, as well as what you're doing to get her back."

"Yeah, part of that is the soldier in me. Search and rescue too, remember? I was a park ranger for five years in between when I served and what I do now. Something about helping people, I guess." He took another sip. "We've both gone through a lot of trauma in our lives too."

"How do you mean?"

"I spent the better part of my adult life fighting in the Middle East. I speak fluent Arabic, for what it's worth."

Gemma leaned forward. "ISIS?"

"Among others. My last operation really messed me up. PTSD on steroids."

"And May?"

Jack set his empty mug down. "Look, I can't say much about her past with her not being here. That isn't fair to her. What I can say is that May's life has been far worse than mine could ever be."

"Gotcha." She picked up her mug. "So, what, you two bonded over each other's misery, is that it?"

Jack could just barely see the smallest of grins form on her mouth as she drank. "You could say that…" He pulled his eyes away from Gemma and looked out over Rome. "There's a connection with her that I've never felt before."

Gemma bobbed her chin up and down. "Sounds like you two were meant for one another."

Jack blinked, suddenly becoming very uncomfortable. "Yeah, sure." He picked up the legion keycard from the table. "Know anyone that can help us with this, with everything, actually?"

Gemma reached for the keycard. Jack handed it over and sat back. "I may know someone, but he is incredibly difficult to get a hold of, as well as just plain difficult to deal with."

"Why's that?"

"Because he's the curator of the Yorkshire Museum."

"Yorkshire? England?"

Gemma nodded. "Spencer Harwood is Northern Europe's foremost expert on the Ninth Legion too. If you have questions, he's your best bet."

Jack rubbed his face. He really didn't want to get another civilian involved. He didn't have a choice, though. Jack's gut told him that wherever the card led, it would be likely to lead to May too.

"Make the call," he said, flopping his hands down to his lap.

Gemma went to stand but stopped. "Okay, but can we go somewhere and take a walk. I need to loosen up a little."

Jack shrugged. "Sure, yeah." She smiled, relief washing over her. "Where did you have in mind?"

16

Gemma guided Jack to what she had said was her personal favorite place to visit in all of Rome. That was high praise, considering her background. Jack didn't ask her why it was her favorite. It would've been an answer built on subjective reasoning. Jack was the tourist here, and he'd trust her judgment.

Who am I to argue with her? he thought.

If they were back in the United States, and their roles were reversed, Jack would've shown her the ropes. And like her, his favorite places to visit would be of his own preferences, not those highlighted by travel brochures.

We'd start with the Seven Sisters Monument.

The memory made Jack smile.

Jack had expected to be taken to places like the Roman Forum, Pantheon, or Trevi Fountain. Instead, he'd been ushered over to a place called Piazza del Popolo. They parked and entered in through a gate called the Porta del Popolo.

"Built in 1475 by Pope Sixtus," Gemma explained. "It was erected atop an already existing gate from Ancient Rome. As you can see, the papacy spared no expense."

"Incredible," Jack said, feeling small.

The gateway was made of marble and sported the typical décor of the time.

Columns? Check. Statues of saints? Check. Jack looked up. *Papel coat of arms? Check again.*

He looked to his right, then to his left, noticing that the walls on either side of the gate were made of different material—red bricks. To Jack, they looked far older too.

Jack tipped his chin toward the left-hand wall. "What's up with the red walls?"

"They are the Aurelian Walls," Gemma replied. "Much older than the gate. Construction began in 271 by a Roman emperor of the same name."

"271?"

"Mmhmm," Gemma replied.

Jack was stunned. "Impressive. How far do they run?"

"Originally, they connected after running a full twelve miles. They are over fifty feet tall in some places."

"Out of curiosity, how thick are they?"

Gemma waggled her hand. "Around eleven feet at the narrowest point."

Jack whistled. "That's one big-ass wall."

"Effective too. They stayed in regular use until the 1800s."

Jack nodded his approval. "When I need a perfect description of 'standing the test of time,' I'll tell people to come here."

Gemma beamed with Roman pride. "Couldn't have said it better myself." She started off beneath the gate. "Come. We didn't travel to this place to only stare at a wall."

Jack faked a frown. "But it's a really nice wall."

He followed her in, surprised to see a heavy military presence. Jack caught up to her and leaned in close. "What's with these guys?"

Two troopers stood directly beneath the arched gateway, while four more meandered about just inside the square beyond it. They wore dark red berets and full camouflage uniforms. Each soldier, a mixture of man and woman, possessed Italian-made Beretta sidearms holstered on their thighs, while also carrying a variety of assault rifles.

Jack examined the first couple he saw. *Beretta ARX160.*

"*Operazione Strade sicure,*" Gemma explained. "Operation Safe Roads. Public security by means of the Italian Army. In this case, we have the Paratrooper Brigade watching our butts. Though…"

"Though?" Jack asked, eyeing another pair of paratroopers.

Gemma eyed the soldiers. "There are a lot more than usual."

Jack looked away as one turned to face his direction. "I'm sure you can thank last night for that."

"Absolutely, "Gemma agreed. "As I'm sure you are aware, we Romans take our history very seriously. An attack on one of our prized monuments makes us feel personally attacked."

"I know the feeling. You should've been in the U.S. right after September 11th. You want to talk about nationalism…" Jack bumped her with his elbow. "Let's hope these guys will dissuade the Legion from doing anything else rash."

"Yes, let's hope. Last night was…intense. Nevertheless, I suppose for you it was just another walk in the park."

Jack looked away from her. "That part of the job never gets easy." They stepped into the interior of the large square, giving Jack a good look at what it held. "Whoa."

A smile overtook Gemma's face. "Yes, whoa."

The enormous, slightly elliptical, public *square* had been sparsely adorned on purpose so it could showcase a singular monument. But that piece of history spoke volumes. It proudly boasted Rome's dominance over Egypt, something the Greeks did too.

Gemma turned and faced Jack, arms out wide. "I give you, the Popolo Obelisk, the obelisk of Ramesses II." She gave Jack a moment to stare in awe before continuing her guided tour. Jack could tell she was thoroughly enjoying herself. "If you include its pedestal, the obelisk stands an impressive 118 feet tall."

Jack let out another low whistle.

"Three of the obelisk's four sides were actually carved under Seti I's rule. The final side was later finished under Ramesses II's, his son's, reign."

"When was it brought to Rome?" Jack asked, gawking as they moved closer.

"Octavian, founder of the Roman Empire, had it brought here in 10 BC."

The history nerd that Jack considered himself was lost in admiration. The atmosphere was inspiring. This was what the U.S. lacked since the country was so young in terms of major civilizations. The only history in the States that was considered "ancient," belonged to the Native American tribes, something Jack was, admittedly, not overly knowledgeable of. Then again, the oldest cultures usually relied on oral accounts versus written word.

Even Bull, Jack's close friend and a man of native Lakotan blood, found the practice to be infuriating sometimes.

Jack looked around, spotting another ten troopers. Two stood guard around the obelisk, one to the north and another to the south. The other eight soldiers were positioned back around the square's perimeter.

These guys aren't playing around, he thought, feeling the hair on the back of his neck stand on end.

Jack wondered how many were at the Colosseum right now, as well as the other famous archaeological sites throughout Rome. Jack estimated that there were around a hundred people visiting Piazza del Popolo at the moment. And so far, he'd seen sixteen troopers. It felt a bit like overkill, and maybe that was the point. The government wanted the people responsible for last night's terror attack to see that the city was very serious, and that they were ready for a fight.

Jack had counted eight legionnaires in total, including the three snipers he knew of, plus however many were up in the helicopter. He doubted that was all of them too. The group could've had dozens of men at their disposal and it wouldn't have shocked Jack.

He took his eyes off the paratroopers, shifting them to the pristine fountain built into the western tip of the oval-shaped, public square. It had a sibling to the east too. Gemma noticed his shift in attention.

"To the west is the Fontana del Nettuno. To the east, we have the Fontana della Dea di Roma—the 'Fountain of Neptune' and the 'Fountain of the Goddess Rome,' respectively."

Jack also spied four smaller fountains situated at either corner of the obelisk's base. "And those?"

"Together, they are called the Fountain of the Lions."

Jack could see why as he approached the fountain to the northwest. The fountain's spout was that of a lion, but one that resembled something you'd see down in Egypt rather than Rome. Jack applauded the architect for keeping the cultural theme consistent.

The pair edged by one of the soldiers just as Jack spotted something he dreaded. A red dot hovered over the man's chest, two inches above his plate carrier. Jack startled Gemma as he diverted paths. He took two steps and dove at the trooper, shouldering into him just as the suppressed round whizzed by them both. It struck the base of the obelisk instead.

Regrettably, the soldier didn't see it. All he saw, and felt, was Jack *attacking* him. He rolled on top of Jack, all while Gemma was shouting at him in Italian.

"There's a shooter!" Jack shouted. "I saved your life!"

The paratrooper stopped what he was doing as Gemma continued to ramble on. He took his eyes off Jack long enough to look up at Gemma, only to be struck in the back of the head by a second round.

Piazza del Popolo erupted in screams as the soldier flopped down on top of Jack. Additional shots rang out as the other soldiers returned fire. Jack wiggled out from beneath the dead trooper, avoiding looking at the fatal gunshot wound. Instead, he picked up the man's fallen ARX160, flipped it into semi-automatic, and aimed up at where the other soldiers were shooting.

There!

Jack just saw a faint reflection of sunlight on glass. He knew from experience that it had been the sun catching the front lens of the sniper's scope. He aimed up at a window overlooking the square and went to pull the trigger. Two shots smacked the ground in front of his feet. Jack knew the sniper hadn't missed by accident. The precision shot to the back of the paratrooper's head was evidence enough that the shooter was a crack shot.

Jack lowered his aim.

"What are you doing?" Gemma asked, shouting over the bombardment of gunfire.

He dropped the rifle at his feet. "I'm saving our lives. Those last two shots were warning shots. They missed on purpose."

"But why?" she asked, flinching with nearly every successive gunshot.

It was obvious to Jack. "They want us alive."

"Run, Gemma," Jack said, pushing her along. "Back to the car!"

A second trooper got taken out by sniper fire. This one was directly behind Jack.

They definitely want us alive.

Now the remaining troopers joined the fray. The one that had been shot behind Jack was still alive. *Dammit!* Jack left Gemma and sprinted to him.

"Come on!" Jack yelled, grabbing the wounded man's vest strap. He half-dragged the soldier into cover behind the same northwest fountain he had been admiring. His radio squawked. Jack ripped it from inside one of his vest pouches. Just because Jack and Gemma's lives were being spared didn't mean Jack couldn't try to save these soldiers' lives too. "Two shooters. One at one o'clock. The other is at our four o'clock."

Gemma rushed into cover beside Jack as someone responded back in Italian. He shoved the radio into Gemma's hands. "Tell them." She did. "Also tell them that it's the same people from last night." She told them that too.

More screams filled the air. Jack looked south and watched as a large passenger van tore into the square. Bullets hit it, but did very little.

"You gotta be shitting me right now with this!" The side door opened and disgorged four heavily armored gunmen. They were each equipped with belt-fed, light machineguns. Jack eyed the rifle he had discarded. "No chance." He, instead, grabbed Gemma's hand and ran north, back the way they'd come.

Gemma could barely keep up as the Piazza del Popolo transformed into a war zone. She glanced back, mouth open like a fish. Her favorite place in all of Rome was being annihilated by members of the Legion.

"I still don't get it. Why haven't we been targeted?" Gemma asked, turning her attention to their retreat.

As Jack had figured out earlier, he realized it was because they wanted him and Gemma alive. He told her as much.

"But why?" she asked.

Jack knew. "May. They're threatened by her—by me. They want to know what I know before choosing whether we're expendable. Which means—"

"Which means we need to keep them from getting you," Gemma finished. Jack nodded. "And now they think I'm involved."

Jack gave her an apologetic look. "Ya kinda are."

A stream of wild shots buzzed by them, impacting the ground to Jack's left.

"Yeah," Gemma said, eyes wide, "I already figured that part out!"

17

Jack and Gemma exited the battlefield of Piazza del Popolo and immediately sprinted west along Via Luisa Di Savoia. They'd gotten lucky with a nearby parking spot. It was just up ahead another three hundred feet from where they were now.

They came up to a north-south flowing side street. Jack didn't stop, either. He darted out into traffic just as a sedan came to a screeching stop atop the crosswalk. Jack leapt, planted his left hand on the hood, and vaulted over it with ease. Gemma kept up, but did so timidly, as a *normal* person should. Once across the road, she quickly caught up with him.

"You're making this look too easy, Jack."

He glanced at her as he ran. "I've...had a lot of practice."

Jack pushed through a crowd of angry locals, causing an older man to drop his groceries. If he wasn't in such a hurry, Jack would've gladly stopped to help him. Unfortunately, this wasn't one of those times.

Gemma didn't seem to get that particular memo. She slowed.

"What are you doing?" Jack asked, flabbergasted.

"You ran into him," she said, speaking softly in Italian.

Jack stomped back to her and grabbed her wrist. The onlookers gave Jack a death stare. "We are trying to not die, remember!" The small crowd took a giant step back. Jack gave them a wide, fake smile and ushered Gemma along. "Come on, dear," he said through gritted teeth. "We need to keep moving."

Gemma apologized to them again and reluctantly followed Jack to his rental.

"Look," Jack said, hustling to the right-hand driver's side, "I know this is a new experience for you. I get that. I really do. But *please* just do what I say, okay?"

She headed around to the passenger side door, opened it, and sat, joining him inside. "Yes, fine, but only if you promise not to harass the locals anymore. Also, we need to go west."

Jack started up the engine, threw the car into drive, and cranked the wheel to the left. "Yeah, sorry, that's not gonna happen. I plan on harassing a lot more people."

Before Gemma could argue, Jack floored the pedal and peeled out of the eastern facing parking spot. From inside the vehicle, Jack could hear the screams of frightened walkers and the blaring horns of enraged motorists.

Gemma clutched her door handle and stiffened her body as Jack weaved through traffic on both sides of the road.

"Directions!" he shouted.

Gemma was wide-eyed, but she was coherent enough to reply. "When you get to the Tiber River, go south, then west over the bridge."

Jack did just that. They power slid through multiple intersections, then shot up onto the short river crossing.

"What now?" Jack asked once they were halfway across.

"Take the right-hand exit and follow it under the road and onto Lungotevere dei Mellini."

"Got it!" Jack shouted, gnashing his teeth. He had to floor the pedal to get around a slower moving sedan.

Jack took the exit ramp faster than he should've. The small Fiat hugged the surface of the road well, though.

"Why are we going so fast?" Gemma asked, shutting her eyes and squealing.

"That's why!" Jack replied, tilting his head back toward the small bridge.

Three blacked out SUVs went charging over it.

"They're chasing us?" she asked.

"Yep, and the only rule of a car chase is *don't get caught*." Jack clipped another car as he entered the next road. "That right there is allowed too, by the way."

More horns blared as Jack pushed their four-banger car south along the banks of the Tiber.

Gemma took a deep breath and sat up some more. "Stay on this road until it dead ends at the Castel Sant'Angelo museum."

"This road dead ends?"

"Yes, but it merges with another. We'll have to go around the northern side of the museum. The southern path is for pedestrians only."

Jack buzzed by other motorists, while routinely checking his overhead mirror. They passed gyms, restaurants, other museums, and gargantuan governmental buildings.

"You'll need to slow and follow the bend to the right," Gemma cautioned.

Jack had every intention of doing so, but then he saw three dark aberrations appear behind him. He wasn't sure what to make of them. If they wanted him and Gemma alive, then surely, they wouldn't do anything that might kill them.

Right? Jack thought, spying slow-moving traffic up ahead.

"Eh, screw it," he mumbled, pulling hard on the wheel. He passed the line of cars, heading straight into the teeth of oncoming traffic. "Hang on!"

Jack skidded around to the right as Gemma had said to do, but then he slammed on the brakes and yanked the steering wheel to the left, *toward* the pedestrian footpath he'd been warned about. After a near-180-degree turn, Jack pounded his palm on the horn. A column of cyclists scattered, many of them falling and tumbling into one another like a comedic waterfall.

Oh, crap. He rolled them forward slowly, getting verbally assaulted from those outside. *Where to now?*

This was one of a hundred things Jack hadn't thought through. What was he going to use as a road? Luckily, Gemma had an idea.

"Up ahead. Keep going. There's a footpath."

"Will we fit?"

She shrugged. "It'll be tight."

Jack gave the car some gas and pushed them along. "Good enough."

A second later, Jack spotted their impromptu throughway. The footpath followed the curvature of the neighboring Tiber River. Beautiful yellow sycamore trees grew on either side of it. This was the cause of the "tightness" that Gemma had mentioned. Jack blared his horn and turned down the path, barely squeezing in between the trees. Their combined canopies covered Jack and Gemma's exodus from above.

Jack sped up, beeping at walkers as he did. His eyes glanced down at the Fiat's speedometer as he drove, growling when he topped out at twenty-five miles per hour.

Better than nothing, Jack thought.

He glanced in his mirror and grinned.

"What's so funny?" Gemma asked.

Jack stuck a thumb over his right shoulder. She turned in her seat and gasped. Their pursuers were too big to follow them in.

"*Perfecto!*" Gemma cheered. She then raised a fist, staring at Jack.

He rolled his eyes and gently bumped it with his own. The car drifted as a result and the passenger-side mirror was torn free by a tree trunk. Jack reacquired the wheel with both hands and smiled sheepishly.

Gemma shook her head, reached in front of him, and started beeping the horn herself.

Jack looked at her.

"What? You can't do it all, tough guy." She pressed down and didn't let up, letting out a string of rapid-fire Italian as she did.

"What'd you say?"

Gemma kept her eyes on the road. "Nothing I'm proud of."

They drove by what Jack guessed was an office building, but then saw the Italian word for *Christian* above the front door. He didn't know, and honestly, didn't care. At this rate, they needed to make it out of the treelined footpath, then past Castel Sant'Angelo, before the legion goons cut them off.

"Come on," he begged, willing the trees to open up more.

But they didn't.

"They stop up ahead. Get ready?"

That perked Jack up. "They do?" He sat straighter and gripped the wheel hard.

Then he saw it. As people and their dogs dispersed, the sycamores waned and gave way to an open expanse of brick flooring. It also gave Jack a great look at the Roman-era mausoleum. Like its more famous sibling, and one of the Seven Wonders of the Ancient World, the Mausoleum of Halicarnassus, the Mausoleum of Hadrian was converted to a castle fortification long after Emperor Hadrian died. That's when its name had been changed to what it was known as now, Castel Sant'Angelo. And like all mausoleums, this one was originally built to house the emperor's remains—his family's remains too.

The only reason Jack remembered anything about it was because of the unique star pattern making up the elaborate tomb's property line. It was something to behold from above.

Jack picked up some speed, frightening no less than a half dozen buskers, musicians and other street performers. Unfortunately, they weren't the only ones now paying attention to Jack and Gemma. A security vehicle pulled up behind them, noisily chasing them with its high-pitch, digitized siren.

What is it with European sirens?

"Hurry…" Gemma begged as another security vehicle joined in.

"Don't worry," Jack said. "We just need to get clear of the mausoleum grounds."

"That's not what I'm talking about." She pointed forward. "That is."

Three squad cars belonging to Italian police skidded to a stop in front of their only exit. Jack had planned on using the pedestrian exit, just like he had done earlier at the pedestrian entrance.

The only other way past the police was through the guardrail separating the museum grounds from the roadway.

Hang on, Jack thought, locking in on the guardrail. He grinned. *Gotcha*.

Jack floored the Fiat.

"Um, what are you—"

"Trust me," he said, glancing at her. "And tighten your seatbelt."

She did, swallowing down her fear.

Jack got them up to forty miles per hour before they smashed through the hip-high perimeter fencing. The fast-moving vehicle decimated the feeble barrier. Jack fought to control the car and did so thanks to a heavier truck. They bounced off it, but straightened their trajectory as they did.

Police gave chase.

"Aw, crap," Jack said, looking in his mirror.

So did the three black SUVs.

He took a deep breath "This just got a lot more interesting."

Jack carefully took his phone out of his pocket and handed it to Gemma.

"Who am I calling?" she asked.

Jack recited the number from heart. Gemma put the call on speaker, hearing it ring twice.

"*Jack?*" Raegor asked.

But Jack didn't hear him. He was too zoned in on the aircraft swooping in down to street level behind the SUVs.

"*Jack?*"

He pounded the steering wheel. "What is it with bad guys and helicopters?" He glanced over at Gemma. "Second time in less than two months!"

"Popular, are we?" she mocked.

Jack growled. "I'd rather not be."

"*Jack!*"

"Sorry, sir," he replied. Gemma held the phone closer to him.

"*What—*"

"Look, just in case we get cut off, it's because we're dead, okay?"

Gemma's eyes darted up to Jack. He shrugged and gave her the best non-verbal apology he could. She looked forward. "Go under the overpass."

Jack nodded and gunned the engine, hearing something clunk somewhere beneath the floorboards.

That can't be good!

Luckily, the tunnel highway was mostly vacant. Jack put on as much speed as he could without feeling like he was going to lose control. The best part about taking the scenic route was that the helicopter couldn't track them.

But they also dropped the call with Raegor.

"Dammit!" Jack shouted, pounding his fist on the dash. He glanced at Gemma. "Not your fault. We'll be fine. Call him back as soon as we get topside, okay?"

Gemma nodded.

"Where are we anyway?" Jack asked.

"This is Via di Porta Cavalleggeri. It's the easiest way to get to the Vatican."

Jack's eyes opened wide. "We're going to the Vatican?"

She smiled slyly. "No. This isn't just a road to the Vatican, Jack. There are other exits along the way."

"Oh," Jack said, feeling dumb. "Right. I should've seen that coming."

Gemma smiled wider. "I can see why she likes you."

Jack's right eyebrow raised to the ceiling. "How so?"

"Handsome, boyish charm, innocent in a way—sincere."

Jack shifted in his seat. "Thanks. So," he said, changing the subject, "what's our exit?"

"Can't miss it. Just head towards the light."

Jack guided them around a scooter. "That's comforting."

"Just look for Via Aurelia, okay?"

"Yes, ma'am. Via Aurelia it is."

The tunnel highway ended abruptly at a light—sunlight, that is. They shot outside like a rocket…and into heavy traffic. Jack was forced to slow, nearly having to stop completely. The first thing he and Gemma did was look for the helicopter.

"See anything?" he asked.

Gemma was extra thorough and put down her window. She stuck her head out and looked up. "Nothing!" she shouted.

Jack let out a sigh of relief, and merged into the flow of traffic, even going as far as using his blinker.

"What are you doing?" Gemma asked.

"Blending in," Jack replied. "Driving like a maniac will only draw attention to ourselves. With any luck, they'll pass right over us."

"Hence the Fiat," Gemma said, understanding.

Jack reached forward and patted the dash this time. "Most popular car manufacturer in Italy."

"Smart man," Gemma said.

Jack shrugged. "I'm not opposed to doing a little homework."

His phone rang.

"So much for calling them back," Gemma said, answering the call.

"What's happening, Jack?" Raegor asked. *"We thought we lost you for a second."*

"You did," Jack replied, flicking his eyebrows at Gemma, "…in a tunnel."

Eddy didn't appreciate Jack's attempt at humor. *"Damn you, Jack. That's not funny!"*

Jack held in his laughter. "I'm sorry, Ed. Couldn't help myself."

"Can it, you two," Raegor said, scolding them both.

"Might want to make this quick, sir. Gemma and I need to vamoose—quick."

"Never mind why we called. What do you need from us?"

Jack thought about what they needed most. "A flight out of Rome to start." He looked at Gemma. "For the both of us."

"*Jack…*" Eddy said, butting in. "*Dr. Conti is—*"

"Valuable to us and in a lot of trouble if she stays behind," Jack finished.

"*I agree,*" Raegor said, getting Gemma's full attention. "*Where are you thinking of going next?*"

Jack had no idea, but then he remembered something Gemma had said. "York."

She gave Jack the same questioning look Raegor and Eddy must've had on their faces.

"*York, Jack?*" Raegor asked. "*Why England?*"

"We might have a lead there. Can you get us on the first available flight?"

Jack heard Raegor say something to Eddy in the background of the call.

"Sir?"

"*Alright, Jack. We'll see what we can do. Head for the airport and we'll call you back with the specifics.*"

Jack forced himself to stay put and not turn back into a stunt driver.

He saw a sense of relief wash over Gemma's face.

"Copy that," he replied. "We're on our way."

18

They'd lost the target vehicle. By the time the airborne team had traced the subterranean highway to its exit, it had been too late. Multiple Fiats could be seen entering and exiting, then dispersing in several directions.

The pilot, an Arab named Zayn, was tapped on the shoulder. He looked back at one of three men in the rear hold. Ajax's job had been to listen in on the police and army chatter. The only reason he'd be interrupting Zayn was if he had received important news.

Ajax held up two fingers. "We'll have company in two minutes!" Even though they were all wearing noise canceling earmuffs with internal speakers, it was still difficult to hear one another speak.

Zayn bit his lip, then nodded. "Roger that. Notify Marcus immediately."

Ajax's face paled a little. Nobody liked to give the *Legatus* bad news. But it was Ajax's job as communications officer aboard the helo. He nodded and placed the call.

Surprisingly, Marcus took the failure better than expected.

"*As soon as you land, cast a net,*" Marcus ordered. "*Put together a friends and family list for Dr. Gemma Conti. Focus on her professional life first with a cross reference concerning the Ninth.*"

"Yes, sir."

"*One more thing... Find out who this 'Jack' really is.*"

"Has his friend not talked?" Ajax asked.

"*No, she has proven to be...difficult. Luckily, time is on our side. We have waited for centuries. We can wait a little longer if need be.*"

"And if she doesn't talk?"

"*Then, she dies, though I have a feeling we'll be seeing Jack very soon.*"

19

York, England

Jack and Gemma's flight to England went smoothly. They had yet to see anything out of the ordinary since losing their pursuers back in Rome. It was a much-needed respite. Unfortunately, the down time had also given Jack a lot of time to think. And naturally, his thoughts had turned to May. He realized that the mission had become second to him, despite pretending otherwise. Only May's life mattered to him now. He had to get that problem solved before he could clearly focus again.

What have you gotten yourself into, Jack? he asked himself.

Gemma waved down a taxi. Jack gave the Leeds Bradford Airport terminal pickup area another glance before following her inside. He ducked his head and plopped into the rear-passenger seat.

"Good afternoon! Name's Jimmy," the cabbie said. His upbeat, chipper accent caught Jack off guard a little. So did the local's gray, handlebar mustache. "Where you off to today?"

"Uh..." Jack began, blanking.

Gemma swooped in and saved the day. "My name is Gemma, and this is my colleague, Jack. We're expected at the Yorkshire Museum."

"That's quite a drive, Miss. Roughly thirty miles," Jimmy explained. He turned and faced them. "Just letting you know before we get underway."

"That's fine," Jack said, buckling in. "Get us there ahead of schedule, and we'll double your rate."

Jimmy grinned. "You've got yourself a deal, mate." He spun. "Hold on to your arses."

That made Jack smile.

Jack estimated that they had at least a half an hour drive ahead of them, more if Jimmy failed in his efforts to get them there quickly. Either way, Jack would tip the man handsomely. Paying off people like this kept them from asking too many questions. Jack could tell the cabbie was a pro too, since he didn't even inquire as to their hurry.

Jack liked Jimmy.

"Care for a little music?" Jimmy asked.

Jack shrugged. "As long as it isn't mumble rap, knock yourself out."

"*Gah*, never!" Jimmy's eyes radiated mischief in his overhead mirror. "Only the classics for me, mate." And with that, the beginning to The Who's *Baba O'Riley* kicked in.

Jack *really* liked Jimmy.

The cabbie cranked it up a little more, essentially giving Jack and Gemma some privacy.

"What else can you tell me about Alexander the Great?" Jack quietly asked, looking at Gemma for a moment. "I only know the condensed version of him. I'm no scholar on the subject."

Gemma sat straighter. The question seemed to focus the historian. This was her lane and Jack could tell she preferred to stay in it, whenever possible.

"Yes, sure. Well, my favorite, less-popular factoid about him is that, as a young boy, he was tutored by none other than Aristotle."

"Aristotle?" Jack asked. "*The* Aristotle?"

Gemma nodded. "The same. A man who many proclaim to be the single-most influential person in history, unless, of course, you're also counting figures such as Jesus Christ and Buddha."

Jack scratched the back of his head. "Whatever floats your boat." He let out a long breath. "Aristotle... Well, that explains Alexander's apparent intelligence. I mean, you don't become as powerful as him without knowing what you're doing, not back then, anyway. Nowadays..."

The corner of Gemma's mouth curled upward. She understood what Jack was implying. In today's world, you could easily fall assbackwards into success, especially if you decided to make a living doing dumb crap online.

They're not all bad, I guess.

Jack did enjoy a handful of "influencers," though only ones that offered something educational or creative. Right now, he was fully engrossed in *Jazza's* YouTube channel, specifically his "Remade Monsters" series. Jack appreciated art, mostly because he was terrible at it.

"Alexander wasn't just some military meathead," Gemma continued. As soon as she said it, she winced and looked at Jack. "I'm sorry if that offended you."

Jack crossed his arms. "Should I be? Am I a meathead?"

"Oh, God no, Jack. You're quite the opposite, actually. You—" Jack's grin froze her in place. Her posture sagged and her chin dropped to her chest. "You're messing with me, aren't you?"

Jack cleared his throat. "What makes you say that?" She glanced over at him again. He gave her a nod. "Please, continue, Dr. Conti."

Gemma gave Jack an appreciative smile. "By all accounts, Alexander was very smart. In fact, I'd even go as far as saying that he was the smartest military commander of an entire generation—maybe ever!"

Jack's military history knowledge was deep, and no, he couldn't argue with her there. There were plenty of great minds throughout all eras of history; Alexander the Great, Genghis Khan, Erwin Rommel, George Patton, even Napolean. It wouldn't be a stretch to single-out Alexander as the greatest ever.

"Okay, so fast forward to Alexander's death," Jack said. "Why can't we find his tomb? What happened exactly?"

"His generals happened."

"Huh?"

Gemma loosened her seatbelt so she could turn and face Jack better. "When Alexander died, a couple of his closest generals fought over his body. Macedonian tradition says that whomever inters the king, officially replaces him."

Jack vaguely recalled something like this. "Ptolemy I, right?"

Gemma smiled. "Very good, Jack. Yes, he was Alexander's favorite general. He went as far as stealing Alexander's corpse and burying it in Egypt for a bit—in Memphis—before his final tomb was ready."

"Memphis? Why there?"

"Well, actually, Ptolemy was still in the process of building Alexander a proper tomb at the time, but it wasn't ready. History tells us that Alexander himself wished to be buried in ancient Libya instead of Macedon, so—"

"So, Ptolemy was actually doing as his king commanded!" Jack finished, getting excited.

"Precisely. To me, it was Perdiccas who was the real enemy in all this."

"Perdiccas?"

Gemma nodded. "He was back in Macedon. He was the one on the other side of this feud. He wanted to bury Alexander in the royal tombs of Aegae, now modern-day Vergina."

Jack gave her a questioning look. "The state in the U.S.?"

Gemma rolled her eyes. "Not *that* Vergina. V-E-R, not V-I-R."

"Is there a West *Vergina* in Greece too?" Jack asked, scratching his head again.

She couldn't hold back her smile. "No idea."

"*Pfft.* Some *expert* you are." She leaned in close, about to reply with something snarky. Jack held up his hands. "Cool your jets, I'm just messing with you again. You really are amazing at this."

Gemma nodded and relaxed. "Thank you. I appreciate that. You're pretty good too."

"Okay, so we have Alexander being temporarily buried in Memphis. Then what?"

The Italian historian shrugged. "Not much else. Ptolemy II, Ptolemy I's son, rose to power and was the one who transferred Alexander to his final resting place in Alexandria. He remained there for over 400 years, until around 200 AD. Then, *poof*, gone."

200 AD, huh? Jack thought. *That's awfully close to when the Ninth Legion vanished too. I wonder...*

"Well, Dr. Gemma Conti, expert in Ancient Rome and Greece, tell me, what do you think happened to Alexander's body?"

"I..." she stared hard at Jack, then relented and looked away, "don't know. I've been digging into it for years, as have countless others, and no one has come up with anything solid. It's as if the location was purposely kept secret, as if someone was trying to hide it."

Or protect it.

"From the Romans, perhaps?" Jack asked.

Gemma bit her lip, deep in thought. "Possibly, but they already had Alexander's remains in their possession for centuries by the time he disappeared. Personally, I think something else was going on."

Ditto.

Jack snorted. "That wouldn't surprise me at all. In my experience, there's *always* something else going on behind the scenes. It's never a straight line to the finish."

The rest of the trip from Leeds Bradford Airport to York was made mostly in silence. Occasionally, Jimmy would ask a question about Jack's musical taste. Gemma hadn't added anything to the conversation. She was too deep inside her own head, trying to put the pieces of the riddle together for what must've been the ten *thousandth* time.

Or she's trying to figure out why this is all happening to her?

Jack hated seeing innocent people get pulled into conflict. It didn't matter if it was during times of war or in his current profession. Gemma didn't deserve to be here, alongside him, on the run from modern-day legionnaires.

"What's that for?" she asked.

"Huh?" Jack asked, blinking out of his own thoughts. "What's *what* for?"

She pointed at his mouth. "That. You're troubled."

"No shit?"

They both shared in a soft laugh.

"I'm sorry that you're here, Gemma," Jack said.

She looked out her window, then back to Jack. "I'm not."

"You're not?"

She shook her head. The motion undid a couple strands of hair. She didn't bother to fix it, either.

"No. If I'm honest with you, and myself, I wasn't happy, Jack. Professionally, I've flatlined. There was nowhere else for me to go and nothing else for me to do—that I *wanted* to do."

"You shouldn't want to do this."

"Why not? You do."

Jack sighed. "Yeah, but my training is a little different from yours, Gemma. While I love history and will do just about anything to protect it, I'm not an academic. I choose to get my hands very dirty."

"Like kill people."

Jack nodded. "Yes. I don't enjoy it, though. I don't seek death. It just sorta comes with the job."

"Well, I have you to protect me," Gemma said, smiling.

Jack knew she was just trying to cheer him up. "Yeah, tell that to May."

They rode in silence for a few minutes. The break allowed Jack to check something on his phone. He went straight to the local Roman news websites, curious to see what information had been released.

Hmmm, not much yet, Jack thought, unsure if they were just being cautious, or if the media had purposely delayed the story. He figured there'd be loads of chatter depicting the Legion in action. *I mean, how often do you see gunmen in high-tech gladiator helmets?*

Jack relayed his concerns to Gemma.

"That is a bit odd," she agreed. "But it could also be nothing—respect for the dead until things are wholly verified."

"Alright, you two, we're here!" Jimmy called out, lowering the volume of the music.

The cab's brakes squeaked as they stopped. Jack gave the grounds outside the front door a quick look, but wasn't all that worried about it. No one knew where they were.

Jack handed Jimmy his company card and opened the passenger door. He slid out, stood, and stretched as Gemma followed him outside.

"Here you go, mate!" Jimmy called out. Jack stepped over to the front passenger side door. He leaned into the open window. Jimmy was holding up his phone. "You sure about the whole double thing?"

Jack playfully shot him a finger gun. "Go for it."

Jimmy shrugged and typed on the device's screen. "You're the boss." He handed Jack his card. "And, done. Pleasure doing business with you, mate."

Jack reached his hand inside and shook Jimmy's hand. "Thanks for the quick service."

"Any time!"

Jack slapped the roof of the taxi, then stood. He was about to turn away and start towards the museum, but got an idea. Something about this entire situation bugged him. Jack was naturally paranoid, but his Spidey Sense was going nuts right now.

"Hey, Jimmy, can I ask you a favor?" Jack leaned back into the window.

"Anything for my best customer!"

Jack looked down the street before he spoke again. "Think you can hang around for a few? We don't exactly have a rental, ya know?"

Jimmy didn't look thrilled.

"I'll make it worth your while…"

The cabbie's face morphed into that of the Cheshire Cat. "Sure, mate, I can hang around for a bit."

Jack shook his hand again. "You're a rare one, Jimmy. We shouldn't be too long."

"Nah, don't worry about it." Jimmy thumbed over his shoulder. "Gonna have a sleep in the back until you're back."

Jack gave the man a mock salute, then stood. But then something else started gnawing at the back of Jack's skull.

"Sorry, one last thing…" Jimmy looked about done with Jack, but he didn't voice any objection. "If, for some weird reason, we don't come back, can I give you a number to call? It's to my boss back in the States."

Jimmy squinted hard at Jack. "What exactly are you expecting to happen in a museum that would prevent you from leaving?"

Jack gave the cabbie a wink. "Anything and everything, my friend."

20

The sun was beginning to set, casting the Museum Gardens in a kaleidoscope of waning light and deep shadows. The 19th-century park was beautiful and sported ruins dating all the way back to Ancient Rome.

How fitting, Jack thought, turning and facing the front doors.

"You sure we can trust this guy?" he asked.

Gemma shrugged. "I assume so. Plus, no one in this part of the world knows more about the Ninth Legion than Spencer."

"It's too obvious, though."

"What do you mean?"

He faced her. "Look at it this way… Wouldn't you think the Legion knows about Dr. Harwood, and his expertise involving the legion? If he really is the foremost expert, then I guaran-damn-tee they're watching him closely."

Gemma looked at the building. "Yeah, sure. I guess that could be true."

Jack sighed. "But…"

"But what?"

He turned and started toward the entrance. "It's not like we have a better option."

"And we did travel all this way…"

The museum entrance was a quaint rectangle that displayed some impressive pieces. If they had more time, Jack would've gladly taken it all in. He loved museums. An archway to their right led into the museum gift shop. Jack would've also liked to peruse its wares.

An attractive blonde was working the front desk. She met them with a smile full of pearly whites, folding her hands atop her desk as they neared.

"Hello, and welcome to Yorkshire Museum," the local said. Her eyes bounced back and forth between Jack and Gemma as she spoke. "Is it just the two of you today?"

Jack looked to Gemma for guidance.

She stepped forward. "It is, but we aren't here as patrons. I am Dr. Gemma Conti of the National Museum of Rome, and we are here to see Dr. Harwood."

"I see, yes." The blonde stood and motioned to the doorway next to the desk. "Please, make yourselves at home while I contact Dr. Harwood."

Jack nodded his thanks and moved for the doorway. "So, whattaya got in here?"

"This is our 'Roman York' exhibit, featuring relics pertaining to the Ninth Legion of the Imperial Roman Army."

Jack's eyes lit up. *Jackpot!*

"Ooh, don't mind if I do."

The first thing Jack found was a fourth-century statue of Mars, the Roman god of war. On the floor behind the deity was a massive map of the Roman Empire dating back to the Emperor Hadrian's rule. The sight made Jack grin.

They had recently buzzed by his personal mausoleum back in Rome during their death-defying car chase.

"Hello, Hadrian," Gemma said, stepping up next to Jack. "It's nice to see you again."

But Jack was already fully engrossed in the next priceless piece. Hanging against the back wall of the exhibit was something Jack had seen online several times. Though incomplete, the inscription was the final known mentioning of the Ninth Legion. Even from here, Jack could see the beginning of their name, plain as day, within the bottom line of text.

LEG VIIII HI, Jack read to himself. *The Ninth Spanish Legion.*

Experts had set the stone fragment into a modern recreation of the entire inscription. The more-recent text was in a bold red and, of course, it was all in Latin.

"Excuse me, Dr. Conti?"

Gemma faced him. "Yes?"

Jack tipped his chin up at the inscription. "Enlighten me, please."

She gazed up at the fragment and stepped closer. *"The Emperor Caesar Nerva Trajan Augustus, son of the deified Nerva, Conqueror of Germany, Conqueror of Dacia, pontifex maximus, in his twelfth year of tribunician power, six times acclaimed imperator, five times consul, father of his country, built this gate by the agency of the Ninth Legion Hispana."* She caught her breath and explained. "This had once been a part of a fortress here in York, when the Ninth founded the city."

Jack looked at her. "The Ninth Legion founded York?"

She nodded. "Yes, but back then it was called Eboracum. The same general that led the Ninth to York went on to became the governor of Britain."

"What was his name?" Jack asked.

"Quintus Petillius Cerialis," Gemma replied.

Jack shuddered and mumbled, "That's a mouthful."

"And a truly great man, if I do say so myself!"

The voice echoed around them. A figure stepped into view from behind a column to Jack's right. He would've been suspicious of where the newcomer now stood, but then he spotted another doorway that led into a different exhibit.

Calm down, Jack. Give this guy a chance.

Spencer Harwood was larger than Jack had expected. He mirrored Jack's height, but was a tad thicker. Jack had expected to see another mousy individual, a male version of Gemma. Perhaps even someone similar to Dr. Lombardi. Spencer was about Jack's age too, maybe even a year or two younger.

"Spencer, it's wonderful to see you again!" Gemma said, shaking the man's hand.

Jack did not.

"It's always a pleasure, Gemma. It's been, what, two years?"

Gemma nodded. "Back in Rome. You came in for a symposium."

"Ah, yes." He looked at Jack. "Another of Alberto's lectures, I'm afraid." His face soured. "I'm sorry to hear about what happened."

Gemma's face now matched his. She may not have always gotten along with Lombardi, but the two had worked side by side for years.

"Yes, it is unfortunate," she said. "I was lucky to survive."

Spencer shook his head. "And to do it all for a legion's eagle…"

"Yeah, weird, huh?" Jack gave him a hard stare. He didn't like any of this.

The museum curator looked at Gemma, then back to Jack. "Did I say something?"

Gemma must've heard it too. "Uh, Spencer, how did you know that Alberto died and that the eagle was stolen?"

Jack folded his arms across his chest. "None of that information has been made public."

Spencer held up his hands in innocence. "I heard about it through the historical community. Everyone is talking about it. Until now, we all thought you had also shared in Alberto's fate, Gemma." Jack didn't budge. "Look, if you two think I had anything to do with it, I will need to ask you to leave."

That couldn't happen. Like it or not, Jack and Gemma needed Spencer's help.

Jack shrugged and relaxed his posture. "Apologies. It's been a wacky couple of days. We're both on edge still."

Spencer faced Jack. "So, you were there too?"

Gemma went to reply but was cut off by Jack. "I was. Met a guy named Theo too, thinks he's a gladiator."

"Am I supposed to know who that is?" If Spencer recognized the name, he hid it well.

"No," Gemma quickly replied. "Please, we need your help with something relating to the Ninth Legion. I told Jack, here, that you are the best in Europe when it comes to the Ninth."

"Yeah. No pressure, pal."

Spencer gave Jack an irritated look before speaking again. "Yes, of course. I've done so much work on the subject that the Ninth are like family to me."

I bet they are… Jack had a bad, bad feeling about this guy.

Gemma looked at Jack but tilted her head toward Spencer. "Show him the keycard."

"Keycard?" Spencer asked. "That's hardly 'ancient.'"

Jack rolled his eyes. "No shit, Sherlock." He retrieved it from his pocket and held it up so the curator could see it. "Any idea why a modern-day mercenary group would be carrying something with the Ninth Legion's insignia on it?"

Jack handed it to Spencer, watching him closely as he did. He immediately noticed Spencer's sweaty brow. The museum was on the cool side. Spencer sweating this much sent up a red flag.

"It's the legion's *nine* too," Gemma added.

He nodded softly. "Yes, it is. A *five* followed by four *ones*. The original Roman numeral for the number nine."

"We know," Jack said. "The more recent IX replaced it centuries after the Roman Empire fell."

"Correct," Spencer said. "Still, I'm not sure why you came to me?"

Jack grinned. Spencer wasn't paying him or Gemma any attention. He only had eyes for the keycard since Jack had shown it to him.

If this thing truly meant nothing to him, Jack thought, *why was he is so enamored with it?*

Jack was pretty sure he could make the man tell them, but he needed to keep it civil, just in case his suspicions about the man were wrong. So, he decided to throw Spencer an empire-sized cookie.

"The people who attacked the Colosseum said they were descendants of the Ninth Legion." Spencer's eyes darted up from the keycard, locking in on Jack. The former Delta operator stepped closer to him. "But you already knew that, didn't you?"

"What?" Gemma asked, looking at Jack. Then she faced her colleague. "Spencer?"

"Why are you sweating so much, Dr. Harwood?" Jack asked. He moved closer, forcing Spencer to take a step back. "It's unreasonably cold in here and damn near beautiful outside." Jack pushed closer again. "And you haven't taken your eyes off that keycard, which tells me you know what it is."

"Jack," Gemma started, "I don't know—"

"Oh, I think you do, Gemma. If Spencer is such authority on the subject, why didn't he scoff at the notion of someone announcing their familial ties to the Ninth Legion?" Jack squinted at the man. "Who's Theo?"

"No one!" Spencer blurted. "I mean...." he looked past Jack and Gemma, then around the room to confirm that they were alone, "maybe we should continue this conversation in my office?"

Jack stepped back and shrugged. "Lead on, Macduff."

Spencer cautiously stepped away and led them away from the Roman York exhibit. He looked over his shoulder a few moments later. "And it's actually 'lay on,' not 'lead on.'"

Jack shrugged. "Eh, whatever, I'm not a big Tolkien guy anyway." The retort upset Spencer enough to get a physical reaction out of him, but not a verbal one. "Or was it Rowling?"

"What are you doing?" Gemma asked quietly.

"Just trying to rattle our boy a little. I wanna see what happens when his head explodes."

"Says the man without a gun..."

Gemma was right, of course. Jack wasn't armed. Flying internationally with weapons wasn't a thing TAC did. An agent figured it out on his or her own or had to land in a major airport or arrive at a chief train station. TAC had locker pickups and drop-offs everywhere. It's how Jack had gotten rid of his firearm in Rome.

He held up his right fist, confident in his hand-to-hand skills. "Don't need a gun, Doc."

21

Spencer led Jack and Gemma to the right, out of the Roman York exhibit, and into a utilitarian stairwell. Stairs led up to the next level, as well as down into the guts of the museum, but there was also an elevator off to the left. Spencer descended the stairs leading into the basement.

This just keeps getting better and better, Jack thought, on high alert.

When they dismounted the stairs, the first thing Jack spotted was a sign pointing them to the restrooms. Jack double checked his bladder situation and figured he'd have to pee before they left.

They took a quick right, passing a baby changing room on their left, as well as the next-door men's room. An overhead sign relayed the women's bathroom was further ahead in the next subterranean corridor. And that's what it was. Jack could feel the weight of the museum looming above his head and the dense, concrete walls squeezing in on him. He wasn't claustrophobic in the least, but there was always something that unnerved him about being underneath so much weight. He honestly couldn't explain it.

Spencer stopped at a nondescript door across from the men's restroom. The only label it contained was a small sign that read, PRIVATE.

Jack looked behind him and grinned. "Your office is next to the shitter?"

Spencer took a deep breath, then let it out slowly. "Do all Americans share your sense of humor?"

"Only the ones I trust." He winked. "Straight-shooting, rigid fellows aren't my type."

Spencer retrieved a keycard that was identical to Jack's legion keycard, except that the emblem on it was that of the museum, not the Ninth. "Well, I guess I have to apologize."

Gemma looked at Jack. "For what?" she asked.

Spencer glanced at Jack. "You and I can never be friends."

That made Jack smile a little. He gave the curator the small victory and stepped back so he could open the door without Jack looking over his shoulder. He did ask the man about the security, though. Nothing about this museum, so far, had screamed "We are state-of-the-art!" If anything, Jack thought the place needed *better* security in place.

"What's with the electronic locks?" Jack asked. "This place feels more lock-and-key to me."

"Very observant. After I took over as Senior Curator in 2009, I secured funding to have the museum undergo a major refurbishment that took nearly a year." He placed his keycard against the door's card reader. Jack heard a soft *click* as the deadbolt released. "Included in that was upgraded security measures at key points, including this room. We added additional cameras too."

Spencer opened the door to reveal...storage.

"Huh?" Jack said, taking in dozens of empty display cases and piles of old signage. "This is your office?"

"No, this is just storage. My office is further back."

He led them down a central hallway past row after row of what constituted as junk. Fifty feet later, they came to the rear wall, and another door.

"Have you ever been down here?" Jack whispered to Gemma.

She shook her head.

Great.

"Here we are." Spencer used the same keycard to unlock it. He turned the handle and pushed his way inside.

Jack was floored by what he saw. The room was roughly the same size as the storage room behind him, maybe fifty feet wide and long. But unlike the glum storeroom, Spencer's "office" was adorned with priceless historical artifacts from all walks of history. Jack did spot several pertaining to the Roman Empire mixed in.

"Okay," Jack admitted, "this is cool."

Spencer beamed with pride. "I thought you'd say as much." He spun and walked backward, arms out wide. Floor-to-ceiling glass cases lined the ten-foot-tall outer walls and another dozen pocked the floorspace in between. "This is where we move pieces to be stored for another time. I thought it best to keep them in the light, instead of locked away in a dusty drawer or cabinet somewhere else."

Jack agreed, which made him second-guess his original thoughts on the curator.

This guy might just be legit, after all, Jack thought, appreciating this guy's point of view.

At the center of it all was Spencer's workspace. It wasn't much, either. The desk was essentially a large, squared U-shape. The left and right sides of the desk each supported a pair of monitors. The forward-facing section of his desk was mostly empty except for a couple of books and a desk phone. There were also two chairs positioned opposite it.

Spencer motioned for them to sit. He continued around to his chair and took it. The alarms that Jack had just quieted in his head were back, and they were blasting.

"Quite the setup you have here," Jack said, looking around. *Too good.* "I'm guessing this wasn't secured in the refurb funding, was it?"

Gemma eyed Jack.

Spencer sat back. "Correct. This was all thanks to a private benefactor."

Jack leaned forward on his knees. "Theo's boss, right?"

Gemma's mouth opened wide when Spencer didn't immediately deny the accusation. Instead, he removed the Ninth Legion keycard from his pocket and tapped it somewhere out of sight beneath his desk. The lock to his office door re-engaged and a second one disengaged somewhere in the back of the room.

"Correct."

Gemma leapt to her feet, but Jack and Spencer did not. So far, Spencer had shown them no animosity or a threat to their safety. He'd been quite the opposite, actually. He'd been a gracious host, even despite Jack's jabs.

Jack reached out and grabbed Gemma's wrist before she could say something she'd regret. Jack was under no illusion that the museum curator was an incredibly dangerous individual. She abided Jack's request for calmness and returned to her seat.

Gemma relaxed as she sat. "Why?"

"Oh, several reasons…"

"Let me guess," Jack said, "one of them is because you also have a descendant from the Ninth Legion, don't you?"

"Yes, I do. Quintus Curtius Rufus, author of the—"

"*Histories of Alexander the Great*," Gemma finished. "Rufus was a first-century Roman historian."

"And like my ancestors before me, I am the private historian for the current Legion." He folded his hands atop his desk. "When I took over as Senior Curator, I offered the museum to be used as a base of operations of sorts." He stood. "Come, I'll show you."

"Just like that?" Jack asked. "Why?"

Spencer shrugged. "Because you cannot leave without my aid, and nor are you in any position to force your way out."

"What makes you say I can't find a way out of here?" Jack asked, looking for a weakness. Then he remembered he was in a locked basement.

"Because, Jack, I am the only thing keeping you alive. This room is being monitored. All I have to do is give the verbal order, and a half dozen, heavily armed men will come in here and dispose of you…and Gemma." He glanced at her. "Apologies."

Jack's shoulders slumped. "Did we just fly from Rome to England only to waltz right into the enemy's secret lair?"

Spencer smiled. "Yes, you did. One of our *lairs*, anyway. Thank you for that, by the way. Made it much easier for us."

"Eat me, *Hard*wood."

Gemma cleared her throat. "How many facilities do you have?"

"Several around the Mediterranean."

With nothing else to add, Jack lifted his hands out to the side, then let them flop down to his legs. "Well, take us to your leader, I guess."

Spencer turned and headed for the back wall of the office. "Oh, they aren't in York. I am in charge here."

That killed Jack. It also meant that May wasn't here. *Damn!* He'd gotten his hopes up for a second. *And now we're prisoners too.*

The trio stepped up to the rear wall. Spencer reached out and gently pushed it. The added pressure caused a mechanism within it to take over. It swung open on a perfectly greased hinge to reveal the top of a stairway.

Spencer stepped aside and smiled. "Lead on, Macduff."

"Har, har," Jack said, stepping through. "You're really enjoying this, aren't you?"

"I am, yes. Now, please, keep moving."

Gemma was next. She stopped, staying close to Jack. "Going down?"

"Yeah, looks like it. Stay close, okay?"

Gemma went as far as to hold Jack's left arm.

Down the rabbit hole we go, Jack thought, contemplating their next move. *I got nothin'.*

"Now," Spencer continued, "who exactly do you and your partner work for? We've had friends of ours look into it but have come up with nothing, not even a parking ticket. That tells me you're government, though we don't know which one."

"Spooky, huh?" Jack asked. "We could work for anyone—even someone more dangerous than your solid-gold *Legatus*."

Jack glanced over his shoulder just as the stairwell came to life in artificial, motion-activated light. Spencer was smartly staying three steps behind them as they descended. Luckily for Jack, he wasn't in a rush. His brain was alight with escape scenarios, but he also needed more intel. So, he'd keep the Legion historian talking for as long as he could until his willingness to divulge information faded.

"I doubt your people are as dangerous as ours," Spencer said. "Now, you and your partner's employers…"

Jack finished his descent, stopped and turned, thumbing over to Gemma. "Who, her? We don't usually work together. We just met the other day."

"Deflecting with humor." Spencer turned his attention to Gemma now. "Does he always do that?"

"Pretty much."

The Englishman eyed Jack. "Based on your partner's nationality and her background, I'd say China, but no, I don't think that's it. Nor do I think it's an American organization. Your ilk might be cowboys at heart, but I doubt anyone over there would be stupid enough to hire a former Chinese spy."

Jack burst out laughing. "You don't know us at all, do you?"

Footsteps came up behind Jack. He spun to see two helmeted legionnaires carrying electric batons. Jack was thrilled to see no guns of any kind. Firing them in confined places, such as a heavily insulated basement compound, was a bad idea. Even suppressed, small-caliber SMGs could do some serious damage to your eardrums.

Spencer looked past Jack, focusing on the new arrivals instead. "Is the live feed ready?"

"Yes, and it's been tested thoroughly," the man on the right replied.

"Good," Spencer said. "Take our guests to Room 2, please."

One of the armed legionnaires circled around behind Jack. The other moved closer to Gemma.

Jack held up his hands. "Easy, fellas. We aren't going to cause any problems."

They pushed onward, retracing the steps the two men had just taken. They stopped between two unmarked doors. The lead legionnaire opened the one on the right.

"Inside," he ordered, stepping aside.

Jack and Gemma cautiously entered to find a ten-by-ten box. If Jack had to guess, it was either a holding cell or an interrogation room. *Probably both*, he decided. The only furnishings it contained were two chairs, a wall-mounted flatscreen, and a massive mirror. Jack knew, for a fact, that the glass was of the two-way variety, and that there were probably already people on the other side watching and recording them.

"You guys ever hear of Brooklyn Nine-Nine?"

But Jack's snark was only met with the slamming of a door. As soon as he heard the deadbolt latch, the voice of Spencer Harwood crackled to life around them.

"*One last time, Jack. Who do you and your partner work for? And, please, do be honest, her life depends on it.*"

The flatscreen blinked to life, showing a live image of May.

She looked terrible.

Jack charged the mirror, pounding the base of his fists against it. "You bastards! I'll kill you all!" But what could Jack honestly do? He knew the answer. For now, it was nothing. He relaxed his hands, laying them flat against the mirror. "Dammit... Fine, what exactly do you want to know?"

"*No, Jack.*" The voice came from May's end of the feed. A single man stepped into view in front of the beaten May. And he wore a gold gladiator helmet.

"You..."

The Italian removed his helmet, showing off a mop of dirty blonde hair, and the same blacked-out eyes as his comrade, Theo, had. "*What you should be asking is what you can do to keep you and your associates alive?*"

Jack looked over his shoulder. Gemma was visibly terrified. She sat, hugged herself, and used her eyes to plead for Jack to do something to save her life.

Jack pushed off the glass and stepped over to the flatscreen. "Make a list. What, specifically, do you need from me?"

The *Legatus* neared the camera. When he was within feet of it, he stopped. "*Well, Jack, to be quite frank, we need your help.*"

22

Eagle County, Colorado, USA

Solomon Raegor sat deep within the bowels of TAC headquarters, elbows on his desk, forehead in his hands. His eyes were closed, and he was alone. So far, both of his agents were MIA. May had been captured on the scene in Rome, and Jack had only recently disappeared since landing in England. Raegor had hoped to get a report from Jack an hour ago, but to no avail.

His phone rang, causing him to snap bolt upright. This was *his* line, not the office's. Only his agents ever called him directly. Not even Senator Wentz, Chairman of the Armed Services Committee, and one of the few people in Congress who knew of TAC's existence, called Raegor directly.

He buzzed Eddy, using his office phone's call button. "Get in here."

"On my way," Eddy said, hanging up.

Raegor grabbed his phone, but calmed and checked the number first. Even though the call was coming through to his personal phone, he still had the ability to trace it. The number wasn't one of theirs. His computer monitor displayed the caller's information, and he saw that the area code was from Leeds, where Jack had landed.

"Who's this?" he asked, answering the call.

"Name's Jimmy Barlow. I'm calling on behalf of a bloke called Jack."

Raegor unlocked the door with a touch of a button that was built into the underside of his desk. Eddy came storming right in. She closed the door and locked it. Now that the room was secure, Raegor put the call on speaker.

"Okay, Mr. Barlow, tell me, what happened to Jack?"

"Um, I'm not really sure, and please, it's Jimmy. Mr. Barlow was my father, and a piece of shite at that." Raegor could see why Jack asked this guy for help... *"I dropped him and an Italian bird off at the Yorkshire Museum. He asked me to wait, but they never came back."*

Raegor looked up at Eddy, who was looming over him, standing on the opposite side of his desk. She quickly began tapping away on her tablet, no doubt pulling up everything she could on the Leeds local.

"And you stayed and called us?" Raegor asked, impressed. "That's very professional of you."

"Yeah," Jimmy said, *"I'm one of the rare ones left around here. Plus, your boy paid me well."*

Raegor rolled his eyes. *You mean 'I' paid you well*, he thought. It was Raegor who secured funding every year and handled most of the agency's finances, after all.

Eddy looked increasingly worried. Raegor held up a calming hand, doing his best to squelch her anxiousness.

"I may not be in whatever line of work you all are in, but I know someone

when they're in trouble."

"Same, Jimmy. Same."

Another call was coming through. Raegor's eyes flashed to his screen. He watched the screen flash Jack's ID number.

Raegor snapped his fingers and pointed at his phone. Eddy quickly dug hers out of her pocket. "Thank you for your help, Jimmy. I'm going to have you talk to my secretary for a moment."

"Uh, sure?"

"Hello, Mr. Barlow," Eddy said, connecting to the call. "Yes, I'm sorry, Jimmy..." She gave Raegor a deep scowl before turning and stepping away. He knew the glare was in response to calling her his secretary.

He didn't respond to her reaction, though. Raegor quickly answered the incoming call. "Jack?"

"What took you so long?"

Jack's excessive personality tended to annoy Raegor sometimes, but not now. He was just happy to hear the man's voice. He didn't want to out Jimmy's involvement, in case someone was listening in, but he also wanted Jack to know that the driver was okay.

"Was on the other line with a new friend of yours. Nice guy."

Jack snorted. *"Ah, okay. Yeah, got it. You should see his mustache. It's pretty epic."*

Eddy hung up with Jimmy in time to hear the comment about the man's facial hair. She met eyes with Raegor and mouthed the word, "mustache?"

Raegor shrugged. It could've been code for something, or, knowing Jack, he was just being Jack. "Are you okay? What about Dr. Conti?"

"About that..." Jack replied, letting out a long, exhausted breath.

He told Raegor and Eddy everything that had happened thus far. The only thing Raegor could come back with was, "Yeah, okay. So, what do you need from us?"

"This is going to sound crazy, sir, but I need clean entry into Saddam's palace in Babylon."

"Excuse me?"

Jack chuckled. *"Like I said, crazy, right? I don't get it, either. That's what they want, and I'm calling you to get it done, like yesterday done. The team from the Colosseum now has me and Gemma, and if we don't cooperate, we're dead, May too."*

Raegor didn't know what to say. The only thing he could was, "Iraq? That isn't going to be easy, Jack."

"I know, but you need to make it happen."

"Yeah, I understand, and we will." He sat back and closed his eyes. "Is it okay if I call you back at this number?"

"Uh... No... I'm getting a hard no." Raegor could hear someone whispering something to Jack in the background of the call. *"We'll call you back in...an hour, really?"*

Raegor's reaction was the same. "An hour? That's impossible."

A third line picked up. *"For your people's sake, I hope it's not."*

"I presume this is the man in charge?" Raegor asked, standing.

"*It is.*"

Raegor snapped his fingers and pointed at his computer. Eddy hurried around and immediately started up their voice recognition software. Besides funding, the toys TAC was given was one of the only other good things about being attached to the American military.

She gave him a thumbs up. She was ready.

"Look, Mister—"

"*It's General, actually,*" the other man interrupted.

"Okay, General, here's the deal. I'm confident we can get you in unseen, but I'm not sure how long it'll take to put an operation like this together. If you want in so badly, then you need to give me the opportunity to do so. A *real* opportunity. Rushing something like a covert insertion into Iraq will not only get *my* people killed, but *yours* too."

The general must've known as much, because he didn't immediately fire back with a response. When he did, it gave Raegor a chance to relax a little.

"*Fine. How long do you need?*"

"Give me two days."

"*Fine, but if I see any of your people on the ground when we arrive, your Jack, May, and Dr. Conti will be shot on sight.*"

The call ended.

Eddy slammed her fist on the desk next to the keyboard.

"Nothing?" he asked.

She shook her head. "Needed a few more seconds."

"I figured as much." He blew out a long breath. "Okay, I have a few calls to make. Can you give me a minute?"

Eddy's eyebrow rose. "Calls? As in more than one?"

Raegor couldn't hide his smile. "You don't really think I'm *not* going to have people on the ground, do you?"

"Is that safe?"

Raegor dialed a number. "For these guys, it'll be like a walk in the park."

23

York, England

Jack got one more good look at May before the flatscreen displaying her image went dark. This was the closest to depressed Jack had felt in some time. He felt helpless. Hopeless too. So, he did as he always did, and he focused on what he could control. He pulled his gaze off the black screen, and shifted it back to the glass.

"Babylon, huh?" he asked.

But he wasn't answered through the speaker system. The door behind him and Gemma opened again. Jack glanced over his shoulder as Spencer Harwood re-entered the room. Two armed legionnaires followed him in, staying put just inside the door.

"Sit!" one gunman shouted.

With nowhere to go, and still too many questions that needed answering, Jack did as he was told and sat.

"There's a lot of good loot still buried over there," Jack continued. "You know, Alexander the Great died in Babylon..."

Spencer stood in front of Jack and Gemma. "Yes, I am aware. Why do you think we're going there in the first place?"

Jack sat up straight. "You know where it is, don't you?"

Gemma matched his posture. "Spencer?"

Spencer folded his hands behind his back and mumbled something before answering. "We've always known," he smiled, laying it on thick.

Jack went to stand, but paused halfway when the two gunmen stepped closer. He twisted his upper body around to look at them, then decided to play it safe and stayed seated.

"Let me get this straight, you know where one of the greatest warriors of all time is buried, and you never once thought to take a look?"

Spencer's bravado faltered. "I never said we haven't tried. In fact, we've tried several times. To gain access would be the highest honor. But without the key, it's impossible."

A key? Jack thought, putting the question in his back pocket.

"Why Alexander's tomb?" Gemma asked, quieting Jack and Spencer's back-and-forth. "You all are descended from Roman soldiers, not the Greek. I understand the monetary value of such a prestigious discovery, but I get the feeling that isn't what this is."

Spencer didn't reply.

Jack pushed him. "If you really need our help, then you need to give us some intel—something we can use."

Spencer squatted in front of them. "The leader of our order—"

"Pony Boy," Jack slipped in. "You know, from *The Outsiders*? Stay gold, and whatnot?"

"His name is Marcus Cerialis, and yes, he is descended from the great Quintus Petillius Cerialis."

Jack motioned for Spencer to keep moving along. "General of the Ninth Legion, founder of York, Governor of Britain... Yeah, we know."

"Yes, well, our records say that, at the request of Nero, Quintus Cerialis put together a kind of secret task-force whose singular purpose was to hunt down the Macedonian's tomb."

"But why?" Gemma asked again.

Spencer stood and paced. "Greed. Nero was, by all accounts, Rome's worst imperator." Jack looked to Gemma for confirmation. She simply nodded. "He wanted the vast fortune for himself, but not General Cerialis. He wanted it for Rome, to expand the empire further."

"Would've probably worked too," Gemma said.

"Why now?" Jack asked. "What's changed since then?"

Gemma's eyes went wide. "The eagle standard! You need it somehow, don't you?"

Jack could sense Harwood wasn't supposed to be divulging so much information, but the man's enthusiasm was overriding his caution. He truly lived for this stuff, regardless of his personal involvement.

"Correct. Unfortunately, Babylon is smack in the middle of one of the most hostile regions on earth. The Middle East has been at war with itself for millennia."

Jack knew that all too well. "And it'll be at war with itself until one side finally exterminates the other."

"Also correct. After all these years, I think it's safe to say that the ideologies of that area will never change."

"Back up a little," Jack said. "You said something about needing a key."

"Yes, it supposedly controls everything that was put in place to stop the unworthy from entering."

Jack glanced at Gemma. "The unworthy?"

"Not in a supernatural way, mind you," Spencer explained. "Whoever attempted this great quest would need to prove him or herself worthy."

"That sounds an awful lot like traps, or possibly a test of some kind," Jack said.

"Once again, you are correct," Spencer said. "Around this time is when the *aquila* was stolen and divided."

"The *aquila*?" Gemma asked. "What does it have to do with this?"

But Jack already knew. "It's your missing key, isn't it?"

"It is. Separated into three pieces and hidden from us."

"Then it was lost to time, yes?" Gemma asked.

The Legion historian bobbed his head. "War, famine, general distrust... For a time, the Legion had lost its way, getting caught up in other ventures, like the Crusades, for instance. The three sacred pieces of our eagle standard were swept away and hidden."

"But who could get close enough to the *aquila* to do it?" That was odd to

Jack. "Oh," he said, understanding. "It was by fellow legionnaires?"

"Yes. There were many traitors in our ranks back then."

The pieces of the Ninth Legion mystery were quickly falling into place in Jack's head. He only had one more question, for now.

"So, the Ninth Legion. What actually happened to them?"

Spencer looked down at his feet before returning his gaze to Jack. "They killed each other."

That was something... Based on what Spencer had told them, it didn't shock Jack in the least. There was a lot going on behind the curtain.

Like civil war.

"What do the pieces look like?" Jack asked, moving the conversation along in a new direction.

"Well, you know the eagle," Spencer replied. "The base is just a small platform with which the eagle sat on. It also contains an exquisitely carved laurel wreath that stands on end."

"Okay, so eagle and base," Jack reiterated. "What's left?"

"The pole of an *aquilifer*, an eagle-bearer."

Jack sat back and cracked his neck. "The guy that carried the eagle standard, right?"

Spencer held up a finger. "And the most important member of a legion. He was to be protected at all costs."

Gemma inhaled hard. Her face lit up. "Alberto said that the storehouse where the eagle was found looked as if it had been a secret room."

"Belonging to one of the traitors within our ranks, yes," Spencer added. "We knew it was somewhere in Rome, but had never been able to zero-in on its exact location. I have records of the traitor's confession. He was caught a couple of days after the *aquila* went missing."

"And the other two pieces?" Jack asked.

"Unobtainable without each other. It seems that these traitors had also been busy over the years."

"Wait," Gemma said. "Each piece is, itself, a key?"

Spencer finally stopped his pacing. "Correct. Very elaborate, I know."

"Smart too," Jack said. "Makes Alexander's tomb impossible to open unless you have the one thing on earth that allows it. And it's not like you can blast your way in. There's no telling how unstable the locales are. One inadvertent explosion and you lose a piece forever—the tomb too."

"Precisely," Spencer replied. "We'd rather wait another thousand years, than potentially lose it forever."

"What happens if the remaining pieces are lost?" Gemma asked.

Just the notion seemed to hurt Spencer. "Then, it's lost. But at least the tomb—our birthright—will never fall into anyone else's possession."

The last back-and-forth made Jack realize something. "You have the base and pole, right?" Spencer looked away. "Wonderful." Jack figured something else out just then. "I take it we aren't going to Babylon quite yet?"

"You're going after the base and the pole first, aren't you?" Gemma asked.

"Correction," Spencer replied, smiling. "*We* are."

Jack sighed. "Figures."

He didn't want to help these people, but Jack knew that if he didn't, one, he'd die, May too. And two, that these nut jobs could find the tomb without TAC's involvement and that would just flat-out suck. This Legion might revere the tomb in some semi-religious way, but they were still nothing but a band of graverobbers looking to make a score.

Jack also knew that if he stayed involved, he could, at least, keep an eye on things until Raegor sent in the cavalry. *Which he will*, Jack thought. He had no doubt about it.

"I'm in," Jack said, standing.

"You're in?" Gemma asked, also standing.

Spencer placed his hands on his hips. "Just like that, you're willing to help us?"

"To find the tomb of Alexander the Great, yeah, just like that. But…"

"But?" Spencer replied.

"I want May back by my side. I will guarantee our help—no bullshit of any kind—but I want her here." Jack pointed at the ground next to him.

"I'll need to confer with Marcus before I can give you an answer."

Jack grinned. "Oh, something tells me he'll play ball."

"And how do you know that?"

Jack folded his arms across his chest. "Because he needs this. He *longs* for it. You do too. And, no offense to anyone else in this organization, but y'all ain't May and me."

Spencer snorted. "You think very highly of yourself, don't you?"

Jack stared hard into Spencer's eyes. "Yeah, bud, I do." Jack clapped his hands together, startling Gemma and Spencer alike. "Wait until you meet my other half! Though, at this point, if you value your ability to breathe, or to conceive children, I'd steer clear of her." Jack looked at the guys behind him. "You too." He brought his attention back to Spencer. "You screwed the pooch by beating on her."

Spencer looked incredibly uncomfortable. "Yes, well, to be clear, I didn't give that order." He glanced at Gemma, the only woman in the room. "Nor do I condone the act."

"Smart man," Jack said. "So, where's this base of yours hiding?"

"Coincidently, right here in York, where the Ninth Legion was once stationed under the command of Marcus' ancestor."

"Eboracum," Gemma added.

"You guys really worship that family, huh?" Jack asked.

"Marcus Cerialis, just like his ancestors before him, is destined to lead us to victory. Tradition is what keeps us focused."

Jack let out a long sigh, softly laughing as he did. "Sorry, but you're wrong. In this case, tradition keeps you subjugated and in line. It holds you back. It's why us Yanks decided to kick your British asses two and a half centuries ago. We saw a better opportunity and took it."

Spencer laughed. "Oh, Jack, if this is you trying to instigate a coup, your words are falling on deaf ears. Every man and woman who has pledged his allegiance to the Legion will gladly die for its cause." He placed his right fist on his chest and his eyes lit up with mania. This was the first time the museum curator had looked the part of a zealot. "*Gaudere Legio Nona!*"

As expected, the two legionnaires watching the door repeated the salute and the phrase.

Yeah, yeah, yeah… To rejoice the Ninth Legion.

24

Rome, Italy

May had lost all sense of time. Theo had popped her with a couple of good shots, not that she'd ever admit it to the man. Based on the quickness of her "interrogation" and the fact that she never lost consciousness, May was confident she was still in good shape physically. Mentally, May was a mess, though people would never know it. One of her greatest gifts was being able to hide her emotions.

Except when it came to Jack.

He obviously had the same shortcomings. May had to admit, his outburst and threat to "kill you all" made her love the man even more. If only she could've seen him. Alas, all she and Marcus had on their end was a camera.

If she was thankful for anything, it was that her captors had forgotten to cover her head again. The sack would've been a nuisance against her swollen skin. The swift beating had focused her, though.

The door behind her opened, letting in the outside hallway's light. Her *cell* had been near-pitch black. The sudden invasion of light forced her to shut her eyes until the slight discomfort vanished. When she did, two men lifted her out of her chair, carrying her, dress and all, backward with ease. May didn't fight them. She figured that if they were taking her somewhere, and doing so with her alive, then they still needed her.

They left the room and turned left. Marcus was there, waiting. He kept pace behind his men, nodding his hello to May as he walked.

"Where are you taking me?" she asked, wincing as one of the men gripped her arm tighter.

"To Jack," Marcus replied, stunning May. "He has agreed to help us." That shocked May as well, though, perhaps it shouldn't have. "He has also guaranteed your cooperation…"

That little nugget didn't surprise May, but it did piss her off.

"Has he now?"

Marcus was enjoying the moment. He smiled. "Yes, he has. He has your people back in the States jumping through hoops for us too."

Damn, May thought, *this has really gotten out of hand. And it's my fault.* If she hadn't rushed into battle, she wouldn't have been captured.

But she wouldn't be here, with the Legion, either.

Even though she was now an operative within the Tactical Archaeological Command, May was still a spy at heart. Getting inside places and burning them down from within was kind of her thing. Jack took down the bad guy from the outside. May did it from places like this, and from situations like this.

"Fine," she said, playing ball. "I'll help."

Marcus sternly gave an order in Latin. His men released May, setting her down gently on her bare feet. She wobbled for a second, but found her footing without the need for aid. She stretched her upper back and her neck. Then she eyed the left-hand wall and stepped over to it. No one stopped her. Why would they? She had nowhere to go. If she lashed out at them, she'd die.

But her rage burned bright, and she needed to throw some dirt on it and snuff it out. She didn't need to put it out completely. May just needed to release a little of it.

She knocked on the wall. "Drywall?" she asked.

Marcus glanced at his men, eyebrow raised. "Um, yes?"

May stepped back, raised her right fist, and put it through the wall. Dust plumed into the air. Then she hit it with her left hand. After rotating two more strikes, and totaling four ragged holes, she faced Marcus again.

"Let's go." May turned away from him. She stopped and looked down at her ruined dress and shoeless feet. She faced Marcus again. "Don't suppose you have a change of clothes?" She picked a piece of loose drywall off her bare shoulder and dropped it. "I can't exactly do what you need me to do in this." She motioned to her hip, specifically the high slit showing it off.

Marcus let out a long breath. "I think I can put something together for you. We have a handful of female legionnaires who are around your size."

"Really? I thought this was just a sausage party."

The corner of Marcus' mouth curled upward. "It was for a long time, but then I realized that soldiers of your sex can get into places the rest of us cannot."

"Sergeant!"

One of the two men behind May snapped to attention. "Sir?"

"Have Angeline help May get changed. Then, bring her to the carport." Marcus turned and stomped away. "We have a flight to catch."

25

York, England

The eagle standard's base was located in York, right next door to the museum, in fact, in the ruins beneath York Minster cathedral. But that's not where Jack was.

It was night now, and he and Gemma had been driven east, away from the city. Ten miles later, they turned off into one of the thousands of farms nestled between York and the sleepy market town of Driffield. Two pairs of headlights flashed on, then off, then back on. Jack's driver stopped and threw the panel van into park.

"Out," Spencer said from the front passenger seat.

Jack really wanted to punch this guy in the back of the skull. But he didn't. Instead, he threw open the van's sliding door and exited, followed closely by Gemma and two random legionnaire guards. Besides Jack and the Italian historian, everyone wore their gladiator helmets. There was definitely an individuality to them all, except for the fact that the helmets covered everyone's faces entirely.

Spencer's helmet featured a subtle metallic mohawk running down the center of it.

Another sported six hornlike protrusions.

Marcus' helmet even had what looked like a crown built into it.

Definitely drinking his own eggnog.

The designs intrigued Jack, but not enough to ask about it.

As they exited, so too did the people in the other vans.

That's when Jack saw her.

May stepped out, hands bound behind her back. Thankfully, one of the other men cut her free once everyone was clear of the vehicle. Gone was her sexy dress. She was now dressed similarly to the Legion, wearing all-black fatigues and combat boots.

Jack tried to hurry to her, but was stopped by one of Spencer's men. Jack stood tall, burning holes into the masked man. "Move." The only response Jack received was a questioning, sideways tilt of the guard's head. Jack looked at Spencer. "Either he moves willingly, or I'm putting his ass on the ground."

Spencer gave Jack a long look before tipping his chin to the other man. The guard stepped aside enough for Jack to shove through him. May was likewise allowed to leave her captors' side. They met halfway, but didn't immediately embrace. Jack just stared at her. They were both illuminated by the three vans' headlights.

"Hey," Jack said, seeing her injuries. He was relieved that they weren't as bad as he had thought. "Who did that?"

"Marcus' number two."

"Theo?" Jack asked. He grinned. "The guy you kicked in the face?"

May matched his grin. "Yeah, him." Her jovialness melted away. "Jack...I'm sorry."

She threw herself into him. Neither one of them shed any tears, though. They just held one another, squeezing the other hard. Jack eventually gave in first.

"Ooh, okay. Mercy. Mercy." He poked at his ribs.

That made May smile again. "Do you ever not hurt?"

"No," he replied, shaking his head.

Jack looked around. The Legion was giving them space while they quietly conversed with one another. He spotted two men keeping an eye on them, one from either group. Jack didn't plan on running, and he needed May to be on the same page.

"Are we really helping these guys?" she asked.

Jack nodded. "Yeah. We need to."

Footsteps approached Jack from behind. May's eyes left him as Gemma slinked in next to him.

"Hello, May," Gemma said, holding out her hand. "It's good to see you're alright."

Jack formally introduced her while the pair shook hands. "May, this is Gemma Conti, from the Colosseum, remember?"

May's eyes opened wider. "Ah, yes. Dr. Lombardi's colleague, correct?"

Gemma shrugged. "Former colleague, I guess, but yes."

"Don't take this the wrong way, but why are you here?" May asked.

"She's kinda here because of me," Jack replied, finding something better to look at.

"You too, huh?" May asked.

Both women smiled at one another.

Jack didn't like that at all. "Don't you two start that crap," he said, shifting a pointed finger back and forth at them. He stared at May. "We got into this mess together. And if I remember correctly, it was *you* who went charging at the bad guy, by yourself. And it was *you* who got captured."

Gemma cleared her throat. "Um, so did we."

"That's not the point!" Jack growled.

Gemma looked at May, then back to Jack. "Then what is?"

Jack grabbed May by the shoulders, gripping them hard. "Don't ever do that to me again." He pulled her in again. "*That's* the point."

They parted enough to kiss, then released one another.

"For what it's worth, he really has been a mess," Gemma added.

"So have I," May admitted. "It's something the both of us are trying to get used to."

Gemma let out her hair, and retied it. "Yeah, don't secret agent-types usually work alone, and with minimal personal hangups?"

"We used to," Jack said. "But that got thrown out the window after Nepal."

"What happened in Nepal?"

May stepped in. "Nothing we can talk about here." She tipped her head over to Gemma. "So, why is she here, exactly?"

"I needed information," Jack explained, "and she was my best option at the time."

"Thank God he came by," Gemma said. "A couple of these Legion guys came over posing as detectives. Jack saved my life."

May took in the surrounding men. "Don't count your chickens before they hatch, Gemma. We aren't out of this yet."

Marcus and, presumably, Theo joined them. The leader removed his golden helmet, holding it in the crook of his elbow. He had the gall to stick his hand out to Jack.

"Marcus Cerialis, General of the Legion."

Jack didn't take the offering. "I know who you are." Jack stuck his thumb out over his shoulder. "Spencer has been very helpful with information."

Marcus' eyes narrowed. "Has he now?"

"Yeah, I don't think he understands the concept of a secret society, or whatever the hell you guys call yourselves."

Marcus huffed an angry breath. "Clearly. Dr. Harwood is very...*passionate*...about our history."

"Where are we going?" Gemma asked, moving the conversation along.

Marcus took in Gemma for a moment before replying. "Tell us, Dr. Conti, why is York significant to the Ninth Legion?"

"It's where Quintus Cerialis and the Ninth settled during the Roman occupation of Britain."

"Eboracum, right?" Jack asked.

Marcus faced Jack. "Yes, Eboracum. And do you know what is currently built atop the ruins of Eboracum's *Principia*?"

"*Principia*?" May asked.

"He means Eboracum's headquarters," Gemma replied. "And he's talking about York Minster cathedral. There is evidence of Eboracum down in its undercroft."

"Correct," Marcus said. "And as I'm sure you've come to figure out, we've had people placed in very important stations throughout the years. One of them being the architect who designed the site's first stone structure back in the seventh century. And ever since then, through war and the passages of time, we've kept watch on the happenings surrounding what would become the York Minster we know."

"What about now?" Jack asked.

Marcus shook his head. "Sadly, no."

"And the base?" Gemma asked. "It's hidden somewhere beneath the church?"

"Correct," Marcus replied. "We routinely check on the entrance down into Eboracum's lower levels, just to make sure."

May stepped forward. "I'm confused. If you know where the thing is, why haven't you just gone in to get it like I'm assuming we're about to?"

"The eagle is the key, May," Jack said. "Without it, they could never enter the...catacombs." He looked at Marcus. "Catacombs, right?"

"Yes, the passages beneath Eboracum were used as burial sites for fallen legionnaires, but I'm not talking about those. There are more chambers past even those. That's what we seek now."

"Spencer said something about there being traitors within the Ninth Legion dating back to when they were stationed in Eboracum," Gemma said, getting everyone's attention. "Are they the ones that built this 'impassable' entry point?"

"They are," Marcus said. Jack quickly watched the man's expression change from stoic, to irate. "And they did it onsite, beneath everyone's noses. By the time they were all rounded up and executed, it was too late."

"I'm guessing it's the same with the eagle-bearer's pole too?" Jack asked.

"It is, but at a different site."

"So, let me get this straight," May said. "We're breaking into a cathedral, in the middle of the night, then descending into its crypts to open a passage into, what, exactly?"

Marcus turned away. "We don't know. There is no written record of what truly awaits us beneath York Minster. The traitors, unfortunately, took that secret to the grave."

"Wow," Jack said, snickering. "You guys really screwed yourselves there, didn'tcha?"

Marcus zeroed-in on Jack. "By all accounts, we did everything we could. The details of their torture are impressive. Techniques were used that would be considered barbaric in today's world."

"And still, they didn't say anything…" Everyone looked at Gemma. "To me, it sounds like they believed in what they did."

Jack took over. "And that tells me we need to proceed with extra caution. If these so-called *traitors* went to these lengths to keep you guys from reassembling the *aquila*…"

"What?" Marcus asked.

Jack shook his head. "We just need to be careful, okay?" He looked to the west, picturing York Minster. "My guess is that we're going to find a lot of dead bodies down there."

"It is a crypt," Gemma added.

He shook his head. "Not those bodies. There will be others. Trust me."

Gemma turned to Marcus. "How are we breaking in? York Minster is an important national monument. Places like that usually have very tight security."

The telltale chop of a helicopter picked up high overhead. Jack closed his eyes. "That's how." When he opened them, he looked at the historian. "We're going in from above."

"But won't that be too obvious?" she asked.

May placed a hand on her shoulder. "I don't think we're casually rappelling down," she looked at Marcus, "are we?"

Marcus grinned and slid his gilded helmet back on. "No, we are not." He spun on a dime. "We leave in two minutes!"

Gemma was obviously confused. She looked back and forth between Jack and May. "What did he mean by that?"

Jack looked up into the night before turning to meet eyes with Gemma. "I don't suppose you've ever been skydiving before, have you?"

26

York Airspace

"How high up are we?" Gemma asked, clutching Jack's left arm tight.

"We are currently sitting at twelve *thousand* feet," Marcus replied.

May leaned around Jack, eyed the Italian, then shook her head.

"Give her a break," Jack whispered. "This is all new for her."

"She shouldn't be here."

Jack shrugged. "Too late for that. Besides, her relationship with Spencer was the reason the band is back together."

May looked at him. "So, we're a band now?"

Jack held up his right hand and counted to two with his fingers. "More of a duo, I suppose."

"Like Sonny and Cher," May said, staring outside the open side door.

Jack grinned. "I was thinking Simon and Garfunkel."

May groaned. "And I wouldn't mind hearing the sound of silence…"

"Thirty seconds!" Theo called out.

Jack checked the buckles on his parachute for the third time. As he did, he gazed outside, cursing the light spray of the incoming storm as it entered the open cargo hold. It had been a few years since Jack had jumped from a perfectly good aircraft—even longer in the rain.

This should be interesting, he thought.

With everything in order, he assisted Gemma with her checks, then turned to help May.

She held up her hand. "I'm fine, thanks."

Jack was enjoying this. "You're jealous, aren't you?"

"Of her?" May asked a little too loud. Gemma snapped her head around and stared at May. She could only give Gemma an apologetic smile. "No offense…"

Gemma shrugged. "None taken. You are clearly a better fit for Jack's lifestyle. This… This is all too much."

"You'll be fine as long as Jack and May comply," Marcus said, leaning forward on his knees. He was sitting directly across from Gemma. He locked in on her, making sure she was listening. "If they don't, Theo has orders to cut you loose midair."

Gemma swallowed and tightened her grip on Jack's arm.

"Threats aren't necessary," May said. "We've already agreed to help you for as long as it's needed."

"Exactly," Jack said. "We get it. There's no need for the theatrics, okay?"

Marcus laughed. "And you expect me to believe you?"

Jack nodded. "Yeah, I do. It's us who shouldn't trust you. As far as I'm concerned, you're still nothing but thieves out for a hearty score." Theo went to stand but was stopped by Marcus. Jack regarded him for a second before returning his attention to the boss. "Good thing you did that. I'd hate for him to get his ass kicked again."

May looked away from him, unconsciously touching her swollen cheek.

Theo smiled.

Jack didn't take too kindly to that. He reached across the narrow gap between them, and yanked a surprised Theo to the door. As he did, he tripped him, taking him to the floor of the cargo hold. Theo landed hard on his back, teetering halfway out over nothing. Multiple sets of hands grabbed at Jack from behind.

"Mark my words," Jack snarled. "You'll be getting yours soon—in spades!" He released Theo and turned to find three weapons pointed at him. He rolled his eyes. "Relax. He has a chute on, remember?"

Theo got up and eyed Jack.

"Enough!" Marcus barked. "It's time!" Theo returned to his seat next to the *Legatus*. "Keep track of your altitude. We will freefall for thirty seconds before popping chutes at five thousand feet. Does everyone copy?" The seven other people within the cargo hold nodded. "Good." He looked at Jack. "And yes, if security should be notified in any way, Dr. Conti makes the rest of the trip at terminal velocity." His eyebrows knit. "Do *you* copy?"

Jack sat back. "Copy." He was done antagonizing this bunch.

For now.

May's hand found Jack's. It stayed there until it was time to jump.

"Dr. Conti, if you will," Marcus said, motioning for her to join Theo.

She gave Jack one last terrified look before linking up with Theo. They were the only tandem divers tonight. Jack had more hours jump time than he could count, and he suspected May had also had her share since she had yet to say anything about it. It amazed Jack that he felt the way he did about May, and yet, still knew very little about her past. Then again, it was the present version of her that truly intrigued him.

Doesn't matter.

"You okay?" May asked. She must've seen him struggling with something.

"Just peachy."

"Go!" Marcus shouted.

Theo and Gemma jumped. The last thing Jack heard from the historian was an ear-piercing shriek.

"Jack, you're up!"

Jack nodded and readied himself. He looked over his shoulder and found May watching him. He gave her a wink, turned, but stopped.

"What's wrong?" she asked.

"What was your mom like?" he asked.

May was caught off guard. "What? I—"

Jack held up a finger. "Hold that thought. I gotta run."

Then, he made a show of his comfort level and casually fell out of the helicopter backward. Before he turned, he caught May leaning outside with a dumbfounded look on her face.

That was the other thing May had done for Jack. She brought the kid out in him. His body was constantly getting beat on, and so was his mind, for that matter. The globetrotting life was fantastic in a lot of ways. It also had its downfalls, however.

Jack was always tired—drained to his core.

He concentrated on the altimeter on his left wrist, while also counting to himself. Beneath him was the outline of York Minster. There was enough artificial light to make the building visible at night. Plus, it was HUGE.

28... 29... 30!

Jack reached behind his back and popped his chute. He quickly found the toggles and began steering himself. He had been slightly off course, but it was nothing a pull here and another pull there, couldn't fix. The York Minster tower was dead ahead, and he pointed himself straight at it. Now in line, he looked up and back, hoping to see May behind him. He couldn't see anything yet, but somehow, he knew she was there.

Theo and Gemma touched down shortly before Jack did. A flashing beacon gave Jack their exact position. Jack also had one on his parachute pack, as did May and everyone else. Yanking down on both toggles, Jack spotted his landing. The tower's roof had a cage surrounding it. Jack had no idea why it had a cage, but it did.

Probably for jumpers, he decided. He landed and realized something. *Or to keep people like us out...*

Jack pulled in his chute and hustled over to Gemma and Theo. She was released from his harness and practically fell into Jack's arms. Theo didn't bother to check on her. He was already digging into his bag. As soon as May landed, Theo ignited a portable blowtorch and began cutting through the tower's protective layer.

"You good?" he asked Gemma.

She didn't audibly reply. All Jack got was a handful of quick nods. Even in the dark, Jack could see that Gemma's naturally tan complexion had paled.

"She okay?" May asked, disconnecting her chute.

Gemma took in May. "Define *good*."

"Did you vomit midair?" May asked, half-joking.

Gemma looked away.

"Oh." Jack's nostrils flared. "I didn't land in it, did I?"

The other legionnaires arrived, one after the other, with Marcus bringing up the rear. Like Theo, each one of them wore their trademark helmets. Jack, May, and Gemma did not.

"Put these on."

Jack sighed. *So much for that.*

He turned to find two of the men holding out additional matte-black helmets. Jack's shoulders fell. He really didn't want to join the team.

"Do we have to?" he asked.

Marcus didn't reply.

Jack took one, and looked inside, recalling something from the last time he held one of them. These things sported a high-end comms system. *That* Jack didn't mind. He slipped it over his head, then attached and tightened a synthetic chin strap. His head was immediately filled with the chatter of Marcus' men.

"How do you activate the mic?" Jack asked.

Marcus shook his head. "They're always hot. We don't speak unless we have to."

Good to know, Jack thought. He hated having to activate comms. It meant he'd have to remove his hand from his weapon to do so. Not that he had a weapon.

Marcus stepped forward. "Lieutenant, status!"

"Ten seconds," Theo replied, concentrating on his job as he spoke. "Almost through."

Marcus eyed his other men. Spencer had joined them, as had two additional team members Jack had not officially yet met, Christos, and a woman named Angeline. Jack figured the latter legionnaire was the person who had given May a change of clothes. She was similar in size to May, but owned the hardest gaze Jack had ever seen. If Theo and Spencer were Marcus' biggest supporters, Angeline wasn't too far behind.

"I don't like this," Gemma said, looking around.

"Your opinion doesn't matter," Theo said as the cut section of cage fell in.

Gemma didn't appreciate the comment. "You remind me of Nero. He was also arrogant and foolish."

"He was a piece of shit too," Jack added, getting a snort out of May.

"That's enough, you two," Marcus said. "Jack, I'm surprised by your lax behavior. I figured someone in your position would appreciate the gravity of it."

"Oh, I do, but I never miss an opportunity to rattle the cage." He stomped his foot. "Get it!"

Gemma shook her head. "That was terrible."

"You get used to it after a while," May said, patting her shoulder.

"Move out!" Marcus ordered, cutting off any additional replies.

Theo dropped in first. Gemma went next. Jack lowered her in, then jumped down himself. May landed next to him in the perfect superhero pose.

"She's such a badass," Gemma said quietly, forgetting that everyone could hear her.

"Thank you," May said, making Gemma look away. She was no doubt blushing beneath her helmet.

"What about security?" Jack asked, adjusting his helmet.

"It's light," Marcus replied. "We have the guards' routes mapped. They shouldn't cause much trouble."

"Are you going to kill them?" Gemma asked.

Jack was wondering that too.

"If it can be helped, no. Our presence must remain undetected for this to work. We can't have authorities tracking us after the commotion we caused in Rome."

"Yeah," Jack said, "that really painted a target on your back."

Marcus faced Jack. "True, it did. But we aren't in Rome, are we?"

"We've accounted for that already," Spencer added. "We even have men on the ground, as we speak, keeping police focused across town."

Jack had to hand it to them. They knew how to cover their own butts.

"I'm sure there are alarms here," he said.

"Of course," Marcus said, "but nothing a child can't bypass. Christos, you're up."

Speaking of a child... The smallest legionnaire hurried forward and vanished further ahead. Yes, Christos was even shorter than Angeline. He was right up there with Gemma, maybe pushing five-two.

The group caught up with him in no time. When they did, they found him kneeling in front of a heavy wooden door. Jack didn't watch him do his thing, instead, he kept his attention on the people around him. He studied Marcus' team, just in case an opportunity arose to fight back.

Something beeped, and it was followed by the snap of metal.

"We're in," Christos announced, shoving the door inward. "Not too hard, not too easy. Just right if you ask me."

The man's accent was decidedly Greek and bounded along like an excited bunny. Christos quickly packed up his gear as he spoke. Then he stood and stepped out of the way. Theo, once again, took point while Marcus kept to the back of the pack.

"You don't lead your people?" Jack asked.

"Oh, I do," Marcus replied, "but I find it much easier to do so when I can see them in front of me."

There was a member of the animal kingdom who operated the same way. The alpha wolf—the pack's strongest—stayed at the back of the pack so he could see everything in front of him, and to make sure no one was left behind. In those terms, Jack respected the idea of operating from the rear. It also meant he trusted Theo greatly to be their point man.

But this isn't nature, Jack thought. If it were him, he'd be in front of even Theo. That's just how Jack operated. He wanted to protect those he led by putting himself in the way of danger, instead of making one of his people do it.

"Sounds like a trust issue," Gemma said, once again forgetting that her words were easily heard by all.

Jack didn't back down, regardless of his true feelings toward the leadership style. "She's right, you know. It's not a good look."

Marcus stepped closer. "And yet, we've survived for two thousand years. I'd say that counts for something, yes?"

Jack shrugged. "Even the Rangers got lucky and won a World Series."

Marcus' body language gave Jack the impression that he didn't understand the reference.

Jack shook him off. "Never mind." He shooed Theo forward. "Lieutenant, if you would be so kind..."

The bigger man huffed in annoyance, but nevertheless, entered York Minster.

27

The air inside the central tower's winding staircase was cool and slightly damp. Jack plodded down the narrow steps, descending between Gemma and May. He glanced over his shoulder and found May staring at her feet, no doubt lost in thought. Knowing her, she was planning, weighing her options.

"Most impressive," Spencer said quietly.

Jack wasn't sure if the guy was trying to start up a conversation, or just talking to himself.

"Yeah," Jack agreed, "not too shabby."

"Not too shabby?" Spencer responded, scoffing at the comment. "This tower is 235 feet tall and is over 600 years old!"

Jack shrugged. "Yeah, pretty neat." He looked back at May again and watched as her exposed eyes squinted more. Jack knew a smile when he saw one, even if her mouth was covered.

Her helmet's design was similar to Jack's except it possessed five vertical slits directly over her mouth. The facemask of Jack's helmet possessed just three slits. Breathing was fine, so far, but he also wasn't running.

"The first Tibetan Buddhist monastery was built in 775," May added. "Makes your church seem awfully…juvenile."

Jack heard the English historian gasp.

The outrage! he internally mocked.

Before Spencer could retort, Marcus shut him up. "Quiet up there!" He hissed his whispered words as loudly as he could.

Jack had to admit it, though, York Minster was an incredible place to visit, especially to someone who enjoyed history as much as he did.

"In all seriousness, it's a nice church."

Theo spun, drew his pistol, and aimed it up at Jack's face. The TAC agent didn't cower away. He didn't even blink. Being in the middle of the two combatants, Gemma threw herself to the stone steps and covered her head.

"Marcus said, 'quiet.'"

"Down boy," Jack replied. It was only until May's hand found Jack's back that he relented. Jack held up his hands in surrender. Then, he pretended to zipper his mouth shut.

Theo huffed and holstered his sidearm. Without another word, he turned and started their descent anew. Jack helped Gemma up and put himself between her and Theo, better protecting her from another of Theo's outbursts.

Seriously, that guy is wound tight!

They exited the confining stairwell and continued out onto a precipitous, outdoor walkway. On Jack's right was the high-peaked rooftop of the cross-shaped cathedral's south transept, its shorter southern arm. To Jack's left was nothing except the open air of York, as well as a fifteen-to-twenty-foot drop down to an additional, slanted rooftop. Jack was confident he could survive the fall. The harsh grade below would act as a slide of sorts. Still, he had no intention of testing his theory. Plus, Jack didn't feel like parkouring down a six-century-old church…at night…in the rain…and cold.

"This sucks," he muttered.

May snorted. "Which part?"

He glanced behind him. "Everything that doesn't involve you and me back in our hotel room."

"Ugh," Gemma said. Jack whipped his head around as they entered another tight stairwell. "Oh, no. I think it's great. It's just been a while for me, is all."

Spencer chimed in next. "I think it's rather repugnant."

"No one asked, *Hard*wood," Jack jabbed.

The Brit quieted, mumbling something incoherently to himself. Jack also quieted, focusing on the next leg of their climb down to ground level. So far, security had been remarkably light, not that he expected someone to be posted on the roof of York Minster tower.

On a cool, sunny afternoon? Sure.

At night, and in a chilling storm? No thanks.

The rain had, indeed, picked up. Thankfully, they were only in it for the short jaunt across the transept roof. The next descent was tricky. The steps were slick with water now. Theo had slowed significantly too. Jack understood why. *This* was the real beginning of their infiltration.

Round and round they went until they came to another heavy wooden door. Theo held up a closed fist and stopped on the bottommost step.

"Christos," he quietly said in their comms, "you're up."

The short and slight Greek slid past May, Jack, and Gemma with ease. Theo stepped aside and allowed the man to do his thing. As they waited, Jack finally got a good, long look at the rifle on Theo's back. It wasn't the same *Heckler & Koch* variant from the Colosseum attack.

This is something else, Jack deduced. *Something custom.*

At first glance, he thought it was a tranquilizer rifle of some kind. That would've been really dumb, though. *Tranq* darts took too much time to take effect, even one loaded with a deadly dose. The other popular, non-lethal option was a weapon that used rubber bullets. Again, it wouldn't have been a smart option. They were designed to incapacitate. They were also designed to discourage and cause pain. Perfect for clearing an unruly crowd.

Whatever it was that the legionnaires were carrying, Jack was interested to see the new-to-him firearms in action.

Their pistols, however, were the real deal. That also made sense, just in case they did need real stopping power. Still, they were at a serious disadvantage if things turned for the worse. Jack pictured a heavily armed group of police storming their way inside. A gun fight with them would be as one-sided as it got.

"Almost in," Christos announced.

"Go for E-rifles," Marcus ordered.

Jack watched the legionnaires shoulder their weapons.

"E-rifles?" May asked.

"Something that a certain firearms developer has been working on," Marcus replied, giving a perfect non-answer.

"The Legion has allies inside weapons manufacturing?" Jack asked.

Marcus sighed. "You'd be amazed what the right amount of money can accomplish these days."

Jack turned and looked up the stairwell. "So, what, you're like a field test team or something?"

"You could say that. They provide the means. We provide the anonymous data."

"What do they do?" Gemma asked.

The door creaked open.

"You'll see..." Marcus replied. His voice was barely above a whisper. "Move out."

Christos stepped aside and allowed Theo to lead the team in. He took up position behind him and the two men cleared the area directly outside the entrance.

"Clear," Theo whispered, his voice coming through loud-and-clear in their shared comms system.

"Angeline, Spencer, you're up," Marcus directed.

Jack, May, and Gemma moved out of their way as the two legionnaires quickly filed inside York Minster. It seemed that the museum curator wasn't just a hands-off academic. Spencer took up sentry position outside the door as Theo, Christos, and Angeline moved deeper into the cathedral.

"Contact," Theo called. Two seconds later. "Target down."

"Two contacts," Angeline said next. After three heartbeats, she announced. "Both down."

"Okay, Marcus," Theo said, "you're clear."

"Move," Marcus said, stepping up behind Jack and the others.

"Only three guards?" Jack asked.

Marcus nodded. "Based on our thorough recon, yes."

Jack was impressed. "Gotta hand it to you. That was well orchestrated."

"My people are pros. We know what we're doing."

Jack led May and Gemma through the breached entry point. The inside of York Minster was something to behold, even if it was mostly cast in shadows due to the time of night. The ceilings were impossibly high and the stained-glass windows seemed to glow in the outside world's artificial light. The moon must've done wonders to this place during a clear, crisp night. Unfortunately, they didn't have that right now. Jack could hear the rain coming down outside.

It surprised Jack when Theo almost immediately descended the steps down to something called the "Undercroft Museum." He was also surprised when a light bloomed in his masked face.

"Freeze!"

Jack raised his hands and looked at Marcus. "Just three guards, huh?"

But just as quickly as the guard had snuck up on them, he was put down. Angeline, the lone female on Marcus' York Minster assault team, snapped up her rifle from behind and fired. There was no explosion of gunpowder, and no muzzle flash. The only indication that the guard had been hit with anything was a strange blue flash of light combined with a stiffening of his limbs.

Then he was on the ground.

"What the hell was that?" Jack asked.

"Taser round," Christos explained.

"*Taser* round?"

The Greek legionnaire nodded. "Sends a quick jolt into the victim's body, rendering them unconscious almost instantly. Similar to that of a policeman's stun gun."

"That explains his rigid posture," May added.

"Yes," Christos replied. He tapped his own chest. "Works best if you aim center mass."

Jack sneered. "I'll remember that." He faced Marcus. "Now, are you sure there aren't any more guards?"

Marcus strode up in front of Jack, but his next words weren't for him. "Theo. Take Angeline and make sure we are truly alone." The two legionnaires snapped to attention and moved off. "Christos, the gate."

"Yes, sir." The Legion's locksmith rushed downstairs and, once more, dropped his bag. He quickly went about cutting the padlock off an iron gate at the bottom of the steps.

28

By the time Jack, May, Gemma, Marcus, and Spencer joined Christos below, he was through.

"Piece of cake." He jammed his tools back into his bag and popped up to his feet. "Like cutting through butter."

Marcus shoved open the gate, but didn't enter. He stepped aside. "Spencer, if you would…"

"Gladly, *Legatus*." The group's chief historian led the way now. "The entrance is this way. Welcome to the *Foundations*."

Jack was next. May and Gemma were close behind. The trio moved as a triangle with Jack in the front. This level owned an eerily low ceiling. The atmosphere beneath York Minster was in stark contrast to what lay above.

"What is all this?" Jack asked.

"This is the *Foundation*s," Spencer repeated. "Not only is it the literal foundation of the cathedral, but it also showcases the foundations of Eboracum, fortress of the Ninth Legion."

Jack saw what he meant moments later. Sporadic security lights illuminated parts of the Undercroft Museum. Within one of them was a sign that described what had been found and how. Spencer also leant his knowledge.

"In May 1967, a survey of York Minster was conducted. It revealed a decimated support structure. The Central Tower was sinking and was near collapse, if you could imagine." Jack visualized it, the enormous cathedral coming down. It pained him to even think it. "Luckily, enough funds were raised to repair the damage. During the subsequent excavations, they found something unbelievable."

Gemma chimed in. "That physical evidence of Eboracum had survived into modern-day."

"Correct," Spencer agreed. His tone darkened. "It was also then that the Legion had to step in to protect it. If archaeologists dug too deep and found the entrance into the catacombs beneath the *Principia*, all could be lost."

Jack understood their fear. If diggers came in and caused a collapse, the entrance that lay deeper, as well as what was held beyond, could be destroyed. Their legacy was in danger too, not just their prize. Jack commended the Legion for wanting their history back. It was their most admirable quality. But, to Jack, the way they went about it was all wrong. They held no qualms about killing innocent people whom also wanted the same thing.

"What did your predecessors do to protect this place?" May asked.

"We did the one thing we could do. We pushed to have it open to the public. We knew that if the community got involved, and if money started rolling in, that further excavations would cease."

"It took years," Marcus added. "But with our help, including sizeable, unnamed donations, all of this was made possible."

"How thoughtful," Gemma said. "Seriously, you preserved an incredible find, while also allowing it to be available for all to see."

"Not all of it," Jack said. "Your reasoning was still selfish."

"Perhaps," Marcus said. Footsteps announced the return of Theo and Angeline. "Report."

"All clear," Theo replied. "And yes, we are sure this time."

"Good," Marcus said, removing his helmet. He took a deep breath. He looked at Spencer, who also removed his helmet. "Continue. We don't have all night."

Jack, May, and Gemma relieved themselves of their headgear. Theo, Christos, and Angeline did not. They kept vigil. Each continued guard duty, holding their E-Rifles at the low-ready, while keeping to the rear of the group.

Spencer nodded and headed deeper into the Undercroft Museum. "Beneath our feet, is an existing road, one that Ancient Romans used regularly."

Jack stepped up to a guardrail and looked down. A worn section of rectangular stones could be seen in the dimly lit space.

"It won't be beneath a road, I'd imagine," Gemma hypothesized.

"No, it's not," Spencer said. "What we are looking for is a secret entrance within Eboracum's *basilica*, its main hall."

We know what a basilica is, Jack thought. He decided to let the man have his moment to shine.

"Where is it?" May asked.

"Our research has pointed us to a very important location, the *aedes*, the regimental shrine, where sacrifices to the gods were made."

"Was it the only way in?" Jack asked.

"We don't believe so, no," Spencer replied. "But it's agreed that it is the only way in today. All other entrances into the catacombs were destroyed over the years due to various reasons."

"Question…" Gemma said. Everyone stopped and gave her their attention. "How are we getting in exactly? I doubt it's as easy as using a lock and key." Her face fell. "You aren't blasting your way in, are you?"

"We are, in fact," Spencer replied. "But I think it's best if Marcus tells you more about it instead of me."

"We are using shaped charges," the leader explained. "It's the quickest way through the rock, while also still being able to take great care of our surroundings."

Jack knew all about the military application of shaped charges. They were used in high-explosive anti-tank (HEAT) warheads, which were commonly used in a bevy of weapons systems; guided missiles, gun-fire projectiles, landmines, torpedoes…

"That's incredibly risky," Jack said. "If you don't get the payload right, bad things can happen."

"How bad?" Gemma asked.

Jack pointed up at the ceiling. "Bring-York-Minster-down bad."

The Italian historian shrank away. "Oh."

"But," Jack continued, "they're right. It's the quickest way through."

May stepped up next to Jack. She supported his statement with just her presence.

"Sir," Theo said from behind. "It's time."

Marcus looked over his shoulder and nodded. "Do it."

Theo and Christos took up point and guided the group forward past unlit signage and an information desk. Relics from Roman-era York had been found and put on display. Jack would've loved to have taken some time to soak it all in. Display cases lined the walls in places, showing off other artifacts from York's past, not just relating to the Roman-era, including the *King's Book of Heroes*.

Since Jack held a deep respect for the lives lost during war, this particular artifact had always interested him. It contained the names of the Yorkers who perished during World War I. The book was mammoth, weighing in at a whopping *9 stone 4*, or *130* pounds, and the cover had been carved from English Oak. It also sported a very medieval-looking clasp. Then, take into consideration that it's twenty-five inches by twenty-nine inches... Jack's favorite paperbacks were only six-by-nine.

They came to an impressively built, glass floor display. Jack had once seen something similar, though on a much grander scale, in Greece, at the Acropolis Museum. To Jack, having the excavation site left intact and preserved like this was a cool way of doing things. He preferred it, actually.

Theo and Christos were already kneeling atop one of the large windowpanes by the time the others gathered around them. The whirl of a drill came to life, startling Gemma. She turned, hiding her bashful face. She was still understandably jumpy.

It took some effort, but the two legionnaires meticulously drilled holes six inches apart and in a circular pattern. Jack estimated that the shape was roughly three feet in diameter.

Enough room for a human and his or her gear, Jack thought.

"What are they doing?" Gemma asked.

May leaned in. "It's our entrance."

Gemma looked to Jack for confirmation. He simply nodded in agreement.

"Alarms?" Jack asked.

Marcus shook his head. "None attached to the floor. I mean, who in their right mind would attempt to break the glass?"

Jack wanted to share the man's cheeky grin, but he couldn't. Jack didn't want to give Marcus the satisfaction.

With Theo's assistance, Christos slipped in a network of tiny, shotgun shell-sized objects into each hole. Every *charge* was connected to a wire, and those wires ran to a square box that sat dead center in the upcoming entry point.

"Remote detonator?" Jack asked.

Marcus nodded. "Yes, though we will have to stay below ground to get a decent signal."

"We?" Gemma asked. "Why do we need to be here?"

The answer was clear as day. Jack and the others weren't going to get the opportunity to escape.

"If one of my people have to be down here during the demolition," Marcus replied, "then *all* of us will be."

Jack didn't argue because there was nothing to argue about. Marcus' decisions were the Gospel to these people—to his captives too. Jack grabbed May's hand, who, in turn, took Gemma by the shoulder. The trio slowly backed away from the glass floor. Marcus' team did, as well. Everyone found refuge behind the information desk.

"Open your mouth," Jack explained to Gemma. "It'll lessen the damage from the incoming shockwave. Equalizes the pressure. Cover your ears too."

"No need to cover your ears," Marcus said, slipping his helmet back on. "These have sound dampeners built in."

Jack wondered if the tech worked the same as electronic, active ear protection. Shooter's ear muffs used directional microphones to take in and measure the strength of a nearby sound, cutting out anything close to a gunshot.

"We ready?" Marcus asked, looking over at Christos. The Greek nodded and held up his detonator. The general took a deep breath, then blew it out. "Proceed."

29

The subsequent explosions were nothing more than a rapid succession of loud pops. Jack felt the impact of each in his chest, but there was little else as far as discomfort was concerned. Jack was more worried about the Undercroft Museum as a whole, than anything to do with himself.

But it held. A handful of exhibits shook and fell, but that was it. Jack and Marcus stood first. The others followed suit. What they saw was a chiseled, three-foot-wide hole in the glass floor. The edges were, no doubt, sharp, but Jack was confident they could avoid injury.

Marcus hurried around the information desk. Jack, May, and Theo did too. They all knelt around the fresh entry point. The ancient foundations of Eboracum lay not four feet beneath it. Getting to the subterranean access point was going to be a challenge, wherever it was.

"Good thing I had a light breakfast," Jack said, standing.

"We never said it was going to be easy," Spencer said.

May leaned out over the opening more. "So, where is this access point exactly?"

"You're staring at it," Marcus replied.

"We are?" Gemma asked.

Marcus nodded. "Our research says that the shrine platform is another fifteen feet to the north." He pointed in the general direction. "All we need to do is descend and crawl to it." His eyes opened. "Then we can open it."

"How?" Jack asked.

"Lieutenant!"

Theo removed his pack, unzipped it, and pulled out a steel box that resembled a smaller version of the Pelican case he had seen at the Colosseum. Jack had a guess as to what it held. Marcus undid the latch, opening the lid with care. Inside was their eagle.

"Test thy courage and enter," Spencer recited.

"Is that supposed to mean something?" May asked.

Jack knew, but Gemma beat him to it. "In Ancient Rome, eagles symbolized a number of things. One of them was *courage*. They also symbolized *strength* and *immortality*."

"Who came up with your 'test thy courage' adage?" Jack asked.

Spencer shrugged. "We don't know, but it's only one of a handful of clues left behind to those worthy enough to use it. But the quote was written in a scroll and was surrounded by an eagle."

"And the lock is down here?" Jack asked. "Just like that?"

Marcus sat and swung his legs around. He dangled his feet in the hole, apparently leading this time. "No, Jack. This is just the seal into the catacombs. The lock is still deeper yet."

Jack sighed. "Wonderful." He also sat and swung his legs into the hole.

"Shall we?"

Marcus nodded and dropped inside.

Jack was right behind him. Both landed, squatting in place. "Don't suppose you have a flashlight?"

Marcus looked up just as Angeline released a pair of small penlights. Both men caught one and swiftly clicked them on. Jack showed his around the historical site, feeling bad for defiling it with his mucky boots.

"So, north?" he asked.

Marcus pointed his light in that direction. It was behind Jack. He turned and added his own beam. They ended at a wall.

"Um…"

Marcus headed off, duck walking where he could. Jack was right behind him. As they headed away, the others descended. Jack and Marcus made it there in no time. Jack immediately panicked. He couldn't see anything that resembled a door, nor was there any symbols cluing them in.

"Now what?" He glanced at Marcus. "More charges?"

Marcus didn't like what he was seeing. "Spencer?"

"Here," the historian said, sliding between Jack and Marcus. "I suspect that time has wiped away what we're looking for."

"Could've been purposely wiped clean too," Jack suggested.

Spencer removed his helmet and sat it down next to him. "Also true."

"But you're sure it's here?" Jack asked.

"Absolutely." He looked at his leader. "I say we blast our way in."

"Hang on," Jack started, "I—"

"Don't have an opinion in the matter," Spencer interrupted. He gave Jack a long look before facing Marcus. "How long have we waited for this moment? This is it, Marcus. We are nearly there."

"I know that," Marcus said. "But Jack's concerns mirror my own." He let out a breath. "Christos!"

"Sir?" the Greek replied.

"I need your advice." The demolition man slid up to Marcus' side. "Is it safe?"

The slighter man examined the rock. "If what Dr. Harwood says is true, then there should be a void behind us."

"But is it safe?" Jack asked, repeating Marcus' question.

Christos ran his hands through his thinning hair. "Yes, I believe it is. Though, just to be sure, I suggest we wait topside."

Marcus nodded once. "Very good. Theo, help him prep another round of charges." Marcus looked back at the group. "Everyone else, return to the information desk and take cover."

Everyone did as they were told. Jack boosted Gemma back up into the museum level of the undercroft, then helped May. He held onto her waist a little longer than he needed to. Her hand found his and she squeezed. Then she patted it.

Time to move, he thought.

Jack hoisted her up. Once she was high enough, May scrambled up onto the floor. She reached down and caught Jack's hand. The four-foot-high climb wasn't at all difficult, but the serrated edges of the glass made it that way. Jack ripped his jacket on the way up.

He sighed, showing the damage to May. "Just keeps getting better and better."

"I'll buy you another one," May offered.

"That's not the point."

She held up the torn section of jacket. "Clearly, it is."

Both turned as Gemma groaned. "Both of you are awful."

May blushed and slid her helmet back on. Jack gave Gemma a grin before also putting his back on.

Everyone else was now back behind the information desk, waiting for Theo and Christos to rejoin them. Jack had no idea how long it would take to prep the next breach. At this rate, they were taking entirely too much time. Then again, was that really a bad thing?

Dammit, Jack thought.

If they all got caught, yes, the Legion would more or less be down for the count, but they would also never find what they were looking for. Jack needed to help them any way he could. He also needed to trust that Raegor was doing everything he could to help on his end. Jack and May needed to succeed. They needed to escape too.

We'll take care of the Legion when the time comes.

Jack checked his watch again. This time, Marcus noticed.

"Have somewhere to be?"

Jack snorted. "Yeah, not jail. Can we hurry it up a bit?"

Marcus checked his own watch. Jack saw a hint of worry in the man's eyes. He was thinking the exact same thing.

"Theo, report."

"*Nearly done,*" Theo replied. "*The entry hole is going to have to be much narrower than the last one, though.*"

Marcus looked toward the three-foot-wide hole in the glass floor. "Doesn't matter. Just get us in as soon as you can. We're running out of time."

"*Copy that.*"

Jack plopped down and leaned back against the desk. "Anyone have a Nintendo Switch?" All eyes turned to him. "No? How 'bout a deck of cards?"

The undercroft went silent, minus the racket Theo and Christos were making below. In that *quiet*, Jack caught Angeline looking his way. The female legionnaire's eyes shifted away from him quickly.

"What's your story?" Jack asked.

Angeline snapped her attention to him. "Speak to me again, and you'll lose your tongue."

Yikes.

Jack held up a hand. "Sorry I asked."

The minutes crawled by. Jack found himself humming the opening number to *The Blues Brothers*.

"Great movie," Gemma said.

Jack smiled beneath his face mask. "One of the best ever."

"You know it?" May asked.

Gemma nodded. "Yeah. Amazing opening sequence."

"Absolutely," Jack agreed. "Love the song too."

"*She Caught the Katy*, right?" Gemma asked.

Jack was getting way too excited, all things considered, but he was also unbelievably bored. His adrenaline had plummeted shortly after getting startled by the fourth church guard. Since then, all they'd done was talk and wait, though he did get quite a bit of helpful information. The Legion's willingness to divulge such juicy details both intrigued and worried Jack.

Were they as bad as they seemed?

Well, Jack thought, *they did kill Dr. Lombardi in cold blood, not to mention several police officers and paratroopers.*

Their willingness to give such information might be ultimately tied to Jack, May, and Gemma's fates.

Dead people don't talk much.

That's what Jack was most worried about. Yes, May, Gemma, and Jack were helping the Legion, but no, that didn't necessarily buy back their freedom. If anything, it made them a trio of loose ends that eventually needed to be cut. They were doing precisely what Jack was doing. They were using the other party's knowledge and connections to get the job done until the other party was no longer of use.

"*We're good down here,*" Theo said through their shared comms system. "*Coming up now.*"

Once Theo and Christos were in position behind the information desk, everyone assumed their blast positions again; helmets on, mouths open. Christos held up his detonator, got a quick nod from his superior, and pressed the all-powerful, little red button.

When he did, the world beneath the team crumbled and Jack fell backwards into an expanding hole.

30

As Jack fell backward, something grabbed his right ankle. He dangled above the collapsed section of undercroft flooring for a moment. Once he stopped swinging, he was able to look up to his feet and see his rescuer.

Correction: rescuers.

Both May and Gemma had snagged his lower leg. May had him around the ankle, while Gemma had the toe of his hiking boot in an awkward headlock. Jack looked back into the hole and noticed a large slab of stone five feet beneath him and a little to his left.

He pointed at it. "Swing me over!"

May nodded, then said something to Gemma. They rocked him back and forth, and with a bit of Jack's help, they were successful in getting him moving.

"Ready?" May asked.

All Jack could do was give her two thumbs up. He kept his arms over his head, hoping he could somehow break his fall without also breaking any of his bones. Either way, this next part was going to hurt.

May counted. "One... Two..." Jack slipped free. "Jack!"

He covered his head with his arms and landed flat on his back. Jack's air left him, and the ledge shifted and tipped toward the hole. He rolled in the opposite direction. The shift in his weight balanced the slab, and it stabilized.

"You okay?" Gemma asked.

Jack waved her off while he caught his breath. He had spared his skull but not his spine.

Gonna need one helluva chiropractor after this.

"Help!"

Jack opened his eyes and rolled onto his stomach, feeling out the slab as he did. Thankfully, it didn't shift again. He slowly crawled over to the edge and looked down. Marcus was buried in rubble. Jack was pretty sure the man's left leg was pinned. Hopefully, it wasn't broken. That was all Jack needed. He also spotted two other legionnaires in the sinkhole-like depression. Jack quickly identified them as Christos and Angeline. Both were shorter and skinnier than either Marcus, Theo, or even Spencer. His guess was proven accurate when Theo appeared next to Gemma.

"Marcus!"

Jack knew what he had to do. "You're doing this, aren't you?" he asked himself. Jack pictured himself weighing as much as a feather. He thought *skinny.* "You're saving the bad guy's life, you idiot." But he was. As much as it pained him to admit, Jack needed Marcus alive. "I'm coming!"

"What?" May, Gemma, and Theo asked in unison.

Jack looked back up at the trio. "Unless you're getting your asses down here too, I don't want to hear it!"

Theo desperately searched for a way in. Jack never doubted the man's intentions. He would've entered the pit whether Jack did or not.

Jack realized something. "Where's Spencer?"

"Where do you think?" Gemma replied. "He ran!"

"I'm here!" the Brit shouted, sliding into view. "Where's Marcus?"

Jack chuckled as he turned and lowered himself down feetfirst. The explosion had caused the ceiling of the ancient catacombs to crumble. Add in the mass of the Undercroft Museum, and you had enough weight to turn the area surrounding the glass floor to kindling.

The top ten feet of the thirty-foot-wide crater was mostly a sheer vertical rock face. From there, the wreckage sloped inward on all sides. But all was not lost. Even from here, Jack could see an opening at the very center of the funnel. Marcus, Angeline, and Christos were all lying between Jack and that opening.

"Theo!" Jack called out. "Get down here and check on your people. I got Marcus!"

"No, I will see to him!"

Jack dropped down, steadying himself on the shifting rubble. He looked back up. "Then you better hurry!"

Jack kept his weight back on his heels so he didn't fall headfirst. He shuffled sideways and slid until he made it to Marcus' side. Now, Jack could see that the *Legatus* hadn't been seriously injured. His leg was merely pinned beneath a large chunk of concrete. Still, Jack needed to be sure.

"You hurt?" he asked.

Marcus gazed up at him. "Why are you helping me?"

Jack shrugged. "Sue me, I'm helpful. And it's not you I'm helping…" Marcus looked up at May and Gemma. "If you die, what are the odds your guard dog cleans house?"

Marcus didn't reply, which meant Jack was right.

"No," he finally said, "I'm not seriously hurt, but I can't get free."

Jack placed his feet shoulder-width apart, then squatted down. He had no idea what his deadlift PR was. It had been quite a while since he'd hit the gym with any regularity.

"Can you help at all?" he asked.

Marcus laid flat and placed his palms under his end.

Jack nodded. "Go." He gritted his teeth and lifted, feeling his lower back pull. Jack dropped his butt lower and drove with his legs. Nothing. "Stop."

They did. Jack yanked his helmet free and tossed it aside. He took a deep breath and wiggled his hips, checking on his spine. Besides the normal discomfort he always felt, he was okay.

"Try again?"

Marcus nodded, then removed his own helmet. He gave Jack a look of thanks. Then placed his palms up underneath his end again.

Jack sidestepped left, getting as close to Marcus as he could. "One, two, three…"

The two men pushed and pulled with all their might. Just when Jack was about to give up, the rubble shifted. Marcus pulled his foot up toward him as Jack took the majority of the weight. He closed his eyes and held it aloft, feeling his face flush as he did.

"I'm free!" Marcus called.

Jack dropped it and fell backward. He collapsed into a pile of rock and metal, paying attention to only his air and not the random remnants poking and prodding him in the back. Marcus stayed put and checked over his lower leg, but nothing seemed too severe. He got up, then surprisingly, held out a hand to help Jack to his feet.

Never one to look a gift horse in the mouth, Jack took the offering and stood. He did so with a moan, feeling a new strain in his back. The pain didn't immobilize him, but nor was it going away anytime soon.

"Marcus!" Theo shouted, dropping down to their level.

The general waved him off. "Check on Christos and Angeline. I'm fine."

Theo didn't like Marcus' lack of need for him. Jack would remember that. It seemed that not only was Theo a devout follower of Marcus Cerialis, but he was also a diehard fanboy and in desperate need of the man's attention.

"Jack?"

He turned and looked up. May and Gemma were waving at him. He gave the women a halfhearted reply with his own wave. It's not that he didn't mean it, Jack was just too tired to do much of anything else.

Marcus limped away, rotating his right foot every few steps as he did. He gazed up at the precipice, spotting Spencer.

"Nice to see you're still in good health, Spencer."

The curator's shoulders dropped. Marcus' dig, plus Spencer's reaction, got a smile out of Jack.

Jack and Marcus joined in on the relief effort, helping tend to Christos and Angeline's injuries. From what Jack could tell, Angeline had more than likely broken her left collarbone where it joined the shoulder. Christos' injury wasn't life-threatening, either, but nor would he be much help. The man had injured his right wrist and elbow badly during his fall.

With everything in order in the pit, Jack returned his attention to May and Gemma.

"Can you get down here?" he asked.

May nodded. "Yeah. We can follow your...*entry*."

Jack grimaced. "Go feetfirst, will ya? I don't recommend the swan dive." He turned and eyed something on the ground in front of him. It was one of the legionnaires' E-Rifles.

"Don't," Marcus warned.

Jack didn't. He stepped back and allowed the man to retrieve it.

Marcus didn't aim it at Jack, but the threat was clear. Even though he had helped Marcus, Jack was still his prisoner.

Once the entire team was back together, Jack, Marcus, and Spencer inched forward toward the hole at the center of the crater. One by one, they each clicked on their flashlights, pointing them inside. Jack instantly spotted something that gave him hope.

"Are those stairs?" he asked.

Spencer tested the edge of the opening with a stomp of his foot, then knelt next to it. "It is." He showed his light around inside, in all directions. "This is it! The entrance survived the cave-in!"

"Most of it, anyway," Jack mumbled.

"Move in," Marcus ordered. Spencer snapped his eyes up to him. Marcus stepped closer. "I said, move in."

Jack shooed him forward with both hands. "You heard the man. Chop chop."

Spencer swallowed back his fear, slid his helmet back on, then went about the task of snaking his way through the narrow, misshapen hole feetfirst. He spoke as he did. Jack could hear the nervousness in the man's voice.

"This must've been a staired entrance, like into a storehouse beneath a business."

"Or a fallout shelter," Jack added, stepping closer.

"Yes, or that," he agreed. "The shrine podium simply covered all this, hiding it in plain sight." Finally, he slipped inside, disappearing from view. Spencer's head reappeared seconds later. "It continues to the north, just as we thought!"

Marcus hurried forward.

"What about them?" Jack asked, motioning to Christos and Angeline. "They can't make this leg."

Marcus stopped and faced them. "You'll need to stay here." He continued before either of his people could respond. "Guard this access point. We may need to leave quickly."

The helmetless legionnaires glanced at one another, then their boss. They both nodded their compliance.

Marcus placed his fist on his chest. "*Gaudere Legio Nona.*"

The injured pair returned his show of respect with one of their own. They placed their fists on their chest and repeated their group's motto.

31

May and Gemma shambled down to Jack. May gently hugged him, while Gemma simply placed a hand on his shoulder.

Both gestures hurt.

"You two okay?" he asked.

Gemma nodded. "Yeah, May took good care of me."

"Good," Marcus said, sitting next to the hole, "we're all here. We will not waste any more time." He shimmied inside and disappeared.

Theo slid in behind Jack, May, and Gemma, leveling his E-Rifle at them. Jack sighed and sat, shuffling feetfirst into the hole. The soles of his boots hit stairs three feet later, but he realized that it was just rubble. Further ahead the way was clear.

Jack grabbed his helmet before continuing any further. Then he repositioned himself, sliding the rest of the way in. He would've landed hard on his ass, but he was caught by Marcus.

"Thanks," Jack said, standing hunched beneath the low-ceiling.

"Don't get used to it," Marcus said. "I'm down two men. I will be needing your help now more than ever."

Jack put his helmet back on. "Oh, so we're equals now, are we?"

Marcus gazed at him. "I didn't say that…"

Jack figured as much. He turned and helped May and Gemma in. The two women owned slighter frames, making the trip quick and painless. Their shorter heights helped them too. Neither one had to fight the six-foot-tall ceiling.

Spencer was ten steps further inside already, playing his light around the stairwell. "This is amazing, don't you think?"

Jack showed his own light around the cramped passage. "It's stairs."

"From the time of Eboracum!" Spencer added.

True… Jack had to remember that everything from here on out was nearly 2,000 years old. It didn't matter if it was something as trivial as stairs. It was still an important archaeological discovery.

And he was part of it.

"I see the bottom!" Spencer shouted, not that he needed to. Everyone could hear him in their comms.

"You know, these are going to be useless down here if we get separated," Jack said, tapping on the section of helmet covering his right ear.

"I know," Marcus replied. "So, let's not get separated, yes?"

"Oh my God…"

Jack and Marcus aimed their lights at the bottom of the steps. They could see Spencer standing, frozen with his own light pointed forward.

"What did you find?" Marcus asked, speeding up.

Jack kept up with him, moving carefully. The steps were shallow and worn.

Spencer stepped further into what was a room outside the stairway. It allowed Jack and Marcus to join him.

Spencer announced what Jack had already figured out. "The lost catacombs of the Ninth Legion."

Marcus continued past Spencer. "Where the greatest of us are said to be buried."

Jack was floored by what they had found. The walls of the large rectangular room contained cut shelves that held the remains of the dead. Each niche, each *loculi*, supported a beautifully carved, stone sarcophagus. And because this place had remained hidden since it had been lost, each and every shelf was currently holding a covered, presumably occupied, coffin.

"Pretty amazing when you get here before the graverobbers do, huh?" Jack said, panning his light around. His comment was meant to be rhetorical. Spencer must've not understood that.

"Says the graverobber."

Jack faced him. "First off, you know nothing about what I've found. Second, I'm not the one who has fantasized about *stealing* from this place." Jack eyed the three legionnaires. "You all have."

"And what about these discoveries you've made?" Marcus asked. The question sounded genuine. "Are you telling me that you didn't take anything from them for yourself?"

Jack turned and took three steps closer to Marcus, making sure the man was paying attention. Jack proceeded to count off some of his finds with his fingers.

"An untold fortune in wartime loot, billions in raw diamonds, more gold than you can imagine… I once had near-immortality at the tips of my fingers, oh, and have any of you heard of Marco Polo's lost fleet?"

Jack faced Spencer as the man's jaw hit the floor. May stepped up next to Jack. "Our jobs are to protect history, not plunder it." Jack zeroed in on Marcus again. "You call yourselves guardians of your people's past. *Pfft.* You sicken me. You're as bad as Nero."

May patted his arm, calming him. If there was one thing Jack despised being called, it was a thief. The diamonds from the Seven Sisters Monument were the only thing that had ever been taken from a find, and those had gone straight to Yellowstone's National Park Service to use as funding. And technically, Jack wasn't the one who had taken them.

Spencer looked down at his feet. "Yes, well, shall we continue then?"

Jack eyed him. "Yeah, *Spence.* That'd be the smart thing to do."

Marcus muttered something in Latin and narrowed his gaze at Jack. Theo drew his pistol, grabbed Gemma, and jammed its muzzle into her side.

"Ow!"

Marcus didn't break eye contact with Jack. "You might just be the most impressive man I've ever met, Jack, but you also need to respect your situation better."

"Is this really necessary?" May asked, holding up two calming hands.

Marcus stepped to within an arm's reach of Jack. "That all depends on whether you two are going to continue to cooperate."

Jack blinked, smiled, and shot Marcus with a playful finger gun. "Sure, why not?" He chuckled and faced May. "Let's keep the good times rolling, huh?"

"Yes," Gemma said, looking up at Theo before returning her attention to Jack, "please do."

As they moved deeper through the ancient catacombs, slotted walls gave way to something the Paris Catacombs were famous for. The walls were now made up of thousands of skulls and random bones. It was, quite literally, a land of the dead.

"Awfully grim," May said.

Something didn't seem right to Gemma. The look on her face said it all. "This makes no sense. Romans preferred cremation to anything like this."

"They did until the second century, if you recall," Spencer said. "Land became scarce and they resorted to this."

Gemma's eyes lit up. "Oh, yes! Overpopulation forced more and more bodies needing to be taken care of. This was the cheaper alternative for most."

Jack looked around. The artistic performance displayed on each sarcophagus was breathtaking. "Something tells me these guys weren't struggling for cash."

"They were not," Marcus said. "The Ninth Legion treated their dead with utmost respect. Dying in the line of duty was seen as an honor."

"Do you know where you're going?" May asked, staying close to Jack.

"In truth, no," Spencer replied. "All of this was kept from us, or lost to time. We just need to keep our eyes open for something. I'm confident it'll jump out at us."

"Oh, God," Gemma said. "I hope not."

Jack sighed. *I was thinking the same thing.*

The main corridor continued for some time. Every so often, they passed by a narrow offshoot, or a secondary chamber. Each one was quickly explored, but all that was discovered was more sarcophagi.

And skulls, Jack thought. *Lots and lots of skulls.*

The worst thing about it all was the smell. It was obvious that this place hadn't been exposed to fresh air in some time, or if it had, the oxygen had sparsely leaked in from random fissures in the rock.

The catacombs shook, freezing everyone in place. Dust billowed into the air, choking and gagging everyone. Even the stoic Marcus Cerialis sneered in disgust.

"*Blegh!*" Jack reeled back and quickly blew a pair of snot rockets. "They're in my sinuses." He wiped his nose with his jacket's sleeve, then saw that it was covered in a layer of the same dust. Jack immediately dry heaved.

May patted his back as his hands found his knees. Jack shook his head like a dog and stood tall. He let out a long breath and closed his eyes.

"That's proper nightmare fuel, right there," Jack said, feeling his heart pounding.

May smiled at Jack.

Spencer stepped closer, looking at May. "You find that humorous—his childish behavior?"

"At least he's authentic. Jack is Jack. He's unapologetic and sincere. What more could you ask for?"

Theo rolled his eyes. "Please…"

Gemma folded her arms across her chest. "For once, I agree with you. Seriously, though, what was that?"

"York doesn't have a subway, does it?" Jack asked.

"No," Spencer replied. "It was the railway. Trains pass by just northwest of the cathedral."

"And the shaking?" Gemma asked.

Jack glanced back at her. "This place is two-thousand-years-old, right?"

That was answer enough for Gemma. The implications were enormous. It meant that, eventually, the catacombs would collapse and be buried forever, or, at least, until they're stumbled upon by an excavation team.

With that, Jack left Gemma and Theo and continued deeper into the Ninth Legion's catacombs. May kept to his side, and they looked for anything that resembled a secret door.

"It's like a needle in a haystack," May said.

"Yeah, and it's a really creepy haystack too." Jack was curious about something. "How far do these things typically go?"

Spencer chimed in before Gemma could. "The Catacombs of San Callisto—they're in Rome—go on for over twelve miles."

"*Twelve* miles?" Jack turned and faced him. "That can't happen if we are to leave before the sun comes up."

"No, it can't," Marcus agreed, "which means we need to keep moving."

"No, we don't," Spencer said, leaving the group.

"Why not?" Jack asked.

Spencer turned and faced them. "Because we're here."

32

The six explorers entered a large, domed room. Jack guesstimated that the ceiling was at least forty feet high. Had they been slowly marching downhill since entering the catacombs? It was obvious that they had.

Stunning art adorned the ceiling, depicting the various Roman gods. Jack recognized Jupiter, Mars, and Neptune pretty easily. One god was featured more prominently than the others. Jack tried to place him, but couldn't. There was also a well-preserved mosaic of the same god on the floor. It sat between two, long, inwardly facing sets of stone benches. The benches themselves were just two single slabs of rock, but they stretched for nearly the entirety of the hall.

At the far end of the space was an altar. It had been constructed on a modest platform, and it all sat within a, likewise, domed alcove. From this end of the room, Jack could see a box of some kind sitting atop it. When his flashlight hit it, it gleamed gold.

Well that's something, Jack thought. He wanted to go inspect it but held back. *We'll get there when we get there.*

"It's a basilica," he said, looking around, "right?"

"It is," Gemma said, examining the oversized god on the ceiling.

Marcus stepped up behind them. "It is, and it's not." They both looked at him, but his eyes were still locked on the oversized deity. "This is a *Mithraeum*."

"He's right," Spencer confirmed. "This is where the Ninth Legion would've come to worship Mithras. There are temples like this, dedicated to him, all over Europe."

"Right," Jack said, rolling his eyes, "perfect explanation. Very insightful, as usual."

Marcus pulled his eyes away from Mithras and met Jack's stare. "Roman legionnaires were known to worship Mithras. *Mithra*, as he was traditionally named, was the Zoroastrian god of light, oath, justice, and covenants. That alone should tell you why a legion of warriors paid him so much respect."

"Admirable qualities, indeed," Spencer agreed.

"Wait, 'Zoroastrian?'" Jack asked. "Ancient Iran?" Marcus' head tilted slightly to the side. Jack briefly explained his knowledge of the subject. "I spent a decent amount of time in the Middle East years back. I may have picked up on a thing or two."

"Back with the military?" the general asked.

Jack didn't take the bait. "So, Mithras was a *Persian* god that *Roman* soldiers worshipped?"

"*Mithra* was the Persian variant, not *Mithras*," Spencer replied. "The Zoroastrians inspired the Roman version of him, yes. Complicated, I know." He continued, turning his eyes skyward. "Either way, legionnaires would gather in temples like this and pray for his guidance and protection. It was also common practice for Christian churches to convert these defunct temples into their own crypts once the religion was introduced, spreading like wildfire through the empire."

"By Constantine," Jack added.

"Correct," Marcus replied. He stepped away, looking around. "But this place looks untouched. I don't see a single Christian relic, do you?"

"I don't," Jack replied. "Which means—"

"We are the first people to step foot in this place since before the time of Constantine," Gemma finished.

"Roughly seventeen *hundred* years ago," Spencer added. "Give or take a few decades."

"Amazing," Gemma said. "What an incredible discovery." She looked at Marcus and Spencer. "I just wish it was under more pleasant circumstances."

"As do I," Marcus agreed. Jack, May, and Gemma faced Marcus. The man's hard eyes softened a little. "Despite what you may think, I do not prefer this method. But it *was* necessary."

"Says the captor to his captives," May said, expertly sliding in the jab.

Marcus shrugged. "I have come to terms with my decisions. I do not regret what I've done, and I will continue to do so until we have our *aquila* back."

"Now what?" Gemma asked. "I don't see another corridor. To me, it looks like this is the end of the line."

May looked around. "She's right. Unless there's a secret passage somewhere…"

Jack started off. "That's *exactly* what it is. Come on."

It has to be the altar, he thought.

As he moved for it, his eyes took in everything his flashlight touched, darting around like a kid with too much caffeine in his system. Jack was tired, but he was also wired. Marcus fell in line to Jack's right, and May kept up with him on his left. Gemma, Spencer, and Theo brought up the rear. Theo hung back a little more than the two historians, though, no doubt trying to keep himself between the exit and everyone else.

Smart man, Jack thought.

They slowed as they neared the altar. The alcove surrounding it was plenty big enough to fit all six people here, but only Jack and Marcus mounted the platform.

"Stay back," Marcus ordered his men.

Jack silently held up a hand. May and Gemma hung back without argument.

The pair stepped closer, studying the stone altar intently. The only thing Jack saw, besides the gilded box, were brown stains. Nearly the entire altar top was covered in them.

"Blood?" Jack asked, but he already knew the answer.

"Yes."

"Sacrifices to Mithras," Spencer added from behind.

Again, Jack had already figured that out.

"What is it?" he asked, staring at the box, but looking to Marcus for answers.

"I don't know," the general replied. "I've never heard of anything like this before." He looked over his shoulder. Spencer shook his head. He was clueless too.

The box lacked any detail, which was odd since the rest of the *Mithraeum* contained such vivid detail. Jack was curious as to why, but who could he ask?

"Think there's something inside?" Jack asked.

"Or beneath it, yes."

Jack leaned in closer, keeping his hands behind his back as he did. "So, it's a lid, is it?" With his face a foot from the box, he glanced up at Marcus. "Touch it."

Marcus eyed Jack with a *Yeah, right!* look.

Jack shrugged. "It's your base, not mine. Be the leader they believe you are." He winked. "Grab it."

Marcus used his nose to blow out a long breath. Jack had successfully gotten under his skin with his last comment. "Theo," he said, turning and holding out his hand. "The eagle."

Theo slipped out of his backpack, looking none-too-pleased about giving up the sacred artifact. He'd been its keeper, thus far. But Marcus was his commander, and he smartly unzipped his bag and handed over the twelve-inch-wide, square container.

Marcus took the case, set it on the altar, and opened it. Inside was their prize.

"Gold for gold?" Jack asked.

"That's what I'm thinking, yes." Marcus looked at the unmarked box. "Why else would you have this here?"

"You think the lock is beneath the box, huh?"

Marcus nodded and lifted the priceless item out of the case. "I do."

"And when the key meets the lock?" The Legion leader glanced up at Jack, then back down to the box. He had no answer for Jack. "Great... Well, let's get on with it." Jack slipped back into his protective helmet, getting a confused look from Marcus. "What? I'm not taking any chances."

Marcus thought better of it and slid his helmet back on too.

Jack then hovered his hands to either side of the mystery box, keeping them each an inch from either side of it. Marcus, in turn, held the eagle aloft above it.

Here we go.

"Kinda feels like the beginning of Raiders, huh?" Jack asked, closing his hands, gently clasping the small-ish box. He tried to slide it towards him, but it didn't budge. So, he tried to push it. Still, nothing. "Uh..." He stood and scratched his head, but only got helmet.

"Try pushing it down," May suggested from behind.

Jack glanced back at her, then looked at Marcus. The other man shrugged. So, Jack did just that. He placed his palms on top of the golden box and pressed. Remarkably, the box—the button—lowered into the altar. It moved slowly too. That shouldn't have shocked anyone, considering its age.

As it continued lower and lower, Jack grew more nervous.

"Something the matter?" Marcus asked.

"Yeah. In my experience, this is when something bad tends to happen."

But it didn't, not yet, anyway. Once the button was flush with the altar, a section of the alcove's back wall *clunked*, then lowered to reveal a three-foot-by-three-foot hole. There, sitting on a simple stone pedestal, was a somewhat bland, yet still incredible, golden rectangle.

Jack and Marcus looked at one another, then skirted around the altar. The others followed them, but stayed back near the altar and watched with nervous energy.

"I don't like this, Jack," May said.

"Me either." He looked back at her. "I'm waiting for the roof to come down, or something."

Gemma looked up. "Please don't say that."

"He didn't mean it literally," Spencer said. He turned his head and looked at Jack. "Did you?"

When Jack didn't reply, Spencer also looked up at the ceiling. He even went as far as stepping back, distancing himself from the others. Jack and Marcus focused on the golden rectangle. An odd pattern was cut into it, showing off a jagged depression.

"It's the lock," Marcus said softly. He raised the eagle over it.

"You sure about this?" Jack asked.

Marcus took him in. "You could step aside, if you'd like?"

Jack snorted. "Yeah, no thanks. I'm not letting you have all the fun."

"Will you please stop pretending this is just some game!" Gemma shouted.

Jack faced her. "But it is, don't you see? All of this." He held out his hands, motioning to the *Mithraeum*. "It's a test." He looked at Spencer. "Back in the museum, before the floor gave way, you said something about our courage being tested, that only the worthy would prevail..."

The curator nodded. "Yes. It was supposed to be an honor to go on this quest. But one would have to prove that they belonged here."

"By defeating a series of challenges along the way," Jack quickly added. "Granted, they aren't particularly difficult challenges, but still..."

"Quiet!" Marcus barked. His voice bounced around the domed temple.

Jack returned his attention to the lock as Marcus slowly lowered the eagle onto it. It fit perfectly, and received a second *clunk* as a reward. The eagle and lock lowered into the floor to reveal a waist-high passageway. Jack and Marcus knelt, shining their flashlights inside.

"Can't see anything," Marcus announced, standing.

Jack stayed put, eyeing the entrance. "Looks like we're going in, huh?"

"We are," Marcus replied, shrugging out of his gear. Gone were his pack and his rifle.

"Is that smart, Marcus?" Theo asked, looking down at the discarded weapon.

"Doesn't matter," Marcus replied, "because if Jack returns without me, you have permission to kill his friends."

33

The first thing May did when Jack and Marcus entered the opening was take in her captors' positions. The museum curator, Spencer, was kneeling in front of it, watching the two men disappear. He would be easy to subdue, possibly kill.

But not the other one.

Theo, the one who had treated May as a piñata, smartly stood farther back. He also had his rifle in his hands, whereas Spencer had his slung around his back. The only way this would work was if she could get the man's sidearm unholstered before being shot in the back with a Taser round.

May removed her helmet and set it on the altar.

Gemma stepped up next to her, also removing her helmet. She placed it next to May's and leaned in close. "Don't," she whispered.

May flashed her rage-filled eyes to the Italian. "Don't do what?"

Gemma tipped her chin toward Spencer. "Whatever you're thinking of doing."

She glanced over her shoulder, seeing that Theo hadn't moved closer...yet. May was about to make her move, but she was stopped.

"Trust Jack," Gemma said softly. Then she reached out and took May's hand. "Please."

May looked at her and saw fear in her eyes.

Dammit.

This was what Jack had asked her not to do anymore. May had been seconds away from risking her life—Gemma's too—to "win the day." Gemma's viewpoint was much different from May's warped perspective. Risking her life was a part of the job in May's eyes, but she wasn't the only one in danger here. Even Jack's life was in the balance if she failed to take down Spencer and acquire his gun.

May didn't like it, but she understood, loud and clear. She gave Gemma a subtle nod, and relaxed her tense shoulders.

"Smart move." The voice came from behind the two women. They turned to find Theo aiming his rifle at May. "Your posture betrays you."

"Does it?" May asked.

She seamlessly, effortlessly switched from hardened operative to seductive temptress. May turned, softening her facial expression, narrowing her eyes on him. Then she gave him the slightest of smiles. May turned her attention to Gemma next, lifting a hand and caressing the side of the Italian's face. May bit her lip, and added eagerness to her eyes.

"Uh, what are you doing?" Gemma asked, face blanking with the unease she was obviously feeling.

She leaned in close to Gemma. "Just go with it." Only when their lips were inches apart, did she snap her attention back to Theo. "How about now? Do you still believe I'm only thinking of the quickest way to kill you and your friend?"

May stood tall. "When you think you know something, it might be safer to assume you don't know anything at all."

She turned away from Theo, flashing a grin at Gemma as she did. Gemma was still lost in the act May had just flawlessly performed.

Gemma blinked out of her stupor. "How long did it take you to perfect that?"

"That?" May asked, chuckling. "*That* was easy." She winked. "*Men* are easy. Now, doing that, while also staring into the eyes of someone you *really* want to hurt..." May squeezed her fists tight, then released them. "That takes years of practice."

34

Jack and Marcus crawled over the eagle, careful not to bump it. There was no telling what would happen if they did.

"Are you sure we can't take it?" Marcus asked, staring back at the artifact.

"If you do take it, are you sure you want to be on this side of the door when you do?"

The prospect of being locked on the wrong side was enough of a deterrent to make Marcus leave it be. Jack led the pair forward, gripping his penlight in one hand as he did. It made him feel like a three-legged dog. His movements were awkward, but Jack didn't dare not make the trek in the dark.

"Anything?" Marcus asked after five minutes.

"Yeah, but I thought I'd keep it to myself."

Marcus stopped. "Really?"

Jack snickered. "Nope. We got nothin'." But just then, the walls and low ceiling surrounding the edge of Jack's light disappeared. It opened further ahead. "Oh, never mind. There's a room up here."

Jack switched his flashlight to his opposite hand and pushed forward. As he neared the opening, he slowed to make sure the coast was clear. He had no idea what awaited them, and rushing into things rarely ever paid off.

Unless you're being chased by bloodthirsty natives, Jack thought.

The pair exited into another temple, though this one was decidedly different from the Roman *Mithraeum*. Jack didn't have to be an expert like Gemma or Spencer to see it. Whoever built this favored a more elegant style, not that Jack could place it.

Marcus noticed it too. He swept his light around the rectangular chamber. It was deep enough that his light failed to reach the end.

That's when Jack realized that this wasn't some retrofitted cave, well, most of it wasn't. To him, the shape was too unnatural. The builders didn't just "use the space," they had cut much of the space into existence. Jack aimed his flashlight up and saw that they had even built a peaked roof over most of the floorspace, as if it were outside in the elements.

"How 'bout that? It's a subterranean temple, roof and all."

"Yes. And do you see the ionic columns?" Marcus asked, pointing to one of them. In all, there must've been dozens. They stretched further than their lights could touch.

"Uh, sure. Ionic…" Marcus looked at him. "What? I have a lot of stuff to remember and ancient column designs ain't one of 'em."

He faced Jack. "It's Greek, *not* Roman."

Jack removed his helmet, sweating hard now. "Greek? You sure?"

Marcus nodded. "Yes. Even though Rome fully adopted the practice of using columns in their architecture, there's one distinct difference between each empire's usage."

"And that is?"

"The Greeks used columns to support their structures. The Romans only used them for decoration. Which do you see here?"

Jack gave the columns another look and instantly saw it. These columns were holding the indoor roof aloft. If Marcus' intel was accurate, and Jack was pretty convinced it was, then this added a whole new layer to their mission.

Marcus removed his helmet. He was wide-eyed—shocked even! Jack had yet to see the man like this. "I think the Mouseions built this!"

Now *that* was something Jack understood. "The Mouseions?" he asked. "As in the Muses? As in Ancient Greece?" Marcus nodded. "It's where the word *museum* comes from, you know? Except I can't fathom why they'd spell Mouseion like *mouse* and not *muse*. Super annoying, if you ask me." Marcus stared blankly at him. "What? Everyone who loves this crap knows who the Mouseions were." Jack looked around, taking in the significance of the hypothesis again. "They were responsible for the Library of Alexandria."

"They were also founded by Alexander's most trusted general," Marcus added.

"Yep, Ptolemy I Soter," Jack said. "Too bad Caesar's men torched the place. The library, I mean."

Marcus looked away, as if he was ashamed. "Not one of Rome's finest hours."

"Take it easy. It's not like you were there." Jack motioned to the room. "All this... You really gotta stop taking it so personally." He eyed the nearest column. "Hang on. Why is this here? I thought York was founded by the Romans long after the fall of Greece?"

"It was, although..."

"Although, what?"

"History says that Rome allowed the Mouseions to continue after they took over." Marcus looked up. "I wonder..."

"You think the Mouseions secretly worked on all this under the nose of their Roman bosses, don't you?"

Marcus smiled and sighed. "I'm not sure of a lot right now. This is all too much, even for me." Jack smiled. "What?"

Jack stepped closer to him. "You know, you're not a *complete* jagoff sometimes." He put his hands on his hips. "You should try to be like this more often."

Marcus squinted, unsure how to take the backhanded compliment. "But none of this explains why this is Greek and not Roman."

Jack chuckled. "That's cute. Come on, Marcus. You, of all people, should know that a lot of secrets have their own secrets." Jack strode away and examined one of the columns, seeing a brown stain on it. "But yeah..." he was now also thinking about what could've caused the discoloration, "it does seem like there was some hanky-panky going on here. And it happened right under your ancestor's foot too."

"Exactly! That's what bothers me the most," Marcus said. "Something like this would've taken *years* to build."

"Okay, so, let's start here. There were no Greek settlements in the area before Quintus and the Ninth arrived, correct?"

Marcus folded his arms across his chest. "Correct."

"So, that would mean that the builders would've had to have been Greek, not Roman, and they would've believed in the old ways too."

"Yes," Marcus agreed, "that makes sense, sure."

Jack shrugged. "Easy. Quintus had double agents working within his own ranks."

Marcus' eyes glowed with rage. "Impossible! The Mouseions were scholars, not soldiers. And every man in the Ninth Legion was a stout believer in the cause—the empire."

"What about the traitors you mentioned earlier?" Jack asked. Marcus tried to rebuke Jack's claim, but he faltered. "What do you say to this… Maybe the people who stole your eagle were really Mouseion agents keeping an eye on things from the inside? Believe me, I've seen weirder." He walked away, heading deeper into the temple. "Plus, you've already laid it out perfectly. This place—this Mouseion temple—was built during Roman rule, not before."

"You know nothing."

Jack glanced over his shoulder. "I know enough. C'mon, let's find your base and get the hell out of here." His light swept to the floor in front of him, to another discoloration. He followed the *streak* to the right, beyond the edges of the Mouseion temple. "Oh, boy."

Marcus quickly joined him, adding his light to the mound of decayed corpses. There must've been two or three dozen of them.

Jack thought back to the discoloration. *Dried blood.* These men had been killed, then dragged here after.

"What do you think happened to them?" Jack asked.

"Isn't it obvious?" Marcus replied, still focused on the gore. "They tried to take it for themselves."

"The traitors?"

Marcus nodded. "Yes. I bet they found this place, but they were cutoff by a legion detachment and killed."

"And how do the Mouseions fit into this?" Jack asked, backing away from the bodies.

"I'm not sure, but it's clear that they played a key role in all this."

They continued deeper through the temple. Shortly after, something glinted in the edge of Jack's light.

"You see that?" he asked.

"Gold," Marcus said, glancing at Jack. "Too big to be the base."

"Yeah, that's what I was thinking too."

Both men picked up their pace. They were at a jog by the time they got to what they had seen moments earlier.

"Holy crap," Jack said, slowing. "It's beautiful!"

35

It was a twelve-foot-tall, marble statue of an unknown woman—unknown to Jack. He dug in deep to his Ancient Greek studies but couldn't pull out anything useful. His best guess was Athena, but he'd seen statues of Athena before, and this wasn't her. Whoever this was, she was less abrasive looking. Less stern. This person was the epitome of elegance. She was calming. Her robes flowed with grace and humility.

The gold they had seen belonged to an oversized U-shaped instrument. Jack was pretty sure he knew what it was, but its presence didn't make a lot of sense to him.

"Is that a lyre?" he asked, estimating the solid gold instrument's length at over six feet.

"It is…" Jack looked at Marcus. He was in awe, same as Jack, but the Legion general's eyes weren't staring at the lyre. He was staring at the woman's feet.

"You one of those weird foot enthusiasts?"

Marcus stepped closer. "The base."

Jack had been so preoccupied with the statue, as well as the enormous gold lyre, that he had failed to see what had caught Marcus' eye. A smaller, less majestic, gilded object sat at the woman's feet.

The base was exactly as he expected it to be. It was relatively flat and rectangular, minus the laurel wreath standing on end. He spotted Latin script on the front edge too, not that he was overly interested in what it said. One thing did gnaw at Jack's mind, however.

"Who's she?"

Marcus blinked and gazed up at the giant woman. "The lyre was the symbol of the muse, Clio."

"Did the Mouseions worship her?"

"Not to my knowledge. They worshipped all nine muses, not one individually. They were the goddesses of science, the arts, and literature. Each one represented a specific area within those arenas."

"Then why Clio?" Jack asked.

"She represented history."

Jack scratched the back of his head. "Makes sense, I guess, since the Mouseions were so heavily involved in that area."

"They were. They took it very seriously," he looked around, "as you can plainly see."

Both men looked at one another, then they cautiously approached the exquisitely produced monument to Clio, the Muse of History.

"I still can't believe this was all done without anyone knowing," Marcus said, kneeling in front of the base.

Jack turned and looked back toward the front of the temple. "Or maybe people did know and they were silenced to keep it from being discovered."

"That is also a possibility, but I can't see the Mouseions operating like that. They were academics at heart. Killing laborers in cold blood doesn't fit their mold."

"Like Spencer, right? An academic, but also a member of a murderous army of zealots." Marcus glared up at Jack. "Hey, I'm just calling it as I see it. Your theory about the Mouseions horribly contradicts your own organization."

Marcus reached for the base, but stopped when his fingers were inches from it. "Is it safe?"

Jack knelt beside him. "I hope so."

"Not very comforting."

"Eh, you want comfort? Buy yourself a Serta Perfect Sleeper. I'm just being real." Jack took a deep breath. "Be careful, either way. The thing it's sitting on might be a pressure plate of some kind."

"You watch too many movies," Marcus said, touching the base. The action caused Jack to close his eyes and turn away.

"Be that as it may," Jack said, "I—"

"Got it."

Jack opened one eye and faced forward. Marcus was holding the ten-inch-wide, square base in both hands, smiling. Nothing horrific had happened. *That's* what made Jack smile. Yes, they retrieved the eagle's base, and they were also still alive.

"Tell me, Jack," Marcus said, standing, "do you love her?"

Jack tripped on nothing as he stepped away. "Excuse me?"

"May. Do you love her?"

Jack looked back up at Clio as he answered. "Well, I mean, I don't know, maybe?" The pair started away. "We only met a couple months ago and—hang on, why am I talking about my personal life with you?"

Marcus stopped and faced Jack. "I was hoping that we could come to trust one another."

"Fat chance," Jack said, snorting.

The other man shrugged. "It was worth a shot."

"Maybe if we'd been given the chance to come willingly from the get-go, and maybe if you and your boys hadn't gunned down Dr. Lombardi without a valid reason, then we could be close to trusting one another right now."

"He disrespected my family."

Jack burst out laughing. "Sticks and stones, pal. Sticks and stones. What about the cops and the paratroopers you killed? Did they say mean things about your fam—"

Jack was interrupted by a groan, then another *clunk*. He knew that sounds like that were usually caused by something opening. Jack spun, sweeping his light around with him, but nothing happened.

"What do you think it was?" Marcus asked.

"I have an idea," Jack replied, beginning his exit, "but I'd rather not wait around to find out if I'm right."

Then, starting at the foot of the Clio statue, the floor fell in, cascading like a waterfall. It chased Jack and Marcus back the way they'd come at an incredible rate. The two men ran as fast as their legs would move. Luckily, it was a straight shot back to the tunnel entrance, though it wasn't exactly close.

"I hate you *so* much!" Jack snarled.

Marcus kept stride with him, tucking the *aquila's* base into the crook of his arm, carrying it like a football. "The feeling is mutual!"

They ran and ran and ran. Jack's lungs burned. Marcus was huffing and puffing loudly, and he was limping on his injured ankle. He fell back a step. Jack growled, grabbed the man's shoulder, and hauled him along for another fifty feet before they finally reached the low tunnel entrance.

Jack pulled ahead and went into a classic baseball slide, entering boots first. He stopped six feet later, turned, and watched as Marcus dove forward. The *Legatus* caught the edge of the tunnel with his free hand. The rest of him vanished.

Jack scrambled to Marcus on all fours, securing his wrist before he could fall. With just his head poking out of the tunnel, Jack now saw the state of the Mouseion temple. The trap had only triggered the central corridor, but it did so from the floor of the Clio statue all the way to here. Jack also spotted what awaited them if they should fall. Marcus' flashlight now lay between two three-foot-tall metal spikes.

Marcus' hand started to slip. Jack squeezed his wrist harder, but had zero leverage. If he had been kneeling or standing, this would've been a piece of cake.

"Give me your other hand," Jack said through clinched teeth.

"And drop the base?"

Friggin' zealots.

"Hand it to me." Marcus shot him an appalling look. "Or…you can fall. Which is it?"

Marcus glanced down at his feet. He was currently hanging two stories above a sea of meat skewers. Jack didn't want him to fall, but if he did, it would be because of his own arrogance and cynicism.

Marcus' hand slipped again.

"Now or never," Jack warned.

Marcus sneered, but shoved the base high enough to reach the ledge Jack was lying on. Jack released one of his hands long enough to slide it to safety. Then, he reacquired Marcus' wrist as the other man snagged the edge with his free hand.

Jack changed tactics and grabbed one of the padded shoulder straps belonging to Marcus' tactical vest. He pulled, relieving Marcus of enough of his own weight for him to clamber up the wall. Once he got a leg up, Jack let go and retreated deeper into the tunnel. As a show of faith, he left the base where it was, making no effort to take it. In reality, Jack didn't care about the base as an individual piece. What he wanted was at the end.

"They really made this difficult," Jack said, panting hard.

Marcus nodded, catching his air. "I may have underestimated the Mouseions. They were more than mere scholars."

"I bet they studied Egyptian trap making to come up with something like that."

"I'm sure they did," Marcus agreed. "But why? Why go to *that* much trouble to keep us from recovering the base?"

"Only the worthy, right?" Jack explained. "Even the Mouseions valued the *aquila*, Marcus. If someone, or someones, could successfully take it from this place, the Mouseions were fine with it. I bet they would've even celebrated the achievement. Or…"

"Or?"

"Or they were also protecting it because they knew where it leads. They would've known about the link to Alexander's tomb, right? I mean, they were Greek, after all."

"So, these traitors. Do you really think they were secretly Mouseion spies?"

"I think it's pretty clear that they were. The civil war within the Ninth Legion makes a helluva lot more sense now, doesn't it?"

Marcus softly nodded. Jack could see the man's eyes darting around in the aura of his flashlight. He was thinking it through for himself.

"You nearly killed yourself for this thing. Why?"

Marcus picked up the base and examined it, revering it with a look of awe. "The eagle standard is sacred to us, as it was to our ancestors."

"It really means that much to you?"

Marcus shrugged. "Why does a cross mean so much to a Christian?"

"Because of what it represents," Jack replied. "Gotcha… It defines the believer in a way."

"Precisely." Marcus' eyes widened and his hands shook. "The eagle *is* us. It is who we are."

"Whoa. Easy there, killer." Jack held up his hands. "Come back down to earth for a second, will ya? I need you focused."

Marcus looked up from the base. "I've never been more focused in all my life."

"That's not what your body is telling me; twitching facial muscles and hands, rigid posture…" He trailed off, looking past Marcus. "What do you think would've happened if we had tried to take the lyre instead?"

The question relaxed Marcus some. "Nothing I care to find out. Now, if you please, you are in my way."

"There he is!" Jack said, celebrating the full return of Marcus Cerialis. He awkwardly turned around and faced the opposite direction. "Glad to have you back, General."

They crawled for a moment before Marcus spoke up again. "Why did you save me back there?"

"For the same reason I helped you back at the cave-in. There are people who matter to me whose lives are at risk. Keeping you alive, is keeping them alive."

"Is that the only reason, or are you just that hellbent on saving people?"

Jack stopped and looked back at him. "I'd like to think I would've saved you, regardless of May and Gemma being involved." He started up again. "But

I also might've let you fall."

36

The duo arrived at the eagle. Jack carefully avoided it, poking his head out as he did. The first person to greet him was May. She grabbed his arm and helped him up, checking him over.

"You okay?" she asked, lifting his helmet off for him.

Jack nodded, wiping away a bead of sweat from his brow. "Yeah. Wish you could've been there."

"What about the end?" Marcus asked, appearing below.

"Oh, right. Yeah, never mind." He and May moved out of the way, allowing Spencer to help his boss up.

May didn't understand what he meant. "What happened?"

"Oh, you know. Same old, same old."

May sighed. "You destroyed another priceless archaeological discovery, didn't you?"

Gemma snorted out a laugh. Jack gave her a quick glare before turning back to May. "Yes—but, technically, it was his fault." He stuck his thumb out, indicating that it was Marcus who had done it.

"Correction," Marcus said, holding up the base, "it was the Mouseions."

Both Gemma and Spencer gawked at the statement.

"The Mouseions?" May asked. "Who are they?"

"You don't know?" Spencer asked.

May shrugged. "If we were in Asia, I'd be more help."

"Fair enough," he said, taking the base from Marcus. "The, uh, Mouseions were Greek scholars. Most notably, they were responsible for erecting the Library of Alexandria."

"Oh," May said, looking at Gemma. "So, they were a big deal."

"Enormous," Gemma replied. "And it also gives us another connection to Alexander himself, rather, his favorite general."

"Ptolemy I Soter," Jack added. "Yeah," he motioned back and forth between him and Marcus, "we had a little powwow about it already."

Gemma stepped up next to May. "For several different reasons, he was ultimately responsible for burying Alexander."

"And these Mouseions are significant to us now?" May asked.

"Could be, yeah," Jack replied.

"Or they could be nothing," Marcus slipped in.

Jack shrugged. "That too. There's still a lot we don't know, but I have a feeling the Mouseions do play a large role in what happened to the eagle." He pointed at the base in Spencer's hands. "We found that at the foot of a twelve-foot-tall statue of Clio."

"What!" Spencer said, gasping. "This was hidden in a Mouseion temple?"

"Deep behind a Roman temple, yep," Jack replied, "and they defended it with a nifty Egyptian trap." He scratched his head. "At least, I think it's

Egyptian." He waved it away. "Doesn't matter. What does is that we now have that to look forward to at our next stop."

"You think there will be additional evidence of Mouseion involvement?" Spencer asked.

Jack nodded. "I'm positive." He pointed at the tunnel. "No way did they build that and then walk away." He eyed Marcus. "I bet we'll find something else wherever your pole is hidden."

"Speaking of that…" May said. "Where are we going next?"

Marcus turned, knelt, and yanked the eagle free of its lock. When it was detached, the wall resealed itself. Now, it was just as it was when they arrived.

"Nijmegen," Marcus replied. "We go to Nijmegen."

"The Netherlands?" Jack asked. "And let me guess, there will be a place to set both the eagle and the base—another lock?"

"Correct," Spencer replied. "That's where we'll find the *aquilifer's* pole."

"And after that?" May asked.

Jack faced her. "Isn't it obvious?" He turned and gazed out at the Roman *Mithraeum*. "Babylon."

Marcus checked his watch. "But first, we need to make it out of here. It's getting late."

"You mean *early*," Gemma mumbled.

Jack looked at his own watch and cursed. "Shit." He slipped his helmet back on. "We *really* need to get moving."

The eagle went back to Theo, and surprisingly, Marcus let Spencer hold on to the base after it was put in a similar Pelican case. After what had happened at the Colosseum, it made sense, really. Having them together, and in the hands of the Legion's leader, a man who had made himself a public figure, would be incredibly dangerous. It was better to keep them separate from one another. If Theo fell, and they lost the eagle, they would still have the base. Same could be said if it were Spencer who went down.

"Now, let's go," Marcus said, descending the altar. He gazed back at the group. "Quickly."

Jack didn't have to be told twice. He and May took off at a healthy jog. Gemma, Spencer, and Theo were next, and Marcus hung back to keep an eye on everything from the rear of the pack.

Their spirited exit slowed as they moved. No one stopped, but everyone's urgency, as well as their strength, diminished. Really, besides Spencer, maybe, everyone here was exhausted and in major need of rest.

Later, Jack thought.

He pictured what they'd find back at the cave-in. Surely someone was bound to find out. Their one saving grace was that the collapse had happened underground. The noise would've been dampened enough to not be heard outside. Then again, who was outside to hear it?

"Are we sure the guards are still down for the count?" Jack asked, seeing the stairs leading up to the destroyed Undercroft Museum.

"They should be," Marcus replied. "The Taser rounds have a minimal effective time of three hours."

"You sure?" May asked, now power walking next to Jack.

"Very sure," Theo replied, speaking up for the first time in ages.

May shot the man daggers with a cold stare. It was plain to see that no matter what Theo said, May was going to take it personally. Jack didn't blame her, either.

Jack placed his foot on the bottommost step and looked back at Marcus. "And what if the guards wake up?"

Marcus gazed up the dark staircase. "Pray they don't."

Noted.

Jack took in a long breath, then made his way back up to the ruined basement of York Minster. Unfortunately, what May had jokingly said about him destroying things was true. Everything Jack touched turned to shit.

That's not true. Jack didn't buy it. He had saved quite a few 'priceless finds' too.

He had also saved a lot of lives.

Jack made it to the rubble, and immediately began crawling on top of it. He kept his movements as quiet as possible in case there was trouble above. When he was a foot from the exit, a familiar face greeted him.

"Thank God," Christos hissed. "Hurry. We have company!"

Jack clawed his way out of the hole and was shocked when the Greek legionnaire thrust his E-Rifle into Jack's arms. Christos only nodded, then turned back to the floor. He was sitting just outside of it, favoring his injured right arm. Jack checked over the weapon under the watchful eyes of Angeline. She didn't make an effort to stop him, though.

They must've decided that this was the best course of action. It was smart too. Jack, May, and Gemma's lives were in the balance, as were the legionnaires. They needed all the help they could get.

When Marcus, Theo, and Spencer exited the subterranean entry point, they were quickly given the low down on the current situation.

"They're here," Angeline said. "You can see lights outside the front door. I give it another minute—two tops—before they force their way in."

"Police?" Gemma asked.

"If we're lucky," Christos replied.

Marcus eyed the rifle in Jack's hands.

Jack faced him. "Do you want my help, or not?"

Marcus sighed, then looked at Angeline. He tilted his head to May. The female legionnaire offered her weapon to her. May happily took it, going over the manual of arms. The E-Rifle wasn't all that dissimilar to most other firearms of the style.

"No lethal rounds," May said.

"What?" Spencer asked, flabbergasted. "We might not have a choice!"

May held her rifle out to Marcus. "No lethal rounds, or I'm out."

"Same," Jack said, backing her up. "These guys are just doing their jobs."

Marcus gritted his teeth, but relented. "Fine. E-Rifle only."

"What's our exit?" Jack asked, back at it.

"Back up to the tower," Marcus replied. "Helo will pick us up there once we call in for extraction."

Jack faced the edge of the crater, happy to see that a path back to the top had been made. Even injured, Christos and Angeline had proven valuable. A makeshift stairway had been constructed out of debris. It was how Angeline had been able to check on the situation outside.

"Better call it in as soon as we get topside," Jack said. "I see a lot more running in our future."

Gemma groaned. "A lot of stairs as well."

Jack glanced at her, matching her displeasure. "Yeah, that too."

37

As soon as Jack leaned out into the high-ceilinged halls of York Minster, he saw something he dreaded. The front doors to the cathedral were forcefully opened and a column of armed policemen filed in. These weren't just regular cops, either. They were the equivalent to the American's SWAT.

Jack returned to cover and looked down at the others spread out on the steps beneath him. "They're armored," he explained, talking barely above a whisper thanks to his helmet's comms unit, "so we're going to have to aim for limbs, instead of center mass."

"The Taser rounds will be less effective," Marcus argued, his voice coming through with a slight tinniness.

Jack shrugged. "Can't help it. If you have to, hit 'em twice."

He was still shocked that he was now somehow leading this outfit. Jack didn't ask for the role, he'd taken it. The last thing Jack was going to do was allow someone else to lead him to failure.

I can fail just fine on my own, thank you.

Spencer and Gemma were in charge of getting Christos and Angeline back to the tower. It would be Marcus and Theo, along with Jack and May, that would be responsible for covering them. Jack was confident that, once they were inside the stone stairwells, they'd be safe, at least until they got back outside.

"Zayn, do you copy?" Marcus asked.

"*We're inbound,*" someone with an Arab accent said, "*see you in ten minutes.*" It took Jack a second to figure out who was speaking. His helmet's radio was also linked to the incoming helicopter it seemed. The voice had belonged to the pilot.

"Ten minutes?" May asked.

"Yeah," Jack replied. "Means we're gonna have to haul ass."

Jack looked over his squad again. Marcus gave him a nod, telling him that they were all ready.

"Are we even sure they'll shoot at us?" Spencer asked, looking up. "This place is a national monument, after all."

"I'm not sure," Jack replied, looking back at him, "why don't you go ask them?"

May gave Jack a look that he guessed was one of amusement.

"Okay, the less shooting the better," Jack said quietly. "Let's try and slip out unseen." He leaned out again. The SWAT officers were almost two-hundred feet away. "Spencer, Gemma, Christos, Angeline, you're up."

Jack waited and watched. He held up his right hand. Then, when the timing felt right, he chopped it downward, indicating for them to move.

"Go."

Spencer edged out, then made a right-handed U-turn, staying low and out of sight. The stairs leading back up to the tower were, thankfully, right behind them. The two injured legionnaires went next, followed by a very unsure Gemma. She gave Jack one last look before squeaking and hitting the deck as a light panned over the stairs leading down to the undercroft. Now on all fours, Gemma made it into cover with Spencer and the others.

The light, however, did not move or go out. Jack, May, Marcus, and Theo were stuck.

Seeing that, the Greek demolitions expert pulled a small object out of his pocket, and held it up for Jack to see. Then, he mimicked as if he was going to throw it.

"Get ready to move," Christos said.

Jack gave him a thumbs up, barely being able to see the man from his current position. Really, Jack could only see the right half of him.

Jack carefully leaned out, only revealing half of his masked face. "We're ready."

Christos chucked the object across the grand hall. It landed within a row of seats in the massive nave that sat between them and the front doors. The policemen's lights instantly flashed over to it, staying there.

Bingo.

"Okay," Jack said, "let's go."

May, Marcus, and Theo exited the stairwell, while Jack held the corner, aiming his E-Rifle at the nearest policeman.

"Clear," Marcus said, taking the next sentry position.

Jack left cover and zoomed around to the others, just as one of the guards startled awake and shouted. "Over here!"

May put a Taser round in his chest, but it was too late. The damage was done.

Multiple lights swung towards Jack and the others.

"Run!" Jack hissed.

His boots squealed on the floor as he hustled for the stairs leading back up to the tower. Jack ducked his head, expecting to be peppered with gunfire. But none came.

I guess that answers that, he thought, feeling his adrenaline pumping. Unlike most people, Jack operated well under a heavy dose of adrenaline.

"Lock the door, lock the door, lock the door!" Jack yelled, last to enter the tightly winding stairwell.

As Jack leapt through, May quickly shut the door and threw the heavy deadbolt.

"What about inside the stairs?" Gemma asked from somewhere further ahead. "Will they shoot at us in here?"

"No, I think we're fine," Spencer replied. "It's clear that they value York Minster more than taking our lives."

"You think they'll let us leave, just like that?" May asked.

Jack wasn't so sure. They had assaulted four guards and defiled the entire undercroft. But they also exposed a previously unfound crypt and a beautifully preserved Roman temple.

Seems like a fair trade, Jack thought, willing the statement to be true.

"We can't take that chance," Marcus said.

"I agree," Jack said. "We need to tread softly."

Theo thought differently. "We could've taken them."

Jack was done. "The only reason we got out of there unharmed is *because* we didn't get into a firefight with non-lethals loaded in our weapons!"

"Which is precisely why we should be using real ammunition!" Theo countered.

Jack opened his mouth to remind Theo of the deal they made, but decided against it. There was no convincing the man otherwise. If he believed that killing these officers was the only way at stopping them, then that's what he believed.

Voices picked up behind Jack. They were far off, back through the door, but that didn't mean the police wouldn't eventually break through and catch up. Jack was gassed and moving slower than he would've preferred.

"*They* don't know we don't have non-lethal ammo loaded," Jack said, thinking aloud. "That could also be another reason why they aren't pushing us harder."

"The stairwell too," May added. "This would be a horrible place to get into a firefight."

"Yeah," Jack said, agreeing. Then he thought of something else. "But what happens once we're airborne?"

Marcus took over. "Zayn, you copy?"

"*I'm here, Marcus. What's the matter?*"

"Please tell me you're close."

There was a moment of silence before the pilot responded. "*Roger that. We're nearly on top of you.*"

"Copy. See you soon."

Jack sighed as they began their single-file march up the steps, plodding onward and upward. No one spoke again until they reached what Jack believed was their halfway point.

"Hey, guys?" It was Spencer. He was at the lead of the pack. "We're about to head back outside. Also, it's raining a lot harder now."

"What's your point?" Jack asked.

"Nothing. Just thought you'd like to know."

Jack wanted the man to shut up and keep moving, but he was too tired to chastise him openly. So, he cursed the man's existence internally, while focusing on the steps in front of him. Their steepness made it impossible to gain any momentum above a steady walk.

Jack was last to make it outside. He had completely forgotten about the middle leg of the climb, the outdoor part with the heavily slanted roofs to either side. And yes, Spencer had been correct. The steady rain from earlier on had been replaced by something close to a torrential downpour. But Jack didn't stop. Nor did he slow. He charged outside, following closely behind May.

The wind was howling around them too, swirling, threatening to pull them from their precipitous perch. The simple hip-high handrail wouldn't prevent someone from being tossed over the side. Jack still couldn't believe that this was the only way up to the Central Tower.

Not exactly the safest of designs, he thought. *And a complete lack of wheelchair access. How rude!*

"The one time we're up here, and we get stuck in the storm of the century!" Jack shouted.

May glanced back at him. "Technically, it's the second time we've been up here!"

Jack flashed her a look. "Don't you start!"

"Come on, you two. You're falling behind!"

Jack leaned around May to see that Marcus was right. The two of them were still thirty feet from the next stairwell. Jack could see the Legion general urging them forward with his hand.

Jack entered the next stairway but suddenly stopped. The *thrumming* of helicopter rotors picked up all around him. He leaned back outside, shielding his eyes as he looked up. A spotlight blinked to life, sliced through the storm, and ignited the ground ten feet in front of him. He jumped back just as the powerful beam swung his way.

He faced his compatriots and pointed up. "That's not our bird."

May dipped her chin. "That's why they haven't pursued us harder." She brought her eyes back up to Jack. "They already had a helicopter in the air."

The timing couldn't have worked out better. Zayn, the Legion's pilot, reported the same thing.

"We have traffic above York Minster. I can't get close enough for extract."

"Yeah," Marcus replied, "we know."

"What should I do?"

Jack was only half-listening. He stepped up to the door, staying just inside it while he mentally went over the roof's layout.

He groaned. "This is really going to suck."

"What is?" May asked.

Jack turned. "The slanted roofs. We can use them to get to ground level." Marcus was about to argue, but Jack cut him off. "Zayn, can you buy us some time, get the other helo to focus on you instead of us?"

The pilot took a second to reply, but when he did, it was with a question. *"I guess, sure. Why?"*

Jack faced the doorway. "Because we're leaving on foot. Wait for new extraction instructions."

"Jack?" Marcus asked, stepping up next to him. "Christos and Angeline can't make that jump."

"With all due respect, Marcus," Angeline said, placing a hand on Christos' shoulder, "yes, we can."

"You sure?"

Christos shrugged, wincing. "What's a little more pain?"

Jack gave him an exhausted laugh. "Yeah. You say that *now*…"

38

A second helo came roaring in, coming to within fifty feet of the police aircraft. The spotlight vanished from the doorway and the enemy chopper turned to face its foe. Jack didn't wait any longer. He hurried outside, gave the drop a second look before vaulting over the handrail and falling.

This is so stupid! he thought.

He tucked his E-Rifle into his chest, wrapped his arms around it, and braced for impact. It came in the form of a loud, hollow *bong*, but also a quick and slippery descent down a near-forty-five-degree slide.

"Oh, shit!" Jack shouted, genuinely surprised by how well his plan had worked. Unfortunately, there was nothing to slow him down or break his fall. "Damn…"

Jack zoomed off the rooftop and plowed straight into a second, hip-high, wall-handrail combination. He crumpled in on himself, absorbing most of the jarring impact with his legs. He moaned, feet straight up in the air at a ninety-degree angle. He stayed there, taking stock of his body. Thankfully, he hadn't been seriously injured.

"Jack?" May asked through their linked comms.

He gave the group a halfhearted wave. "Still alive, but be careful. There are no brakes."

Two seconds later, he heard a pair of *bongs*. Jack spun and sat up in time to see May and Marcus sliding down to him. They had smartly headed farther out into the maelstrom before jumping. By doing so, they would avoid colliding into Jack.

Jack got to his feet while watching something odd. Spencer was helping Gemma over the edge. He even went as far as dangling her lower before releasing his hold on her wrist. She flailed, spinning in midair. She hit the rooftop on her stomach instead of her back, and was propelled straight at Jack feet first.

"Aw, nuts."

Gemma was thrown back first into Jack's chest. He took her mass as solidly as he could. He wrapped his arms around her, stumbling back, and bounced off the handrail. His lower back took the entire force, which wasn't appreciated. Both of them fell hard. Jack let go, grabbing at his ruined lumbar area.

"Oh my God, Jack!" Gemma shouted. "I'm so sorry!"

He swiped at her leg, patting it. "It's fine. Everything…is fine."

May came to check on them as the rest of the Legion descended. From his lower vantage, Jack watched Christos and Angeline finish their death-defying exodus writhing in pain. Neither had suffered back or lower body injuries, however, the shockwave caused by their landing had still been damaging.

Last to go was Spencer.

"Come on, *Hard*wood!" Jack shouted, sitting up. "Get your ass in gear!"

Marcus stepped up next to May. "Get moving, Spencer, or you get left behind!"

That got through to the visibly terrified curator. He climbed over the railing and tried to dangle down lower, but all he did was compromise his grip and fall. Spencer landed in the worst position possible; headfirst and facing up.

"Catch him!" Marcus shouted, sliding into position with Theo.

Jack went to get up, but was held down by May. She was, of course, right. Jack doubted he could've helped all that much. He was still hurting from his *and* Gemma's falls.

The thickly built legionnaires absorbed Spencer's weight and momentum admirably, but were still driven backward. Spencer was much heavier than the petite Italian. Jack couldn't keep himself from smiling when the trio went down in a tangle of limbs and curses.

Gunfire erupted overhead. Jack couldn't see which helicopter was shooting which. It didn't matter, either.

Jack pointed at the next stairwell. It sat to the south, inside another Gothic spire, a cookie cut version of the one they had just exited. It also contained another hefty wooden door. Jack rushed for it, grabbing the handle and pulling.

Nothing.

"Christos, can you get us through?" he asked.

The Greek limped up next to Jack. "I'm sorry, no. My bag was buried in the cave-in."

"We can shoot out the lock," Theo suggested.

While certainly effective, the gunshot could also attract the attention of anyone within earshot.

"Can't risk it," Marcus said. "It might be heard. We need to find another way down."

Jack spun and looked across the perch, seeing an identical door. He didn't move to check it, knowing it would also be locked.

"We could jump?" Everyone looked at Gemma. She was leaning over the railing and looking down. She looked up to seven sets of stunned eyes. "What? It's only ten feet. Can't be much worse than that was." She pointed at their makeshift slides.

Jack turned west and gave the drop a look. She was right. It was only ten feet—the height of a basketball hoop. The next roof was flat, and it belonged to a two-story building attached to the cathedral, though Jack had no idea what was inside.

"It's a gift shop," Spencer said. He pointed to a square gray section further to the west. "That's a roof access hatch. We can get in through there."

"Then what?" May asked. "Are we just going to waltz right out the front door?"

Jack grinned. "That's exactly what we're going to do."

"Marcus, Theo, lower me down as low as you can. Once I'm there, Spencer, you and Theo lower Marcus down. Keep going until everyone is back together."

Marcus nodded. "Do it."

Jack tossed his leg over the railing, sitting on it for an uncomfortable moment. May put a hand on his shoulder.

"Be careful."

Jack smiled, not that she could see it. "Oh, you know *me!*"

A gust whipped around them, threatening to peel Jack off the rail. He clutched it with both hands and squeezed with his thighs, reminding him of that time he miserably failed to ride a mechanical bull. But this time, he held on, waiting for the wind to die down. When it did, he looked at Marcus, who again, nodded. Jack threw his other leg over the edge. Marcus grabbed one of Jack's wrists, while Theo secured the other. Now, he just had to hope that the legionnaires didn't purposely drop him.

They didn't.

Jack's ten-foot drop became a more-manageable six-foot drop.

"Now," Jack said.

They let go. Jack's balky knees and back managed the impact well enough. He stumbled away, but quickly got back into position beneath Marcus as he was lowered down. Jack could almost touch the man's feet now.

"Okay, let go," Jack said.

Theo and Spencer released their commander. Jack readied himself, somewhat catching Marcus as he landed. Then, both men looked up and waited for the others. May was next, followed by Gemma.

The four of them worked together to catch the injured Christos and Angeline. Jack had to admit, those two were troopers. They didn't complain once.

With them safely atop the gift shop, Jack, May, and Marcus returned to the wall and looked up. Spencer was going next this time.

Smart move, Jack thought, guessing that was Theo's choice. Allowing Spencer to move at his own pace had been a terrible decision before.

As he'd done earlier, the curator scrambled, kicking his feet when he didn't need to.

"Stop kicking!" Jack shouted. Spencer kicked again. "Oh, just drop him already!"

Theo did.

Spencer fell the rest of the way and was easily caught. He stood tall, but didn't look at Jack.

"Pansy," Jack mumbled.

"What?" Spencer asked.

Jack looked around. "Huh? Who said that!" He pointed up. "Don't look at me. We still have Theo to catch."

Spencer reluctantly turned away from Jack. The two of them, plus Marcus and May, gathered beneath Theo as he climbed over the railing. The door leading into the stairs burst open. Theo brought up his E-Rifle and unloaded a bevy of Taser rounds at whomever was rushing him. As a result of the bedlam, Theo teetered and fell. He ragdolled over the edge, plummeting into the foursome waiting below.

His chaotic landing flattened all four of his comrades.

Jack was on his side with a foot resting atop his head. He had no idea whose foot it was, either. He also felt a hard lump in his back. If he had to guess, it was a helmet.

Slowly, they separated. Jack was beyond shocked that no one had been hurt. He ducked as one of the helicopters swooped in low.

"Zayn!" Marcus shouted. "We're here, on top of the two-story building!"

The black aircraft slowed, then stopped with its landing struts level with the roof. "*I see you! Get in now!*"

The group rushed to the southern edge of the building. They needed to be careful. They were still a good twenty-plus feet above the ground.

Zayn got as close as he could. The rotors were dangerously close to the attached cathedral. If they touched it, the chopper would be a total loss.

"Go!" Marcus shouted, rushing forward. He leapt the four-foot gap, planted a foot on the strut, and rolled into the open side door.

Jack and May were close behind. Once inside, they helped in Gemma and Angeline. Theo didn't wait for Spencer or Christos this time. He quickly made it inside the aircraft.

Spencer didn't look so sure. Neither did Christos, for that matter. They gave themselves a little extra room, then both took off at a sprint. Christos stumbled, but Spencer caught his good arm and kept him moving.

Gunshots zipped past the two men. Spencer abandoned his aid of Christos, planted his foot on the ledge of the roof, and dove headfirst across the gap, clipping Angeline as he sailed by.

"You idiot!" Angeline hollered, groping at her injured shoulder.

Jack glanced to his right and up, spotting a flash of light. It had been from the muzzle of a rifle. The SWAT team had broken through the locked, wooden door.

Another volley of projectiles forced Christos to cover his head and shuffle his feet. Even with very little forward momentum, he still attempted the jump, missing the landing strut entirely. He fell, but somehow caught the strut with his hand! He dangled like Schwarzenegger for a second as the helo rose and banked away from York Minster. Additional gunfire peppered the helicopter.

The Legion leader didn't care. He leaned outside and reached for his man's hand. "Christos!"

"Get him inside. We gotta go!" Zayn shouted.

The police aircraft was nowhere to be seen. Jack wasn't sure what happened to it. He couldn't see any wreckage. It was possible that it was damaged but not severely enough to crash.

"Grab him!" Zayn shouted.

Dammit.

Jack joined Marcus on the strut. May held the back of his belt, while Theo held Marcus'. They each swiped at Christos' hand but missed. His other arm was tucked into his chest and immobile. If the man hadn't been injured, he wouldn't have been in this situation.

Damn you, Marcus, Jack thought. *You did this.*

Then, forty feet above the pedestrian-only footpath outside of Minster Yard,

Christos looked into Jack's eyes and fell.

39

Eagle County, Colorado, USA

"You've authorized a nighttime jump into Iraq?"

Raegor opened his eyes and met Eddy's. "I have, yes."

Both sat in his office. Raegor was still at his desk, a place he'd been for what felt like two straight days now. Eddy didn't look any better than he felt. He was rundown and, at this point, he doubted his body could handle another cup of coffee.

Eddy leaned forward with her elbows on her knees. Even though her face was currently frozen in a look of exhaustion, Raegor could also see the worry in her eyes.

"Solomon… You authorized an insertion into Iraq, with known terrorists working alongside a man who we both consider to be more than just another field agent."

Raegor glanced away. Ever since he and Jack had gone gallivanting into the Pacific in search of some mysterious island, he really had begun to think of Jack as more than his subordinate. During that chaotic mission, the two men had grown close and become friends.

The upcoming jump wasn't what bothered Raegor, it was the fact that Jack was involved.

May too, he thought, knowing what would happen to Jack if something awful happened to her. A man in Jack's mental condition would react as you'd expect—terribly.

Jack's PTSD had gone into a type of remission since joining up with TAC. Raegor was proud of him for several reasons, but none more than him getting his head right. Raegor couldn't count how many soldiers he'd once commanded that ended up in institutions or prison.

Or worse, he thought. *One too many funerals too.*

"Look, Eddy, I'm not asking for your approval. This situation stinks, we both know that." He leaned forward and folded his hands atop his desk. "I'm doing whatever I have to do to get our people home alive and not in an unmarked body bag."

Eddy sat back. "You know what'll happen if this goes sideways, and Jack and May are discovered, or worse, killed, right?" She lowered her eyes for a second, then brought them up to meet his. "You'll lose TAC. An international incident in enemy territory involving a military organization that doesn't technically exist, led by a dead man, will need a scapegoat."

"Exactly." Raegor grinned. "I'm already dead, Eddy. What could they possibly do to me that's worse than losing Jack?"

Eddy didn't argue. "What about the other side of this? Aren't your friends in JSOC or Army command, or whoever the hell let you do this… Aren't they in danger of going down too?"

Raegor pushed away from his desk and stood.

Eddy stood too. "Solomon? What aren't you telling me?"

"The deal I made to get this to happen... The only way I could was to offer my job as collateral."

"What!" Eddy was understandably shocked. Then she became enraged. "You can't do that! You had no right!"

"I have every right, Agent Marker!" he shouted back, making Eddy flinch. Raegor still owned a booming voice despite his near-fatal bout with cancer. "I alone have that right."

Eddy stepped closer to his desk and jabbed a finger at him. "But you didn't have the right to do it without talking to me first." She turned away, visibly upset. Raegor could hear her sniffing back tears. When she faced him again, they fell. "Ten years, Solomon. I've stood by your side for *ten years*. Never once have you done something like this, especially without me knowing."

Raegor circled around his desk and embraced his close friend and trusted number two. She hugged him back. When they parted, he explained.

"I didn't tell you because you would've gagged me, locked me up, and melted down the key."

She grinned. "Damn right I would've." She wiped her eyes. "And TAC? What happens if things do go sideways?"

Raegor couldn't look at her while he answered. "TAC, as well as her assets, will be seized and, if necessary, its employees will be re-tasked or let go completely. Apparently, unless I'm in charge, we aren't needed." He faced her again. "Would you believe that there are some who don't appreciate history as much as you and I do?"

"Really, you don't say?" She sighed. "What about Senator Wentz? What does he have to say about all this?"

"Officially, he knows nothing, per the usual. This is a sensitive matter, especially for a politician. Can you imagine what would happen if people knew that he knew?"

Eddy gazed up at him. "Yeah, I can... And what happens to you? It's not like you can return to active duty or be 're-tasked' to another division."

"I wouldn't, even if that was an option. Besides, aiding and abetting terrorists doesn't exactly look good on the ol' résumé."

"Oh," Eddy said, clearly understanding what he meant. "I see." She stood, showing remarkable resolve, not that it surprised Raegor in the least. "So, I guess we should get to work then."

"There's nothing we can do until we talk to Jack again."

Eddy smiled, stood, and placed a hand on her friend and mentor's shoulder. "That's not what I meant."

Raegor knit his eyebrows. "I don't follow."

"What I'm saying is, that we should get to work on covering your ass *if* this mission does, in fact, take a jog to the left." He held up a hand to stop her. She pushed it down. "You don't get to be the only hero here, Solomon. If there's a way to get you clear, then we're taking it, regardless of if you approve of it or not. First things first, we'll need to get you out of the country." A smirk slowly formed on her face. "And I think I know just the man for the job..."

All right, I'll bite, Raegor thought. He was honestly curious who Eddy had in mind.

He slipped his hands into his pockets. "Who?"

Eddy had the gall to snicker. "I think it's better you don't know—yet." She turned and headed for his office door.

"Eddy," he said sternly. But she didn't stop. She simply opened the door, then glanced back at him.

"Excuse me, but I have a call to make." Her eyes shifted to his desk, specifically his phone sitting on top of it. "And so do you."

She left.

Raegor looked at his phone, took a deep breath, then returned to his chair. He sat and dialed the number.

40

May couldn't believe what Raegor had put together! And what was even more impressive was the small amount of time in which he'd done it. They had a direct path into Babylon, to Saddam's palace.

After Jack had gotten off the phone with Raegor, he looked concerned, and not about the jump.

"What's wrong?" May had asked once they were in private.

They sat in a private jet, halfway to Nijmegen. Jack stared out the window. He was so absorbed with the view that May wasn't sure if he had heard her.

"It's Solomon," Jack replied, still looking outside. "He... He wasn't himself."

"How do you mean?"

Jack faced her. "Something's bothering him. Other than this." He motioned to the interior of the plane, but clearly meant their situation.

May put her hand on top of his. "Any idea what it could be?"

He shook his head. "No. But I could definitely hear it in his voice."

"What about Eddy. Can you call her and ask?"

"Nah." He patted her hand. "I doubt it's a big deal. Besides, I don't think Marcus will let me use the phone again."

May agreed about Marcus not letting them make another call. But she didn't agree with Jack about whatever was bothering Raegor not being a big deal. If it bothered Jack enough for him to mention it, then it must've been something.

May didn't pretend to know Raegor well. She had only met the man in person a few weeks ago, and only the one time. She had talked to him and Eddy several times on the phone, but had only physically been in their presence once.

So, as she'd done countless times before, she'd trust Jack's gut.

Something is definitely wrong.

41

Nijmegen, Netherlands

Similar to the city of York, Nijmegen was also founded by the Roman Empire. In 98 AD, Emperor Trajan built a fortress where modern-day Nijmegen stood today, stationing Legio X Gemina's 5,000 troops there. "The Twins' Tenth Legion" stayed put until 103 AD, when they were eventually reassigned and moved to the Roman military camp of Vindobona, modern-day Vienna, Italy.

Another Roman legion moved in not long after, Legio VIIII Hispana, the Ninth Spanish Legion. This was their last known, confirmed, location. The trail abruptly ended sometime around 120 AD.

"So, this is it, huh?" Jack asked, looking around the Waalhaven marina. "This is where the Ninth finally bit the bullet?"

No one answered.

He took his eyes off the one-thousand-foot-long harbor and faced his fellow looky-loo tourists. With him was May, of course, but also Marcus and Spencer. Theo was back at their private hangar getting their gear together with two new additions to their team.

Angeline didn't make the trip to the Netherlands due to her busted collarbone. Neither did Christos. The Greek demolitions expert, regrettably, fell to his death the night before while they made their escape. Jack dealt with death in a, sometimes, off-putting way. He battled stress and exhaustion in the same way.

He looked at the water again. "I'm sorry about Christos. I really did try to help him."

"I know." Marcus turned away. "Thank you for your efforts."

"Where's the entrance?" May asked, stepping up next to Jack.

"Sixteen hundred feet behind us," Spencer replied.

Jack looked at him. "Then why are we here?" He pointed at the murky water of the Dutch marina.

"Because," Marcus replied, "the pole's location is deep underground. When the Nijmegen fortress was torn down and replaced, a village was built directly on top of it. Then, a major metropolitan city, population 736,000."

"For years, we've tried to find another way in," Spencer continued. "But there just isn't a viable one."

"Then how do you know the pole—where it's held—still exists?" May asked.

"Because of down there," Marcus said, kneeling and eyeing the water.

Jack glanced at May. "It's underwater?"

"Technically, no," Spencer replied. "But the only way to get to the entrance nowadays is from underwater, rather, through an ancient storm drain." He shrugged out of his backpack and retrieved an iPad. He unlocked it and showed

Jack a single image. "One of our fellow legionnaires found this a couple decades ago."

The picture was black and white and grainy as hell. But even with the poor resolution, Jack could see it. The Roman number nine had been carved into a wall somewhere—the original VIIII, not the more modern IX. It was faint, but still legible.

"This is down there?" Jack asked, pointing at the water.

"It is," Spencer replied. "We never went in because we needed the eagle and base first. Plus, it's a protected site."

"The Dutch government knows about it?" May asked.

"Indeed. That's the other main reason we haven't gone in."

Jack also recalled them talking about why the Legion hadn't gone in to York Minster until last night. They had been afraid of damaging the entrance, as well as what might be hidden on the other side. It was a kind of measure-twice-cut-once situation.

Don't go in unless you're absolutely sure, Jack thought, respecting the decision.

"And see that?" Spencer asked, pointing to a blur of gibberish. "This is a warning."

"What's it say?" May asked.

Marcus stood. "To be careful with one's fortune."

"Fortune?" Jack asked. "Treasure?"

Marcus shook his head. "No. Fate."

"Wonderful..." Jack muttered, rubbing his face. "How deep is it here?"

"Fifteen feet, give or take," Spencer replied. "We'll be using scuba gear too, if you care to know."

Jack shrugged. "No biggy for me. I've clocked my fair share of hours beneath the surface, not that I enjoy open water."

"You don't like the water?" Spencer asked.

"*Open* water; oceans, lakes, even deep ponds. Pools are fine, though. If I can't see what's around me, I don't want to be in it."

Marcus eyed him. "I take it you aren't fond of sharks then?"

"I like them just fine, but you'll never catch me swimming with one." Jack faced him. "It ain't their fault, either. If you came strolling through my living room unannounced, I'd attack you too."

"When do we begin?" May asked, getting the conversation back on track.

"Nightfall," Marcus replied. "The lighting is poorest at the east side of the marina. We'll slip in there and swim over to the entrance."

Jack stepped up closer to the water's edge. "Where's the actual entry point?" he asked, trying to envision it.

"Ten feet below your toes," Spencer replied. "We'll need to cut through a grate, but other than that, the way should be clear."

"You see," Jack said, "that's a word I hate."

"*Grate?*" Spencer asked, looking confused.

Jack stood. "No, *should. Should* lacks clarity. A lack of clarity can lead to some pretty terrible happenings, especially when you're underwater."

"I have confidence that we'll be just fine," Marcus said.

Jack really wanted to say something about his *confidence* and how it got Christos killed, but he kept his mouth shut.

For now, Jack thought. *I can rattle his cage again later.*

"Besides the fact that the Ninth were stationed here before their disappearance, is there anything else we should know that could help us?" May asked, turning and facing the city.

Spencer tapped his chin and he thought. "Other than the imperator at the time being Trajan, and the fact that he was Hadrian's predecessor, no."

"Hadrian?" Jack asked. "The Mausoleum of Hadrian—Castel Sant'Angelo?"

"The same," Spencer replied.

Marcus held up a hand. "That's enough. Let's head back." He checked his watch. "We have five hours until we head out. I suggest we use that to rest and prepare."

Jack glanced at May and yawned. "You won't get an argument out of me. I could definitely use a nap."

42

It was after midnight when Jack and the others arrived back at the Waalhaven marina. With them were Marcus, Theo, and Spencer. Two more legionnaires waited in two separate vehicles down the road. They would act as lookouts, and the group's de facto getaway drivers. Jack prayed that they'd end up being only their drivers and that there'd be no "getting away" from anyone.

Gemma had been left behind back at the hangar housing their plane. Jack was honestly pretty surprised when Marcus had announced they'd be using one. Apparently, the Legion was wealthier than he'd originally thought. Thinking back, it shouldn't have shocked him. If the guys really had been around for the better part of two millennia, then it would make sense if they had accumulated a vast fortune.

"Ready?" Marcus asked, kneeling in the shadows to the east.

Several businesses lined the water here, butting up right against the water's edge. The five-man team was currently taking advantage of the cover the buildings gave them. Six lampposts lined the 500-foot, concrete shoreline. Their reach was limited, and the spaces between as dark as the sky itself.

"Yeah, we're ready," Jack replied.

He gave May one last look before slipping on his full-face dive mask. The best part about these models was the comms system. The quintet would be able to speak to one another clearly while underwater.

All of them held high-powered spotlights too. Jack had wanted to test it on the water's surface but decided against it since it would give their position away. Another mentionable accessory was the glowing red LED attached to each person's ankle. Once activated, they'd be able to see one another as they swam, which was good, because the water was really dark, as most marina water was.

At least the ones I've been to, Jack thought. Some were downright nasty.

Once they were all in their masks, Marcus checked their comms. "Comms check."

"I have you," Jack said.

"I do too," May added.

Spencer gave Marcus a thumbs up. "Same."

Theo didn't reply.

Marcus touched his arm. "Theo, do you copy?"

"I do," the quieter man replied. "But I do not think they should be here." He tightened the straps of his waterproof pack. "We do not need them."

"I'll be the judge of that." Marcus sat, and swung his finned feet over the edge. The water's surface was another foot or two beneath them. "Let's go."

Everyone sat next to one another. Then, one by one, they each lowered themselves into the water as quietly as they could. Jack entered with minimal noise, as did May. Spencer was a little more careless with his entry, but not

Marcus and Theo. They moved as silently as Jack and May had. That told Jack, right away, that Spencer wasn't as seasoned as the rest of them.

Hopefully, he doesn't freak out.

They stayed together and sank lower. Once they were ten feet beneath the surface, Marcus powered on his handheld light. The instrument possessed a handgrip similar to a pistol. Jack found his tethered to his waist. He grabbed at it for a moment, feeling a slight restriction in his movements thanks to his wetsuit.

Jack hated wetsuits. Still, it was better than nothing.

The water was incredibly cold on his exposed neck and hands. Thankfully, the rest of his body was covered. He still felt the cold, but it was much more manageable than if he wasn't wearing a wetsuit.

"Okay," Marcus said, "follow closely and don't wander off. It's very easy to get turned around down here."

"We know," Jack said. "This isn't our first rodeo."

Marcus stared him down. "Activate beacons."

The five divers reached down to the device strapped to their ankles, switching them on.

In the aura of their combined light, Marcus glanced at the number two. "Lead the way."

Theo nodded and got moving.

Jack pictured their position from above. Their entry point was supposed to be along the southern embankment, ten feet below the surface.

Four hundred feet later, Theo slowed. Jack continued around the larger man, seeing the grate they were supposed to cut through.

"Wait here," Theo said, kicking forward. As he swam, he undid two buckles along his left thigh, then quickly ignited a marvel of engineering.

An underwater blowtorch.

Fire in the water, Jack thought, watching intently.

Jack stared in awe and watched the legionnaire expertly slice through the iron bars. While he worked, Jack took in the entrance itself—its size. It was going to be a tight fit with their dive tanks, but even a man of Theo's girth should fit okay. The biggest problem wasn't the circumference, it was what it would feel like to be in a metal tube while underwater.

Jack looked at Spencer.

"What?" the curator asked.

"You gonna be okay with this? I'm asking for everyone."

Spencer turned away. "I'll be fine."

"Because, if you're not," Jack pushed, "you could easily kill someone."

"I said, I'll be fine!" Spencer twisted his body to the left and faced Jack. "Are you deaf?"

Jack tapped the side of his mask. "No… I've been talking to you this whole time."

A muffled *clunk* announced the successful removal of the grate. Theo let it drop to the bottom of the marina, reattached the extinguished blowtorch to his leg, then headed inside.

"You two next," Marcus said, shining his light on Jack and May.

Jack nodded, then held out his hand to May. "You first."

May eyed him as she swam past. She didn't say anything. May just met Jack's eyes and kept swimming. He waited for her feet to disappear before working himself inside. Jack paid close attention to the connections on his tank. If he bashed one the wrong way, there was a chance he'd cut off his air.

Once Jack was totally inside, he looked over his shoulder and watched Spencer haphazardly follow him in.

"What?" the Englishman asked, noticeably annoyed with the attention Jack was giving him.

"Oh, nothing," Jack replied, facing forward and pulling at the water.

He caught up with May in no time, falling into rhythm behind her and Theo. Jack didn't confirm whether Marcus was at the back of the pack. Jack knew he would be. Instead of instigating unnecessary conversation, Jack kept quiet and concentrated on his breathing.

The five divers slowed as they neared the end of the line. The tunnel ended at a large, square, manmade chamber. As soon as Jack aimed his light up, he saw that the room wasn't entirely flooded.

He kicked for the surface. When his head broke through, he saw the wall.

"Huh," he said, "kind of uninspiring if you ask me."

The wall was just a wall, maybe eight feet tall and wide. The only blemish on it besides years of wear was their VIIII and the mysterious warning about one's fortune. May surfaced next to him, looking straight up when she did. Jack had been so focused on the wall that he hadn't taken in the ceiling. Directly above him was another grate, but this one belonged to a modern drainage system.

"Where are we?" he asked.

"We are below the ruins of a Roman temple and bathhouse," Spencer explained. "What you see is a drain at its center."

May looked at the curator. He was wading next to them, as were Marcus and Theo. "Why didn't we enter through here?" She pointed at the grate.

"Because the ruins are a popular tourist stop," Marcus replied. "We couldn't risk being seen."

Jack didn't argue. He brought his eyes back down to the wall. "What about that?"

"The symbol has been here for a very long time, though we're not sure how long, exactly."

"You don't know?"

Spencer shook his head. "No. Best guess is since World War II."

"Why then?" May asked.

Marcus took over. "The Legion used the war as cover to pick up its search for clues of the surrounding area. It would only make sense that it was then."

"And the text?" Jack asked.

Marcus faced him. "Longer."

"And the government knows about it?"

He nodded. "Yes. But because of its location, in the sewers, it is not widely known or promoted."

Jack gently patted the surface of the water. "Can't imagine why." He turned and faced the wall again. "So, I take it we're going through that wall?"

"We are," Marcus replied. "Theo, if you would?"

Theo nodded and swam over to the wall in question. Jack was surprised when the big man hoisted himself mostly out of the water. He couldn't see anything from here, but there was apparently a ledge of some kind beneath him. Theo slid off his rugged backpack, knelt, and quickly unzipped it. Jack knew an explosives kit when he saw one. He looked up, thinking about what was above them.

"Is that safe?" he asked.

"Are demolitions ever safe?" Marcus asked back.

Jack gave him the win. "Touché."

"We only need a hole big enough to slip through," Marcus explained. "It should hold up just fine."

There's that word again.

To be safe, Jack backed up as much as he could. He wanted to be as far away from the detonation as possible. Plus, if shit really did hit the fan, he could go under and escape. May smartly stayed close. Spencer looked back at them, then returned his attention to the wall. He must've thought better of it, because he also joined Jack and May.

Marcus did not move away. He stayed put at the center of the space, staring at the wall the entire time. Even after Theo had finished wiring it and re-entered the water, Marcus didn't move. He just waded in place, in the middle of the square room. Theo swam to his side, holding a small, clear detonator in one hand, keeping it above the surface of the water.

Without looking at his man, Marcus simply said, "Do it."

Beep.

The space rumbled. Dust fell. The water shook, hit by the shockwave of the explosion. Jack felt it in his head and chest, though it wasn't nearly as powerful as the one beneath York Minster—before everything collapsed.

Jack Reilly, Historical Wrecking Ball, he thought, mentally blocking out everything he'd destroyed since joining up with the Tactical Archaeological Command.

As the dust settled, the five explorers pushed forward. Marcus and Theo climbed up to the ledge first. Jack wasn't too far behind when the other men stuck their heads inside the fresh hole. Jack sat in waist-deep water thanks to the ledge. He grabbed the back of his mask to remove it but was stopped.

"I wouldn't do that," Marcus said.

Jack twisted his upper body around and looked up at him. "Why not?"

Marcus faced the hole again. "Because you're going to need it."

Jack climbed to his feet and squeezed between the two legionnaires. What he saw gave him the chills. It was another network of Roman catacombs. The trio stood at the top of a tall stairway leading down, further underground...and it was flooded.

The entire thing was flooded.

43

Out of everything Jack had seen since his first mission with TAC, this was by far the oddest, most bone-chilling one yet. Jack still couldn't believe it. He was swimming through a second network of catacombs. And like the crypt beneath York Minster, this one was populated too.

Some of the stone sarcophagi were still sealed and in the place of honor within the shelves to either side of Jack. Others were not. Lids were open, and the weathered, sodden remains of the dead were everywhere, preserved by the chilling temperature of the water. The water inside was much colder than it had been out in the submerged tunnel.

Should've worn gloves, Jack thought, opening and closing his hands.

Bones littered the floor. Thankfully, there were no bodies floating around aimlessly. That would've really ruined Jack's day.

"You okay?" May asked.

She and Jack swam at the back of the pack this time. Spencer was ten feet ahead of them with Marcus and Theo another twenty feet ahead of the curator.

Jack glanced at her. "I'm cold, and if this place is as big as the last, we'll be down here for a while."

"There's no reason to believe these catacombs are built in the same manner as the ones in York," Spencer said.

"Why's that?" Jack asked.

"Well, these would've been designed by different people. Nijmegen wasn't founded until 98 AD. That's twenty-seven years after Eboracum. Also, Nijmegen wasn't as prominently mentioned in history as Eboracum was, so one would think that the empire wouldn't spend as much money here."

Jack looked around. "This don't look like no low-budget tomb to me."

"Compared to some, it is," Marcus confirmed. "While impressive, this is nothing compared to some of the others I've seen."

"How are we on oxygen?" May asked.

Her question spooked Jack for a split-second. He hadn't even thought to check.

"As long as we don't waste any more time," Theo replied, "we'll be fine."

Typically, in hostage situations like this, wasting time was the thing to do. Wait it out long enough and devise a plan while doing so. But not now. Jack didn't feel like drowning today.

That feels more like a Monday thing.

"We have an opening up ahead," Marcus announced.

Spencer glanced over his shoulder. "See, told you. Definitely not the same design."

Jack rolled his eyes, churning his legs a little faster now. He'd been conserving his energy, but the prospect of more open space, and fewer bones—maybe even getting out of the water—was too much.

Marcus and Theo entered first, both of their lights sweeping around what Jack could tell was a vast cavern.

"It's another *Mithraeum*," Marcus announced. "Though much larger than the one in York."

"How much larger?" Jack asked, nearly close enough to see.

He stopped kicking and floated the rest of the way, coming to a stop next to Marcus. The Legion general gave him an astonished look. "*Much* larger."

Jack's mouth fell open. "Whoa. You ain't kiddin'."

The team floated in place atop an overlook. Unlike the temple back in York, this one's ceiling was mostly at the same height as the catacombs behind them. The floor, however, dropped away another one hundred feet. Jack's light barely made it to the bottom, which honestly surprised him.

"Water's much clearer here," he said, spotting something below. "Hey, guys, a little more light?"

May, Marcus, Theo, and Spencer added theirs to his. A large square altar stone could be seen in the center of the room. It was much bigger than the one in York too, and like its brother, this one was also built on top of a raised platform.

"Let's move," Marcus said, starting off. He didn't dive, but instead, just made his way into the middle of the cavernous space.

Jack was right behind him. He tilted his spotlight to the left and discovered multiple rows of stone pews. Jack followed the circular arrangement and found other pews encompassing the altar.

"There's enough seating for hundreds of people," Jack said.

"More if you include standing room," Spencer added. "This is unprecedented."

May swept her light around the temple. "Thought so."

"What'd you find?" Jack asked, flipping himself right-side up. May's light was pointed back at the wall, to the right of the overlook.

"Stairs," May replied. "Was wondering how they got down there," she glanced at Jack, "unless, of course, they had gills."

Jack snickered.

"There's more over here," Theo said, pointing his light at the opposite side of the overlook.

"I don't get it," Spencer said, more to himself. "Why isn't any of this recorded?" He spun and faced Marcus. "We knew something was here, but never did I imagine *this* is what we would find."

It was clear that Marcus didn't know, either. He glanced at Jack. "Yes, well, some secrets have their own secrets."

"Down there," May said, pointing.

The four men followed her outstretched hand to where the back wall and floor met. They each added their lights to hers. A tunnel entry became clear as day in their combined beam.

"Think that's it?" Jack asked.

"It must be," Marcus replied. "I don't see anything else." He turned and faced Spencer. "Thoughts?"

The curator nodded. "It's worth a shot. Even if this place wasn't built by the same exact people, I'd imagine their construction practices would still be close."

"Thinking there's another hidden door?" Jack asked.

"I do," Spencer. "Again, that's *if* the builders here followed the York design."

The divers angled themselves down and kicked for the bottom. The pressure was starting to become a problem for Jack. He wasn't in danger of freaking out or anything, but it was becoming uncomfortable for him.

They reached the bottom just as Jack was thinking of turning back. He thanked Mithras when he spotted stairs heading back up toward the surface.

"Very promising," Spencer said.

Jack edged closer. "Yeah, that all depends on what's at the end."

"After you, Jack," Marcus said, staying put.

Jack sighed and spun around. "Oh, so now I'm leading, huh?" He didn't argue with the man. Jack only looked at May and tipped his head back toward the tunnel. "Shall we?"

May silently kicked forward and followed Jack in. The steps angled up aggressively.

"How do you think it flooded?" she asked.

"Not sure. Could be a number of reasons," Jack replied. "But based on where we are, I'm going to say this is all river water that slowly made its way inside after this place was abandoned."

"Or," Marcus added from somewhere behind Jack, "it could've been flooded intentionally. Remember the bodies we saw in the Mouseion temple?"

"How could I forget?" Jack replied. "But yeah, that's also a possibility."

"You think the Mouseions flooded this place to keep it from being found?" Spencer asked.

Jack bit his lip and nodded. "Yeah, actually. Now that I think about it, that's the obvious answer. If this place did flood, who would have the technology to reach it?"

"No one," May replied. "At least, not until diving equipment was invented."

Jack's light hit what looked like a pane of glass. It wasn't one, but to Jack, that's what a beam of light looked like when it struck the bottom of the water's surface.

"We've got a void," he announced.

"Air?" Spencer asked.

"No clue. Just because there's no water, doesn't mean there's breathable air."

"He's right," Marcus said. "Many caves are full of CO_2."

"How do we check?" Spencer asked.

Jack swam while he thought. Then it dawned on him. "Anyone have a lighter?"

"A lighter?" Spencer asked.

Jack's theory was sound. It was a simple one too.

Fire can't exist without oxygen.

"I have one in my pack," Theo replied.

Jack's head broke the surface at the same time as his light. When it did, he saw that the water stopped perfectly even with the floor of another temple. This one was much smaller, and seemed to be a private prayer room of some kind. It also lacked any of the more refined qualities of the other temples Jack had seen recently. In reality, this was merely a cave. He estimated the circular space's size to be roughly twenty feet across with a twelve-foot-tall ceiling.

One by one, the others surfaced alongside him. As they did, Jack took in the temple's only occupant.

"Well, hello again, Mithras."

44

Instead of a grand painting of the Roman god, there was a well-preserved, nevertheless simple, ten-foot-tall statue of him.

"It must be here," Marcus said softly, staring at the figure.

Jack looked back at the guy and saw the manic look in his eyes return.

I wonder what Babylon will do to him? he thought.

"Theo?" Marcus asked.

The Legion lieutenant slid out of the water and set his backpack down on the dry floor. He smartly kept his mask on while he did. Jack was secretly hoping he forgot, inhaled pure CO_2, and fell unconscious.

Oh, well. A boy can dream.

Theo pulled out a classic Zippo lighter and flicked open its top. With a quick snap of his thumb, he ignited it.

The flame burned bright.

"That's a good sign...right?" Spencer asked.

"Only one way to find out," Jack said, trusting his gut. He removed his dive mask, keeping it close, just in case. He inhaled and smiled. "We're clear. It's dank, but still breathable."

He got his feet beneath him and climbed out of the water, ditching his air tank as he did. Jack stretched his back, still eyeing the statue.

Marcus stepped up bedside him, also without his mask and tank. "What do you bet the statue is really a door."

Jack glanced at him. "I'd bet the farm on it."

They looked away from one another and marched forward. The statue wasn't as large as the one of Clio, and nor was it as defined.

Not that it matters.

He looked over the statue carefully, trying to spot a place for both the eagle and base to go. He checked the pedestal first, but found nothing out of the ordinary.

"Think it's another pressure plate?" Jack asked.

"I'd imagine so, yes," Marcus replied. "Although, I don't see anything that supports it."

May joined them and looked up. "What about up there?"

Jack and Marcus craned their heads back. The two men had been so focused on the pedestal that they hadn't given Mithras himself much attention. The god was standing in a regal posture, spine straight, shoulders back, chin up. His left hand gripped a scepter. Its bottom end touched the ground. But the god's right hand was out in front of him, and his palm was turned up.

"That's it," Marcus said. "The eagle and base go in Mithras' hand."

Jack and Marcus turned to find Theo already digging into his pack for the required items. He handed them to his superior who, in turn, took them without acknowledging the man's effort.

Jack took the opportunity to poke the bear a little. "What can I say, he's a bit jazzed." He even went as far as to softly slap Theo on the arm. "Still, you're a good pack mule."

"Lift me," Marcus said, standing directly beneath Mithras' outstretched hand. When no one moved, Marcus snapped his head around and shouted, "Lift me!"

Theo and Spencer got moving. Jack and May stepped back, letting the legionnaires do all the work for once. May threaded her freezing left hand into Jack's right, and the duo waited and watched.

Marcus stepped into the other men's clasped hands and was lifted skyward. Jack's lack of effort didn't go unnoticed.

"You're enjoying this, aren't you?" Spencer asked, annoyed.

Jack grinned. "You know I am."

Marcus wobbled as he was lifted higher. "Focus, Spencer."

Spencer shot Jack a venomous stare before turning his full attention back to the task at hand. He and Theo leaned back and lifted Marcus higher. Once Marcus was nearly at eye level with Mithras' upturned hand, he gently placed the stacked eagle and base in it, shifting it around until it clicked into place.

The result was instantaneous.

The god's arm rotated down twenty percent at the shoulder, activating an ancient door lock as it did.

Jack thought back to when they unlocked the back wall off the *Mithraeum*. The lock had simply lowered into the ground to reveal a hip-high tunnel entrance. But that's not what happened here. In this case, Mithras was dragged backward by some unseen force. Marcus was kept aloft while everything unfolded. All three legionnaires were glued in place.

Mithras, the eagle, and the base continued backward until they entered another room. Jack and May followed the statue with their lights.

"Come on," Jack said, pulling May forward. He wanted to see what was on the other side before the Legion goons could.

The pair entered the newly formed doorway, slowing as they did. Jack inspected the four-foot-wide, ten-foot-long passage. Seeing nothing of note, he and May continued through. As for Mithras, he had stopped six feet past the exit point. To enter the next room, they had to step around the god.

Jack went left.

May went right.

They rejoined one another around the back of Mithras, shining their lights out over the next space.

Jack's shoulders fell. "C'mon, man. Really?"

"What is it?" Marcus asked, hurrying to catch up. He stumbled to a stop next to Jack.

Jack ran his hands through his wet, matted-down hair. "Nothing good."

"You aren't kidding," May said, looking at Jack.

Marcus stepped forward, leaving the others behind as he took in the next space. Something inside Jack told him to stay put, that something was wrong. The only thing in the entire one-hundred-foot-wide cavern was an odd circular object built into the center of it.

"Marcus, stop," Jack said, grabbing his shoulder. "I don't like this."

"Do not tell me what to do," Marcus said. "Not when we are so close."

Jack shrugged. "Fine. You dying would definitely even the odds for May and me."

The Legion general, turned and glared at Jack. "What is it that bothers you?"

Jack stepped closer to him. "The floor."

Marcus faced the center of the cave again, and aimed his light at the floor. It was recessed below a five-foot-high, outer ring of stone that was itself four feet wide. The five-man exploratory team stood on a landing of sorts. It overlooked the floor, one that was constructed of countless stone tiles. Each one had been carved from the same material as the cave itself and measured roughly three feet by three feet. Everyone shined their lights on the floor, showing off hundreds, maybe even thousands, of them. And each and every single one was covered in a sign of the zodiac.

Between them and the floor were a dozen stone steps leading down.

What the hell is going on? Jack thought.

"And that?" May asked, focusing her light's beam on the circular object built into the center of it all.

To Jack, it looked like the "Big Wheel" from the long-running television game show *The Price is Right*. He doubted that's what it really was, but that's what it looked like to him. He thought back to all the water behind him, deciding it could be a water wheel of some kind.

"It's a wheel," Spencer said.

"Really?" Jack asked. *Huh. I guess I was right, after all.*

. Theo's light landed on a stone support on the left side of the vertically installed wheel. "He's right. Look."

Unfortunately, they couldn't see the other side of the wheel from where they were standing.

Spencer looked around, shining his light over the tunnel leading back to the flooded prayer room. "Up here," he said, finding something.

Jack turned and immediately recognized the text as Ancient Greek. "Well, I guess we know who built this room."

He gazed over his shoulder at Marcus.

The Legion leader nodded his agreement. "The Mouseions."

"What's it say?" May asked.

Spencer cleared his throat. "To control one's fortune is to deny one's self the most basic principle offered to mankind."

"And what's that?" Jack asked.

Marcus faced the wheel. "That we are never truly in control."

With that, he descended onto the first step. As soon as his foot struck, the entire cave rumbled and the statue of Mithras slid back into place before anyone could react with anything other than confusion.

"Dammit, Marcus, what are you doing?" Jack snapped.

"Beginning the test of fate." He faced them, holding out his hands. "Don't you see. This place has been dedicated to the Greek god, Tyche. In Rome, she was Fortuna, the goddess of fortune, personification of luck. And that..." he said, turning and aiming his light on the wheel.

Jack finished his explanation with a sigh. "The honest-to-God *Wheel of Fortune.*"

45

"Okay, guys," May said, "what are we doing here?"

Jack pushed aside the rage he felt for Marcus and focused on the situation. "We defeat the trap."

"How?" Spencer asked.

Jack pointed at the wheel. "That. It's gotta be the wheel."

"And the zodiac symbols on the floor?" May asked.

"They're connected to Fortuna," Spencer replied. "The Wheel of Fortune was prominent during the Ptolemaic dynasty, back when it belonged to Tyche."

"Ptolemy?" Jack asked. "Him, again?"

"It seems so," Spencer replied. "And with both the zodiac and Fortuna being linked to fate…"

Jack's shoulders fell. "It's a game of chance."

"A game?" May asked. "Does this look like a game to you?"

"You know what I mean!" Jack yelled back. "It means there isn't any method. There's no pattern. It's all about blind luck."

"It's another Mouseion test," Marcus said, barely speaking loud enough for anyone to hear. "From the beginning, this has been about worth. Are we worthy enough to proceed."

Spencer nodded. "He's right. The Greeks and Romans believed in fate and luck as much as anyone."

"Wonderful." Jack gazed out at the wheel. "So, what, we spin and hope we don't land on 'bankrupt?'"

"What are you talking about?" Spencer asked.

Even May looked confused.

"Oh, right," Jack said, "it's an American thing. There are a couple of game shows with wheels that spin. Both are games of luck. *The Price is Right* has the vertical wheel. *Wheel of Fortune* doesn't, oddly. And…" Everyone turned and stared at him. "You know what, never mind."

"A game," May said. "Okay, sure, we turn it. Then what?"

"And to which symbol?" Spencer asked.

Theo stepped forward, looking very sure of himself. "It's Aries."

"The god of war?" Jack asked.

Theo shook his head. "No, the zodiac symbol."

Jack spotted one twenty feet from him. He squinted at Theo. "How do you know that?"

Theo's eyes darted away, as if he was uncomfortable with the answer.

"Theo?" Marcus asked.

The bigger man met Jack's stare. "Because, Aries lives for competition and will do anything to succeed."

Jack's hands found his hips. "You read horoscopes?"

Theo rolled his eyes. "The point is, that we need to believe we will succeed for us to do so. More importantly, we also have to believe in whoever goes out there and spins that wheel."

All eyes turned on Jack.

He raised his hands and flopped them down to his side. "Aw, what the hell? Why not?" He looked at Theo. "So, Aries, huh?"

Theo nodded. "Its symbol is typically that of a ram's head."

"Copy that," Jack said, turning and heading out onto the recessed floor. Footsteps came up behind him. He didn't have to look to see who it was. He knew it was May. "What are your thoughts?"

"Sounds pretty ridiculous to me."

"Just *pretty* ridiculous?" Jack asked, getting a smile out of her.

The pair made it to the wheel and stood in awe of it. Up close, it was so much more spectacular than back by the exit.

"What do you see?" Marcus asked, shouting across the fifty-foot expanse.

"Why don't you come out and see for yourself?" Jack asked, knowing the man wouldn't risk it.

Jack studied a raised area around the wheel. The same zodiac symbols encompassed the wheel, twelve in all.

"Hang on..." Jack said, thinking.

"What is it?"

He pointed at the ring of symbols. "I think we've got this all wrong. There isn't a predetermined outcome. We're playing by Vegas rules here." Jack looked up at the fifteen-foot-tall wheel. "It's a game of luck."

"With a one-in-twelve chance," May added. She faced Jack. "I don't think we should do this. There has to be another way out."

"What's wrong?" Marcus asked.

"Besides everything?" Jack replied, still staring into May's eyes.

May turned and explained. "We think it's a game of chance, not trust."

Marcus hurried down the steps. He was closely followed by Theo and Spencer, though the curator wasn't as quick as Theo. Spencer hung back a little, clearly frightened by the game board.

And that's what you are, isn't it? Jack thought.

Marcus and Theo stopped within five feet of the raised ring of zodiac symbols. Spencer, foolishly, strode right up to it and reached out his hand to touch one.

"Don't!" everyone else shouted together.

Spencer flinched and snapped his hand back into his chest. He gave the group a sheepish look then stepped away.

Jack gave the other four members of his team his attention. "We're being made to choose which symbol to bet on."

"What's the currency?" Spencer asked.

"Our lives," Jack replied. "And no, I have no idea how many spins we'll get."

"Could be just the one," Marcus suggested.

Jack nodded. "That it could."

"No, I don't think so," May said. "A one-in-twelve chance is hardly proving your worth. That doesn't feel right based on what the Mouseion builders have shown us."

"And the symbols on the floor?" Spencer asked.

"Not sure," Jack replied. "But I think it's best if you all wait up there." He pointed back to the top of the short staircase.

May stepped forward. "Sorry, Jack, but this is a two-person job." She moved closer to the ring of symbols. "My guess is that someone has to stand on a symbol while another person spins the wheel."

"Yeah," Jack said, looking at his feet, "that was my guess too. I was going to stand on the closest one to the wheel and spin it too."

May smiled. "Thought you could do this without me, huh?"

Jack shrugged. "It was worth a try."

"Which symbol?" Spencer asked. "If this is nothing but luck, it doesn't really matter which one, does it?"

"You were born in July, right?" May asked, looking at Jack.

"Yeah, why?"

"Because...I'm placing my bet." May eyed the ring and hopped up onto a crab symbol—the symbol of Cancer. The room rumbled again. "Better get spinning, Jack."

The legionnaires took off running across the fifty-foot-wide expanse. While they ran, the harsh rumbling became nothing more than a soft vibration. Still, whatever May had triggered was active beneath their feet.

If I were a betting man, I'd say more spikes. Jack gazed up at the wheel. *Oh, I guess I am.*

He climbed over the ring of symbols and up onto the platform displaying the real-life Wheel of Fortune. The vertical water-wheel-looking-thing contained carved zodiac symbols on each end and, as expected, there were twelve. Two ionic columns held the wheel in place and there was a post connected to each that ran through the center of the wheel. There was even a metal arrow constructed in the shape of a simple triangle. In Jack's head, that was the selector on the game show wheel.

He looked over his right shoulder, at the legionnaires. The trio had made it back to the *safety* of the overlook. "Ready?"

Spencer replied with a "No."

Jack understood the dread that was laced in the man's voice. It was currently sitting in Jack's gut.

He looked over his left shoulder, giving May a sorrowful look. "Ready?"

She nodded. "I trust you, Jack."

Jack let out a long breath. "That makes one of us."

He gripped the side of the wheel and spun.

46

The wheel spun surprisingly well, considering how old it was. Jack watched it finish two whole revolutions before slowing. As it did, he tried to track the Cancer crab, but lost it once it disappeared out of view. He spotted it again, but his heart sank. It continued past the triangle indicator, ending up on the other side once the wheel came to a stop.

On the Aries ram.

"Son of a bitch!" Jack cursed, kicking the base of the wheel.

That's when he remembered that he was wearing nothing but a pair of water shoes. He groaned in agony, but quieted when the cave groaned even louder. He forgot all about his big toe and turned to watch the sections of flooring depicting the ram's head fall away, released by some unseen mechanism.

"Oh, crap," May said, reading his mind. "Jack?" She faced him.

"I know," Jack replied, not knowing what else he *could* say.

"Aries, really?" Spencer yelled.

Jack stood tall and looked his way. "Hey, numbnuts, you are more than welcome to switch places with me."

"What are you going to do, Jack?" Marcus' question had been sincere.

He shrugged. "Nothing to do but keep spinning."

"Should you pick another symbol?" Marcus asked.

"No," Jack replied. "Resetting the odds is never the right answer. The way I see it is that we now have one less wrong answer."

"We are also now short of a potential right answer too," Spencer added.

Jack stared him down, getting the man to shut his yap. "When we're done here, I'm going to throat punch you."

Theo kept quiet, per usual, and knelt. He aimed his spotlight into the nearest trap hole to him, looked around for a bit, then stood.

"Care to share with the class?" Jack asked.

"Thirty-foot drop into water," Theo replied. "Fall, and you drown."

Jack turned back to the wheel and gripped its edge. "Good to know."

He yanked it downward as hard as he could, hoping he could get an extra half-turn out of it. If he did, the Cancer crab would end up on the right side.

Turned out that he had pulled too hard.

The crab ended up two symbols beneath the indicator, landing on a rudimentary bow and arrow. He pictured the constellations in his mind's eye.

Sagittarius?

Jack didn't know for sure, and honestly, he didn't care. You didn't have to know what they meant for them to match up. Every section of flooring depicting a bow and arrow fell. Theo, once again, pointed his light into one of the trap holes.

"The water's rising."

Jack's face fell. "That's not good... So, the water rises with every failed attempt. One too many and this entire place floods."

Marcus said something to Theo and pointed at the blocked exit. Theo stepped away and dropped his pack in front of it.

"Let me guess…" Jack said, not having to finish his question.

"We need to try," Marcus replied.

Jack waved him off. "No, I agree. Blow the shit out of it." He looked over at May. She looked even more scared than at any point when they had been in Nepal. "Hey," Jack said, getting her attention, "we'll be fine." He smiled. "Do you still trust me?"

She nodded. "You, yes. It's this place I don't trust."

Jack gripped the wheel for the third time. "Ditto."

He pulled, only, this time, he did so at half-power. Jack watched in agony as the wheel trickled around.

"Jack, what happens if the wheel doesn't complete a full rotation?"

He was concerned with that too. Jack glanced over his shoulder at May, but didn't have an answer.

The wheel stopped one symbol away from Cancer, but on the wrong side of the crab. The wheel had only finished most of a rotation, not the entire thing. The cave shook as *two* different symbols fell away.

"Virgo and Taurus," Spencer called out. "What happened?"

"Nothing!" Jack shouted back. "Doesn't matter."

"Um, Jack," Marcus said, kneeling and looking down, "we don't have much time."

Dammit, Jack thought, aiming his own light below. He could just see the top of a raging body of water. He guessed it was being fed in from the flooded *Mithraeum*. It could've also been coming in from the Waal River too.

"Shut up and focus."

"What?" May asked.

Jack waved her off. "Nothing." He caught her staring at him, and he put on the best fake smile he could. "Don't worry about it, babe. We got this." She nodded, visibly shaking. Jack's face grew more serious. "We got this."

May wiped her eyes and inhaled deeply. "We got this."

Jack faced the wheel, mumbling to himself. "Alright, you prick, I'm only going to spin you one more time, and you *are* going to land on that stupid little crab, okay?"

He let the wheel fly, pulling it as hard as he could. Jack stepped back and prayed for it to land on their symbol. May had chosen Cancer because it was Jack's zodiac. She'd chosen it because she believed in him.

Come on, Fortuna. Don't let her down.

The wheel whirled around just as Jack heard the sloshing of water. He looked down and saw that the rising waters had nearly made it to the game room's floor.

"Jack…"

He looked over his shoulder, but May wasn't looking at him. She was staring at the wheel. Jack faced forward just as the wheel stopped on their crab.

"Yeah, baby!" Jack hollered.

The cave replied with an agonizing whale call and a snap of something that sounded important.

"Uh-oh," Jack said, stepping away. He tripped on something and went down on his back. "What the... Oh."

He gazed between his legs as a tall, thin, cylindrical object rose out of the stone platform. Spotlights ignited its golden surface and voices called out, not that Jack could hear what they were saying over the rushing waters.

That's when Jack's back got wet.

"Time to go!" Jack said, yelping as he stood. He snagged the *aquilifer's* pole from its mount. A small door had opened and allowed the pole to be raised to meet its champion.

"The water's still coming!" May yelled.

"I know. I'm guessing that snap we heard was something breaking that shouldn't have!" He pointed to the others. "Gonna have to swim for it!"

May nodded, gave Jack one last look, then dove into the raging subterranean tumult. Jack was right behind her. When they both surfaced, they each took an end of the pole and kicked for the overlook that was close to taking on water.

Another explosion rang out overhead.

"It's open!" Marcus called. "Swim, dammit, swim!"

"You think he's concerned for us, or the pole?" May asked, between breaths.

"Do I really have to answer?"

He was pulled under and tossed around by an incredibly powerful current. Jack nearly lost the end of the pole too. If he had, he'd have been pulled even deeper. But, as it were, he was yanked up to the surface. When his head broke, he found May and Marcus holding the opposite end.

Jack waved his thanks and climbed onto the steps leading up to them. Once he got his feet under him, he let go, happily handing over the pole to Marcus. No one stuck around to marvel at the third and final piece of the Ninth Legion's lost *aquila*. Yes, the eagle standard was finally complete, but it didn't matter if none of them made it out alive.

Jack was the last through the tight squeeze in the back of the Mithras statue. He snaked his body past a jagged edge, hearing bedlam coming up behind him. Jack didn't want to look, but he did. Somehow, a wave had been created, and it was coming straight for him.

"Brace for impact!" he yelled.

The pressure of it hitting his legs shot him through the confined space, all the way through the tunnel, and halfway into the prayer room. He tumbled to a stop, taking out May, and Spencer as he did. Jack lay on his back for a moment and caught his breath.

"Now I know how a torpedo feels."

Spencer climbed to his feet. "More like a wrecking ball..."

Jack nodded. "That too."

By the time Jack got to the flooded stairway, Marcus and Theo already had their masks, tanks, and flippers on. Jack yanked his mask on, snagged his flippers, and tossed his tank over his shoulder.

Then he jumped in, barely missing the quickly advancing wave.

He went under, but forced himself to remain calm. Jack allowed his flippers to fall to the steps as he slid into his tank. Once it was buckled in place, he reacquired his flippers and slipped them onto his feet, forgetting about his aching big toe. He grimaced, but the pain subsided. The cold-ish water temperature helped mightily. Luckily, Jack was pretty sure he had avoided breaking it.

May floated into view next to him. She gave him the universal sign for "okay," asking him if he was, indeed, okay.

Jack gave her a thumbs up in return and the pair descended along with the others.

"Can everyone hear me?" Jack asked, testing his comms. "Everyone alive?"

"Better than alive," Marcus replied. "We now have the entire *aquila* in our possession."

"You're welcome, by the way," Jack said. He then looked at May and asked the most pertinent question. "So, Babylon?"

"Yes," Marcus replied, "we go to Babylon."

47

Eagle County, Colorado, USA

Eddy hung up. Unfortunately, Jack's South American contact was unavailable at the moment, though he did promise to call back as soon as he could.

She tossed the burner phone on her desk and sat back. "Stupid criminals…"

Never in Eddy's life did she think she'd be calling in favors from people like Jack's smuggler friend down in Colombia. And never in her life, did she think she'd ever have to set up her boss' potential withdrawal from his own country. Everything Eddy was doing was a guaranteed career ender. She'd never have a government job again, let alone one within military intelligence.

Her desk phone buzzed. *"Eddy, to my office, please."*

She sighed and depressed a quarter-sized blue button. "Yes, sir."

Eddy pushed away from her desk, crossed her semi-spacious office, and opened the door. As always, TAC was prime with activity. The central hub of their underground, mountain headquarters was mostly made up of cubicles. Private offices, like the ones Eddy and Raegor possessed, ringed the outside of the main floor. They had agents all over the world neck-deep in all types of missions. Most were involved with investigatory work or surveillance right now. Lately, Raegor had saved the juiciest ones for Jack.

We're working him too hard, Eddy thought. A smirk formed on her face. *Damn you Jack for being so good at your job.*

She crossed through the center of the hustle and bustle, saying her hellos as she did. Depending on the goings-on, Eddy could go days, even weeks, between seeing certain people. She and Raegor had no set schedule like a lot of the office employees had. The two executives operated whenever they were needed.

She stepped up to Raegor's door, lifted her hand to knock, but didn't get to. A buzz announced the releasing of the deadbolt. Eddy gave the camera above the door a small salute and entered.

"Something troubling you, Solomon?" Eddy asked, shutting the door behind her. He gazed up from his computer and stared at her. "You know what I mean…"

He finished typing something, then gave Eddy his undivided attention. "You're going to want to sit for this."

Eddy sighed and slumped into one of two chairs opposite Raegor's desk. "Hit me with it."

Raegor tapped his fingers on his desk before speaking. Eddy knew the man well enough to know something was bothering him more than usual.

"Solomon, what's wrong?" she asked.

"I just got off a call…with Delta command."

"What?" Eddy asked, sitting bolt upright. "You contacted JSOC?"

He nodded. "I still have a couple of people I trust."

"Are these friends in the loop?"

His eyes darted away, quickly returning to Eddy. "Not officially."

"Dammit, Solomon." Eddy's hands went to her face. "This is so much worse than I thought. If the committee finds out you've been in contact with unapproved people…"

"Let me worry about that."

Eddy would have to trust him. She did too.

"Fine." She sat straighter. "Okay, so tell me about this call you made. Are you sure this is a good idea?"

"Not at all, but we don't leave our people to the wolves."

Eddy held up her hands. "I know, but nor do we involve a Delta strike team. But since that ship has sailed, what was said on the call?"

Raegor smiled, throwing Eddy off a little. "I found out that one of the team leaders used to serve under Jack for nearly two years. Just got off with him and his squadron's commander before I called you in."

Eddy sat forward. "They let you speak directly to a Delta team leader?"

Raegor gave Eddy a sly grin. "All these years by my side, and yet, somehow, I still surprise you?"

"Yes, Solomon Raegor, you are truly an enigma," she said, rolling her eyes. "Still, I can't believe you told him about Jack's involvement."

He shrugged. "I told him what he needed to know. Jack is in the hands of a terrorist group and needs some help. His commander left it in his hands since this isn't technically an official operation."

"Which means this soldier's career is also at risk." Raegor didn't dispute the statement. Eddy calmed and sat back. "So, what did this team leader say?"

Raegor stood, looking very much the part of a retired Army General. "He said that he'd go to hell and back to bring our boy home."

48

Iraqi Airspace

Jack would've preferred a HALO jump to the normal kind, but he understood the reasoning behind the decision not to. First and foremost, there were people involved in this insertion that had no business being here.

Unlike the dive mission beneath Nijmegen, Gemma was coming along this time. Jack was thankful for it too. He hated not having her within shouting distance. Her safety meant everything to Jack since it was his fault she'd gotten involved. Skydiving had been the easiest part so far. The flight in had been unnerving. The crew inside the C-130 Hercules was sparse, but those onboard couldn't help themselves but stare. Luckily, everyone's faces were covered, and with simple black ski masks this time.

Marcus had agreed to have his people forego their usual headgear, opting for a less memorable appearance instead. The Legion's gladiator helmets were, no doubt, in talks throughout particular circles. If they had worn them here, Jack had no doubt they'd be apprehended, or worse, killed.

Jack was also thankful for the lighting below. Saddam's palace was a major tourist attraction now. Tall street lamps dotted the grounds surrounding the palace, giving the incoming force an easy target to hit. Jack was also appreciative for the lack of light atop the palace's roof, their landing zone.

He hadn't waited for one of the legionnaires to jump first; as soon as they were ready to go, Jack had stepped forward and jumped. As he had expected, May wasn't too far behind him.

Jack's E-Rifle shifted, even though it was strapped tightly against his chest. Yes, he and May were, once again, armed. With the end in sight, Marcus had thought it best to have as many people armed as possible. He also agreed that casualties needed to be kept to a minimum. A blood-soaked battlefield wouldn't be easy to hide, but unconscious guards would be.

Now! Jack thought, ripping his chute's cord.

It quickly unfurled and caught, cutting his airspeed down tremendously. He navigated himself into position above the southern rooftop and waited for touchdown. There really wasn't anything else he could do.

Marcus' intel said there shouldn't be anyone on the roof after dark. Jack prayed he was right. He knew, for a fact, that the guards would be carrying lethal rounds. If there was someone stationed up top, Jack, along with everyone else, would be easy pickings to anyone looking up, even against the night sky.

He landed in an awkward run, turned, and pulled in his billowing parachute. He quickly wrapped it up in a ball, then ditched his rig. As the others landed around him, Jack loosened his rifle's sling, then shouldered the weapon, aiming it toward a set of exterior stairs. Only after all ten of the team members safely landed did anyone speak.

It was Jack.

"Clear," he said, whispering into his tactical radio.

Once again, the Legion had come prepared. They outfitted everyone with an above-average comms system, one that was also built into a hardy pair of active ear protection, much like the helmets had possessed. They similarly sported the miniature, noise canceling microphones.

Everyone wore a hefty plate carrier too. Jack *really* appreciated that. The only real difference between the non-legionnaires and legionnaires were their lack of deadly sidearms. Those were loaded with traditional ammo in case they ran into a real firefight.

Jack was going to do everything possible to keep that from happening.

The ten-man team gathered in a tight circle to review their game plan. It was a simple one too.

"Okay, everyone," Marcus said, showing off the six-foot-long *aquilifer's* pole attached to the side of his pack. "We get in, neutralize the guards, then head for our entry point." He looked at Theo. "Take your team and sweep this entire palace. I don't want anyone sneaking up behind us like they did in York, is that clear?"

"Copy that," Theo said, glancing at Jack.

Jack enjoyed that little dig, because that was exactly what had happened back in York. It didn't help that their intel had been wrong. There had been four security guards instead of three. That was the first time Jack had seen the Taser round in action. The flash of blue light was particularly neat.

"Spencer and I will lead our civilian guests down to the lower levels via the back stairs." Marcus looked around. "Is everyone clear?"

He received a bevy of confirmations in a mixture of verbal and nonverbal responses.

"Okay, my team, switch to channel two. Theo's will use channel three. Channel one will override both. Do not use it until we are all back together or unless it is an emergency."

Of the new members of the ground force, Jack recognized one of them.

Zayn, Marcus' Arab pilot, had joined the fun. Jack thought that made sense. They were in Iraq, after all. As it turned out, the police helicopter had been damaged while fighting the Legion's chopper. Zayn had verified as much shortly after Christos' fateful fall. There was another man of the same ethnicity. He'd been introduced as Xavier shortly before they had loaded into the C-130.

The third newcomer was a man of American origin, not that he was an American anymore. Damien had fled the states some time ago. Jack had no idea why, but that's what the legionnaire had told him.

The final addition was another Italian named Aldo. He'd yet to say anything at all. Even the hardened Angeline would have said more to Jack by now.

Jack broke formation and turned so he could see their entry point into the palace. Luckily for them, getting in would be a breeze. Shortly after Saddam had been captured, his recently finished Babylonian palace had been ransacked. Everything had been destroyed or stolen. For a short time, it had been used as the Americans' base of operations for the area.

Jack would've loved to have seen it, but that had been before his time. By then, Jack had been deployed to the Middle East, but not in Babylon. In fact, Jack had never been to Babylon, until now.

"Move out," Marcus said. "See you soon."

The two teams split up, each entering the palace from different directions. Jack's "Academic Team" headed for the eastern side of the roof, while Theo's "Strike Team" headed west.

Marcus fell in line next to Jack as they headed off.

Jack checked his watch. "Based on the current time, I give us four hours to get in and out. The out is going to be tricky too."

Marcus agreed. "Either way, we need to hurry."

"What about our exit?" Spencer asked. "Did Zayn come through?"

That was the question everyone was pondering. The Arab pilot had contacted an old contact from years back. Supposedly, he was going to have three vans here by the time the ten-man team needed to leave. Zayn had been up front with his contact's lack of reliability, but it had been their only option.

Raegor had been just as forthcoming when he had called Jack back. He had said that he'd secured their entry but had no way of getting them out. That's what had forced Zayn's hand. Jack knew Marcus would still attempt the operation, regardless. He was too close to turn back now.

Jack slung his rifle over his shoulder and, with Marcus' help, disassembled a five-foot-wide section of barrier. A wall blocked a central horseshoe section of the roof and was made of worn construction sheetrock and rotten wood. With the way now clear, Jack took up arms again and entered, eyeing their entry point.

They moved without their weapon lights on. No one was to use them if at all possible. The interior of the palace was supposed to be dark. If anyone outside saw ten, high-powered lights darting around inside it would surely arouse suspicion. So, they moved by starlight.

Jack slowed as he neared the eight-foot-tall window frame. Like all the other windows, it too was missing. A heavy tarp had been attached to keep the elements at bay. Marcus sliced it to ribbons in seconds. As he sheathed his knife, he stepped aside so Jack and Spencer could enter.

Jack crept forward, moving like the dead. He leaned in through the new opening, but relaxed. The space on the other side consisted of one large room, not unlike a loft. It was empty save for a few random piles of junk and construction debris. He stepped through, knelt, counted to ten, then gave his people the go-ahead to join him.

"Clear," he whispered.

Everyone else filed in, moving quickly and quietly. Marcus continued across the room, stopping just inside an open door.

"Spencer, stay with Gemma," Jack ordered. "May, watch our butts."

"Gladly," May replied.

Jack smiled, stood, and pushed across the room to join Marcus at the doorway.

"You two really are awful," Spencer said.

"Someone's jealous," May cooed, teasing the curator.

Jack didn't add to the barrage. With him being so close to another room, he kept quiet. Marcus inched forward, hugging the left side of the doorframe.

"Right side is clear," he whispered.

Jack mimicked his movements, but kept to the right-half of the door. The left side of the next room was also devoid of life.

"We're good," he said, slipping inside.

At the center of the room was an unrailed, spiraling staircase cut to mirror the square stone walls encompassing it. As Jack expected, they were on the top floor. They needed to make it down to the first level of the palace, which, based on the Legion's intelligence, contained a total of three floors.

"Not as glamorous as I expected," Jack said.

"This isn't the main staircase," Spencer explained. "The double staircase leading down to the foyer was immaculate before the Americans defiled it."

Jack rolled his eyes. "Dude, it was Saddam. If anything, we didn't do enough." Jack looked around. "Should've burned it to the ground."

"Enough," Marcus said. "None of that matters now. Besides, we want to stay away from the central part of the floorplan for now." He glanced at Jack. "That's where Theo's team is headed."

Jack understood. It seemed that the guards hung out around that part of the palace.

"Copy," Jack said. "Where are we headed anyway?"

Marcus headed for the stairs. "The throne room."

"The throne room?" Gemma asked. "That feels a little too high profile for a secret entrance, don't you think?"

"Actually, I believe it's the perfect place," Spencer replied. "Think about it from Saddam's point of view. Who's going to disturb his throne? To me, there is no better place."

"I guess so, sure," Gemma said.

She looked at Jack. All he could do was shrug.

"How has no one found it?" May asked. "It's been two decades since Saddam was captured."

Spencer smiled. "I'll show you."

49

Eagle County, Colorado, USA

The burner phone vibrated atop his desk. Raegor's eyes darted over to it, leaving his computer screen to do so. He'd been anxiously awaiting this exact message. He hovered his hand above the disposable device before picking it up and turning it over to see the screen. The message contained two words, and the sender's heavily encrypted number.

"Package delivered."

Raegor gripped the phone and sat back, letting out a long breath. His nerves were fried, his hands shook, and his sleep-deprived mind was much too exhausted to properly rest.

"I'm going to need another vacation after this…"

He looked at his desk phone, dialed Eddy's extension, then hit the blue call button.

"Sir?" Eddy asked.

"It's done."

His statement was met with a brief pause. *"What do we do now?"*

"We wait."

Raegor ended the call and stood. He plucked the burner phone from the top of his desk and nonchalantly tossed it onto the floor. The wall behind him held the tool of the phone's inevitable destruction. Raegor lifted the signed baseball bat off its mount, squeezing its handle hard in a classic grip. He even took a couple of practice swings, recalling his high school days. Raegor had played a little ball in his teenage years.

He lifted the bat, tilting the barrel so he could re-read the signature again.

Todd Helton.

Helton was a legendary first baseman for the Colorado Rockies. Jonathan Yates, Raegor's current persona outside of the office, attended a few Rockies games from time to time. The bat had been a gift from Eddy after their first year together in TAC.

He sighed. "Sorry, Todd."

Raegor hefted the wooden bat over his head. His office's soundproofing would provide the perfect cover for what he was about to do. As if he were chopping wood, Raegor brought it down on the phone six times, completely obliterating it. The next time he left TAC HQ, he'd scatter the pieces in trash cans throughout the town.

He knelt, using the now-chipped piece of sports memorabilia as a cane. Raegor set the bat down beside him and began picking up the phone's remnants. He pictured Jack and May as he did, wishing there was more he could've done to help them.

It's up to you now.

50

Babylon, Iraq

Once again, Jack led the Academic Team. The going was slow thanks to a handful of improvised barriers. The top floors looked like they were off-limits to tourists from what Jack could tell, which was a shame. The decision made the three-story-tall palace two-thirds smaller. If Jack came all this way to see it, he would've been pissed to discover that!

They'd made it to the landing between the second and first floors without so much as hearing a guard, let alone seeing one. Jack's foot hit the next step and he froze. A light bloomed to life somewhere out of sight. Its owner had yet to reveal himself, and when he did, he simply walked past the foot of the stairs. He didn't give them a second glance.

Jack knew how easy it could be to be lulled into a false sense of security. He'd been in the same boat dozens of times when he was with the National Park Service. More often than not, the job had been pretty mundane and uneventful.

That's what was happening here. The guard had probably never dealt with a nighttime trespasser before, or if he had, it had only been once or twice.

Probably walks the same route too, Jack supposed.

Jack let him pass. Once he was out of sight again, Jack descended quickly to the bottom floor. He spotted the man further down what constituted as the main hall. Jack checked the other end first, leaning out and looking to his right to make sure no one was coming up behind him. Confirming that he was alone, Jack shouldered his E-Rifle, recited a silent apology, and shot the guard in the base of the neck.

Blue flash.

Man down.

May joined him, rifle jammed tightly to her shoulder. "Nice shot."

Jack glanced at her. "You're not helping."

"Head north," Spencer instructed.

North was in the direction of the incapacitated guard. Jack continued forward, stopping when he reached the man.

"Give me a hand with him." May slung her rifle around to her back and helped Jack drag the unconscious man into the adjacent room.

They stepped lightly, passing multiple rooms and corridors.

"Right here," Spencer said.

Jack didn't verbally acknowledge him. He just leaned out into the next intersection of hallways and cleared it. Then he slinked right, heading east. Jack expected to be met with more resistance, but since stumbling into the first guard, he'd seen and heard nothing.

Don't jinx it, dummy, Jack thought.

The rooms here were much bigger, not that Jack could identify their original use. The looters had done a number on the place. Spray-painted graffiti coated every wall in sight. Most of it was in Arabic, however there was also quite a bit in English too.

"English graffiti?" May asked quietly.

"From the Americans stationed here," Spencer replied. "They certainly left their mark."

Jack was done with the Brit's comments. "The UK sent soldiers here too, you know?" He ground to a halt and spun. "As did Poland and Australia. Many more countries followed once the dirty work was done." He stepped toward Spencer. "The more you say, the more it confirms that you don't belong on the field of battle. You don't belong *here*. You belong in your precious museum, where it's safe." Jack tapped his own chest. "I was on the ground. I saw countless men die while trying to rid the world of this maniac." Jack motioned to the palace as a whole. "You can say what you want about the people who sent us here. I'd probably agree with a lot of it. But you don't get to say a *damn* thing about the people who fought here!" He snarled. "If I had been here when they found that rat hiding in his hole, I would've put a bullet in his head and called it a day."

He turned away from Spencer, calming himself down. May put a hand on his shoulder.

"Jack," May said, "Spencer wasn't defending Saddam, he—"

Jack stopped her with a raised hand. "Don't." He looked at her. "Just…don't."

Marcus cleared his throat. "Can we proceed?"

Jack huffed out a breath and did just that. He shouldered his rifle and continued forward, clearing doorways as they passed them. The other guards would be fairly predictable. They'd have their flashlights on as they wandered through the hallways. What Jack really hoped, was that most of them would just be lounging around, waiting for shift change.

"It's just up ahead," Spencer said.

Jack slowed, then held up a fist. Only he kept moving. He heard movement inside the throne room. Then voices, but Jack couldn't tell who was speaking. Five feet from the opening, he heard a familiar voice.

"Throne room is clear. All guards are down."

It was Theo; he had switched over to channel two to announce his team's success.

"Copy that," Marcus replied. "We're just outside. Everyone switch to channel one."

Jack reached down to the radio on his chest rig and rotated the channel selector over one spot.

The *Legatus* zoomed around him and entered the throne room first. Several handheld flashlights winked to life next. Jack was about to say something, but thought back to the guard he'd shot. He also had a flashlight. If someone down in the village below the palace saw it, they'd probably just think it was a guard and not an armed ten-man team of mercenaries, explorers, and scholars.

Jack watched Theo drag one of the guards into the next room and out of sight. He joined Marcus at the center of the throne room, looking very satisfied with himself.

"Do you know why Saddam's engineers constructed this place here?" Marcus asked, pointing at the floor. "It could've been anywhere in Babylon, yet they chose this exact spot."

Jack relaxed and slung his E-Rifle around his back. "I'm guessing it had something to do with our entry point."

"Correct. Although, lucky for us, none of his men could get in."

"More traps?" Jack asked.

Marcus replied, "No, actually." That surprised Jack. "From what we've heard, he had tried to dig through. When that didn't work, he tried blasting his way in. Nearly collapsed his palace in the process. As the years went by, he slowed his obsession and focused on other things. Then, the U.S. invaded in 2003."

"You're welcome, I guess."

"Did the U.S. get in?" May asked, stepping up next to Jack.

Marcus faced them and smiled. "They never even knew to check."

"How do you know all of this?" Gemma asked. She and Spencer joined the conversation. "I understand that your knowledge is deep when it pertains to the ancient past, but these are all things that have happened in the last two decades."

Jack agreed. "I thought you said you didn't have people in the area."

"We don't. Not anymore..." He looked over his shoulder. "Xavier." The second Arab legionnaire turned and headed over to them. "Years ago," Marcus continued, "we had people on the ground while this palace was occupied by invading forces." He stepped aside, giving room so Xavier could join them. "Xavier's father was a part of it. He was hired as a guide and translator. And as I'm sure you've deduced, he also kept watch on the entrance."

"And once coalition forces abandoned this place," Xavier explained, "my father was also forced to leave. If he had stayed, it would've invited too many questions."

"Even now," May said, "after twenty years of access, you haven't tried to enter."

Marcus looked at her. "But we have."

"You have?" Jack asked, looking at where the throne would've sat.

A two-step, halfmoon, raised platform sat built into the western wall of the throne room. The floor of the platform was made up of cream-colored marble tiles, while black, possibly midnight-blue, tiles covered the wall behind it. Everything was set into an arched alcove. Jack was honestly a little disappointed at the design. It was rather bland considering the way Saddam usually spent his money.

His people's money.

"Yes, we have tried," Marcus replied. He looked at Spencer and tipped his chin toward the throne platform. "Show them why we haven't proceeded any further."

The museum curator mounted the platform, explaining what he was doing as he did.

"Did you know that Saddam thought of himself as Nebuchadnezzar II's son? He believed that he was destined to rebuild Babylon to its former glory—to the heights of what the Babylonian king had attained. Saddam was rather mad, wasn't he?" Spencer looked back at Jack. "He flattened a village to build all this, you know?"

"Not a great way to win over the people," Jack said.

"Come on, now. Do you really think someone like Saddam Hussein cared about what the people thought of him?"

Jack gave Spencer that one. Saddam was a dictator, after all. He did what pleased him.

"The tidbit about Saddam believing he was a king's son was how we found the way in," Spencer explained, pulling out his flashlight and kneeling. He clicked it on. "Look at this."

Jack stepped forward, mounting the short platform and taking a knee next to the Legion's historical expert.

"What am I looking at?" Jack asked.

"This," Spencer said, pointing to one of the dozens of dark, six-by-twelve-inch, marble tiles. They had been attached to the back wall in a vertical position. "If you look carefully, you can see the side profile of Nebuchadnezzar II." Jack leaned closer, barely seeing what Spencer was pointing out. "Yes, I know, the spray paint isn't helping any."

Jack spotted it. "I see it. What's so special about it? We already know Saddam was gaga over the old king." The corner of Spencer's mouth rose. "What?"

"Press it." Jack looked at him. "Go on. Press it."

Jack reached out his gloved hand, laid his palm flat against the tile, and pushed.

It sank in with the telltale *clunk* of a catch unlocking.

Spencer's smirk transformed into a wild smile. "There's six more."

Jack stood and searched the wall for the others. He found two more without any help. Spencer already knew where they were, that was obvious. He quickly depressed three more, then stepped back.

"The seventh one is incredibly difficult to find. It took me hours to find it the first time."

"You've been here before?" Jack asked. "On the ground and in person?"

Spencer nodded. "Yes. I've toured this place twice before on behalf of the museum. Now, about the last tile…"

"It's over there," May said, landing her light in the top left-hand corner of the tiled wall. Spencer looked at her. His peacock-like bravado had taken a hit. She shrugged. "I have good eyes."

"And yet, you see something in him," Spencer said, motioning to Jack. The Brit then had the gall to point up at the tile. "Give us a boost, will you?"

Jack shook his head, put his back against the wall, and cupped his hands. Spencer stepped into them, and Jack lifted him as high as he could. He swiftly pressed the tile with another audible *clunk*. Jack lowered the man down as Marcus stepped up onto the platform.

"Saddam's engineers went all out, huh?"

"They did," Marcus replied. "They knew this was significant, but didn't know just how significant it was. You ready?"

Jack shrugged. "For what?"

Marcus pressed his left shoulder into the center of the wall. "Help me."

Jack added his right shoulder to it. The two men met eyes before Marcus nodded. When he did, they pushed as one. The wall retreated, revealing a rectangular, obviously hand-cut, hole in the floor. Jack sidestepped it, spying stairs as he continued to push the unique door backward. Six feet later, it stopped.

"This it?" Jack asked.

Marcus stared into the dark void. "It is. We are about to finish a two-thousand-year-old journey." He took a deep breath. *"Gaudere Legio Nona."*

His men repeated their motto.

To rejoice the Ninth Legion.

Jack shined his flashlight into the hole. "Alright, let's see what we have."

51

Marcus and Spencer led the troops into the earth. After continuing west for fifty feet, the stairs began to tightly spiral downward and to the right. The ten-man team marched down them for a couple of minutes before finally exiting into an empty, twenty-foot-wide, square chamber.

Jack was confused by what he *didn't* see. "Um…"

"Your confusion is valid," Spencer said. "We've deduced that this room has never been used. Not even by Saddam. There may have been a plan to use it as a bomb shelter, but as you can clearly see, it was spared."

"No graffiti, either," May said. "No one's been down here since Saddam was captured, I bet."

The team spread out, silently waiting for whatever was about to happen, to happen. May stepped across the center of the room and froze. Then she picked up her foot, drawing the attention of everyone else.

"I see you've found the next lock," Spencer said.

Jack stepped over, knelt, and inspected the discovery. He wiped away a light layer of dust to find a hole with a ring of text around it.

"Don't suppose you've translated this?" he asked, recognizing the language. He looked up at Gemma. "It's Greek."

"We have," Spencer replied. "It says—"

"*No stranger is to enter*," Gemma read aloud. "*Whoever is caught will himself be responsible for his ensuing death*. It's a warning to those seen as strangers—outsiders—to those unworthy of stepping foot any further."

"That it is," Marcus added.

Gemma gently grazed the engraved text with her fingertips. "It's eerily similar to the inscription found on Temple Mount in Jerusalem."

"Jerusalem?" May asked.

Gemma nodded. "Yes. The warning there was also carved in Ancient Greek. First century BC, if I'm not mistaken."

"You are not," Spencer said.

"Unworthy…" Jack said, replaying the warning in his head. "That sounds awfully familiar, doesn't it?"

Marcus reached over his shoulder and pulled the pole free from the side of his bag. "It does."

"Think they're connected by more than just chance?" Jack asked.

"We do," Marcus replied, still staring at the small engraving. "We believe that whomever carved the Temple Mount warning stone may have also carved this one."

Jack scratched his chin. "That would make them a Mouseion too." He sighed. "I guess we can expect some pretty nasty defenses beyond wherever this thing leads us."

"That was our assessment as well," Spencer added.

Gemma's left hand went to her mouth, and she stroked the text again.

Jack touched her shoulder. "You okay?"

"This," she said, lightly rubbing the letters.

"What about it?"

She looked up at Jack. "This was carved by a Mouseion scholar."

"Yeah, and?" Jack asked, not putting it together.

"This room belonged to Ancient Babylon, Jack." She returned her eyes to the engraving. "This was built by Nebuchadnezzar II and later modified by Alexander the Great's men."

Jack looked around with new eyes. *Alexander may have stood here, as did so many other great men.*

"So, this is as far as your people have ever gotten?" Jack asked, confirming the intel.

"It is." Marcus faced Theo, holding out the eagle-bearer's pole. "Assemble the *aquila*."

Spencer dove at the chance to assist Theo in rebuilding the Ninth Legion's long-lost eagle standard. Jack was surprised Marcus hadn't demanded to do it himself. Jack faked a cough and turned away, lowering his line of sight down to the general's left hand.

It was shaking.

That's why, Jack thought. *He doesn't want his men to see him so nervous.*

Everyone stepped back to give the two legionnaires some room to work. Theo handed the pole to Spencer, then slid out of his backpack. He unzipped it and pulled out, not one, but two small Pelican cases.

He unlatched the first one to reveal the laureled base. Theo took great care in how he handled the priceless artifact. Jack appreciated that. Spencer did too, for that matter. The Legion lieutenant lifted the base above the pole. This was the first time Jack had gotten a close look at the base. There was a hole that went straight through it. Theo guided the base down onto the pole. It stopped with three inches of the pole jutting out of the top.

"Is that it?" Jack asked.

Theo nodded. "The pole is not a perfect cylinder. It's narrower at the top."

"Interesting design," Gemma said. "I doubt it could be precisely replicated."

"No, it cannot," Marcus said. "We've tried, using measurements based on past *aquilas*." He glanced at Jack. "Yes, we have that information too. Our biggest problem was that we didn't know the weight of the gold that had been used."

"Or the length of the pole," Spencer added. "We found a handful of discrepancies along the way that had given us cause for doubt…until now."

"I bet the exact weight is what really matters," Jack hypothesized. "Every lock we've come across has used a pressure plate."

Marcus eyed the eagle as Theo removed it next. "I agree…"

Jack wasn't sure Marcus had actually heard him. He couldn't ask him, either. Marcus was off in la-la land at the moment.

Theo hefted the eagle higher, then eased it onto the exposed tip of the pole. Like the base, it slipped on without issue. Everyone held their breath, even

Jack. This was a historic event. This was the first time a Roman Legion's *aquila* had been seen in this condition since the empire had been in power.

Jack grinned. He couldn't help it. "Okay, that's awesome."

Marcus stepped closer. "Yes, it is…" He placed a closed fist on his chest and bowed his head. The other legionnaires did the same thing, paying respect—no, reverence—to their sacred relic.

Jack didn't respect anything these guys did, but he did understand what this moment meant to them. He kept his mouth shut and let them enjoy it. And, in all honestly, Jack was thoroughly enjoying the moment too. Marcus opened and shut his hands several times, before reaching out and accepting the assembled eagle standard.

He slowly walked in a circle as he spoke. "I thank each and every one of you for assisting in this grand occasion." Jack assumed that also meant him—May and Gemma too. "We have done it. It is our time, our right, to see that our ancestors' mission finally succeeds." He stopped and turned. "The eagle-bearer shall lead the way." Then he lowered the *aquila* into the lock. "Eighteen hundred years of waiting…"

"Does anyone else find it strange that we're using a Roman key to open Greek locks?"

"Without knowing how connected both empires were to all this, no," Spencer said. "I—"

Jack heard the pole touch bottom a foot inside the hole. When Marcus released it, the entire twenty-by-twenty-foot-wide floor rumbled.

Then it descended.

Jack looked at May. "Going down?"

All she could do was shrug and go along for the ride.

52

The ancient elevator stopped five stories down. Jack had no idea what kind of engineering feat had been completed to produce such an industrial marvel, especially one made out of heavy stone. Ten flashlights whipped around, illuminating the next, two-hundred-foot-wide, circular space.

Three quarters of it was nothing except a deep, dark chasm. Jack personally checked one side, pointing the beam of his light into it. The blackness effortlessly absorbed it. The bottom was barely visible. Either way, a fall was a death sentence. Jack swallowed back a rising discomfort and took two giant steps away from the edge.

The eastern portion of the space was *not* abyssal in nature. More stairs greeted them. They were as extensive as their twenty-foot-wide lift, but five times that distance in length. They looked to be in good enough condition to cross, but Jack wasn't going to offer his services as the guinea pig.

He hoped it would be Marcus or Theo at this point.

The stairs ended at a clifftop, one that was lower than their elevator's platform. The grounds atop the precipice seemed to go on forever. Jack's handheld light didn't reach the back of the cavern. He, instead, aimed his E-Rifle at it and ignited its mounted light. The more powerful beam sliced across the darkness with relative ease, showing off a tall archway cut into an, otherwise, solid rock face.

"There's our door," he said, tracing the edges of it with his light. "Looks like it's about thirty-ish feet tall and half that much wide."

Marcus reached for the *aquila*.

"Hang on," May said, stopping him. "How do we know this thing won't return to the palace and leave us down here?"

Marcus looked at her. "We don't." He plucked the eagle standard free of the lock, indifferent to what *might* happen. "All that matters is what's in front of us."

"I can think of a few other things," Gemma mumbled, quickly turning away from Marcus before he could give her a death glare.

Jack waited for the floor to rise, but it didn't. He eyed the lock, deciding that the *aquila* would have to be reinserted for that to happen. He looked straight up, realizing something.

"We're leaving an awfully messy trail."

"Can't be helped," Spencer replied. "Like Marcus said, all that matters is what's in front of us."

Jack snorted. "You say that now. What happens if the Iraqi authorities figure out what's up before we leave?"

Spencer's posture changed. It had gone from courageous to uncertain in the blink of an eye. He looked up, then back down to the archway. "Yes, well, perhaps we should get moving."

Everyone turned to face the steps leading down to the clifftop entrance.

The grounds beyond the stairs were mostly empty save for eight statues lining a central passage. Jack had no idea who they depicted. It was too dark and they were still too far away to get a definitive look.

Jack and Marcus each stepped up to the edge, but no one moved. Jack turned his head and looked at him. "The eagle-bearer leads the way, right?"

Marcus huffed a breath because he knew Jack was right. Marcus' dramatic show back up in the palace basement would lose its luster if he were to back down now. He hefted the *aquila* up, holding it out in front of him in a very professional manner. Jack was impressed that he could hold it like that with it being solid gold and all.

The first step came and went with no consequences. Seeing that it was safe, so far, Jack was about to follow but stopped. He'd wait as long as he could.

He felt something jab him in the back. Jack glanced over his shoulder to find Theo standing behind him. "You're next."

Well, that didn't take long, he thought.

Jack decided to stay nonconfrontational. He dismounted the elevator platform, stepping exactly where Marcus had stepped. May shadowed Jack, following suit. Soon everyone was descending the subterranean steps in a single-file line. Theo fell in line behind May and Gemma was slotted between him and Spencer.

Jack looked down at the rifle in his hands, then threw it around to his back and tightened the sling. As he did, he craned his head around and looked at May and gave her a tired smile. Her eyes darted down to the rifle. The question was clear.

Why?

"I'm more concerned with falling to my death right now than getting into a gunfight."

May tilted her head to the side in thought, but must've agreed. She also cleared up her hands by tossing the rifle around her back.

The legionnaires did not. The only one that wasn't presently armed was Marcus since he was carrying the *aquila*.

When they reached the bottom, Marcus must've had enough light to identify the statues.

"It's them," he said, voice filled with wonder. He looked back and forth as he continued past the first two. "It's them..."

"Who is them?" Jack asked. All he saw were a bunch of classic Greek statues, women wearing flowing robes.

Jack's answer came from behind him. Gemma stepped out of line to get an up-close look at the woman to their right. "It's the Muses."

"Oh," Jack said, "that makes sense." He quickly counted them. "Hang on, I only count eight. I thought there were nine?"

"There are," Marcus said from further ahead. "Clio is missing."

Jack studied each of the Muses. "Oh, yeah. I don't see a lyre anywhere."

Spencer headed for the second Muse on the left. "I suspect we'll see her soon. As we've come to find out, the Mouseion builders fancied her—what she stood for, I mean."

Jack was betting on it. There was no possible way they wouldn't be seeing Clio down here.

Marcus paused just outside the archway. Multiple lights illuminated its interior, showing off a floor made of gorgeous mosaic tiles. When Jack stepped up next to the general, he immediately recognized the pattern that was built within the artwork.

"A staff with wings and two snakes... That's Hermes' caduceus, is it?"

Marcus glanced at Jack. "It is."

May, Gemma, and Spencer joined the pair to look over the ominous design choice.

"I thought Hermes was the god of medicine and travel," May said.

"He is," Spencer verified, "but he was originally used as a *psychopomp*?"

"A what?" Jack asked. He'd heard the term before, but had no idea what it meant.

Gemma stepped closer but didn't enter. "A *psychopomp* is an entity who is charged with ushering souls from the world of the living to the world of the dead."

"Isn't that Charon's job, Greek ferryman of the dead?" Jack asked.

"I'm impressed," Spencer said.

Jack shrugged. "I read the Percy Jackson books a while back. I'm an expert now too."

Spencer couldn't take it. He stepped away from the group for a moment to collect himself.

"That still doesn't explain why Hermes' caduceus is here," May said.

Gemma knelt. "Like Charon, Hermes is also sometimes seen as the conductor of the dead. However, it's very rare nowadays. I believe this is meant to be another warning."

"So, not good times?" Jack asked.

Gemma looked back and up, meeting Jack's gaze. "No, Jack, not good times."

Jack sighed. "Figures."

"I agree," Spencer said, rejoining them. "To me, this reads as 'cross the seal and enter the underworld,' or something like that."

Gemma nodded.

May leaned around Jack to look at Marcus. "It looks like the eagle-bearer is not only our leader but also responsible for his party's safety."

Gemma stood and faced the group. "And their deaths."

"More traps, huh?"

The Italian historian shrugged. "They have been consistently in use."

"Tests to verify that we are, in fact, worthy," Spencer added.

Jack softly patted Marcus on the back. "Well, my dutiful *aquilifer*, onward."

Marcus turned and faced Jack, making his right eyebrow rise in question. "No onward?"

Marcus jammed the eagle standard into Jack's hands. "Yes, *now* onward." Marcus stepped back, grinning ear to ear. "Congratulations, Jack, you've been promoted."

"Yay…" Jack halfheartedly cheered. He gazed up at the eagle, then stepped through the archway. He paused after the single stride and faced Marcus again. "One question." Marcus' hands found his hips and he waited. "Is there a pay rise?"

Marcus stepped up to Jack and shoved him in the chest. "Get moving, eagle-bearer."

Jack turned away from him and eyed the darkness beyond. "I'll take that as a no…"

53

They marched due west from what Jack could tell. As they crossed the floor, the mosaic tiles gave way to smooth stone and an advancing downward grade. Jack checked his watch. They had been walking for almost ten minutes.

"We must be beneath the Euphrates by now," he said.

Jack pictured the famous river. It and its sibling, the Tigris, were considered two of the most important waterways in history. They had supplied Ancient Mesopotamia with sustainable life, assisting in creating the grandest empire of the time.

Babylon, Jack thought.

"We are close, yes," Marcus agreed.

"No wonder this has never been found," May said.

The Legion general nodded. "Everyone has always been fascinated with the river's eastern shoreline. To think, all they had to do was look to the west."

"And down," Jack added. "We've gotta be pretty deep by now."

"That we are."

May looked up, then back to Jack. "Refresh my memory, what's to the east of the palace?"

"The heart of Ancient Babylon," Spencer replied. "The city's ruins, the majestic Lion of Babylon, a replica of the Ishtar Gate, and, if you care to believe, the remains of the Tower of Babel."

"The Tower of Babel?" May asked. "I thought that was a myth?"

Jack gave her a wink. "We can look into it later."

"What are you—" Gemma started. "Wait, do you hear something?"

Everyone quieted and listened. Then they stopped. Jack heard something, for sure. He closed his eyes and tried to picture what it could be. Presently, all he could pull from the sound was static—white noise—or possibly…

"Water," Jack said, snapping his eyes open. "There's an underground river up ahead."

The ten-man team started up again, picking up their pace from earlier. Their fast walk turned into a subtle jog as they grew nearer.

"A river beneath a river?" Gemma asked.

Jack gave her a quick look. "I've seen stranger things."

May snickered. "Same."

The arched pathway gave way to another cavern.

"Oh my God," Gemma said, showing her light around the space.

It was then that Jack realized that she had yet to see either of the two Mouseion temples they'd found thus far. And like the others, this one was just as uniquely designed and constructed.

It reminded Jack of the one in York, the one dedicated to their missing Muse, Clio. Marcus' ionic columns were present. But unlike the York temple, this one had no roof, as well as no floor. In the latter's place was a raging river.

"What the hell is this?" Jack asked, flabbergasted. "You're kidding me, right?"

Stretching across the moderately-sized hollow, Jack counted twenty-four columns in all, twelve on each side. The cave itself was wider than it was long. Jack guessed it was roughly eighty feet from where he stood to the other side.

The team stood on a sizeable landing. In the center of it was a ten-foot-tall platform. On the side facing their entry point was a narrow flight of steps. No one scaled it, though. Everyone was too transfixed on the river.

Its surface was roughly eight feet beneath their boots. The drop didn't concern Jack. The river's speed did. There was no one in their group that could maintain their footing without being swept to—

Where, exactly? he thought. Jack followed the easterly flow and, unfortunately, discovered his answer. *Oh.*

"That's not good," he said.

Nine more lights joined his to perfectly illuminate dozens of impaled skeletons. Jagged spikes lined the walls down at water level. The river itself continued harmlessly beneath them, into a low opening in the rock.

"Note to self," Jack said. "If you fall, you get skewered."

He tore his eyes away from the dead and returned them to the water. "If this is the Underworld," Jack said, "then is this Styx?"

"It could symbolize that, sure," Spencer said.

"It does."

Jack spun and found Gemma staring up at the wall above the doorway. He spotted an engraving similar to the one back in the Wheel of Fortune *game* room.

"What's it say?" he asked.

She lowered her light and faced him. "This room is called the 'Crossing of River Styx.'"

"Of course, it is," Jack said, looking at the torrent below them. "Sometimes I really hate being right."

"Billion-dollar question..." May said, stepping up to the river's edge. "How do we get across?"

"Traditionally, it would be by boat," Gemma said, "though there is nothing traditional about this place. It is magnificent, however." May stared at her. "What? How can you not appreciate the construction?"

"Easily," May replied, emotionless.

"I don't see a boat," Jack said, checking the other corners of the pit, just in case.

Theo placed a foot on the bottommost step of the central platform. "What about up here?"

Jack looked at the eagle portion of the *aquila*, then met Theo at the base of the steps. The bigger man removed his own foot from the bottom step and moved aside. Jack took a deep breath and started his ascent, holding the eagle standard in front of him as if it were a bow staff.

Ten feet higher, Jack arrived at the top. There was nothing there except another small hole. But then he spotted something around the hole. He knelt and wiped away a layer of grime to find more Greek text.

"Gemma? A little help, if you would?"

Light footsteps followed Jack's request. The Italian historian arrived a few seconds later, joining Jack atop the platform. She took a knee next to him and quickly translated the text.

"It says, 'The Hero's Path.' And like May said earlier, Hermes was classically seen as the god of travel. It looks like the Mouseions decided to combine the different aspects of Hermes' character into a singular personification."

Jack pushed himself up. "I guess this is it then."

"Looks like it," Gemma said, also standing.

Jack tilted his head toward the steps. "You might want to stand clear."

Gemma nodded and descended the platform, relaying what she and Jack had found.

He lifted the eagle standard and aimed for the hole in the platform. Jack pictured Gandalf the Grey, but instead of shouting "You shall not pass!" he bellowed, "You *shall* pass!"

The base of the pole fit perfectly, sinking a foot before bottoming out. Once it did, the platform shook. The tremor continued into the landing, spooking the others, causing them to give the river a larger buffer.

There was no way for Jack to prepare himself for the next part. Additional ionic columns began rising out of the water, one after the other. When they all stopped, they were perfectly even with Jack's platform.

His eyes darted around the room, already seeing a pattern.

"It's an obstacle course," he said softly. Then, he looked down at the others and repeated what he'd said louder. "It's an obstacle course!"

"And it's soaked," May said.

Jack's enthusiasm was deflated a bit. "Yeah, it is. Thanks, Hermes."

Out of nowhere a heavy ticking picked up, reverberating around the temple. Jack spun, trying to find the source, only stopping when he figured it out. He looked down at his feet.

May understood as well. "Why does that sound like a timer?"

"She's right!" Gemma shouted, holding her hands over her ears. "It's speeding up too!"

Jack looked down at May, then to the *aquila* in his hands. "Sunnova bitch!" He turned, removed the eagle standard from the lock, and jumped. Not only was this some kind of ancient obstacle course, it was also a test of speed.

"The *aquila!*" Marcus yelled. "Jack, no!"

But it was too late. Jack was already airborne between the first and second columns, *aquila* in hand.

He estimated that the gap between each column was five feet, and yes, they were all wet and extremely slippery. Jack would've gone faster, but then he'd run the risk of falling and becoming a shish ke*Jack*. He needed to move quickly, but he also needed to keep his balance and timing.

The third column was to Jack's right. He made the jump, then turned back to the east and made another jump.

The fifth column was to the north, and the sixth and seventh were back to the west. When his feet struck the seventh column, the first one fell, returning to the river. The second column had stayed put, for now, but Jack knew it was only a matter of time until, it too, sank.

Columns eight, nine, and ten cut straight across the cavern, to the south. Jack gave himself a little extra room. He took two steps and leapt. When he hit his jump's peak, he saw that the top of the next column was slathered in something that resembled algae.

Oh, crap.

Jack hit it and slipped. Luckily, he only landed flat on his back, instead of continuing over the edge. His air left him, and he wheezed.

The second column fell.

Then the third.

"Get up, Jack!" May shouted. "It's speeding up again!"

Jack could hear it too. The ticking had definitely picked up.

He climbed to his feet, his lower back aching. He collected himself, and made the next two jumps without issue. Jack took a moment to catch his wind completely, watching as the fourth column fell. Now, he only had five between him and death.

"Move your ass, Reilly," Jack muttered through gritted teeth.

The eleventh column was to the east and the twelfth to the south. Jack completed both jumps as columns five, six, *and* seven fell together. Jack watched it all unfold, eyes open wide. He gazed up at the eagle, wishing he had wings.

"Too bad I don't have a Red Bull on me…"

He landed on top of the fourteenth column in time to see four more columns plummet back into the water.

"Whoa!" Jack shouted, feeling his footing falter as the column beneath him shuddered.

Jack leapt just as it fell. He didn't stop again. Jack jumped, and then jumped again. A second landing and platform greeted him to the west. He lobbed the priceless *aquila* over to it, then dove as the sixteenth and final column fell. Jack lost his footing, and his escape fell short.

He fell but snagged the edge of the ten-foot-tall platform with one hand. Jack dangled in the air, hearing a pair of female voices cheering loudly for him.

Using his free hand, Jack reached up to the ledge and caught it with his gloved fingertips. The glove's heavy texturing aided in his ascent greatly. Jack reset his grip and hauled himself up onto the platform. He rolled onto his back, breathing hard as he did.

"*Jack?*" he heard in his headset. It was May. "*You okay, Jack?*"

Jack turned his head and looked across the water. He gave the group a thumbs up, then slowly got to his knees. The *aquila* survived just fine too. Jack brought his eyes up enough to see a second archway. This one was identical to the one behind him over on the first platform.

He reached for the eagle standard, and once he wrapped his hand around it, Jack jammed it into the locking mechanism. When he did, the room came to life again, but this time, there was no timer. The columns returned to the height of the platforms, looking sturdy and unfailing.

It didn't shock Jack that May was the first one to test the obstacle course. She flew over it with ease. It also helped that she hadn't been forced to rush through it like Jack had. Still, she needed to be careful. The river was still surging below them. One false move and May would fall.

She stopped once she made it to column number sixteen. May was breathing hard, but otherwise looked fine.

"You okay?"

Jack nodded and got to his feet. "Yeah, I think." He cringed, feeling his knees protest the movement. "Been better too."

May smiled. "How about a vacation once we're done?"

Jack let out a laugh as May successfully completed the Crossing of River Styx.

54

Marcus was the last of the group to make the journey across Babylon's River Styx. When he did, he looked over the eagle standard before even recognizing that Jack was still alive. The man was more concerned with the *aquila's* wellbeing than that of Jack.

Why am I not surprised? Jack thought.

"I'm fine, by the way," he said.

Marcus looked him up and down. "Then why do you look so tired?" With that, Marcus descended the platform, leaving Jack in shock. Was this his way of teasing Jack?

"Asshole," Jack mumbled.

Marcus stopped three steps below Jack and turned. "Excuse me?"

Jack's eyebrows raised. "I said, 'let's go.'"

He yanked the pole free and held it out for Marcus to take. But the general didn't accept the offering. All he did was smile. The reaction was enough for Jack to spin and heave the *aquila* into the river. But he didn't. To do so would mean his death. May and Gemma's too.

"Nice work, eagle-bearer," Marcus said, turning and descending.

"Eat me, General."

Marcus didn't acknowledge the juvenile come back. He just finished his descent and continued forward to the exit. It, like the entrance, was nothing more than a large, open archway. Jack relaxed, knowing this would all be over soon. And when it was, he would gladly unload a full thirty-round-magazine of Taser rounds into every legionnaire he could.

Jack lifted the eagle standard, casually teetering it on his right shoulder. He wasn't going to carry it like Marcus had, as if he was leading some kind of marching band ensemble.

Marcus eyed him as he moved to the front of the pack. "What? It ain't *my* flag."

"You could still respect it," Theo snapped.

Jack didn't look at the man. He just continued past him. "Oh, I do respect *it.*"

Plainly, Jack respected the artifact, just not the people who idolized it.

He passed beneath the next archway, relying on May and Gemma's light. The women walked on either side of him. Their presence was reassuring, and incredibly brave, considering their present location.

The next passage was much shorter than the last one, a hundred yards at most. It ended at another arched doorway. The room beyond it was less grand, more normal in size. All ten team members piled in. Thirty feet from the entry point was another stairway that led deeper underground.

"Again?" Gemma asked.

"Looks like it," Jack replied, heading across the space. "Stay here, okay?"

May and Gemma nodded, keeping their lights fixed on the floor in front of Jack. He edged closer, studying his future footfalls closely. Nothing happened, thankfully. He made it to the next set of steps without conflict.

In the light, Jack also spotted something he dreaded. Not only was this, yet another, spiraling staircase, but the walls on both sides of it were filled with three-inch-wide holes. If Swiss cheese had been a wall, this was it.

"Looks like another trap mechanism." He glanced over his shoulder at Marcus. "More spikes." Jack returned his attention to the holes. He sighed. "What is it with these people and spikes?" But Jack knew why. Spikes would've been cheap to produce, and they were extremely effective. There wasn't a lot that could go wrong when your only job was to stab.

"Okay, we're good," Jack said.

The others joined him, but kept back a few feet, for now. As the light shifted, Jack noticed more Greek text engraved in the floor in front of the top step. There were also two symbols on either side of the text that he recognized but couldn't decipher. Jack lifted his eyes, following the steps down, seeing that one of each symbol graced an individual step.

They're random too, he thought. *There's no pattern.*

"Gemma, Spencer, you're up." The two historians stepped up next to Jack. He pointed at the text with the tip of the *aquila's* pole. "Down there."

Gemma and Spencer knelt to inspect it. Spencer rubbed his fingers over the text, clearing away a little debris. He and Gemma quietly conversed with one another.

"What does it say?" Marcus asked with a noticeable amount of aggravation.

Jack looked back at the man. "Hey, relax, will ya? They're doing the best they can."

Gemma looked up at Jack and gave him a thankful nod. Then she explained what they had found.

She pointed at the main text. "This says 'Siblings at Arms.' And look," she pointed at the left-hand symbol. "The diamond with a cross attached to its lowest point is the symbol of Athena, Greek god of intelligence and military strategy."

"And this," Spencer continued, tapping the other symbol with his finger, "the circle and arrow, is the symbol of Ares, the—"

"God of war," Jack finished. "And Athena's brother." Jack gazed down the stairwell. "Siblings at Arms, huh?"

"Yeah," Gemma said, standing, "Siblings at Arms… What do you think?"

He decided not to overthink things. This one felt pretty obvious, anyway.

"We avoid the steps marked with Ares' symbol," he said, turning and facing the group.

"You sure?" Marcus asked.

"Nope," Jack replied. "And please, if you'd like to test my theory for yourself…" Marcus didn't budge. Jack turned back toward the steps. "Yeah, didn't think so."

"Jack, there's something else."

He found Gemma kneeling again, brushing away more dust from the left-hand side of the trap title. Jack spied another hole in the floor. He gripped the eagle standard hard and lifted his foot to step over it but was stopped.

"Jack, don't," May begged, grabbing his arm. He met her eyes. "I mean, is it necessary to activate it?"

Jack looked at the stairwell, then back at May. "What happens if we don't?"

She relented and released Jack's biceps.

"I agree, for what it's worth," Gemma said. "I don't think the Mouseions were foolish enough to allow safe passage without the use of the key."

"Yeah, that's what I'm thinking too." He hovered the pole over the hole. "Okay, be ready, *and* be very careful with your footing." He gazed back at the group. "One bad step might kill us all."

Gemma and Spencer both tried to swallow down their fear but took matching steps away from Jack and May. May moved closer, in full support of what Jack was about to do.

She placed a hand on his shoulder and squeezed. "Do it."

Jack lowered the eagle standard into place, activating the "Siblings at Arms" trap.

There was the expected *clunk*, then nothing.

"Is that it?" Spencer asked.

Jack went to pull the *aquila* free but thought better of it. "Looks like I'm going last." He met Marcus' intense stare. "I don't know what'll happen if I remove the eagle."

Marcus joined Jack at the top of the stairwell. "Then it looks like you'll have to go first instead." He turned his head and looked at May. "Pray that your partner is right."

Marcus' tone had changed noticeably since they'd left the elevator. There had always been a twitchy edge to him, like the manic eyes of an overstimulated TV preacher. Marcus' *crazed* side revealed itself every time another piece to the two-century-old puzzle was fit into place. He'd dived deeper and deeper into his own zealous beliefs with every obstacle cleared. Soon he would be completely unhinged and extremely dangerous.

But Jack also knew there was a positivity in all of it. Marcus' thoughts would become clouded and he'd act irrationally. Like he had said, moments after the elevator had stopped.

All that matters is what's in front of us.

Jack wanted to interject, but May didn't allow it. She held up her hand and stopped Jack before he could even formulate a single word.

She gently touched his filthy cheek. "I can do this."

Jack stood tall and gave her a reassuring nod. "Think skinny." She looked down at her lean body. "Dammit, you know what I mean. Just be careful, okay?"

This time, May gave *him* a playful wink and stepped forward, eyeing the next stair with great care.

"Avoid the Ares symbols, right?" she asked.

"Yeah, avoid the Ares symbols."

May took a deep breath. The first step down featured Ares' emblem. She skipped it. The next one sported Athena's diamond and cross. She firmly planted her boot atop it.

Nothing.

"Oh, thank God," Gemma said, gasping.

May looked back at her and gave her a nod, then the trained operative continued her descent.

"Okay, people," Marcus said. "Let's get moving. May, if you could, call out the patterns as you come across them." He pulled his sidearm. "Jack and I will bring up the rear together."

Jack eyed the lethal pistol. It wasn't loaded with Taser rounds. "What's with that?"

Marcus' pupils were dilated and his facial muscles spasmed as he attempted a cheeky grin. "I'm not taking any more chances. This is our time and nothing—*nothing*—will stop us."

55

The way was steep and treacherous. Luckily, May was light on her feet and, thanks to her training, and her toned core and legs, she possessed the balance of a world-class gymnast. She studied each step carefully, then made her move, uncaring what the next one would bring. She focused on only what was directly in front of her. Thinking two steps ahead wasn't a viable option here.

"Nice and easy," she told herself. This was the hardest part of her new life. "Your life is the only one at risk."

Her thoughts turned to Jack. May needed to replicate his need to help others. It's what made him so good at what he did. He truly cared about what happened to someone else. Now, May didn't like it when an innocent life hung in the balance, or worse, when someone died that didn't need to. But she'd been trained to not let it bother her more than a skin-deep reaction of sadness. May would just shake it off and continue on.

That's not you anymore.

She jumped over an Ares step, landed gracefully, then turned. "Okay, Gemma, you've got this."

The Italian historian wasn't May. Actually, she was the least capable of any of the people here. Even Spencer had navigated the traps relatively well, minus a few mumbled complaints and deer-in-the-headlights looks. But not Gemma. She was wholly out of her element.

Gemma snorted. "Says the operative who's been doing this her entire life…"

"Fair enough," May replied. "But that doesn't take away the fact that you can do this too."

Gemma gave May a small smile. Then she gritted her teeth, eyed her landing, and jumped. May reached back over the two Ares steps she had just cleared and pushed against Gemma's forward momentum. She gripped the abdominal portion of Gemma's shirt until the Italian was back in control of her body.

"Okay, that was only a one step jump," May said. "The next one is twice that."

Gemma nodded and waited for May to vacate the targeted step. May turned and completed another two-step jump, using the wall to balance herself upon landing.

"I'm ready," Gemma said.

May nodded but noticed something. "I can't reach you this time, okay?" Gemma nodded, but didn't look at peace with the observation. "Remember, you've got this."

May sighed. *This feels an awful lot like babysitting.* Still, she needed to help Gemma. Besides being the right thing to do, there was another reason to aid her. May had no idea what would happen to the rest of the team if Gemma should falter and set off the trap.

She looked around. *It might kill us all.*

Gemma went airborne—and stuck the landing!

"Yes!" May cheered.

"Keep moving!" Theo shouted. He was behind Gemma and at the mercy of her and May's speed.

Gemma snapped around on the man, showing impressive bravery. "Would you like to switch places?" She faced May again and gave May a nod of thanks. "I can do this."

May spun and continued forward, proud of Gemma…and herself.

She'd look back and verify that Gemma was still holding her own, but no longer did she help her stick the landings. Gemma had gained the confidence she needed to take care of herself.

May mentally walked herself through the steps as she made them.

Skip one. Skip two. Skip none. Oh, sweet. She was thrilled to see two Athena steps back-to-back.

May looked up from her feet and saw that she was nearly done. She relayed that to the others.

"I see the end." She studied the next few jumps, seeing something dreadful. "You'll need to skip three Ares steps to reach the bottom, though."

"Three?" Gemma asked.

"Yeah, did you say three?" Spencer asked from somewhere further behind her.

May sighed. "Yeah, I did."

But before she got there, May still had two more jumps to make; another two step and a one step. She was getting tired too. The hard landings were doing a number on her feet and ankles, as well as her knees and lower back. And the stress of it all was giving her a headache.

She jumped, easily clearing the one Ares step. Then, without waiting, she jumped again. May felt her right ankle give a little on the impact, but she completed her last two step jump without a problem. To be sure, she tested the weakened joint.

"You okay?" Gemma asked.

May waved her off. "Fine. You?"

"Been better."

May eyed her landing and dove forward with extra gusto. She sailed head first over the three Ares steps and turned what could've been a harsh landing into an athletic roll. She tucked her right shoulder in, hit the floor, and popped back up to her feet.

Gemma eyed her with her hands on her hips. "Showoff."

May shrugged. "If it makes you feel any better, I think I jammed my shoulder a little."

"It does, actually." Gemma finished her second-to-last jump. "I didn't think robots could feel pain?"

May rolled her eyes and stepped up to the bottom step. "Alright, Dr. Conti, you are nearly there. Give this one all you've got."

Gemma's jovial expression morphed into a serious one as she concentrated on not dying.

She went airborne, doing exactly as May had said.

Uh-oh.

Gemma hit May like a bulldozer, knocking her to the floor. Gemma miraculously stayed on her feet, looking very pleased with her efforts. She spun and found May flat on her back. Eyes wide, she hustled over and offered her *coach* her hand. May took it and was hauled to her feet.

"You okay?" Gemma asked.

May dusted herself off. "Yeah, I'm fine." Her eyes took in the stairs. "But what about Jack?"

56

Jack gave Marcus a head start before following him down. But first, in order to do so, Jack needed to remove the key from its lock. He needed to pull the *aquila* free. Unfortunately, no one knew what would happen. And like a lot of the things that had happened over the course of a couple of days, Jack would have to trust in his innate ability to stay alive despite the odds.

"Alright, guys," he said, speaking into his comms, "here goes nothing." He yanked the eagle standard free. When he did a sound like a stone grinding against itself filled the air around him. He flinched, then stared at the eagle. "Aw, nuts." Jack went airborne. "Go, go, go!"

Marcus didn't need to be told twice. The *Legatus* picked up his pace, as did the men in front of him. Everyone jumped in rhythm with the person in front of them. To Jack, it resembled the most wicked game of Leap Frog he'd ever seen.

Spikes on either side of the top step activated, impaling nothing but air. As soon as they snapped shut, the next stair's trap activated—even the Athena steps!

"Oh, shit. Please, move," he begged. "We are in serious trouble!"

"I know!" Marcus shouted back. "I'm going as fast as I can!"

The remaining men were being chased deeper into the Babylonian underworld by what Jack would describe as a serpent of chomping spikes. He followed Marcus, knowing he would be going faster if he didn't have the guy in his way.

"Ah!"

Jack looked past Marcus to watch Damien, the other American, go down. Before he could cry for help, he was impaled by a dozen spikes and instantly killed.

"Oh, God!" Marcus said, gasping in horror, and worse, stopping.

"Dammit, Marcus, move, or we're next!"

The general looked back and past Jack, right into the maw of the advancing spike serpent. His eyes went wide and he turned and fled, moving faster than before. Jack followed, but he also got an idea, waiting for Marcus to disappear from view due to the curvature of the stairwell.

Jack landed next to the very dead legionnaire and swiftly relieved him of his sidearm. He jammed it into the front of his pants, concealing it with his shirt. Then he started his escape anew.

"Thanks, pal."

Even though Jack was nowhere near safe, he did feel better about his situation knowing he could now properly defend himself, when the time came for it. He knew it would too. Once they completed this grand adventure, Jack, May, and Gemma's usefulness would run out.

Jack made it to the last handful of jumps, but found himself moving too quickly. His momentum carried him forward too much. He was forced to jump again without being able to set his feet. But really, he had no choice. The spikes had sped up and were nearly upon him.

He watched as Marcus went airborne over the bottom three Ares steps. Jack was still two jumps behind him.

Schink!

The noise startled Jack. He glanced over his shoulder to see that the spikes were now only a foot behind him. He shouted in surprise and fear. Jack bunny hopped forward, then jumped again. This time, he planted the eagle standard pole into the last Athena step, using the *aquila* as a pole vaulter's pole.

Jack tucked his leg in and cleared the last Ares step but was caught from behind and slammed to the floor. His bell rung from the landing. He saw stars and felt slightly nauseous.

"Jack!" May cried, rushing to his side.

Jack lay on his left arm, *aquila* still clutched in both hands.

"What happened?" he asked, blinking hard.

May leaned over him and checked his back. Once she was done inspecting the damage, a grin formed on her face. "The spikes caught your rifle."

Jack shook his head, clearing the cobwebs some. "That explains the whiplash then." He released his hold on the eagle standard and tried to slip out of the rifle's sling, but couldn't. He looked up at Marcus. "A little help?"

The Legion general unsheathed his knife and stepped over Jack's prone form with a killer look in his eyes. Jack shrank back, and quickly snatched up the *aquila*.

He gave Marcus a sheepish smile. "The eagle-bearer leads the way?"

The *Legatus* huffed a breath and cut Jack free of his ancient bonds. He stood and slipped his blade back into its place on his hip. "Yes, he does."

Gemma came over and assisted May in getting Jack to his feet. "You okay?" she asked, inspecting an oozing wound underneath his hairline.

Jack touched the injury and winced. "Yeah—*ouch*—never better." He stood on his own, using the eagle standard as an improvised cane. "At least I've got myself a walking stick." May gave him an unamused glare. "Seriously, I'm fine."

"You don't look fine," Gemma said. She grimaced when Jack's dirty finger came away red after having been in his hair.

May shook her head. "To be fair, this is how he normally looks…"

Jack frowned at the comment, even though she was mostly right. Jack really did get the crap kicked out of him on a regular basis.

Gemma faced the staircase. The spikes were still engaged. Jack was curious how they were going to deactivate the trap. The spikes that had killed the American legionnaire had immediately returned to their home in the wall holes. But these hadn't.

"Oh, eagle-bearer…" Jack rolled his eyes and found Marcus standing off to one side of the room. "If you would be so kind…"

The only blemish in this room was a tiny six-inch-wide square in the floor near the left-hand wall. Even from here, Jack could see the hole.

And there's my answer.

Jack lifted the *aquila* back onto his shoulder, then dropped it into the hole with a bang. Every legionnaire in the room stared at him with murder in their eyes. Jack didn't care. He just looked back and watched as the spike trap reset itself. When it did, a gruesome scene unfolded.

"Oh, God!" Gemma said, covering her mouth with her hands.

A river of blood slowly flowed down the center of the steps. Its origin, the dead legionnaire, that was thankfully out of sight around the corner.

Jack looked away, finding Marcus still staring at the blood.

"Sorry, 'bout your friend," Jack said, "but you know what they say about us Americans?" Marcus wasn't in the mood, but he faced Jack. "We're like the Highlander. There can be only one."

With that, Marcus socked Jack in the jaw. The TAC operative went down like a sack of potatoes, holding his mouth as he did. May, once again, tried to come to his aid, but she didn't get there.

The Legion general drew his pistol and aimed it at May's chest. She skidded to a stop, raising her hands as she did.

Marcus' eyes never left May, nor did he blink. "I am through with your insults, Jack. Next time you disrespect me or my people, she dies." He snapped his attention down to Jack. "This is my promise."

Jack quietly gave Marcus a nod of understanding. The man was unhinged and would follow through with his threat—Jack was sure of it.

Marcus lowered his aim and stepped away. May carried on and helped Jack to his feet. Now, his lip was split from the solid, straight right. He licked it, feeling the sting. The pain focused him, though.

A smirk formed on his face. *But you aren't the only one with a gun, are you?*

"Why are you smiling?" May whispered.

Jack blinked, cleared his throat, and wiped the expression off his face. "Nothing." He looked at her. "It's nothing…"

"It's never nothing with you."

Jack couldn't argue that.

"Move out!" Marcus shouted. "Eagle-bearer, up front!"

Jack hefted the *aquila* back onto his shoulder and made his way to the front of the group. Theo didn't move out of his way.

"Move," Jack said, earning a sneer. "I said, *move*. This team's most important member needs to get through." Jack leaned around Theo and looked at Marcus. "The *aquilifer* was a legion's most important member, right?"

"You are not a member of this legion."

Jack tapped the base of the eagle standard. "This says otherwise. I doubt the great Quintus Cerialis would let some lowly peasant carry his eagle, am I wrong?"

Marcus gritted his teeth. "Theo, let him pass."

The bigger man stepped aside. As Jack went to step past Marcus, the general ensnared Jack's arm. "Remember what I said."

Jack ripped his arm out of Marcus' grasp. "And remember who it is that's leading you to your long-awaited victory."

Gemma stepped forward. "He's right. None of you would be here without Jack."

The historian straightened her posture and marched up next to Jack and stopped, looking as confident as she ever had. May followed Gemma's example and took her place by Jack's side, flicking her eyebrows at Marcus as she did.

"Shall we continue?" Jack asked.

Marcus let out a long breath. "Proceed."

Jack gave Marcus a slight bow and left the room. The next tunnel pushed onward, straight and true. Jack slowed and heard the sound of running water again.

Oh, man. Come on!

"Is that the river again?" Gemma asked.

"Can't be," May replied. "Can it?"

Jack glanced over his shoulder and shrugged. He had no idea. "I guess it's possible that we're headed back to the east."

"If we are, then that'll put us underneath Styx and the Euphrates," Gemma confirmed.

"Yeah, it will," Jack agreed. "But why?" He stepped into the next cave. "Oh, that's why."

57

The Mouseions outdid themselves with the next chamber. The ceiling rose fifty feet off the floor and was perfectly smooth. There wasn't a single imperfection in sight. Like several other rooms, this one was circular, but unlike the other rooms, ninety-nine percent of the available wall space was covered in cascading water.

Jack would've gladly called it the Waterfall Room, but surprisingly, that wasn't even the most amazing thing here. Sitting in the middle of the cave was the largest trumpet Jack had ever seen. It filled the space admirably too. Jack guessed it was about thirty feet tall and twice that long, and it sat on top of a stone pedestal that was nearly as tall as Jack.

And it was brass.

Jack definitely wasn't expecting something this big to be made of anything other than stone or perhaps an exquisite marble.

This wasn't your modern-day trumpet, either. It didn't have any buttons or valves. To Jack, it resembled a straightened-out military bugle. The brass instrument was typically used as a single-calling device. Throughout history, the bugle had been used to relay orders, signal surrender, or used at military funerals to indicate that the deceased soldier had been laid to rest.

But it had also been used to tell a fighting force to charge!

Jack pictured a column of medieval-era men, blowing the instrument in celebration, and not with their butts, like in *Monty Python and the Holy Grail*.

"A Roman tuba!" Spencer said, voice trailing off.

"A tuba?" Jack asked, facing the curator.

The Brit nodded. "You can call it a trumpet if you'd like, but centuries ago, it was known as a tuba. It was very common to have three-dozen tuba players in a single Roman legion too."

Jack headed out into the middle of the room, looping around to the right so he could get a look at the *tuba* in its entirety. Upon entering, they had been near the instrument's mouthpiece. Now, ninety degrees to the right, Jack was able to take in the entire discovery.

"Please tell me I'm not the only one seeing a trumpet of this size for the first time?" he asked.

No one said otherwise.

Gemma stepped away from the group. "Is that a lyre?"

Jack had been so transfixed on the mammoth brass instrument, that he had yet to appreciate the detail in the design. Carved into its solid-marble stand was, indeed, a lyre.

"It's the Heroic Trumpet of Clio!" Spencer said, eyes wide.

"She has a trumpet now?" Jack asked, getting Spencer's attention. "First an ancient guitar. Now this. Was she and the other Muses in a Roman-era ska band?" Everyone stared at him. "What? I'm just trying to wrap my head around this, same as you."

"Could you do it quieter, though?" May asked.

Spencer cleared his throat and continued. "As the Muse of History, Clio would sometimes be seen blowing a Roman tuba, signaling that another daring tale was about to be told."

Gemma looked at him. "But why is it here?"

"You got me," Jack said, looking around. Except for their entry point, the entire cave was wall-to-wall with waterfalls. His gaze stopped on the mouthpiece. "Hmmm. Brass, huh?" He handed May the eagle standard. "Eh, what the hell?"

Jack started towards the mouthpiece of the tuba.

"What are you doing?" May asked, getting everyone's attention.

He spun, walking backward now. He shrugged. "When in doubt, blow!" Before she could say something, Jack continued. "Trumpets are also used for celebratory purposes, right?"

"Um, yes?" Spencer replied.

Jack glanced back at him. "Maybe they're telling us we're near the end?"

"What are you doing, Jack?" Marcus asked.

Jack positioned himself behind the mouthpiece. He grinned. "I'm gonna blow my horn."

And he did.

Jack applied his lips to the end and blew as hard as he could. The action resulted in a deafening, concussive force that reverberated around the spherical cave, bouncing back and forth like mad.

As Jack pushed in more air, something astonishing happened. The ceiling, just opposite of the open end—the bell—cracked, and the waterfall's force in that section lessened.

Bingo! He thought, forcing more air through. *There must be something behind it!*

The ceiling cracked again, cutting off even more water. Jack's vision began to blur a little, but he kept blowing. As the ceiling crumbled, Jack released his tight-lipped hold on the mouthpiece, wiping a string of drool away from his chin as he stepped around the instrument.

Now, the water only dripped, and instead of a wall of falling water, there was a set of massive, forty-foot-tall stone doors with, yet another, lyre engraved into the center of them. The symbol itself must've been at least half the height and width of the doors.

The entire group hurried over to the beautifully carved door. The artistry was incredible. All the Muses were represented, but none of them held a candle to the prominence of Clio and her lyre.

These people really did worship her, Jack thought.

Jack met May on the way, relieving her of the eagle standard. As they neared the doors, Jack slowed and took it all in. Waterfalls now lined either side of the doors.

"Fantastic..." That's all Jack could come up with. He looked away from the doors, catching May staring at him. "Right?"

She smiled and returned her gaze to the four-story-tall stone gates.

"What do you suppose is on the other side?" Spencer asked.

"What we've been waiting for our entire lives," Marcus said, stepping closer. "Jack," Jack took his eyes off the doors, and found Marcus staring at him. "Open it."

Jack silently nodded and carried the eagle standard over to the doors. As he expected, there was a hole in the floor not ten feet from the gorgeous ornate carving. Jack bypassed the hole and stepped up to the doors themselves.

"Jack," Marcus warned.

Jack didn't pay the man any attention. He simply, gently, raised his hand and caressed the bottom of a Muse's dress. The detail was so lifelike. The way the dress billowed seemed real.

"Jack?"

He turned. May had stepped forward a little. Her eyes said enough. She was ready to go. Jack gave her a small nod and slid the *aquila's* pole into what would hopefully be the last lock.

The doors ground open, revealing a dark void beyond. As everyone moved closer, and added their flashlights, the sight of what waited for them made Jack drop the *precious* eagle standard at his feet.

He stepped over the felled *aquila*, leaving it where it was. He was too entranced to care. The next room wasn't really a room at all. It was more of a corridor or something resembling the inside of York Minster.

A great hall?

But instead of the high arched ceilings displaying precisely fashioned, stained-glass windows, the walls displayed what must've been years' worth of man-hours of intricately produced engravings. Jack clicked on his own flashlight and headed further inside, never once taking his eyes off the walls.

The one on the left started with a beautiful valley of trees and farms, dotted with homes. He even saw people meandering about.

He shifted his gaze to the right-hand artwork, confused by what he saw. It depicted what was obviously a funeral. The deceased individual lay inside a dome of some kind, which was odd. What hit Jack the hardest was the thousands of people in attendance. Jack got the feeling that if the artist had more room to work, he would've added even more people.

The only sound other than that of the fading waterfalls were that of the nine-man team's footfalls. Everyone was in just as much shock as Jack. He stopped fifty feet later, understanding what all of this was now.

On the left was a young boy with what must've been his father. They stood atop a pedestal with a large crowd gathered around them. Both wore crowns.

Jack shifted his attention to the opposite wall. It featured a single warrior holding a sword. Instead of a crowd of onlookers gathered at his feet, he was in front of a sea of death.

"It's him," said a quiet, female voice. Jack tore his eyes away from the relief. Gemma stood, staring at the same piece of art that he'd been looking at. Tears streamed down her face. She looked at Jack. "It's Alexander."

"She's right," Spencer said, looking as choked up as Gemma. "This is a celebration of his life, similar to what you'd see in a church, but pertaining to Christ."

"Alexander wasn't a god," May said, holding the eagle standard in her hands.

Jack held out his hand and accepted the *aquila* back. May closed her hands around his for a moment. They met each other's eyes and simply stared.

"To his people he was," Gemma countered, breaking their concentration. "Kings of the time were considered living gods to some."

May didn't argue. Jack wouldn't have argued, either, not when he was going up against the likes of Gemma or Spencer.

"Does this mean..." Marcus said, turning in a slow circle.

"It does," Spencer replied. "We've done it."

All nine explorers turned and faced the other end of the long, tall hall. The end was barely visible in their combined light.

Jack had anticipated that he would see another set of gigantic doors. Instead, there was only a narrow archway. Jack respected the decision to go easy on the exit. It would've taken away from the majesty of all this.

He couldn't wait; Jack pocketed his flashlight, lifted the eagle standard, and took off at a jog, as did everyone else. In this moment, they were all equals, lovers of history with a desperation in their hearts to see this to the end. There wasn't a single individual present that didn't appreciate what surrounded them.

The tomb of Alexander the Great, Jack thought. *I can't believe it!*

Jack looked behind him, finding a combination of warriors and scholars following close. He then looked at the artifact in his hands. Everything that was happening felt ridiculous. It *was* ridiculous. Yet, here he was, holding the actual Ninth Legion eagle standard in his hands, leading a legionnaire detachment to the Macedonian's lost tomb.

With thirty feet to go, Jack slowed to a fast walk. He didn't stop when he arrived at the narrow, four-foot-wide archway. Jack continued inside at a steady pace. Like everyone else, he needed to see what was waiting for them. He decided to carry the *aquila* over his left shoulder so he could reignite his own flashlight. Jack held it out, but something caught his eye further in.

There was light inside the next room, but not just any light.

Blue, purple, and green light?

Jack once more pocketed his flashlight. Twenty feet later, he exited the passage and fell to his knees. He peeled off his earmuffs and removed his ski mask, tossing them both aside.

"It can't be..."

Not only was it one of the most beautiful sights he'd ever seen, even on par with the Valley of Petals, but it was a place that, until now, was supposed to be pure myth. Like the Valley of Petals, there was nothing in history that said this place existed, either—zero evidence, whatsoever.

The ceiling was covered in a glowing carpet of blues and purples, but also dotted in green here and there. That's what Jack had seen back in the tunnel entrance. He knew what was causing the colorful display too.

Bioluminescent fungi.

There were stalactites throughout the breathtaking growth too. And if you only gave the carpeted rock formations a quick glance, it resembled plant life being suspended from the ceiling.

Jack's tear-filled eyes stared into it in wonder. The ambient light gave the entire cavern enough light to see by. To Jack it felt like an eternal dusk. It calmed him some. The same type of luminescence could be found in several places along the floor too.

A waterfall graced each of the rectangular cavern's four corners, as did the tide pools beneath them. They weren't as powerful as the ones back in the trumpet room. These felt purposely regulated, as if the builders wanted them to be more peaceful. This place was meant to be serene.

A narrow stream ran across the floor in front of Jack. The same tributary seemed to loop around the entire cave, reconnecting with the four tide pools as it did. Directly in front of Jack was a gently sloping stone bridge that spanned the stream, allowing access to what lay beyond.

What lay beyond was a Greek temple that mirrored the Parthenon in Greece. Majestic columns formed a perimeter around the central floorspace within the structure. This temple owned no roof, though. The supports had been attached directly to the cave's ceiling. Even from here, Jack could see that the glowing fungi had begun to spread down a few of the columns.

"Jack?" May asked, kneeling beside him. "What... Where are we?"

He sniffed back his tears and looked up at her. "Think about where we are, May."

Jack turned his attention back to the subterranean paradise, specifically to the plant matter attached to the ceiling and the grounds surrounding the temple. "This isn't just Alexander the Great's tomb. It's the Hanging Gardens of Babylon."

58

The others entered behind Jack and May. Each one of them, no matter how hardened they'd become over the years, were taken aback by the magnificence of the Gardens. Jack stood to murmurs. The legionnaires sounded shocked by what they saw, confusing Jack.

He looked at Spencer. "You're shocked by all of this?"

The curator nodded, mouth open. He blinked hard, dragging his mind back into the present and out of the clouds. "We... Nothing we have describes this. The Hanging Gardens are supposed to be a fairytale."

"Does this look like a fairytale to you, oh, *great* Historian of the Legion?" Marcus asked, wheeling on Spencer with disdain in his voice.

Spencer shrank back. "Marcus... I'm telling you the truth. There is nothing in our people's combined records that tell of this being here! It was the Mouseions—it must've been. *They* hid this from us!"

Jack looked away from the confrontation. "They hid it from everyone. Pretty impressive, if you ask me."

"What do you mean?" May asked.

Jack motioned to the cave as a whole. "There is zero evidence of this actually existing, yet everyone accepts it as one of the Seven Wonders of the Ancient World. The other six have been confirmed by a number of reputable sources, but not the Gardens." He looked at Gemma. "Nebuchadnezzar II was said to have built this, right?"

She nodded. "Yes, though, like you said, there is no physical proof to the claim. In fact, there's a lot about Ancient Babylon we don't know, despite how powerful and influential the kingdom was."

"Hmmm," May mumbled.

"Have something on your mind?" Jack asked.

She looked at him like he was an idiot. Of course, she did. "Is it just me, or does it feel like the historical record has been tampered with?" She faced the group. "There are facts that *should* be known, that aren't. Something smells funny to me."

"The Mouseions..." Marcus said, his voice trailing off. "They deliberately altered history to keep all of this hidden. I bet they hunted down all traces back to this place, physically removing it from record."

Spencer looked at his feet and quietly said, "Until there was nothing left."

"How do you hide the Hanging Gardens of Babylon, not to mention everything we had to get through to even make it here?" Gemma asked.

"Don't forget York and Nijmegen," Spencer added. "Can you imagine what all of it cost to build? It must've been astronomical!"

"Speaking of costs..." Jack said, looking around. "Does anyone see any treasure, because I sure as hell don't."

That snapped everyone out of their comatose state.

"That is unfortunate," Marcus said. "Maybe there's another chamber?"

Jack had no idea, but that didn't feel right.

"Yeah, I'm not sure about that. This feels like the end to me." He looked at May, then Marcus. "I think *this* is the pot of gold at the end of the Mouseion rainbow."

Spencer's eyes opened wide. "Alexander's fortune financed all this?"

Jack shrugged. "That's my guess, yeah. Like you said, the costs must've been astronomical. Imagine how many people they had to payoff too."

"Clio was the Muse of History, correct?" May asked from out of nowhere.

"Uh, yeah?" Jack replied. "We've kinda covered that already."

She rolled her eyes and continued. "And the Mouseions, the original history protection squad, worshiped her for what she stood for?"

Jack glanced at Gemma. "Yes?" she replied.

May scratched her head. "Yeah, I have to agree with Jack. There was never any treasure here." She turned and looked out over the Gardens. "*This* was the Mouseion Holy Grail, not a pile of gold and jewels."

Jack could hear Marcus seething with rage. He hissed as he breathed in and out. "And the Macedonian's tomb?"

Gemma perked up. So did Jack.

He faced toward the temple. "How 'bout we go find out?"

Jack left the others, descending a short, three-step stairway. He continued along a designated pathway constructed of one-foot-wide, square, stone pavers. The grounds around him were pocked with more of the glowing fungi. Jack wasn't a mycologist in any way. The only real relationship he had with a mushroom was on pizza or in miso soup.

Looking around, Jack assumed that they had been maintained like any garden would, but not now. Besides the main, winding footpath, Jack could see snippets of additional pavers beneath overgrown sections of mushrooms and other random fungi that Jack had no shot of identifying. The one commonality between the plant life was their evolutionary gift.

"Kinda reminds you of the Pandoran plant life from Avatar, huh?" Spencer asked.

Jack agreed. "Yeah, it does, though I hope there isn't a tribe of big blue hunters here too."

"How does it shine?" Theo asked.

Jack had learned that Theo didn't usually speak unless it was important, or he needed answers. So, Jack gave him one.

"Bioluminescent fungi. Most likely *Armillaria mellea*, the most common of its kind."

"How do you know that exactly?" Gemma asked bluntly. She caught herself quickly. "No offense."

"Ouch, thanks, Gemma. If you must know, I've been spending a lot of time underground lately, and I was curious. So, one day, I looked it up. Found a cool video online about it. Don't quote me, but I think it's something about them developing another means of energy production other than photosynthesis. Can't do that without sunlight. I think it's some kind of internal chemical reaction called...called..." he snapped his fingers, "chemosynthesis!"

"Statues up ahead," Marcus said, staying otherwise silent.

Jack saw them up ahead. A pair of statues graced the next courtyard, but before they could get there, they needed to cross their first obstacle since entering the fabled Hanging Gardens of Babylon.

"Let's see..." Jack said.

The footpath ended at a quaint stone bridge. It arched over an eight-foot-wide stream that Jack now saw had been hand cut to allow water to flow freely through the cavern. There was no shoreline in the traditional sense. The cave floor ended at a perfectly shaped edge.

"It's humid in here, isn't it?" Gemma asked.

Jack hadn't been paying attention to the air, but he did find it rather thick. "It's probably what keeps everything growing down here. The moisture in the air waters everything."

Jack tested the foot of the bridge. It didn't so much as groan. The craftsmanship on display here was like everything else he'd seen from the Mouseions. Perfection. Jack mounted the bridge and made it halfway before stopping. He stepped over to the left-hand railing, clicked his flashlight back on, and aimed it into the water. The stream wasn't all that deep. Jack was pretty sure his head would stick out of it if he were to get in and stand upright.

"See anything?" May asked, joining him.

Jack clicked off his light and looked at May. He smiled. "You look good in this light."

She rolled her eyes and began her descent.

"'You look good in this light?'" Gemma asked, repeating Jack's question as she stepped up next to him.

Jack shrugged. "It was meant to be a compliment."

The Italian historian could only shake her head and follow May.

Spencer was next to grace Jack with his presence. "Women, right?"

"Like you'd know..." Jack said, spinning away, and leaving the stunned curator in the dust. He hurried to catch up to the woman he just accidentally insulted. "May, hang on. I—"

"She's one of the Muses, isn't she?" May asked, stopping and staring at one of two statues. This one was to their right.

"I think so, yeah," Jack replied, momentarily forgetting why he had rushed to May's side.

There was another Muse off to the left of the next footpath. Both of them were roughly thirty feet from it. They each looked inward toward those who graced the walkway.

"Are they guarding this place?" she asked.

Jack looked around. Then, he remembered what he'd been told about Muses. "No, I don't think that's it."

"How do you know?"

He placed his hand on May's lower back. "I mean, I don't know for sure, but they're Muses, right? I'd wager that they're just keeping an eye on things, but not the way a guard dog would. The Muses didn't do that kind of work.

They are here to be celebrated, not called upon for battle."

Jack also spotted a lump in the cave floor to the northern side of the statue. There was one across the way on the southern side too.

Benches?

He looked back, then up, trying to reorient himself. If they had really cut back under the Euphrates and Styx, then yes, they were, in fact, traveling east. *Which means my directions are sound. The Gardens run west to east.*

He pictured him and May sitting together, relaxing and taking all of this in.

May! Jack just remembered why he had rushed to catch up to her.

"Sorry about the 'look good in the light' thing, by the way."

She shrugged. "Eh, it's nothing. I know what you meant. And thanks, by the way. But do me a favor, next time you want to compliment my appearance, don't say that I look good while we're deep inside a half-lit cave filled with trippy mushroom light," she looked at him, "okay?"

Jack smiled. "Deal." His eyes darted away, but then landed on her again. "Still...you do look nice."

May chuckled softly, then tilted her head toward the temple. "Thanks, Romeo. Come on."

As they continued their exploration of the Hanging Gardens, Jack confirmed that the streams did, in fact, connect via waterfall tide pools. The leg of water that flowed north and south originated from the same place as the streams that flowed east to west.

There were several other bridges deeper in the Gardens. Jack counted two on the left, as well as two on the right. All four of them spanned the pair of eastern running streams, giving their patrons access to the grounds on the other side of the tributaries. And if the design was symmetrical, then there was another bridge hidden somewhere behind the temple.

"What do you think this place is, two-hundred-feet-wide?" Jack asked, mentally calculating the cavern's dimensions.

"Give or take, yeah," May replied. "And the length? I say it's twice that. Maybe even more?"

Jack had an idea. "Hey, Gemma, Spencer, do either of you know how big the Parthenon is?"

The two experts conversed with one another for a second.

"About one hundred and twenty feet by two hundred and forty feet," Gemma replied.

Jack gauged the width of each column, then added them together. Then he did the same thing to the spaces in between.

"Yeah, this is pretty close to that. A little smaller, but not by much."

"Uh, guys?" Gemma asked, slipping between Jack and May. She pointed into the temple. "Is that who I think it is?"

Jack looked at Gemma then May, before returning his attention to a lump in the middle of the temple floor.

May silently mouthed the only question that mattered at the moment. "Alexander?"

The three of them took off at a sprint.

59

They slowed as they neared the steps leading up into the temple. There were only three of them, but they were taller and deeper than usual. Jack would risk falling if he rushed up the stairs.

He made it to the top first. He didn't wait for May, Gemma, or anyone else, either. Jack charged inside, power walking between a pair of robust ionic columns.

Thanks, Marcus, Jack thought, unsure if he should punch the man instead. Jack was filled with an excessive amount of useless information as it was, and he knew that little tidbit was going to stick around for a long, *long* time.

He, once again, slowed as he approached two giant stone…tablets? Jack wasn't sure what they were, actually. They were perfectly spread apart and angled toward the middle of the structure. There were also two more of the things on the other side of the temple's lone occupant.

This was the first time they'd gotten any inclination that this place had also been used as a tomb. Until now, it was *just* the Hanging Gardens of Babylon. Jack's feet felt like lead now. He struggled to move, and not out of fear or exhaustion.

It was out of absolute wonder.

Standing watch at the center of the temple was the very recognizable Clio, the Muse of History. As Jack had expected to see, she was holding her lyre. She was also standing over the Macedonian himself.

"Alexander the Great…"

As Jack neared, his brain finally processed exactly what he was seeing. Yes, the missing Macedonian king had been laid to rest here. And yes, it was in a sarcophagus. But this wasn't like any sarcophagus that Jack had ever seen before, or heard of.

Alexander lay on a beautifully chiseled, marble base. It sat in the center of the temple and was roughly four feet wide and eight feet long. The pedestal was covered in intricately produced horses, soldiers, gods, a castle, rolling hills, and even a few of the Muses.

Then there was the lid.

"Can someone explain to me why Alex is inside Snow White's glass coffin?"

Gemma was dumbfounded. The only response she had was to shake her head vigorously.

May was equally as perplexed but didn't show it as openly.

The lid was made entirely of glass. It covered the deceased king like the top of a slow cooker. There weren't any seams in sight, either. This was one, single piece of morphed glass.

"Look at him!" May said, stunned. Her eyes were locked in on Alexander, and her bottom lip quivered.

Jack did see him, and he felt like how May looked.

"It looks like he died yesterday," Jack muttered.

He moved to the side of the coffin to get a better look. Alexander didn't look like he had died in 323 BC. His skin was intact, as was his flowing, dirty blonde hair. He'd been handsome in the past, but it was clear to see that he'd been ill before he had passed on. His cheeks were sunken in and his body's musculature had atrophied, though that was difficult to confirm beneath his regal robes.

The only other item beneath the domed glass, other than Alexander, was his crown. It sat atop his chest.

"What are you..." Marcus skidded into view, opposite the coffin from Jack. "What is this?"

Jack didn't blink. He couldn't! He was too afraid he'd miss something else astounding.

"They must've built this before his death," Gemma said quietly. "It's the only way they could've gotten him covered so quickly."

Spencer stepped up to the foot of the sarcophagus and gently laid his hand on it, staying quiet. "Unbelievable."

"I've heard of something like this before," Gemma said quietly. "It was first described by Aristotle in the fourth century BC."

"What was?" Jack asked.

"The first diving bell ever recorded," Spencer replied, staring at the king. "Constructed entirely of glass by the world's foremost glass makers—*Macedonian* glass makers." Spencer lifted his hand and headed around to where Marcus still stood. "Legend says that Alexander used one to explore beneath the surface of the sea. Back then, it was simply a solid-glass covering that would be lowered upside-down into the surf, trapping breathable oxygen inside."

"Incredible..." Marcus whispered, wide-eyed. "Absolutely incredible."

Jack turned away from Alexander's remains. He didn't even know if that was the right thing to call his body since it was still technically here. To him, remains were usually skeletal and completely devoid of recognizable features.

But not Alexander.

Jack had intended to do nothing except get his heart rate under control and get his emotions in check. This was why Jack loved this job so much. Being here, in this place, was worth more than any treasure to him.

Treasure... Jack thought, looking around. *Are you really gone?* His eyes landed on one of the four sizeable stone tablets. *Hmmm.* Jack slowly turned in a circle, giving each of them a quick look before returning his attention to the one at the northwest side of Alexander's coffin.

There was clearly text engraved into them. In fact, the entire ten-foot-wide by twenty-foot-tall tablet was covered in what would most likely be Greek lettering. For these things to be here, surrounding Alexander, they must've been extremely important.

"Hey, Gemma?" Jack asked.

"Yes?"

"Follow me, will ya?"

Jack headed for the tablet. Gemma and May were hot on his heels. Even Spencer had joined them. His presence made sense since his entire existence had revolved around the gathering of information. The guy lived for knowledge. It was actually a very respectable quality.

And the only one he has.

The text was fairly small. Jack had to squint to even recognize some of the characters. Gemma didn't seem to be struggling with it. Even before she'd reached it, Jack could see her mouth opening and closing as she read bits and pieces to herself. Then she hurried forward.

"I can't believe it!" she said.

"What is it?" May asked.

Gemma skittered to a stop in front of the tablet, running her fingers beneath the words as she read. "It's their history." She looked at Jack and May. "It's the entire history of the Mouseion Guard."

"The Mouseion Guard?" Marcus asked from next to Alexander's sarcophagus.

"That's what she said," Jack replied.

Marcus left the Macedonian's side and ventured over to the northwest tablet. Theo came with him, but not Zayn, Xavier, or Aldo. They were still gathered around the great king's body, deep in conversation with one another.

"Here!" Gemma said, leaning in closer. "This talks about their hierarchy. Um, yes, okay…"

"What does it say?" Marcus demanded.

Jack held up a hand. "Chill. Let her work."

Marcus didn't like Jack's response, though he didn't berate Gemma again, either.

"Okay, so far, we have Ptolemy I and his son, Ptolemy II."

Spencer slid in beside her. "That makes sense. They founded what would become the Mouseion Institution in Alexandria. That is a historical fact."

"Yes, it is," Gemma confirmed, looking back at him. "But maybe it was the other way around. This makes me think they founded the Mouseion Guard first, and the institution was merely a result of it." She faced the tablet again. "There's also three other names of significance." She squinted. "No, wait… This can't be."

"What is it, Gemma?" Jack asked.

"Cassander, Antigonus, and Seleucus."

May glanced at Jack. "Are we supposed to know who they are?" she asked.

"The *Diadochi!*" Spencer said, stepping away. "This changes everything!"

Jack was getting frustrated. "Will someone please explain why these people are so freaking important?"

"They are the Successors," Marcus explained. "They are the rival generals who divided Alexander's kingdom after his death. The wars between them are legendary."

Jack looked at Marcus, then stuck a thumb out towards the tablet. "But this makes it sound like they were best buddies."

"Because they were," Gemma said, running her filthy hand through her hair. "They lied about their relationship with one another."

May asked the only question that could be asked. "But why?"

Gemma quickly translated the text. She stood tall and faced Jack. She opened her arms out wide. "To hide all of this." Her arms flopped to her sides. "They lied so they could keep the rest of their empire focused on war and not what was happening behind the scenes."

May blew out a long breath. "That's…brilliant."

"They were some of the brightest minds of the time," Spencer added. "We shouldn't put all of this past them."

"Still…" May said, gazing back at the tablet.

Gemma knelt as she continued to read. "The *Diadochi* took an oath while standing over their fallen king, to keep a promise they made to him."

"What promise?" Marcus asked.

Gemma gave Jack a long look, combined with a smile, then looked at Marcus. She knew Jack was going to like this next nugget. "To protect history."

Jack's eyes opened wide. "Whoa."

"You said it," Spencer said, fumbling with his hands. "This is bigger than huge."

"Like Gemma said at the beginning," May said, "this changes everything. The entire separation of Alexander's kingdom was a coverup."

"But to protect history?" Marcus asked. "Are you sure?"

Gemma nodded. "I am. They formed the Mouseion Institution as a way to formally protect what they found here, and what it represents, as well as its secret protectors, the—"

Marcus' eyes went wide. "The Mouseion Guard." He looked west, back toward their entrance, no doubt picturing the obstacles that had been laid in their path. "It was the Mouseion Guard that built all this—that erased all evidence of it."

"It seems so," Gemma said. "A secret society within a society."

"Where does all of this fit into the historical timeline?" Jack asked.

Gemma looked back in on the tablet. "Immediately after Alexander's death, what would become the Hellenistic Period."

"What happened after that?" May asked.

Even Jack knew that. "The rise of the Roman Empire." He laughed softly. "It's perfect." He glanced at Marcus. "That's how they got people inside Rome. The Mouseion Guard never left. They continued to operate deep within the Roman Empire, no doubt taking advantage of Rome's resources and connections to continue working on all of this."

"But the Hellenistic Period was nearly three *hundred* years long," Spencer said. "Are you telling me that the Mouseion Guard stayed active for three centuries?"

Jack nodded. "Very active. Like thousands-of-sleeper-agents active."

Marcus shut his eyes and turned his face down to the floor. "You were right, Jack. They had agents within Rome's legions." He opened his eyes and looked at Theo. "Within the Ninth Legion."

"I'm confused about something," May said.

"Aren't we all?" Jack asked.

She ignored him and continued. "How is it that Alexander's body is here? I know he died here, but I figured he'd be returned home to Greece."

"Very astute observation," Gemma said. "Give me a second, will you? This might take a while."

Jack shrugged. "Take your time. It's not like we're going anywhere."

She nodded her thanks, then took a moment to collect her thoughts. "Okay. History tells us that Ptolemy I, Alexander's favorite general at the time of his death, stole the king's body from the men of another general back in Greece, Perdiccas, while Alexander's remains were en route to Macedon. Now, without understanding Ptolemy's true motives, this would just seem like a run-of-the-mill, opportunistic power grab, right? But it wasn't!"

"What are you getting at?" Marcus asked.

"I'm getting there… It's said that Alexander wanted to be buried in Libya, in the Siwa Oasis, but Perdiccas went against his king's wishes and attempted to bring him home to Macedon."

Gemma coughed, but kept her lecture going at light speed.

"Alexander was, instead, spirited away to Egypt and interred in Memphis until his final resting place was ready. Think about that." She looked at Jack. "With everything we now know, I'd wager that *this* place was always supposed to be Alexander's tomb, possibly even years before he actually died."

Spencer wandered around to the other side of the tablet. Jack hadn't even thought to check it for more text.

"Um, fellas?" he said. "You should see this."

Jack and May went around to the right. Gemma and Marcus went left. When they rejoined one another, they stopped and stared. Spencer was on one knee, inspecting the decomposed remains of a body.

Jack stepped closer. His eyes weren't locked on the deceased, but rather, what he was wearing.

His robe, while decrepit and rotten, featured a red sash with a very familiar emblem on it.

"It's Clio's lyre," Jack said, putting it all together. He met eyes with Marcus. "The lyre is their symbol—the symbol of the Mouseion Guard, protectors of history."

They're us.

60

"He's one of them," Jack said, kneeling next to the corpse.

Everyone gave Jack and Marcus room to investigate the dead man. He'd been hidden from view, tucked behind the mammoth tablet with ease. Jack inspected the man's hands. They each held an object—a tool.

"A hammer and chisel?" Marcus asked.

Both men turned and faced the tablet. There, near the bottom, was an unfinished engraving.

Gemma knelt next to Jack and immediately began translating it.

"After nearly four hundred years of existence, I am the last of my order," Gemma read, wincing as she read. It hurt her to read such a statement. "We've been betrayed by one of our own, one of our brothers."

Jack glanced at Marcus. He'd been talking about the same thing.

"Nero's pet," Gemma continued, her voice softening, "General Cerialis, has killed so many already."

Marcus' eyeballs were about to bug out of his head. Jack smartly stood, pulling Gemma to her feet as well. Both gave the legionnaire more room in case he broke out into a tirade.

Marcus stood, calmer than Jack had expected. "He is named?"

"Yes," Gemma said. She looked down at her feet. "The timeframe works out too," she glanced up at Marcus and Spencer, then stepped back, "but you already know that... Sorry."

Spencer faced his commanding officer. "We were lied to?"

"It appears so," Marcus replied, balling his hands into tight fists. "If this is true, then Quintus did not put together a taskforce to find Alexander's tomb. He already knew where it was." He gnashed his teeth in anger. "He hunted down his own men. He...betrayed them, the Mouseion Guard."

"Then, that would make us Mouseions too, wouldn't it?" Spencer asked.

Marcus floated his hand over the sidearm holstered on his hip, but he didn't unholster it. Jack casually folded his hands in front of him. They now lay directly atop his concealed pistol. If things went south, he'd need to be the quicker draw.

"We are," Marcus said. "And that's who disassembled the *aquila* to hide this place from Quintus and Nero." He looked around. "They saved this place from that tyrant." His face was emotionless, frozen in time. "But we are still legionnaires...and traitors." He looked at Jack and tapped his own chest. "*We* are the traitors," he pointed at the body, "not them."

Jack knew what the man was going through inside his head. He'd been very clear about his feelings for the people he had thought had betrayed his ancestor. But as it turned out, it was Quintus Cerialis that had been responsible. He had been the one to turn on his own people within Ptolemy's secret protectors.

"What about the nickname General Cerialis is given?" Jack asked, trying to sound as genuine as possible, which he was. "'Nero's pet?'"

Neither of the legionnaires replied.

Gemma took the opportunity to give her own opinion, one Jack trusted to the fullest. "He saw an opportunity and took it. Nero must've found out what had been going on and offered the general a deal."

Jack stepped toward Marcus, hands raised, showing no threat. "He was trapped, Marcus." The Legion general looked up at him. "You know damn well what would've happened if he had refused that psychopath..."

And that's exactly what Nero had been. Nero had been, by all accounts, nuts.

Marcus sneered. "I would've sooner cut my throat than cut a deal with that filth!" Tears welled in his eyes. "Quintus Cerialis was a despicable traitor!" Marcus eyed Spencer. "He chose gold over his brothers." Marcus blubbered like a child. "He chose gold over his brothers…"

Jack was honestly heartbroken. He didn't need to like Marcus to feel for the guy. His entire life, and that of his ancestors, had been a lie. He'd performed countless atrocities, all in the name of something he wasn't.

"Even after hundreds of years, they dutifully served Alexander and his generals," Marcus said to no one in particular.

Jack looked around at all the solemn faces. Even the other three legionnaires had joined them in time to hear that their existences were a shame.

"To be fair, I think we're really glossing over how much of an asshole Nero really was." Jack lifted a hand to put on Marcus' shoulder, but decided against touching the man. He liked his hand where it was. "If Quintus didn't do what he did, there's a good chance you wouldn't have been born. That's gotta count for something, right?"

Marcus laughed. "I bet you would've loved that."

"Hell no. I mean, you've been just as much of an asshole as Nero was, but I would never wish that upon someone." He thumbed over to Theo. "Well, maybe him."

Theo stepped toward Jack.

"Stand down, Theo," Marcus ordered.

Marcus' number two didn't respond. He closed the distance between him and Jack with another giant step.

Jack was stunned when Marcus slid between them. "I said *step down*, Lieutenant." He looked around the temple, then over his shoulder at Jack. "Our war with them is over."

That perked Jack up. He turned and took May by the hips and brought her in for a quick kiss.

Then, Jack realized something. He grinned. "Did we just reform the villain?"

May sighed. "Yeah. Kind of cliché, don't you think?"

"Better than being at the wrong end of a firing squad."

Theo spun and stomped away.

Marcus relaxed. He closed his eyes and tilted his head back. "All those years wasted. And for what?"

Gemma stepped forward. "It's not too late, you know?" Everyone except Theo gave her their attention. "It's time to choose, Marcus. Are you the general of the Ninth Legion's descendants, or are you the leader of the modern-day Mouseion Guard?"

"What are you doing?" Jack hissed, not that it mattered. Marcus could hear him.

"What I can," Gemma replied. "Besides, it's not like we can arrest him or anything. He can do whatever he wants from this moment forward."

"But he killed your boss," May said. "Jack and I were there. It was in cold blood. They killed a bunch of cops too."

"And what about the paratroopers back at Piazza del Popolo?" Jack asked. The mere mention of Gemma's favorite spot in the Rome-turned-battlefield stung her.

She looked away from Marcus. "I know. And for that I cannot forgive him." She looked at him again. "But it's not me who needs to forgive him." Marcus faced her. "He needs to forgive himself."

"Enough!" Everyone's attention left Gemma and Marcus and darted over to Theo. The biggest man in the room turned, eyes on fire. "I will not simply walk away after everything we've done to get here."

"Theo," Marcus said in a calming voice, "I—"

"Will listen to me!"

Marcus held up his hands in surrender. "Alright. Go ahead."

Theo snarled. "You've become weak over the years, Marcus. Your behavior here has confirmed as much." Theo stood impossibly tall. "You are not fit to lead us anymore."

Jack expected Marcus to draw his pistol and put two in Theo's gut. But he didn't. Marcus' shoulders sagged. The man was utterly defeated by the revelation learned here.

"You're right," Marcus said quietly. "I am not fit to lead you." He gazed up at his long-time number two. "So, I won't. I resign as your general."

Not only did that shock Jack to hear, but it blew Theo's mind. It also pissed him off more.

"Just like that, you quit? Just like that?"

Marcus looked around again. "Yes, I do."

Theo barked something in Latin. Zayn, Xavier, and Aldo came to his side.

Jack, May, Gemma, and even more surprisingly, Spencer, came to Marcus' aid.

The two groups eyed one another before anyone spoke again. When someone did speak, it was Jack.

"Looks like we've got ourselves a good old-fashioned Mexican Standoff." He, once again, placed his hands in front of his concealed pistol. "How 'bout we settle this in a way that no one gets hurt."

"Tell that to Damien," Theo said.

"Technically, he tripped and killed himself," Jack said. "That's on him."

Theo's lips morphed into a scowl. "Sorry, that came out wrong."

May sighed. "It usually does with you." Then she mocked Jack. "You look good in this light…"

Gemma couldn't hold back her laughter.

"You find this funny?" Theo shouted, quieting the Italian historian quickly.

"No one does, Theo," Marcus said. "Stand down…please."

Theo grinned. "I don't follow orders from you anymore." He looked at the legionnaires standing beside him. "And neither do they. We are here for Alexander's fortune. We are here to finance our rise from the shadows."

"You still don't get it," Marcus said. "There is no fortune. No rise. There never was. We should be taking this news and contemplating our next move, not killing one another like Quintus and his men did."

Theo didn't reply. He just dug his right foot into the floor more, getting into a classic boxer's stance.

Uh-oh.

"Hey, Spencer?" Jack asked.

"Yes?"

Jack leaned around Marcus and looked at the Brit. "When things get ugly, do me a favor and look after Gemma, will ya?"

The curator silently nodded, then looked at Gemma and gave her a nervous smile.

Marcus stood to Jack's left. May stood to his right. The two non-combatants were on either end of the five-man line.

"Just to be clear," Jack said, speaking to Marcus but staring at the men twenty feet across from him, "I still hate you."

Marcus let out a long breath. "The feeling is still very mutual."

61

Jack couldn't believe that he was teaming up with Marcus. However, Jack wasn't sure if Marcus was really fighting alongside him, either. This felt more like Marcus fighting to *not* fight at all. He was obviously confused and wanted to avoid further conflict in any way possible, but the only way to avoid conflict was to destroy the men standing twenty feet across from him.

No one drew their pistols, or raised their E-Rifles. May was armed with the latter.

But Spencer has both, Jack thought, wondering if there was a way to get his sidearm into May's hands. *No, he'll need them both to protect Gemma.*

Everyone here was trained in the art of taking the other's life. Luckily, the stalemate continued. Jack needed to get Gemma to safety *before* bullets started to fly.

"Gemma, Spencer," Jack quietly said, "go."

The legionnaires across from Jack stared at him. He doubted that they'd be opposed to Jack making his side of the contest a shorthanded one. Thankfully, no one tried to shoot Gemma as she took a step backward. Seeing her success, Spencer also began to backpedal. Neither were stupid enough to turn their backs, either.

Jack could tell that Theo was itching to get moving. But Jack could likewise see the indecision in his eyes. This was going to end with somebody's death, possibly multiple somebodies.

"Leave," Jack said, eyeing Theo.

"Excuse me?" Theo replied.

Jack repeated himself. "Leave. If you value your life and the lives of your men, you'll leave."

"And if you value yours, you will shut your mouth."

"Oh, I value my life." He tilted his head right. "Hers too. Heck, I'm even down to save Marcus' skin right now, and I don't even like the guy."

Theo squinted at Jack, tilting his head slightly to the right. "Why? Why defend Marcus after everything he's done?"

This topic had always been a struggle for Jack. To most, Marcus didn't deserve anyone's help. If anything, he deserved to die.

"Because it's the right thing to do," May replied.

Jack was impressed. He smiled. "What she said."

Out of the corner of Jack's eye, he could see Marcus look at him before returning his attention to Theo and the others.

With Gemma and Spencer gone, it was now three on four. Jack only possessed his pilfered pistol. Marcus had a pistol and an E-Rifle. His body language suggested he'd be going for the lethal option. May only had her E-Rifle, and it was currently slung around on her back. She was also still holding the eagle standard, gripping the pole hard.

What are you planning? Jack thought.

Theo moved first, going for his sidearm, just as Jack had anticipated.

Working from concealment was nothing new to Jack. He habitually practiced drawing from both a shoulder holster, and his waistline. He lifted his shirt, fumbling for the pistol's grip for a moment. Without a proper holster to keep it positioned correctly, the gun had sunk lower into his pants, making it difficult to grab on the first try. He got it on the second try and did the only thing he could do. He made himself a smaller target by diving backward.

As he did, he saw the *aquila* go sailing into the air, directed at the man to Theo's left, Aldo. The legionnaire instinctively abandoned his rifle to protect the sacred relic from being damaged.

Midair, Jack aimed his pistol at the man and shot him in the gut. The *aquila* struck Aldo in the chest as he grabbed for the wound instead. Both impacts knocked the man to the ground.

A split second after Jack pulled the trigger, he was struck in the left forearm by a Taser round. The painful jolt knocked the gun from his two-handed grip as he landed flat on his back.

May brought her E-Rifle around. Not only had Aldo's attention been taken by the airborne eagle standard, but it had caught Xavier's attention too. He stood to Aldo's left. The result was Xavier getting his rifle up too slow, though he did get a round off in time to strike May in the thigh as she knelt to take her own shot.

Her electric round struck Xavier in the left eye. If the penetrating power of the projectile didn't kill him, the shock radiating through his brain did. He fell face first to the temple floor, unmoving.

Marcus and Theo traded blows, shooting one another.

Marcus' bullet slugged Theo in the center of his armored chest rig, punching the air from his lungs. If he hadn't been wearing a protective rig, he'd be dead.

The ex-Legion general wasn't so fortunate. Theo's shot was much more successful, striking Marcus in the meat of his left shoulder.

Zayn had been the only combatant not injured in any way. He had also flinched during the first round of gunfire, and had yet to pull the trigger. He aimed his rifle at Marcus but didn't get a shot off.

Spencer leaned out from behind the northwest tablet and sent a volley of Taser rounds into the lone, upright gunman. They hit home and incapacitated the man. He fell forward with a healthy thud of skull on floor.

Theo reacted by snapping his sidearm up and forcing Spencer back into hiding behind the tablet with a series of trigger pulls. Two hit nothing but air, but one smashed into the priceless relic.

Jack clambered to his feet, leaving his pistol, and running north. "Scatter!"

He made it three steps before he realized that May hadn't gotten up.

"Run!" she shouted, favoring her right leg.

Jack turned, and was about to come to her rescue, but was driven back by a pair of wild shots from Theo. The big man had sat up, but was leaning hard to his right. His compromised posture was making it difficult to get a bead on Jack as he turned and fled.

Jack made it to the northern edge of the temple, and was about to leap across the three-stepped entrance but was, instead, sent tumbling down them due to getting pounded in the upper back by a jackhammer. Jack landed hard on his side, rolled, and finished his chaotic, painful exit on his stomach.

For a moment, he just lay there, feeling out his injuries with a series of deep inhalations. Breathing was difficult, but he'd been in this situation before. In a couple of minutes, he'd be fine—still in agony—but alive.

"Oh, Jack!" called Theo. "You forgot something!"

Jack tried to remember what he could've forgotten. The first things that came to mind were his gun and the eagle standard that May had—

May!

Jack launched to his feet, uncaring what his body was telling him. He quickly looked for Gemma and Spencer, but couldn't find them. He could've really used the curator's sidearm right about now. Marcus was missing too, for that matter. Jack knew the man wasn't dead. He'd seen him dive for cover behind the southwest tablet, shortly after taking a round to the shoulder.

Jack cringed as he climbed back up the steps. He kept a column between him and Theo, just in case. He continued to look for his backup while he climbed.

But Marcus, Gemma, and Spencer were still missing.

"Where are you guys?" Jack went to activate his headset, but remembered that he had tossed it aside after entering the Hanging Gardens. He sighed and called, "Marco?"

"Polo!"

Jack froze. It had been May who had responded, and it sounded like she was hurt.

He lifted his hands, favoring his throbbing left arm as he did. The Taser round had, essentially, given him a dead leg in the muscles of his lower arm. He couldn't even begin to move his fingers without sending a shocking jolt up his arm and into the meat and nerves encompassing his shoulder and scapula.

He stepped out from behind the column and kept going, re-entering the Parthenon-sized, roofless temple. Jack looked up at the beautiful, glowing ceiling. He loved that the Mouseion builders had kept the ceiling intact instead of tearing the fungi down or simply blocking it with a traditional roof.

Theo held a pistol to May's head. She cringed, having to put most of her weight on one leg. Jack couldn't imagine the pain she was feeling if his arm hurt as bad as it did. Theo wasn't in perfect condition, either. He was still having a hard time standing fully upright.

The Legion goon dug the muzzle of his gun deeper into May's temple.

May hollered.

"Stop!" Jack yelled, stopping fifty feet from Theo and May. "You win, okay?" He glanced back over to the nearest tablets, but Spencer was gone. Marcus and Gemma were still missing too. Jack cleared his throat and held out his hands. "All of this is yours." Theo looked around, pleased with the prospect of owning the Hanging Gardens of Babylon. Jack pointed at May. "Just let her go."

Theo dug the pistol's muzzle in a second time, smiling when May squirmed. "No," he replied, meeting eyes with Jack again, "I think I'll watch you suffer instead." His eyes turned ice-cold. "Tell me, how do you think it will feel to watch your love die?"

A sharp cough was quickly followed up by something striking the back of Theo's skull. His face went blank, and the gun fell from his hand. He lurched forward and dropped, dead before he hit the temple floor.

Jack stared at him. "It would feel just like that."

May dropped to one knee, grabbing at her thigh with both hands. Jack rushed forward, scanning the temple grounds for the source of the killing blow.

"Where's Marcus?" May asked.

Jack held out his hand and helped May up, taking on half of her weight. "I don't know."

The footsteps of a single man caught both Jack and May's attention. They snapped their heads to the west and watched as a black-clad soldier entered the temple. Jack was stunned to see someone else down here. He was also too far away for Jack to identify, and the tactical half mask covering his nose and mouth didn't help.

"Fan out!" the newcomer shouted. "Secure this room!" Jack looked around but couldn't see anyone else. The soldier, who was obviously a team's leader, pulled down the mask and smiled. "After all these years, I'm still watching your butt."

Jack squinted, shocked when he recognized the soldier. "Keno Dyson?" Jack made sure May could support her own weight again before leaving her and wrapping his arms around his old Delta teammate. "What the hell are you doing here?"

That last time Jack had seen Keno was just before he was discharged from service, so five years ago. He'd been on Jack's Delta team for two years and, as it seemed, been promoted to team leader. Keno had been with Jack during his fateful mission in Mosul.

They parted and May limped up next to Jack. He, once more, wrapped his arm around her waist.

Keno studied May for a second before answering. "A friend of yours called in a favor. A *dead* friend."

That made Jack's eyes open wide. Never in his wildest dreams did he think Raegor, who was legally dead, would ever call in this type of support.

"Marcus," May whispered, looking around.

Right!

"Tell your men," Jack said, "there are two friendlies and one unfriendly out there somewhere."

"Gemma, Spencer, and Marcus, he's the leader of this group," May explained.

Jack didn't know what to think of Spencer. Was he friend or foe now? He had helped when it mattered most, so Jack had decided to give him the benefit of the doubt.

"Copy that," Keno said, relaying the message into his comms system.

While he did, Jack turned to look at the mayhem from their standoff. Two of the men still lay where they were. Jack figured that both were dead. Xavier looked like he had his brain fried, and Zayn may have suffered a fatal blow to the head after Spencer had stunned him. The third man, the one Jack had shot in the stomach, had successfully made it around to the opposite side of Alexander's glass sarcophagus. As of now, he was face down, lying in a pool of blood.

Then there was Theo. His body was twenty feet from Zayn and Xavier's, but he was just as dead.

"Okay, they're on it," Keno said, keeping his eyes on their surroundings while they talked. "So, what has Jack Reilly been up to since leaving the military? Your boss wasn't exactly forthcoming about what you do. Last I heard, you got a job as a park ranger after retiring." Keno looked up at the cave ceiling, then over at Alexander's coffin. "This doesn't look like Yellowstone to me."

Jack shrugged. "You'd be surprised how easy it is to get lost out there."

Keno eyed him and grinned. "Is that what happened?"

"I'm afraid it's classified," May said, putting the discussion to rest.

Jack gave Keno a wink. "I'll tell you over a beer someday."

"You better." The Delta team leader gazed at the columns to his right. "I mean, we are standing inside the Hanging Gardens, after all." Then, he glared at Jack. "And don't even get me started on the shit we had to navigate to even find you."

"Don't forget about him, either," May said, pointing at the coffin.

"Who's he?" Keno asked.

Jack smiled wide. "Alexander the Great."

The stoic soldier choked on his own air. "Is that who that is? Looks like he died yesterday!"

"I said the same thing," Jack said, taking in the sight of the eerily fresh corpse.

Keno held up a hand and listened to a call coming through. Jack and May couldn't hear the other end of it, but with how relaxed Keno's stance was, Jack wasn't worried. If it were bad news, Keno would've acted as such.

"My people are inbound," Keno explained. "Found your friends, though one of them is dressed like these men here." He pointed at the four dead legionnaires.

Oops.

"Yeah, a lot has happened recently," Jack explained. "But you have my word, he'll cooperate."

May draped her left arm over Jack's neck and reset her footing. "When can we leave?"

Keno's expression darkened some. "Not until tomorrow night, unfortunately. It's too close to sunrise for extraction." The three of them looked east, hearing footfalls. Gemma and Spencer were led in by two soldiers. Spencer had his hands up in surrender. Jack was happy to see that Gemma wasn't being treated as a suspect. She did hang close to the curator, however. "There's also a chance we might never leave."

That punched Jack in the stomach. "Why do you say that?"

"We tripped a switch after coming in through that ancient elevator shaft. Damn thing closed on us." His eyes burned. "Seriously, Jack, what the hell is with all those traps? And how the hell did you get through them the first time? They were already deactivated by the time we got to them." Keno blew out a calming breath. "Don't suppose you have a way to reopen the lift?"

Jack and May eyed the eagle standard lying next to Aldo's remains.

"As a matter of fact, we do," May replied, grinning ear to ear.

Looking around, Jack noticed something. "Where's Marcus?"

Keno asked, speaking into his comms. "Do we have eyes on that unfriendly?" His face said it all. "Nothing, so far."

Damn, where the hell did he go? Jack thought.

Then it hit him. "The water! It has to have an outlet somewhere."

Keno understood, quickly repeating Jack's suggestion. "Check the water. Look for an outlet." He looked at the two Delta operatives. "Gibby, go help. Duck, stay here and keep an eye on our *friend*."

"'Gibby' and 'Duck?'" Jack asked.

Keno shrugged. "Gibson and Donald."

"What about the throne room door?" May asked, kick-starting another round of worries in Jack.

"Oh, shit," Jack said. "Yeah, that would be bad if it was still open."

"No idea," Keno added. "Hopefully, it closed too, or else we'll have the entire Iraqi Army waiting for us."

"What about the guards?" Jack asked, piling it on higher.

Keno sighed. "We'll have to deal with that when we deal with it. Nothing we can do right now."

"The E-Rifles might help with that," May said, pointing to several lying about. "Non-lethal rounds. Ask Jack, they worked like a charm on them last time."

Keno closed his eyes and rubbed them. "Please don't tell me you shot a guard with one of those things."

"Fine, I won't."

Keno left them to privately converse with his people. Both Jack and May relieved two of the legionnaires of their pistols. Even though Jack doubted Marcus would attack them right now, he wasn't taking any chances. And it was pretty obvious that he'd escaped somehow.

Two of the men searching for Marcus had, indeed, found an outlet tunnel as wide as the streams themselves. It was very possible that Marcus had escaped that way. Jack doubted he'd head back to the elevator with a Delta assault team on location. Jack truly did believe what he had thought beforehand.

Marcus didn't want to fight anyone right now.

Jack looked up at the ceiling again. "You gotta admit."

"What?" May asked.

"There are worse places to spend the day."

With May's left arm still draped around his neck, she used her free hand to gently caress his chest. "Worse people too."

62

Eagle County, Colorado, USA

The mission had been a success in many ways. Jack and May had discovered the fabled Hanging Gardens of Babylon, while simultaneously uncovering the final resting place of Alexander the Great. They had also made it out of Iraq.

Raegor stood behind his desk, inspecting the chip in his autographed bat. Eddy sat across from his desk. Both were relieved but utterly exhausted.

"So, are you going to tell me who you called on my behalf or not?" Raegor asked, facing her. "I think I deserve that."

"Fine, but you should probably sit down first." Raegor didn't budge. "Oookay. Don't say I didn't warn you." She smiled wide. "Hugo Nunez."

Raegor's legs turned to Jell-O and he fell into his chair. "The Colombian smuggler?"

"The same," Eddy replied, clearly enjoying his reaction. "He and Jack have stayed in touch."

"Why him, Eddy?"

She shrugged. "I figured who better to help smuggle someone out of the country than someone who's been smuggling things his whole life."

"Dammit, Eddy, what you're talking about is human trafficking!"

Her right eyebrow rose. "You do know that's how we'd get someone out of the country, right?" Raegor opened his mouth to say something but was cut off. "Sorry, Solomon, but you're worth it."

Raegor grabbed the water bottle from atop his desk, opened it, and drained it. "Worth it enough to contact someone like Hugo Nunez?" He let out a tired laugh. "I'm not sure if I should feel grateful or disappointed?"

Eddy stood and retrieved another bottle of water from Raegor's private mini-fridge. She handed it to him before sitting back down.

"I guess that depends on what you think of Hugo."

Raegor took the bottle and opened it. "Exactly."

EPILOGUE

Babylon, Mesopotamia
323 BC

Alexander was dying. Fever had nearly taken him days ago, but the great warrior had valiantly fought to stay amongst the living. Rumors of foul play had begun to circulate through the king's camp. But Ptolemy knew better. He had watched Alexander live a reckless life for years. Each time his king, his friend, grew ill, it was worse than the time before. Something was sapping Alexander's ability to fight off this latest illness, even at the youthful age of thirty-two.

"Ptolemy, my friend..."

The king's general knelt beside him and grasped his offered hand. Alexander winced. Whether it was the movement that pained him, or Ptolemy's legendary grip, he did not know. Nor would he ask.

"I'm here, my king."

Alexander smiled weakly. "You... You are the strongest one, Ptolemy. The loyalist one. It is you who will lead in my absence."

Ptolemy looked up into the eyes of the other generals, Cassander, Seleucus, and Antigonus. Only these chosen few were permitted to be in the king's presence during his final hour.

The other generals turned to Ptolemy, put a fist to their chests, and bowed. They accepted him as their new leader.

"What of this place?" Ptolemy asked. "What of the Great Garden?"

Alexander leaned up from his bed, showing a strength everyone had thought left him. "Protect it." He gazed at the others, fighting off unconsciousness. "Protect the knowledge we've collected."

The other generals, once again, placed a fist on their chests and bowed.

Ptolemy also bowed. "I promise. This place will not be defiled."

Alexander laid his head back. "I have one last request."

"Anything," Ptolemy said, gently raising their clinched hands, kissing the top of Alexander's.

The king smiled. "I would like to be buried here...in this paradise."

"As you wish," Ptolemy replied. "Everything is already being prepared, per your instructions."

Alexander had ordered a very specific style of sarcophagus. It had been produced in record time by men working around the clock.

The task of interring Alexander in the garden would not be as easy as it sounded. Macedon traditions allowed the king's successor to assert their right to rule by simply burying their predecessor. Others would want to do the same thing, both here in Babylon, and back home in Greece.

Others like Perdiccas, Ptolemy thought. *He cannot be trusted.*

Perdiccas, like the men standing before their ailing king, was a general of the Macedonian Empire. Ptolemy had always found the man to be overly hungry for recognition. If given the chance, Perdiccas would attempt to seize control of Macedon, as well as Alexander's hard-fought empire.

Ptolemy, the present generals, and another handful of select men, would need to do some substantial planning for this to work. In doing so, Ptolemy would also have to make himself something he wasn't, the villain.

So be it.

It also meant that Ptolemy wouldn't be going home anytime soon. But he'd have to worry about that later. Plus, he had always possessed a deep love for Egypt. The first thing he'd have to do was switch the king's body with another. Luckily, along with Alexander's failing health, gone were his looks too. He was now a shell of a man. It had happened quickly this time. Alexander had barely eaten anything in the last two weeks. If the illness wasn't killing him now, starvation was.

"Ever faithful." Alexander closed his eyes. "Thank you for your service, my friend." He let out a long breath, then fell still.

The king was dead.

Ptolemy released Alexander's hand and stood. Those in attendance placed their fists on their chests and bowed. They stayed in this posture for some time, praying to the gods that they watch over the late king.

Ptolemy opened his eyes, signaling the others to do the same.

"What now?" Cassander asked.

The favored general gazed at his comrade, then back down to Alexander's corpse. "We do as our king commanded."

"What of his remains?" Antigonus asked.

Ptolemy sighed. "If we are to do what I believe is necessary, then we will need to work deep within the shadows. Few can know of our purpose. There is also the risk of being counted as an enemy of our homeland."

"All of us?" Seleucus asked. "Are we all to become the enemy of the people like Perdiccas?"

Ptolemy stepped away from Alexander's body, taking in the wondrous gardens. "No." He faced them again. "Just me." The grumbling commotion picked up within the ranks. Ptolemy slammed his fist against his breastplate. "I choose this!" They quieted. "The rest of you may return to Macedon, but not before we come up with a long-term solution, yes?"

The others bowed.

"First things first, find another recently deceased and place him in Nebuchadnezzar's palace."

"Will the men not suspect foul play?" Cassander asked.

"No," Seleucus replied. He motioned to Alexander. "This is not what they remember."

"We can cover him too," Antigonus suggested.

Cassander looked troubled.

"Yes, General?" Ptolemy asked.

"These ideas are grand and all, but how are we going to do such a thing?"

Cassander asked. "There are too many eyes. They will come to us for answers."

Ptolemy knew Cassander was correct. This wasn't going to be easy. "We divide his kingdom."

The others gasped at the near-blasphemous statement.

"We are to become enemies with one another?" Antigonus asked, stunned.

Ptolemy held up a hand, silencing them. "Hear me out, brothers. We will divert our people's attention away from all of this. You and I will assume control of Alexander's kingdom, playing the roles of greedy, power-hungry foes."

Seleucus scratched his chin. "It's brilliant." He looked at his brothers-in-arms. "Think about it... There will be such a panic—an uproar even. Chaos will ensue."

"Yes," Antigonus agreed. He faced Cassander. "As you said, they will come to us for answers, but also for guidance."

"Cassander?" Ptolemy asked. "Do you not agree?"

He softly laughed. "Do I agree, no. Is there a better option to fulfill our king's last request, also no." He brought his eyes down to Alexander. "We must only include our most loyal men. To ask anyone and have them reject us... It will mean their deaths." He looked up at the others. "Does anyone disagree with that?"

No one voiced their objection.

Antigonus stood tall. "So, what of the kingdom? Who takes which region?"

"I believe we can come to an arrangement in the pending days," Ptolemy replied. "We each have unique knowledge of the different lands, but I believe we will do this juncture a disservice to decide on that now."

No one argued.

Ptolemy gave each of the three men in attendance a hard stare before speaking again. "Are we all in agreement?" They each looked at one another and nodded. Ptolemy held out his hand. "Then we are bound to one another by honor, to fulfill our king's dying wish."

Cassander laid his hand atop his. "For the king."

"For the king," Antigonus repeated, placing his hand on top of Cassander's.

Seleucus' hand followed. "For the king."

In that moment, an idea came to Ptolemy. "We will honor Alexander. We will pray to Clio, the Muse of History, for her guidance." Ptolemy placed his other hand on top of the group's hands. "All hail the Mouseion Guard!"

The others responded as one. "All hail the Mouseion Guard!"

Ptolemy smiled. "Welcome, Generals." He released their hands. "Now, come. We have much work to do."

Chamonix, France
Present Day

It had been a month since Marcus and his legion had discovered Alexander's tomb with the help of Jack, May, and Gemma Conti. But everything Marcus and his brethren had worked for—everything their *ancestors* had worked for—

had been for nothing. The Macedonian's tomb, as well as its magnificent location within the fabled Hanging Gardens of Babylon, had been slathered in blood. And worse, Marcus had discovered that his ancestor, Quintus Cerialis, had been the traitor, not the Mouseions. He had turned on his own people.

Just like me, Marcus thought, playing back the moment he became the Legion's adversary.

He still agreed with his decision to disband from the group. He just regretted the way it had happened. Marcus had teamed up with the enemy to "win the day." But now, after thirty days, Marcus didn't feel like he'd won anything. He'd actually lost everything. Marcus had even lost the Hanging Gardens. He attempted to scout the palace one night, but had been spooked by something lurking in the shadows of the grounds surrounding it.

It felt as if someone had been watching him. So, he left. Plus, it wasn't like he was getting in. The Americans had not only taken away the tomb and the garden, but they had also taken away the *aquila,* the only way underground.

"It was taken by thieves," he muttered, walking down the darkened alleyway.

As noble as their intentions might be, Alexander's tomb wasn't the Americans' to protect. They had stolen it from Marcus, rightful General of the Mouseion Guard. With Spencer detained, and Theo, as well as countless others dead, this was the first time in his years of leading that Marcus truly felt alone.

He was on his own.

The fact that his people had been the traitors had scarred Marcus deeply. This was also the first time in his life that he'd been without purpose. He knew this day would eventually come, but he hadn't expected it to happen this way. No one could've anticipated it. Quintus Cerialis had betrayed his own brothers for Nero—for profit.

So many years wasted, Marcus thought.

He snarled and pushed that thought aside, instead focusing on his present mission.

Marcus wanted Alexander's tomb back. Unfortunately, he knew there'd be no way to rip it away from the Americans without a full-scale assault. To do that, Marcus would need an army. And with the Legion unavailable, Marcus' only choice was to ask for help from people he didn't trust, which in itself was a problem.

Marcus hated dealing with mercenaries. At least the Legion had a cause. The people he was about to hire only cared about the health of their bank accounts.

Chamonix was only six miles northwest of the Italian border. It always amazed him how easy it was to hide in places so close to home. He didn't think about it too much, though. Marcus rarely ever questioned the good in this life. Instead, he focused on the bad, and tried to work out a way to eliminate it from his life.

Like Jack and his friends.

But as much as it pained Marcus to admit, Jack and his clandestine organization had been the only reason the Legion had even stepped foot in the

Gardens.

"And now, it's time to take it back."

Left arm in a sling, Marcus continued to the end of the alley. He could see the door he sought from here. Inside was his contact, the mercenary liaison. Once price was negotiated, Marcus would be allowed to mingle with his newfound team. Until then, he was at risk.

He stepped up to the door at the very end, but didn't knock. He was told not to.

Marcus gave the doors on his left and right a good, long look, before gazing up at the camera mounted above the liaison's door. Once his face was revealed, a mechanical buzz announced that the door had been unlocked. A second later, a slight man with a long, narrow nose opened the door.

"Peter Accardi, I presume?" he asked through a thick French accent.

Marcus confirmed his alias with a nod. "And you must be Mr. Beaufoy."

"Yes, I am."

Marcus looked around, uncomfortable being outdoors. "Shall we continue this conversation inside?"

Beaufoy shook his head. "No, this will do fine. No one can hear us." He motioned to the buildings lining the alley as well as the handful of doors leading into them. "We own this property." Beaufoy eyed him hard. "My first question is, did you really think I wouldn't know who you really are?"

Marcus went on high alert. "I don't know what you mean."

"One month ago. The terrorist attack on the Roman Colosseum."

The former legionnaire sneered. "I am *not* a terrorist."

Beaufoy smiled. "I'm sure you're not. Still, your recent history brings us unnecessary risk."

Marcus stepped closer. "Twenty men, five *million* dollars."

The Frenchman's eyes opened wide. "Five million, you say?" But the liaison still didn't agree to the deal. "Why offer so much? And what are you after that requires so many men?"

Marcus shifted his stance. "Do you always ask this many questions?"

"Yes, I do, Mr. Accardi," Beaufoy replied matter-of-factly. "I like to properly vet my potential clients. It's how we don't end up in *your* situation."

"Be careful, Mr. Beaufoy," Marcus hissed. "You aren't talking to some simple-minded criminal."

Beaufoy stepped closer. "Neither are you, Mr. Accardi." His face hardened. "Or should I say, *Marcus Cerialis*."

The doors to either side of Marcus burst open. Ten armored soldier-types came filing out. Each held Belgian-made FN SCAR assault rifles. They surrounded Marcus in a halfmoon, cutting off any escape, weapon lights blazing.

Beaufoy stepped aside and allowed a man dressed in civilian clothing to exit his base of operations. The newcomer held up his identification, showing off the agency he represented, the General Directorate for Internal Security, France's domestic intelligence agency.

Beaufoy glanced at the agent, then Marcus. "Sorry, but they got here first."

"DGSI," the agent announced. "Marcus Cerialis, you are under arrest."

The semi-circle of armed men closed in. Marcus smartly held up his right hand, deciding to play a card he had kept for just this occasion.

"The Colosseum attack," he said.

"What about it?" the agent asked.

Marcus glanced at the ten gunmen. The DGSI man responded by holding up his hand. The other men lowered their aim to the ground, but they didn't relax their posture. There was nothing Marcus could offer that would exonerate him from any wrongdoing, but at least he could take down as many people as he could.

He slowly reached into his jacket's pocket. When he did, all ten rifles were leveled at him again. Marcus plucked a tiny black object from inside, holding it between his thumb and forefinger. He offered it to the agent in charge.

He took the thumb drive and looked it over. "What is this?"

Marcus grinned. His team's gladiator helmets not only contained a crystal-clear comms system, but it also had the ability to record everything that was said within it. "This is three days' worth of audio recordings."

"Why should I care?" he asked, shrugging.

Marcus' grin turned into a full-fledged smile. "Because, on it are the voices of multiple American operatives who willingly helped me."

The DGSI agent's eyebrows lifted. Then he motioned for his men to move in. Two stepped up to Marcus, but they did not handcuff him due to his slung left arm. Both men simply gripped his jacket from behind. Marcus allowed it too. Fighting back would only mean his death. As long as he was alive, he stood a fighting chance.

Marcus was led away.

"What will I hear?" the agent asked.

The pair holding Marcus' jacket stopped and spun him around.

Marcus eyed the thumb drive. "That I'm not the only guilty party. The U.S. knowingly funded the other agents. If I were you, I'd have a word with them about it."

The DGSI agent pocketed the evidence and stood tall. "Yes, well, we shall see."

Marcus smiled. "I'm sure you will."

I've got you now, Marcus thought. *Jack, you and your friends are finished.*

If you enjoyed this book, would you mind heading on over to its Amazon page and
leaving a quick review? It lets me know that you liked, which makes me want to continue the series.

Just click the link below.

Amazon.com Page for the Jack Reilly series:
The Jack Reilly Adventures

Thank you, Matt

ABOUT THE AUTHOR

MATT JAMES is a full-time storyteller and the international bestselling author of over thirty-five titles, including THE CURSED THIEF, THE BLOOD KING, THE LOST LEGION, and ORIGIN. He specializes in globetrotting archaeological thrillers that fans of James Rollins, Clive Cussler, and Ernest Dempsey will devour! Matt's work is heavily influenced by the likes of *Indiana Jones*, *The Mummy (1999)*, *Uncharted*, *Tomb Raider*, and *National Treasure*.

He lives twenty minutes from the beach in sunny South Florida with his amazing wife, three beautiful children, a lovable pitty, and an overly dramatic black cat.

Go to **MattJamesAuthor.com** and subscribe to his newsletter for early and exclusive news and updates! You will NOT be mercilessly spammed with junk mail. And don't forget to click the FOLLOW button on his Amazon page to receive new release alerts!

YOU CAN VISIT MATT AT:

Website: MattJamesAuthor.com
Newsletter: MattJamesAuthor.com/Newsletter
Amazon: Matt James on Amazon
Facebook: Facebook.com/MattJamesAuthor
Reader Group: Facebook.com/groups/MattJamesReaderGroup
Instagram: MattJames_Author
X/Twitter: MattJamesAuthor

Printed in Great Britain
by Amazon